I0739658

Stories, Tales, & Fables

MARQUIS DE SADE

Stories, Tales, & Fables

Translated by R J Dent

Contra Mundum Press   New York · London · Melbourne

Stories, Tales, & Fables
© 2025 R.J. Dent;
translation based on
Historiettes, Contes et Fabliaux,
1787–1788 & 1782.

First Contra Mundum Press
edition 2025.

Library of Congress
Cataloguing-in-Publication Data

De Sade, Marquis, 1740–1814
Stories, Tales, & Fables /
Marquis de Sade

—1ˢᵗ Contra Mundum Press
Edition

656 pp., 5 × 8 in.

ISBN 9781940625720

   I. Sade, Marquis de.
  II. Title.
 III. Dent, R.J.;
 IV. Translator.
  V. Heine, Maurice;
 VI. Author.
 VII. Apollinaire, Guillaume;
VIII. Author.
 IX. Éluard, Paul;
  X. Author.
 XI. Masson, André;
 XII. Author.
XIII. France, Anatole;
XIV. Author.

2024952715

Contents

Stories

Tales & Fables

Non-Fiction

Essays on Sade

Introduction

R J DENT

The stories in *Stories, Tales, and Fables* were written by the Marquis de Sade in the years 1787 and 1788 when he was imprisoned in the Bastille. The collection was written after Sade had written *The 120 Days of Sodom* and *Justine*, yet the stories are very different in tone to those two libertine novels.

Stories, Tales, and Fables was not published in Sade's lifetime; the collection was first published (as *Historiettes, Contes et Fabliaux*) in France in 1926, due to the efforts of Maurice Heine, who included Sade's novella, *Dorci, or The Unpredictability of Fate* in the collection. Heine wrote a foreword to the collection. It is included as a foreword to this translation of *Stories, Tales and Fables*.

This collection is divided into two parts: *Fiction & Non-Fiction*.

The first half of the book is comprised of *Stories, Tales, and Fables* in its entirety, with the stories, as Heine explains, in the order that Sade intended. *Dorci, or The Unpredictability of Fate* is included in this collection, as is *Dialogue Between a Priest and a Dying Man*.

The stories in *Stories, Tales, and Fables* are in the order Sade listed them in the contents page of his notebook, and are in the same order in which they appeared in *Historiettes, Contes et Fabliaux* when it was first published in 1926.

Stories contains eleven stories, some of which have a fantastic or supernatural theme. These include *The Serpent*, *The Ghost*, and *An Incomprehensible Adventure*. There are also shorter anecdotal-style, faux-pas sex comedies such as *The Horse-Chestnut Flower*, *The Obliging Husband*, and *Always the Same Way*.

Tales and Fables collects together several cruel tales containing elements of the sexual abuse and physical torture that can be found in Sade's libertine novels. These tales include *Émilie de Tourville*, *The Marquise de Télème*, *The Punished Husband*, *The Lady of the Château de Longville*, and *The Confidence Tricksters*.

Tales and Fables also includes *Augustine de Villeblanche* which, because it is almost the only eighteenth-century short story with a lesbian theme and contains a moving plea for tolerance and acceptance, should perhaps be better known than it is.

Tales and Fables also contains several of Sade's proto-feminist tales, such as *The Murdered Brothel-Keeper*, *Room for Two*, *The Prude*, *The Self-Made Cuckold*, *The Duped Judge*, *Retaliation*, and *The Lady of the Château de Longville*, all of which emphasize Sade's oft-stated belief that women should be considered equal to men and should, like men, be free to make their own life choices. Sade constantly rails against the way women are treated by men, often making his characters speak out against the social inequalities between men and women, some of which, such as arranged marriages and property rights, are inscribed in law. An example of this can be found in Ranville's closing speech in *The Self-Made Cuckold.*

Throughout the collection, particularly in *The Duped Judge* and in *The Marquise de Télème, or the Effects of Libertinism,* and *Dialogue Between a Priest and a Dying Man,* Sade makes plain his disdain for the judiciary, the French government, organized religion, and his own era's lack of morality. He also utilizes his sexually-themed narratives to reveal his belief that nature is responsible for the drives of the libertine.

There are subjects and locations that Sade returns to: his penchant for writing about sodomy has resulted in two stories in this collection, *The Obliging Husband* and *Done As You Require* having, apart from the names of the characters, almost identical plots and situations. Location-wise, some of the stories *(The Provençal Haranguer, The Duped Judge,* and *The Husband Who Said Mass)* are set near Provençal and Aix, which is the region where Sade's family home, the Château La Coste, is located.

One of the stories, *The Marquise de Télème, or The Effects of Libertinism,* has two incomplete final pages in manuscript. Sade took the initial idea for the story from an anecdote he read in a letter, as he mentions in his preface to this collection. He intended to rewrite the story so that it took place during the Terror, but the story remained in its incomplete form. The last few paragraphs of *The Marquise de Télème, or The Effects of Libertinism* appear in note form, with several narrative lacunae. The translating process has thereby necessitated a small amount of reconstruction of the missing parts, simply for narrative cohesion.

Non-Fiction is divided into two parts: *Non-Fiction* by Sade and *Essays on Sade,* which is non-fiction *about* Sade by other writers. The non-fiction by Sade consists of an essay, a letter and a Will, and *Essays on Sade* consists of five essays by other writers about de Sade and his work.

Non-Fiction collects together several of Sade's more significant non-fiction works. His insightful essay on fiction, *Some Thoughts on the Novel,* is included, as is his *Last Will and Testament.* Also included in this section is *My Grand Letter,* the letter Sade wrote to his wife from Vincennes Prison, outlining his defense against his enemies, his explanation of certain events in his life, and an overview of the tenets of his libertine philosophy.

The final section, *Essays on Sade,* includes essays by Guillaume Apollinaire, Paul Éluard, Maurice Heine, André Masson, and Anatole France.

Apollinaire's essay, *The Divine Marquis,* is the essay that arguably began the literary rehabilitation of the Marquis de Sade by freeing him from the label of clandestine pornographer and positing him, and ultimately re-establishing him, as an important and major writer of French literature. Maurice Heine's essay *The Marquis de Sade and the Gothic Novel* echoes much of what Sade himself says in *Some Thoughts on the Novel.* Masson, Éluard, and France's essays address different facets of Sade's work, with Éluard focusing on Sade the revolutionary; Masson on Sade's sadistic imagination.

Anatole France's curious essay *Notice* was originally written as an introduction to Sade's novella, *Dorci, or The Unpredictability of Fate*, published by Charavay Frères in 1881. The essay is divided into two parts: the first is a brief biography that focuses on many of the more sensational aspects of Sade's life. France misrepresents or exaggerates facts in several places; the second part is an overview of the writing, editing, and publishing history of *Dorci, or The Unpredictability of Fate.* It is included here so that the essay's hysterical tone can provide balance to the other essays that are more deferential in tone.

Although Sade's literary rehabilitation is underway in this first quarter of the twenty-first century, it is far from complete, as can be ascertained by the fact that this is the first ever English translation of *Stories, Tales, and Fables*, which, for a collection of stories completed in 1788 by a major French writer is negligence bordering on the criminal.

Foreword

*to an Original Collection of Short Stories
and Longer Tales* (1788)[1]

D. A. F. DE SADE

There is an obligation placed upon every writer to conform to the tone and style of the age in which he lives. This goes some way to explaining why the present author has been effectively forced to make the serious tales of this collection extraordinarily solemn, and contrarily to over-write the comedy of those stories placed among them with the intention of lightening the general mood and hopefully causing the reader's frown to alter to a more pleasing aspect.

Everything degenerates with age.

Be that as it may, it must be stated clearly that in the writing of these stories, we have given ourselves the freedom to follow an impulsive path, so that some of these tales we now set before the reader do not always accord with current moral values, which are often as chaste as they are tedious.

If we have not always been very virtuous, we have always been true.

Nature is, by its nature, more often crooked than straight, and its twists and turns have to be followed. This is what we have done with these stories. No one can claim, in writing of this sort, that he has shown virtue achieve true victory unless the subterfuges of vice which assail it relentlessly from all sides have not been strongly detailed & described.

Let us speak plainly. Over time, tastes grow jaded, minds deteriorate, and the reading public quickly tires of romances and comedies. A discerning author has no alternative but to serve up his wares highly seasoned if he wishes to succeed.

Consequently, in several of the tales in this collection, we have used a technique that is quite new. It is a technique we feel justified in using, although unfortunately bigots will protest, no matter how dramatic the effect is that the technique produces.

The basis of all stories, all tales, seems to be that a young woman is loved by a young man of her own sort, and whose affections are then crossed by a rival she dislikes, and who dislikes or disregards her. If the rival wins, then the heroine is, as is usual, very unhappy.

In our current age (for the present must always be the writer's starting point) and given the depravity of modern mores, it seems that the novels which we read always have a denouement in which someone insists on driving young women to despair.

In view of the generally recognized simplicity with which a woman can console herself for having been given in marriage to an unpleasant husband, why should we, as readers, need to be made to feel particularly sorry for any young lady who has been thrust into the arms of a man like that?

It was this consideration which led us to add a further dimension to the usual age and ugliness in our portrayal of the man who uses force or violence in order to impose his will and his ways on the heroine. We color him with a touch of vice or a hint of lechery in order that he instills real fear into the young creature he sets out to seduce. The result of this is that these young women find themselves facing a fate infinitely more terrifying than anything they have ever known or feared, which, in terms of the story, cannot help but be infinitely more interesting.

We feel that most would agree that if an ugly old man were to become the lord and master of a young woman, she may very well become deserving of our sympathies. Yet her predicament could hardly be considered a major catastrophe; after all, a new outfit and a young lover would easily make her forget her woes. But if, on the contrary, either the old and ugly husband or a rival lover turned out to be capable of unimaginable depravity, abhorrent conduct, bizarre tastes, cruel and despicable impulses, and threatened to subject the young, defenseless victim to an unending series of mental and physical tortures, would we not shudder as we read of his subjugation of the young lady?

Heartless or careless readers will be scandalized by the deployment of devices that emphasize wickedness, although they are devices that are much underused by writers nowadays. But for the more adventurous readers, those who are more spirited, hence more discerning and who will happily read anything as long as it is interesting, for them, there is an altogether different set of thrills in store. These readers are aware of how wayward nature really is and they follow it along its tortuous path, determined to study people, to understand them, and to shed tears over the terrible things that will invariably befall them if they fail to apply the principles of virtue as a corrective to the influence of their impulsive temperaments on their weak and cowardly souls.

There is no doubt that it was wise to keep the more outrageous examples of hedonism well-hidden during more virtuous, more honest times, when even the word "love" was hardly ever mentioned. But with the increase in perversity contained in modern mores it has been possible to reveal this hypocrisy and say to mankind: this is what you have turned into, so now you have to change your ways for you are repulsive, an abomination.

Were the people of antiquity, or those from the age of chivalry, aware of the existence of the type of depravity we have just mentioned? Were there authors who deliberately excluded it from their portrayal of human nature? Boccaccio, Bandini, the Duchesse d'Alençon and our troubadours all made extensive use of it, and was that not the reason their works proved so popular?

In order to be interesting today, a writer is no longer restricted to writing about jealousy, revenge, and ambition, but instead is free to write about other, stronger passions that will strike chords in the reader's heart and make them vibrate resoundingly.

This new style of writing calls for a degree of judgment and control, so that even the most modest of women may read us without so much as a frown crossing her features.

And yet, we readily admit that there is more than a dash of earthiness added to our humorous tales, for as a man of profound wisdom once observed: "It is perfectly acceptable for an author to use comedy in a tale, and even to take certain liberties which would be quite out of place in a serious work."

It is a form of writing that great men have never been ashamed to attempt.

We hope that respectable ladies will shed tears as they read our tragic tales and smile a little knowingly at those stories which seem slightly lewd, sure in the knowledge that all of them are meant to amuse and entertain and as such will cause neither fright nor corruption.

And as for *puttane*, they will continue to walk their own vice-strewn path and undoubtedly not wander far from it.

In the humorous tales collected here, we do not inflict any harm on virtue, and we most certainly neither encourage nor promote vice. That leaves the clergy, which we do ridicule, but that is of no concern as no one bothers to listen to them any more... and as for bigots, all they are concerned with is their reputations, rather than issues, so they will not dare criticize.

There remain the insignificant, ephemeral compilers of thirty ill-conceived, badly-plotted volumes a year, those who are not so much writers, but rather absurd assemblers or ridiculous plagiarists who, by means of their poor efforts bring literature into disrepute. They become enraged when they see that these tales of ours are written with a scrupulous regard for the very language that they cannot help but mangle every day, and they hate that these tales grip the reader's attention by means other than their own monotonously repetitive and mediocre plots and devices.

Consequently, they do their best to stir up trouble for us. We, of course, despise them utterly. We stand so far above them that we do not notice they exist. We cannot hear their feeble sneers, nor shall we ever stoop to respond to them. In fact, to mention them at all, even in passing, or to pay them the scantest attention would raise them from the mud that their trivial scribblings have damned them to forever remain in.

It only remains to point out that these tales are all new. Only "The Enchanted Tower" has some basis in history. A small element of "The Marquise de Télème," is taken from an anecdote in one of Madame du Noyer's letters. Other than those, not one of these stories is modeled upon an existing source. Hopefully, it can be seen from our willingness to admit this and to point it out that we have no intention of trying the patience of our readers by trying to pass off borrowings or thefts as our own. Whoever writes in this genre must either be totally original or else stay away from it entirely. We shall now present the parts of the two tales we have mentioned which can be found in the sources we have identified.

The Arab historian, Abul-Coecim-Terif-Aben-Tariq, is an author barely known by our modern readers. In his brief sketch of "The Enchanted Tower," he wrote:

> *"Rodrigue, a decadent prince, obsessed with voluptuous pleasures, summoned to the court the daughters of his vassals, and there abused them. Among them was Florinde, the daughter of Comte Julien. He raped her. Her father, who was in Africa, received this news through a coded letter from his daughter. He recruited some Moors, and returned to Spain at their head; Rodrigue did not know what to do, as there were no funds in his treasures, and there was no place to hide. He decided to go in search of the Enchanted Tower, near Toledo, because he had been told that it held vast sums of gold. He entered it and saw a statue of Time poised to strike with a huge club. On a stone nearby was an inscription, warning Rodrigue of all the misfortunes that awaited him. The prince went on and saw a large vat of water, but no money. He retraced his steps and gave orders for the tower to be closed and locked securely. A thunderbolt struck the tower and destroyed it, leaving ruins & rubble.*

Despite these disastrous predictions, the prince as-
sembled an army, fought a battle for eight days near
Córdoba and was killed. His body was never found."

That is all that history has provided us with as source
material. Let the reader now carefully read our story and
then judge as to whether or not the extra plot points and
the details we have added justify our contention that
the story should be regarded as entirely our own.

With regards to the genesis of "The Marquise de
Télème," if the reader turns to volume 2, page 202, of
the *Letters of Madame du Noyer*, then they will find an
anecdote about a woman from Champagne who travelled to Paris to take part in a court case. It was not long
before it became obvious she would lose her case. A
rich moneylender who was infatuated with her offered
to pay for the best lawyer and to cover all of her legal
fees, in order to ensure that she won her case. In return,
she had to make herself sexually available to him. She
agreed to his terms and went on to win her case. She
returned home to her husband, but soon guilt began to
make her very ill. Her husband questioned her, insisting
on knowing the cause of her unhappiness. Finally, she
confessed everything. She was forgiven by her husband,
who informed her that what happened was not her fault
and that she did what she had to do to win her case.
The woman recovered and subsequently lived with her
forgiving husband as happily as could be expected.

That was the basic situation, the crude, slightly ludicrous outline that we used to create one of our most tragic and hopefully absorbing tales. If anyone takes the time to compare that rather vague outline with our finished tale of virtue and nobility under duress, then we are certain it will be seen that we can quite rightly claim the honor of being the actual and the original author of "The Marquise de Télème."

We have used nothing from the past as a guide for any of the other twenty-eight tales. We would be more confident of earning the approval of the modern reading public if we had imitated Richardson or Rousseau. But alas, these tales are fashioned in our own image, and consequently the reader who has a closed mind need read no further, as there is only that which is not very well-known to be discovered within these pages, told with a boldness of outlook which is unlikely to suit everyone's tastes.

If these stories do not please you, we acknowledge that the fault is ours alone, as we sought no outside help to bolster our feeble talents.

Foreword
to *Stories, Tales, and Fables*

MAURICE HEINE

To Pascal Pia

I

On the first day of October 1788, Donatien Alphonse François, (Marquis) de Sade, a prisoner at the Bastille by *lettre de cachet*, drew up a *Catalogue raisonné* of his works. He began by compiling a detailed inventory of the short stories he had written and recorded that there were fifty of them, including sixteen stories, thirty tales or fables, one incomplete story, one redrafted as a play, and two stories the author wished to suppress.

However, one hundred and thirty years later, only a dozen tales have appeared — eleven of them in 1800, solely due to their author's efforts, under the collective title of *Les crimes de l'amour (The Crimes of Love)*. A twelfth story was published in 1881, due to the rather malevolent care of Anatole France, under the title *Dorci ou la bizarrerie du sort (Dorci, or The Unpredictability of Fate)*.

After a meeting with Guillaume Apollinaire, we agreed to combine our efforts to search for and publish all of Sade's *disjecta membra*. Our work was interrupted by the disaster of Apollinaire's premature death;

the task we started has now been taken up and continued by the *Société du roman philosophique,* a society specifically founded for the study of the man and his work.

If one acknowledges from the outset, as the author has asked us to, that of his completed tales, there are thirty-seven short stories that he would have acknowledged as his. However, the three available manuscripts containing those stories are all more or less damaged and we have only managed to recover the complete texts of twenty-three of those short stories, to which are added the beginning and two fragments of a twenty-fourth, as well as a curious variant; a story that has been rewritten in the form of a fable.[2]

Since this is a serious attempt to recover missing stories, the other thirteen short stories are currently identified only by their title, sometimes also by their outline or because of some note fragment that was, until recently, considered to be of little importance. There are, however, certain indications — such as the recent public sale of a notebook containing the text of some of them — that allow us to hope that their loss is not definitive and that a later publication will make the author's complete works available.

II

Sade used the interminable stretches of time he had during his imprisonment in Vincennes, then in the Bastille, to take extreme care over his manuscripts. He wrote prolifically and methodically: first, he construct-ed a plan that he developed logically and if necessary reworked, with rewritten sentences being added to the preliminary manuscript. Then he wrote a second draft as an authentic manuscript based on the first draft, in fine, neat writing. He wrote fast, which allowed him to follow a thought to its conclusion, and to add additional thoughts as they occurred to him. His pages had little in the way of excisions, but they were sometimes corrected during a reading, and often loaded with references from a mysterious notebook of supplements and marginal additions. This is Sade's "yellow notebook," which can only be compared, because of its architecture, to certain manuscripts of Marcel Proust. Lastly, the final version was written in exquisite handwriting set within a border of red ink, in the "beautiful notebook," with its pages of medium-weight ivory Holland laid paper.

The man who began a literary career at the age of fifty-one, with the thunderbolt that is *Justine*, devoted himself passionately to the art of writing. He knows that he will become, he feels that he is, a man of letters, with all the force of his pride. The likelihood is that it was his own work that he himself judged in this haughty note:

"There is neither tale nor novel in all the literature of Europe where the 'horror' genre is taken to a more terrifying and more pathetic degree."

Nevertheless, even though he claims to have a mastery of the horror genre, a genre that he does not respect in the least, Sade neglects no method of deriving the greatest effect from it. Here is how he announced his collection of tales:

> *Tales and fables of the eighteenth century by a Provençal troubadour; this work is in four volumes & each tale has an accompanying illustration; these stories are intertwined so that a humorous or slightly risqué tale (but one that is always constrained by the rules of modesty and decency), immediately follows a serious or tragic adventure…*

We had hoped, although it is a hope now dashed, to be able to present this curious sequence of tales to the reader. As we know, Sade broke the sequence himself by publishing eleven heroic and tragic tales drawn from this collection of thirty tales, and the uncertainty of the fate of five others prevents any attempt at reconstruction.

The same drawback applies to the stories: Sade intended for them to take their place in the second volume of the *Portefeuille d'un homme de lettres (Portfolio of a Man of Letters)*, a work that adhered to the literary tastes of the time. The collection was to be comprised of a mixture of literary and philosophical stories brought together with a selection of dark fables. However, with the exception of the "Publisher's Warning" and a few scattered fragments, the *Portfolio* remains untraceable, and it is unrealistic to think of ever publishing the ten stories that we know of in their intended format.

So, we have decided to compromise by putting all of the available stories into the same volume and under the single title of *Stories, Tales, and Fables*. It is not exactly as Sade would have presented it, since one of the stories, *The Confidence Tricksters*, was earmarked for deletion, according to a note by the author.

The manuscript contains stories that have been mixed together creatively, according to the imaginative plan Sade drew up. The first part contains stories; the second part contains two different kinds of stories: tales and fables. In one instance, the author was able to draw from the same subject to create a story and a fable.

III

The order that we have adopted for these twenty-five stories is, with the exception of the lacunae, the order Sade indicated for them in his *Catalogue raisonné*.

The spelling & punctuation are in accordance with modern usage, but the text differs from the autograph manuscripts only by the restoration of a few errors or omitted words. However, in establishing the text, the "beautiful notebook," which has been reduced to a few sheets, was of no help, & so it is the "yellow notebook" from which the stories have been taken. Therefore, this publication is not based on the final version of each story, but on a draft that has been in fact reread & corrected by the author.

This errata notice is necessary, essentially, as it fully explains certain examples of negligence, or even rarer inaccuracies over which purists could take issue. Let critics therefore attribute these errors, not to the Marquis de Sade, a writer far superior to most of his contemporaries and many of the leading French novelists of the revolutionary era, but rather to his persecutors and the irreparable consequences of their attempting to censure and censor his works. Sade has a complex œuvre, and the Gallic irony & Provençal humor that make us laugh today is unexpected from the master of mutilations.

IV

What dying in 1814 meant for that bitter old man was that he would share the end of his life with the death spasm of the Revolution that he had served. It was fortunate that he then slept for a century & thereby avoided the contempt, the ignorance, the outrages and the stupidity of the nineteenth century, during which he somehow managed to be constantly slandered.

To confuse the celebration of his centenary with the unleashing of a world war, in which his worst conclusions were finally verified, was, for the great misanthrope, to achieve a perverse posthumous glory.

Nothing written by Sade, the man, should remain unknown.

Maurice Heine

Stories

The Serpent

At the beginning of this century, everyone knew that the Magistrate's wife, Madame C—, was the kindest & most beautiful woman in Dijon, and everyone who called on her inevitably saw her sprawled on her chaise, openly holding & caressing the large, white snake which will be the subject of this anecdote.

— This animal is the best friend I have in the world, she once said to a foreign lady who came to see her, and who seemed curious to learn the reasons for the love that this attractive woman had for her snake.

— I was passionately in love once, she continued. My lover was a very charming young man, who had to leave me to go and fight in the war. Before he left, he made me promise that, regardless of whatever I was currently doing, I would, at certain appointed times, go alone to a private, solitary place, and pleasure myself until I had satisfied my passionate desires.

— One day, at five o'clock in the evening, in order to keep my promise, I had gone to a bower at the end of my private walled garden, where I removed my clothes. Oh, the walled garden was so secure and so private that no creature, let alone one of this species, could have entered it. I had just started to pleasure myself when I suddenly saw between my spread feet this charming creature which you now see me worshipping so devotedly.

— My instinct was to run away. But before I could move, the serpent reared up in front of me, and somehow, I'm not sure how, seemed to ask me for mercy. It then seemed to promise me that it did not want to hurt me. So here's what I did: I paused and looked very carefully at the large, white creature.

— Seeing that I was now still and quiet, it slithered nearer. It came closer and closer, coiling and uncoiling a hundred times at my feet, coiling around one foot and then the other. I could not help but put my hand out and touch it; it moved its head toward my hand and I gently stroked it. Emboldened, I took it in my arms and dared to lower it onto my lap. It wriggled there, then settled, then seemed to sleep.

— After a while I felt myself becoming restless, agitated… I was aware of myself crying involuntarily; my tears fell onto the slumbering creature. Awakened by my tears, it turned its head and looked at me, then, it sighed and slowly moved over my body and rested its head on my breasts… the movements of its undulating body caressed me. Then the snake settled and fell asleep again. Its movements had increased my desires and my body reacted accordingly.

— Oh! Oh, good God! I cried. And at that moment, I knew my lover was dead. I sprang up, dressed, and left that terrible place, taking this snake with me. In spite of myself, I felt a curious bond with it and did not want to be parted from it.

— You'll no doubt interpret my experience as you please, Madame, but eight days later, I learned that my lover was indeed dead. He'd been killed and had fallen at the very hour this serpent appeared between my feet. Since then, I have never wanted to separate myself from this magnificent creature; either its death or my own are all that will separate us. Although I have married since then, it is under the express terms that this snake will never be taken away from me.

Having told her visitor her story, the Magistrate's wife then picked up her serpent, leaned back, placed it on her breasts, and made it coil itself around her upper body several times for the benefit of the lady who had asked her about it.

Providence, how inexplicable your decrees are, if this adventure is as true as the whole province of Burgundy assures me it is!

The Gascon Officer's Dinner Bill

Louis XIV had granted a Gascon officer a gratuity of one hundred and fifty pistolas. With his document affirming this in his hand, the officer entered, without being announced, the home of Monsieur Colbert, who was seated at the dinner table with some lords.

— Which of you gentlemen, the officer asked, in the accent that revealed his homeland, which one of you is Monsieur Colbert?

— That's me, Monsieur, replied the minister. What is that document you have there?

— It's nothing hugely important, Monsieur. It's a gratuity of one hundred and fifty pistolas that I've come to collect from you, Monsieur.

Monsieur Colbert, who could immediately see how the Gascon officer could be used as a source of entertainment and amusement, politely asked the man's permission to finish his dinner, and in order to make him less impatient, he asked the officer to sit down at the table with him.

— Gladly, replied the Gascon, taking a seat at the table. I have not yet dined.

The meal was eaten and the minister, who had had time to have the first clerk notified, told the officer that he could go up to the office and that his money was waiting for him. The Gascon duly arrived at the office and handed over his gratuity document, but the clerk only counted out a hundred pistolas.

— I sincerely hope you're joking, the Gascon said to the clerk. Can you not see that my gratuity is for a hundred and fifty pistolas?

— Yes, Monsieur, replied the bureaucrat, I can see your gratuity document very well. However, I am holding back fifty pistolas for your dinner.

— By God, fifty pistolas for dinner! It only cost me twenty sols at my inn.

— I'm sure it did, but at the inn, you don't have the advantage of having dinner with the minister & his noble guests.

— Well then, said the Gascon, in that case, Monsieur, keep all of it! I'll bring a noble friend of my own here tomorrow and then we'll be even. (By this, of course, he meant King Louis, who had given him the gratuity.)

The Gascon officer's answer and the joke that had occasioned it amused the minister and his guests for a few moments, after which fifty pistolas were added to the Gascon's gratuity.

The Gascon officer returned to his country, praising the dinners of Monsieur Colbert, Versailles, and the way in which official business is conducted by men who don't want to end up dead and floating in the Garonne.

The Effective Subterfuge[1]

There are many, many foolish wives who imagine that
— provided they do not "go all the way" with a man —
they may indulge in certain discrete dalliances without
giving offence to their husbands. It is a point of view
which not infrequently gives rise to consequences far
more dangerous than if their fall were to be complete
and utter. The case of the Marquise de Guissac, a lady of
quality from Nîmes in Languedoc, furnishes the clearest
proof of the proposition which we have expressed in the
form of a general truth.

Giddy, scatter-brained, vivacious, having a modicum
of wit and pretty manners, Madame de Guissac believed
that a handful of flirtatious letters, written and received
between herself and the Baron d'Aumelas, would have no
untoward consequences, firstly because no one would
know about them and secondly, because if by some mis-
chance they were to be discovered, she could prove her
innocence, since she had done absolutely nothing to
incur her husband's displeasure.

In this, she was very much mistaken.

Monsieur de Guissac, being an exceedingly jealous
man, suspected that a correspondence was being carried
on, questioned a chambermaid, and got hold of one of
the letters.

There was nothing ostensible in it to justify his fears outright, though it contained infinitely more than was required to feed his suspicions. Caught in a cruel state of uncertainty, he armed himself with a pistol & a glass of lemonade and burst angrily into his wife's bedchamber.

— You have betrayed me, Madame! he cried in a rage. Read this letter. It tells me everything I need to know. The time for wavering is past. I leave you to decide the manner of your death. He waved the lemonade and the firearm. Poison or the pistol?

The Marquise spoke in her own defense. She swore to her husband that he was mistaken, saying that it was true that she might be guilty of imprudence, but she was absolutely innocent of any crime.

— You are an unfaithful woman and I have been deceived by you for the last time, said the furious husband. I refuse to be fooled ever again. Come, decide immediately, or else I'll use this pistol to bring about your hasty demise.

Poor Madame de Guissac, frightened out of her wits, opted for the poison. She took the glass of lemonade from her husband and drank.

— Stop! ordered her husband when she had swallowed part of the glass's contents. You shall not die alone. Despised by you, deceived by you, I no longer have a place in this world.

And having spoken, the Marquis took the drink from his wife and drained it in one gulp.

— Oh, Monsieur, said Madame de Guissac. You've now made both of us reach a fatal moment. Would you therefore permit me a confessor, as well as the opportunity to embrace my parents for a final time?

The Marquis sent word; the Marquise's parents were summoned. The hapless woman threw herself into the arms of the couple that had brought her into the world and protested her lack of guilt. She did, however, find it difficult to find the words necessary to reproach her husband; he believed he had been deceived by her, and, after cruelly punishing his wife, he had meted out the same punishment to himself. The Marquise's only course of action now was to accept her punishment & surrender to despair. Her tears flowed copiously.

The confessor arrived.

— At this cruel conclusion to my life, the Marquise said, it is my wish, for the consolation of my parents and for the honor of my memory, to make a full & public confession.

And so she proceeded, aloud, to confess everything that she believed she had done wrong throughout her life.

The Marquis listened attentively, but as the confession drew to its conclusion, he heard no mention of the Baron d'Aumelas, except a brief reference to some over-familiar, flirtatious letters the Baron had written. Quite certain that his wife was unlikely to resort to deceit during the very confession she had requested, the Marquis stood up, elated.

He clasped his father-in-law & his mother-in-law to him in a single embrace.

— Take heart, he said to them. And may your daughter forgive me for causing her such a fright. She gave me cause to worry, and I used it to justify giving her a few moments of anxiety in return. There was no poison in the drink we both drank. She may set her mind at rest — and so may you both. Let her remember this: not only should a truly good wife never do any wrong; she should never do anything that might suggest that she has done wrong.

It was with enormous difficulty that the Marquise recovered from the lamentable state to which she had been reduced. So utterly had she believed the drink's poison was working on her that in the heat of her imagination, she thought she could already feel the onset of the agonizing symptoms that herald death by poison.

Trembling, she stood up and went to her husband. Her relief at his revelation banished her suffering. The young woman thoroughly assimilated the lesson of the whole dreadful episode. She vowed that thereafter, she would avoid doing anything that might be construed as wrong. And then she kissed her husband.

The Marquise was true to her word. She lived with her husband for over thirty years, and during all that time, he never once had cause to reproach her for anything she did.

The Murdered Brothel-Keeper

It was during the Regency period that an extraordinary event occurred.[2] It was so extraordinary that it is still worth repeating — even today.

Firstly, it offers an insight into clandestine sexual activity, which no one can ever shed too much light on.

Secondly, it is the story of three brutal murders, the perpetrator of which was never caught.

And so, [we will now present the various] theories regarding what might have happened, after which, we will relate how it actually ended.[3] By presenting the details in this way, we hope the dénouement will be a lot less horrifying.

Monsieur de Savari was an elderly bachelor, who had been ill-served by nature.[4] By way of compensation, he was excellent company, and a man of profound wit who regularly entertained the very best of society in his home on the Rue des Déjeuneurs.[5]

It is said that one day, he decided to turn his house into premises for prostitution of a very singular kind. Ladies of quality, exclusively, married or single, who, beneath a cloak of the deepest secrecy, wanted to enjoy sexual pleasures and gratification with impunity, found they could call on him at any time and he would always provide several partners more than ready and able to satisfy them. His discretion was impeccable and every woman who visited his establishment was able to collect as many roses as she desired, without any risk of harm from the thorns of public knowledge that such arrangements can be susceptible to, a risk that many regular illicit liaisons have a tendency to become.

At social events, if any of those women or the young ladies happened to meet the man or the men with whom she had taken pleasure from the evening before, then she would give no sign of recognition, nor would any of the men who had provided her with satisfaction do or say anything to draw attention to her or to mark her out from the other women there.

This particular agreement between parties meant there was no jealousy in any marriage. There were no vengeful husbands, no angry fathers, no separations, no divorces, no women banished to a life in a convent, in a word, none of the disastrous consequences that this kind of arrangement would normally entail.

It would be difficult to find a more convenient arrangement, although, undoubtedly, this plan would be too dangerous to offer nowadays. Indeed, in our own century, in which the depravity of both sexes has crossed all known boundaries, and if the monumental success of the service were to be generally known, it would be a matter of grave concern that it might give a certain type of person the notion of reintroducing something very similar. Therefore, it is expedient that we now recount the cruel fate that befell the man who invented it.

Although Monsieur de Savari has become very rich from the service he had devised and which he so efficiently managed, he nonetheless restricted his domestic staff to one servant and one cook, so as to have the minimum number of witnesses to what went on in his house.

Late one morning, one of his acquaintances arrived at his house and asked if he could stay for lunch.

— You are most welcome, replied Monsieur de Savari. It will be my pleasure. And just to prove it, I'll have my butler go and get you a bottle of the best wine from my cellar…

— Just a moment, the friend said, as soon as the butler had received the order. I believe your butler sometimes switches the wine… I know which racks hold which bottles, and, with your permission, I'd like to follow him down & see if he really does fetch a bottle of your best vintage.

— Very well, said the master of the house, deciding to humor his guest. I'm sure you're wrong about La Brie, but you have my permission to follow him into the cellar and watch what he does. If it weren't for my disability, I'd come with you.

Monsieur de Savari's acquaintance left the room, entered the cellar, picked up a crowbar and smashed the butler's skull in. He then made his way into the kitchen and murdered the cook using the same method, even killing a dog and a cat that got in his way as he crossed the room. Finally, he returned to Monsieur de Savari's dining room and without hesitation, murdered his defenseless host in the same way he had dispatched his staff.

Remaining totally calm and, without feeling the slightest shred of remorse for the brutal crimes he had just committed, the heartless killer opened a book on the table, and on a blank page quietly wrote down the way in which he had killed the three people & the two animals. Careful to touch nothing else, nor to take anything, he left the house, locking it behind him, then disappeared.

As always, there were too many people visiting Monsieur de Savari's house for the murders to remain undiscovered for long. When several people knocked and no one answered, someone realized that, of course, the owner of the house could not have gone out for a walk. So they broke down the doors and immediately saw the grisly remains of the unfortunate man, his staff, and his animals.

There was a clock in Monsieur de Savari's dining room. It was decorated with a skull, beneath which were carved the words: *Look at this and use your time wisely.* Not content with detailing the murders on the page of the book for everyone to read, the audacious murderer had also pinned a note to that clock. The note read: *Look at his life and you will not be surprised by his death.*

It was the kind of crime that attracted a lot of attention. Monsieur de Savari's house was searched thoroughly, but the only item that was found which may have had some bearing on the whole case was an unsigned letter, written by a woman, addressed to Monsieur de Savari, and which contained the following words:

"We are lost, my husband now knows everything! You must find a way to get away. Only Paparel can talk him out of what he has planned. For God's sake, get him to speak to him, otherwise there is no hope of salvation."

A man named Paparel was interviewed. He was a kind man, who kept excellent company, and he worked as a treasurer at the War Office. He admitted that he knew Monsieur de Savari, but he also said more than a hundred notable people, many from the court and the city, had called regularly at the dead man's house. One of the most notable was the Duke de Vendôme, he said, adding that by comparison, he, Paparel, was probably one of Monsieur de Savari's lesser acquaintances.

Several people were arrested and almost immediately released. Eventually, enough was known about the service the dead man had provided for it to be very clear that if enquiries were continued, there would be innumerable ramifications, namely that half of the city's husbands and fathers would be compromised and left open to ridicule, and that a good number of people of the highest rank would find their lives and careers ruined. For the first time in their lives, the magistrates involved used prudence, rather than severity to judge the case.

And so, the whole affair was concluded there.

The result of the death of the unfortunate man, no doubt deemed too guilty to be mourned by honest people, was that no one was prepared to step forward to avenge his death.

His loss made no difference to virtue, but vice was affected for a long time. Most affected were the merry band of gigolos who had found so many blossoms to pluck, thanks to that sweet child of Epicurus; also affected were the pretty priestesses of Venus who had come daily to burn incense on the altars of love, who now bitterly mourned the demolition of their temple.

And that is how everything is measured. A philosopher, on reading this account, would say: if, out of a thousand people implicated in this adventure, five hundred were happy and the other five hundred unhappy, the outcome is balanced, therefore neutral. But if the calculation shows that there are eight hundred unhappy people, because of the deprivation of pleasures caused by the murder, against only two hundred who happen to gain from it, then Monsieur de Savari did more good than bad, and the only culprit was the one who killed him out of resentment. I will leave the matter to you to decide as I move on to another subject.

The Stuck-in-the-Mud Bishop

It is a rather peculiar thing that some pious people have the idea that certain letters of the alphabet arranged in such & such a way can, taken one way, infinitely please the Lord, and taken another way, cruelly offend Him; and this idea is undoubtedly one most pleasing to any of us who like to offend devout gentlemen.

Among those people who considered some words beginning with the letters "c" & "f" to be particularly offensive was the former Bishop of Mirepoix, who many, at the beginning of this century, considered to be a veritable saint.

On his way one day to see the Bishop of Damiers, his carriage wheels sunk in one of the quagmires that was a typical hazard on the lesser roads that separated those two cities: no matter how hard the coachman tried, the horses could not move forward.

— My lord, said the coachman finally. As long as you are sitting there, my horses will not budge.

— And why not? the Bishop asked.

— Because, in order to make my horses pull the carriage free, I need to swear at them, and Your Grace says that God is opposed to swearing, or what some call "bad" language; but we'll be stuck here forever if He will not allow me to swear at my horses.

— Very well, said the Bishop, making a sign of the cross. Swear away, my son… but only a few choice words — enough to get your horse moving and no more.

And so, the coachman swore, the horses pulled the carriage free, and the Bishop arrived at his destination without incident.

The Ghost

Of all the things in the world in which philosophers profess the least faith, the first and foremost is ghosts. However, the extraordinary experience I am about to report is backed up by the sworn statements of several witnesses and is recorded in a number of respectable journals. If it did happen, and according to what has been said since, and according to the authenticity it had at the time, then I maintain it should probably be believed. It will, of course, be necessary, in spite of the skepticism of the most stoic of disbelievers in the supernatural, to persuade oneself that, even if all the tales of ghosts are not true, at least there are some very extraordinary things about this tale which render it very likely a real occurrence.

A large woman, Madame Dallemand, whom all of Paris knew at the time as cheerful, frank, naïve and good company, had been living for more than twenty years as a widow with a certain Ménou, a broker who lived near Saint-Jean-en-Grève. One day Madame Dallemand was having dinner at the home of a Madame Duplatz, a business woman with whom she was on friendly terms, when in the middle of a party game that had begun once everyone had left the table, a servant came to ask Madame Dallemand if she would follow him into a nearby anteroom, as a person of her acquaintance wanted to speak to her on a matter of some urgency.

Madame Dallemand said that she would wait because she did not want to disrupt the game. The servant went away, then came back, insisting so much that the lady of the house was compelled to intervene & urge Madame Dallemand to go and see what the person wanted.

Madame Dallemand went into the anteroom and immediately recognized Ménou.

— What business is so urgent, she demanded, that it can force you to come and disturb me like this, in a house where you are not known?

— Very essential business, madam, replied the broker, and you must believe that it is so, for I have obtained from God permission to come and speak to you for the very last time in my life...

At these words, which did nothing to indicate a man in possession of his senses, Madame Dallemand became very confused and, staring at her friend whom she had not seen for a few days, she became even more frightened when she saw how pale & disfigured he was.

— What has happened to you? she asked him. Why are you saying these sinister things to me and why are you in the state that you're in? I'd like you to start making sense & explain clearly & quickly what has happened to you.

— Something fairly ordinary has happened, Madame, said Ménou. After sixty years of life it was time, apparently, to leave my life behind. But thanks to Heaven, I am dead, but I am here now. I have paid nature the tribute that all men owe it, and my only fault is that I have forgotten you in my last moments, and it is for this fault, Madame, that I come here to ask your forgiveness.

— Listen to yourself! You're talking in riddles. There is no reason for such madness! Either go away and regain your senses or I'll leave.

— Do not leave, Madame. My unwelcome visit will not last much longer; I am near the time limit that the Lord has given me; therefore hear my final words before we leave each other for ever… As I told you, Madame, I am dead. Very soon you'll know the truth of what I am telling you. I have forgotten you in my will, and I have come here to make amends for my oversight. Take this key, and go to my house at once. Behind the wallpaper at the head of my bed, you will find an iron door, and if you open it with the key I've given you, you'll find it's the door to a safe. Take all of the money out of that safe which is behind that door, locked by that key. No one knows about that money, certainly none of my heirs. It is yours, so take it and use it as you wish. But do it now, so that no one can cheat you of it. Farewell, Madame, do not try to follow me…

And Ménou disappeared.

It is easy to imagine how troubled Madame Dallemand was as she entered her friend's living room; it was impossible for her to hide her perturbation. She quickly explained.

— The claim deserves to be investigated, said Madame Duplatz. Let's not waste a moment.

Picture it, if you will: they called for horses, they got in the carriage, they were conveyed to Ménou's house...

He was lying in his coffin, just inside the door. The two women went up to the apartment; as the master's friend, she was too well known to be refused, so she went through every room she wanted to. She arrived at the one she had been instructed to go to. She found the paper-covered iron door, opened it with the key that Ménou had given her, and found the money inside.

These are undoubtedly proofs of friendship & gratitude, examples of which are, unfortunately, not frequent. They must also make us forgive those who return from the grave and frighten us, and the many fears they cause. Let us instead look carefully at the reasons that lead them to make an earthly appearance and become visible to us.

The Provençal Haranguer

During the reign of Louis XIV, there was, as we now know, a Persian ambassador who was traveling through France. The French king liked to attract travelers from all nations to his court, in order that those visiting personages could admire his greatness, and perhaps take back to their country some sparks of the rays of glory that he radiated to the ends of the earth.

As he passed through Marseilles, and reached Aix, the ambassador was very warmly received there.

The committee of the Council of Aix, perhaps with jealousy motivating them, had no wish to be outdone by Marseilles, a city that they considered, for very little reason, inferior to their own.

The Council committee had one concern: what sort of public speech (known locally as a harangue) should they write and have recited in honor of the visiting Persian ambassador?

Of course, to have someone read the harangue aloud in Provençal would have been pointless; the Persian dignitary, they had been informed, would understand very little French. This problem gave them considerable pause.

The committee deliberated. It had never needed much incentive to sit and deliberate. Any pretext was enough: a peasant trial, a theater controversy, any issue involving prostitutes, all were grist to the committee's mill. These controversies were mulled over endlessly by the committee members, since it was no longer legal for them to exercise their rights, as they had under Francis I, to use fire and iron to subjugate a town, nor to douse those flames with the blood of the town's unfortunate citizens.

And so, the committee deliberated. How could they manage to have the harangue translated into Persian in time? No matter how much they deliberated, they could not find a solution to the problem, which was simply that no one in Aix-en-Provence could speak Persian.

Despite this, with time running out, the harangue was nonetheless written in French. Three celebrated lawyers had worked on it for six weeks.

By some miracle, a sailor who spoke Persian was found in one of the lesser districts of the city. He had been in the Levant for a long time and he spoke Persian almost as well as he spoke his own patois. He was briefed and after negotiating his fee he accepted the task. He quickly learned the harangue and translated it into Persian without difficulty.

When the day arrived the haranguer was given a jacket that had once belonged to the mayor. He was also lent the best wig available and although it was a little loose, it successfully lent him the required appearance of being dignified. Once he was ready he walked out to meet the ambassador followed by all thirty members of the Council committee. He had rehearsed his speech to perfection and, knowing Persian etiquette and customs as well as the language, the haranguer had specifically requested that those of the committee who followed him stand behind him and do absolutely everything he did.

The committee thought that this was a very good idea.

The ambassador and the haranguer met in the arranged place. The haranguer bowed low and the too-loose wig fell off his head and landed on the ground at the ambassador's feet.

The committee members, giving no thought to anything other than ingratiating themselves with the ambassador by following the haranguer's instructions and example, pulled off their own wigs and threw them to the ground at the ambassador's feet. They then bowed simultaneously, presenting the Persian dignitary with the tops of their bald or balding skulls.

Realizing the extent of the committee members' faux pas, the haranguer tried to cover it over by beginning to recite the complimentary harangue.

When the ambassador heard the speech being delivered in his own language, he was horrified.

— You evil man! he yelled, putting his hand on his saber. You speak my language, but you are not Persian! You must be one of Mahomet's renegades; therefore I must punish you for your crime; you must immediately pay for it with your head!

— No, no, no, no! the haranguer protested. I'm not a follower of Mahomet.

Behind him, the committee parroted his words in unison:

— No, no, no, no! I'm not a follower of Mahomet!

The haranguer gesticulated wildly, protesting his innocence.

The committee members imitated his gestures and protested their innocence.

The ambassador looked furious. He drew his saber.

The haranguer realized that not only was he not being listened to nor understood but also that he was now in mortal danger.

Out of desperation, the haranguer did the only thing he could do under the circumstances: he dropped his trousers in order to prove to the enraged ambassador that he had never been circumcised, and was therefore as Christian as Saint Christopher was.

The thirty committee members immediately imitated his actions, all of them standing there, their trousers around their ankles and their flaccid members in their hands as they waved their foreskins at the ambassador, proving, without any shadow of a doubt, that they too were as Christian as the haranguer & Saint Christopher.

How the ladies watching the event from their windows must have laughed at such an unseemly display.

By now, the ambassador was quite confused; but not, specifically, insulted. He realized that the haranguer was not guilty of what he had accused him, so he sheathed his saber, then clicked his heels and bowed by way of apology. As he did so, he thought to himself:

Now I understand why these people always have a scaffold erected here. They are so obviously incompetent that they must simply need to do everything over and over again, until they get it right. The scaffold must be there to incentivize the more useless of these dull creatures.

Later, an artist was commissioned to capture the momentous day; he had already drawn the spectacle as it occurred. He painted it, but his painting was ultimately rejected. It was thrown into a fire and the artist was banished. It never occurred to the committee members that they were burning an image of themselves, as they were a part of the painting.

— We look like imbeciles to outsiders, said the committee chairman. Is this what we want? Even if it isn't, we have proven it to all of France, for all time to come. We certainly don't need a painting that will preserve it for posterity. In time, no one will remember our good intentions. Instead, they will, we hope, remember us as they remember Mérindol and Cabrières. As far as I'm concerned, it's far more honorable to be regarded as murderers than as idiots?

Always the Same Way

There were very few men in the world that were as liber-tine as the Cardinal de ... whose name, given his current healthy and vigorous existence, I would ask that you allow me to keep to myself. His Eminence had made arrangements in Rome with one of these women whose unofficial trade was to supply the debauched with objects of desire necessary for the satiation of their passions. Every morning she brought his Eminence a young girl aged between thirteen to fourteen years at most. The good monsignor enjoyed the type of inappropriate intercourse that the Italians and some Parisians have famously made their main source of delight. This meant that when the young girl was finally allowed to leave the clutches of His Eminence, her virginity was as intact as when he had first embraced her, and therefore, she could be resold as a virgin a second time to another libertine.

The procuress was perfectly aware of the cardinal's tastes and she was, on a daily basis, committed to providing the young girls he found so delectable.

However, there was one particular day when she was unable to locate the desired object and instead, out of necessity, decided to use the prettiest choirboy she could and dress him as a girl.

She took a particularly pretty young boy from the Church of the Apostles and carefully prepared him.

She put him in a dress, arranged his hair, applied some subtle makeup, and used all of the illusory paraphernalia that she had at her disposal in order to deceive the holy man of God. However, it had obviously proved impossible to provide the boy with the part of the anatomy that would have ensured him a total resemblance to the sex he was impersonating, although this particular deficiency did not bother the procuress very much…

— The Cardinal has no interest in that particular part of a girl's anatomy; he does not touch it, nor does he try to enter it, she said to her assistant who was helping her prepare the deception. He will almost certainly want to use her the same way he always uses all of the girls; it's always the same way, so we have nothing to fear…

The procuress was serious. She was probably unaware that an Italian cardinal has such a refined and delicate sense of taste that he is unlikely to ever be deceived by such an obvious ploy.

The "girl" arrived and the Cardinal pounced on her and pushed her into the desired position. He thrust into her and on the third stroke, the man of God stopped his exertions and exclaimed:

— *Per Dio santo, sono ingannato, questo bambino è ragazzo, mai non fu puttana!*

He then turned his victim over and examined the crotch; the small organ he saw there was the incontrovertible proof of his suspicions.

However, there was no mishap that was ever too daunting to overwhelm a prominent inhabitant of the Holy City. Aware that his status demanded he must always rise to the occasion, His Eminence plunged in up to the hilt, perhaps muttering, at the crucial moment, like a peasant who has been served truffles instead of potatoes:

— Ah, always the same way!

When the cardinal was done and the boy taken away, His Eminence took the procuress to one side for a quiet word.

She quickly explained her reasons for the substitution.

— Madame, he said to her, chuckling. I do not blame you for your attempted deception.

— Please forgive me, Monsignor.

— As I just said, I don't blame you. However, if it happens again, you must not fail to let me know. I may not notice during the heat of the first time, but I'd certainly notice it during the less-frenzied second time.

The Obliging Husband[6]

All of France knew that the Prince of Bauffremont had more or less the same tastes as the cardinal we have just talked about. He had been given a very naïve young woman in marriage, and whom, according to custom, had been instructed by her mother, of all people, only the day before regarding her daughter's wedding night duties.

— Without further explanation, her mother had said, because decency prevents me from going into certain details, I have only one very important thing to recommend to you, daughter. Beware of the *first request* that your husband makes in the bedchamber. Say very firmly to him: *No, Monsieur! That is most definitely not the way that an honest woman comports herself. You may avail yourself to anywhere else as much as you like, but with regards to* that, *no, certainly not...*

Not entirely certain as to what *anywhere else* referred to (and actually, completely confused on that point), the young woman nonetheless went to her marriage bed that night determined to use her mother's interdict, should it be needed.

They lay in bed and the Prince, in order to demonstrate principles of honesty and decency that no one would have suspected he even possessed, requested that they do things (at least for the first time) in the traditional manner. In other words, he merely offered his wife the chaste pleasures associated with the hymen.

But the well-educated young woman immediately recalled her mother's advice, and hastily deploying all of her resolve, she said to the Prince:

— No, Monsieur! That is most definitely not the way that an honest woman comports herself. You may avail yourself to anywhere else as much as you like, but with regards to that, no, certainly not...

— But, Madame... the Prince protested.

— No, Monsieur! No matter how hard you may persist, you shall not alter my decision!

— Very well, said the Prince, confused, but nonetheless impressed by the similarity of his bride's taste to his own, and by her single-minded insistence on him providing her with that pleasure.

— Madame, I sincerely hope that it will give you the same satisfaction it gives me. I should be very upset and angry if it were said that I had done anything to displease you!

Without further ado, and following her interdict, the Prince drove his engorged manhood home between the twin globes of his bride's beautiful derriere.

And let it be clearly stated that it is best if mothers do not to instruct daughters who are newly married as to what duty they owe their husbands.

The result will inevitably be consternation, with the daughter possibly resenting her mother for some time after.

An Incomprehensible Incident, Attested to by an Entire Province

It was less than a hundred years ago that we still had, in several places in France, weak-minded individuals who still believed that it was only a matter of giving one's soul to the devil, with certain rituals, both cruel and fanatical, to obtain everything they wanted from that diabolical entity.

It is no more than a century ago that the event that we are going to speak of occurred in one of our southern provinces, where it is still attested today in the registers of two cities and verified by several personal testimonies that would convince even the most skeptical.

Reader, you may believe it, or you may not; we mention it only after having verified it. Obviously we cannot guarantee it as a fact, but we can certify that more than one hundred thousand souls did believe it, and that more than fifty thousand can still attest today the authenticity with which it is recorded. If you will allow us, we will disguise the province and the names and proceed to tell you of it.

Since the days of his youth, the Baron de Vaujour had combined the most unbridled libertinage with a taste for all sciences, and especially those which often mislead man, and make him lose precious time in reverie and illusions that he could use in infinitely better ways.

He was an alchemist, an astrologer, a sorcerer, a necromancer, a reasonably good astronomer, and a mediocre physicist.

At the age of twenty-five, the baron, master of his own estate and therefore his own destiny, claimed he had found in his books a ritual whereby one could, after sacrificing a child to the devil and by using certain words and certain gestures during that execrable ceremony, make the devil appear and, on using one's own soul as payment, obtain from him everything one wanted.

The baron was determined to attempt this horrific ritual. If it worked, he would insist on living happily until his sixtieth birthday, of never lacking money and, until he reached the agreed age, of always having full use of all of his faculties which were to provide him with the most eminent degree of strength, prowess, and stamina.

The baron committed the heinous act, and this is what happened.

Up to the age of sixty, the baron had an annuity of fifteen thousand livres. He, however, constantly spent hundreds more than that, without ever falling into debt.

At the age of forty his sexual prowess was at its peak and there was no end to the succession of attractive women he regularly serviced, one after the other, in a single evening. The orgies he indulged in were legendary.

On one occasion, when he was forty-five years old, one of his friends bet he could not service twenty-five women in a single evening, one after another — for a hundred louis. He did so effortlessly and gave the hundred louis to the twenty-fifth women.

Another time, approaching fifty, he organized a card game. He watched the game carefully, but refused to take part.

— Regrettably, I cannot join in, as I don't have any money! he said.

The other players refused to believe him and exhorted him to join the game. Finally, tired of their carping, he went to a dark corner of the room and made a number of strange gestures. He returned to the table and tried to put ten thousand louis on the turn of a card.

The other players refused the bet. The baron asked why. As a joke, one of the players said the money he'd offered for the card wasn't enough. There was some laughter.

The baron made his way back into the shadows and made the same strange gestures again. Returning to the table yet again, he began to pull huge wads of money from his pockets. The other card players were astonished. This incident was later attested to by several witnesses.

At the age of fifty the baron married a delightful woman with whom he lived very happily. He had seven children with her. Of course, as a dedicated libertine, he was often unfaithful, committing infidelities that his wife often suspected. However, she must have realized it was simply in his nature to be promiscuous for she never argued with him about it.

They lived at his château, and men of learning and distinction came to see him there, for he enjoyed their company and their insights.

Unfortunately, as he approached the age of sixty, a deep melancholy began to affect him as he remembered his infernal pact. He thought of the human sacrifice he had performed, right in that very building, and wondered whether the devil might reappear soon, demanding his wealth, his health, or his soul. The baron began to grow melancholy and distant, until his precious wife began to wonder what was wrong with him. He began to become withdrawn as more and more time passed, until finally, in the last few days of his fifties, he hardly ever left his château.

On his birthday, precisely at the moment the baron became sixty years old, a valet entered the room and announced that a stranger, having heard of the baron's intelligence, had asked to have the honor of speaking with him. The baron, distracted for a moment, so therefore not thinking about what had been preoccupying him constantly for the last few years, gave instructions for the guest to be brought to his study.

Seated at his desk, the baron watched as a well-dressed stranger was shown in and immediately began to discuss the high sciences with the baron, who answered all of his questions. The monsieur's way of speaking seemed to indicate he was from Paris. As the conversation continued Baron de Vaujour suggested that the two of them take a walk around the château gardens. The guest accepted the invitation and the two philosophers made their way out of the château.

It was one of the seasons where all of the peasants were working in the fields. Some of them, seeing the Baron de Vaujour walking alone, but talking and gesticulating as though he had someone with him, thought that he had most likely lost his wits, and so hurried to alert Madame. However, there was no response to their continued knocking on the château doors, so the good people then retraced their steps and kept a watch over the baron, who quite clearly imagined he was walking and conversing with a real person. He was talking loudly and waving his arms around, as people do during heated or controversial moments.

Finally our two scholars strolled along an avenue that ended in a kind of walled garden cul-de-sac, from which one could only exit by retracing one's steps. Thirty peasants watched them, thirty were later questioned, and thirty all swore that Baron de Vaujour had entered the walled garden alone, gesticulating wildly as he walked along.

After about an hour, the person he thought he was with said to him:

— Baron, you don't recognize me, do you? Have you forgotten the promise you made to me in your youth? Have you forgotten how I fulfilled it?

The baron began to tremble.

— There is no need to be afraid, said the visitor. I haven't come here today to control your life. But, if I wished, I could take you away and take away everything that is dear to you and reclaim all of my gifts. Go back to your château and you will see what a sorry state it is in and then you'll know that it's just punishment for your many crimes. I love crime, Baron; I lust after crime, and yet, my peculiar fate compels me to punish crime. Go back to your château, I say, and change your life! I shall grant you five more years, so you still have a while to live. Do you hear me? You will die in five years. However, your hope of one day being with God will not be taken away from you, provided you change your ways. And now I must go!

And the baron, on finding himself alone, & aware that he had not seen anyone leave his presence, quickly retraced his steps. He described the man to every peasant he met and then asked them if they had seen him entering the bower accompanied by a man of that description.

They each replied that he had entered it alone, that they had been so frightened at seeing him gesticulate to no one, had gone to warn madam, but had found that there was no one at the château.

— No one, exclaimed the baron, deeply disturbed. But I left my wife, my seven children & six servants there.

— There was no one there, Monsieur, one of the peasants said.

The others agreed.

With a deep sense of foreboding growing inside him, he ran to his château and hammered with his fists on the door. There was no answer so he broke down the door and ran inside. Blood was streaming down the stairs; a portent of what was about to happen to him. He opened the door of a large room, and saw his wife, his seven children, and his six servants, all dead; their bodies strewn on the ground, each lying in a different position in a pool of their own blood. He fell to the floor in a faint.

A group of peasants whose statements are still available to be read, entered & saw the same horrific sight. They put their employer into a chair and as he revived, he began beseeching them to give his wife and children the last rites. He then made his way on foot to the Grande Chartreuse where he died after five years of absolute devotion and piety.

We refuse to comment on this inexplicable event. It occurred, it was witnessed, but it cannot be explained. We must do all we can to avoid believing in illusions, but when something is universally attested, and there is a kind of singularity to it, we must simply bow our heads, close our eyes, and say: *I do not understand how the planets float in space, so there must also be things on earth that I will never comprehend.*

The Horse-Chestnut Flower [7]

It is alleged, although I cannot vouch for it with any certainty, that certain learned men claim that the horse chestnut tree most definitely possesses the same smell as the abundant seed which nature has placed within the loins of men for the reproduction of their species.

One day, after church, a young girl of around fifteen years of age, who lived at home with her parents, was walking with her mother and the Abbé, a family acquaintance, down an avenue of horse-chestnut trees, the flowers of which were filling the air with their very distinctive scent.

— Oh, mother, what a very intoxicating smell, said the girl, not realizing from where the scent emanated. What is it? It's a smell I recognize.

— Be quiet, daughter, the mother replied tersely. Don't make remarks of that kind, I implore you.

— But why not, mother? I don't see why I shouldn't tell you that I've smelled it before. I most definitely have.

— Thank you. That's quite enough! snapped the girl's mother.

— But, mother, I recognize it. Really I do.

Failing to understand her mother's response, the girl turned to the Abbé.

— Monsieur Father, please tell me, I beg you, what's so wrong with me telling my mother I recognize that smell?

— Mademoiselle, the Abbé said, adjusting his collar and speaking in a calm *&* measured tone. There is absolutely nothing wrong in the fact itself. However, we are walking along an avenue of horse-chestnut trees, and botanists are generally in agreement that the horse-chestnut flower —

— Yes? the girl interrupted. The horse-chestnut flower...?

— Mademoiselle, the Abbé said. They smell of spunk.

Tales & Fables

The Theology Teacher

Of all the subjects that are instilled in a child's head when working on his education, the mysteries of Christianity, although, without doubt, one of the most sublime parts of a young person's education, are not those that are introduced with the utmost ease to a young mind.

For example, persuading a young man of fourteen or fifteen years of age that God the father *&* God the son are one, that the son is consubstantial to his father and that the father is consubstantial to the son, et cetera, no matter how necessary it may be for a happy life, is more difficult to comprehend than algebra.

Therefore, when one wants to impart the details of the subject successfully, one is obliged to employ certain material explanations, certain physical methods, which, however unorthodox they are, nevertheless help a young mind to comprehend the complexity of this most mysterious of subjects.

No one was more deeply dedicated to this method than the Abbé Du Parquet, tutor to the young Comte de Nerceuil, who was about fifteen years old and already as handsome as a young man can be.

— Abbé, the Comte said to his teacher one day, in all honesty, consubstantiality is a subject far beyond my ability to comprehend; it is absolutely impossible for me to grasp that two people can make one. Explain this great mystery to me, I beg you, or at least demonstrate it in a way that I can grasp.

The honest Abbé, whole-heartedly dedicated to successfully educating the young Comte, was determined to teach his pupil everything that would one day make him an important and powerful leader of society. On hearing his pupil's request, he thought of a rather pleasant way of ironing out the difficulties that were currently stymieing the Comte, for where explanation fails, nature must necessarily succeed.

He brought home a young girl aged thirteen or fourteen and having instructed her in detail, he gave her to his young pupil.

— Well now, my young friend, he said to the Comte later, do you now comprehend the mystery of consubstantiality: do you find it less difficult to understand how it is possible that two people are one?

— Oh my God, yes, Monsieur Abbé, said the teenager, exuberantly. I have learned quite a lot about the subject now. It was surprisingly easy; I am not at all surprised that this mystery is, as is said, so joyful to heavenly people, for it is very sweet and enjoyable when two attempt being one.

A few days later, the Comte begged his teacher to give him another lesson, because, he claimed, there was still something in the mystery that he did not quite grasp and which could only be explained by participating in it once again, as he had already done.

The diligent Abbé, most amused by this request made by his pupil, brought the young girl back and the lesson began again. This time, during the lesson, the Abbé was so singularly aroused by the deliciously delightful view that the Comte de Nerceuil's companion presented to him when she consubstantiated herself with the Comte, that he could not resist putting himself forward as a third part of the explanation of the evangelical parable, and the fleshy delights that he had to touch and move in order to make the lesson clear ended up totally inflaming him.

— It seems to me that it's all a little too hurried, said the Abbé Du Parquet, putting his hand on the young Comte's back and slowing down his movements. There is far too much elasticity in the movements, from which it follows that the consubstantiation is no longer as intimate as it should be, and therefore presents a poorer understanding of the mystery that is being demonstrated here. However, said the reprobate Abbé, releasing his student and positioning himself beside the girl, if we proceed, oh, yes, in this way...

— Ah! Oh, my God! the young girl groaned. Both of you together makes me feel full, Monsieur Abbé. I feel quite a pleasurable sort of pain.

— Well, said the Comte, testily. This particular demonstration seems quite pointless to me. What more does it teach me about the mystery?

— Can't you see, my dear pupil, that I'm teaching you all of the sacred mystery at once? It's the trinity, my boy... Today, it's the trinity that I am demonstrating for you.

The Abbé gasped with pleasure.

— Oh, God, he groaned. Another five or six such lessons like this one and you will be a Doctor of Divinity at the Sorbonne.

The Prude, or the Unexpected Encounter

Monsieur de Sernenval was about forty years old, and had an income of twelve or fifteen thousand livres a year, which he spent quietly in Paris. He was no longer involved in the business in which he had made his money and was quite content to live without distinction except for the honorable title of burgher of Paris, with the possibility of an aldermanship at some future point. He had recently married the daughter of one of his former colleagues; his wife was twenty-four years old.

No one was as fresh-faced, as milky-white, as voluptuous, or as fleshily sensual as Madame de Sernenval. She was not built like the Graces but she was like a veritable goddess of love. She did not have the bearing of a queen, but she exuded sensuality and carnality without effort.

Her eyes were tender and languorous, her mouth was pretty, her throat firm, her body curved and inviting, as though solely designed to provoke desire. Most men, given the choice between her and one of the few truly beautiful women in Paris, would have chosen her.

But Madame de Sernenval, despite having so many physical attractions, had some very specific psychological defects... an unbearable prudishness, an exaggerated kind of virginal modesty, and an excess of devoutness that was so ridiculously excessive that it was impossible for her husband to persuade her to appear with him socially.

Taking bigotry to the extreme, it was very rare for Madame de Sernenval to want to spend an entire night with her husband, and in those very rare moments she deigned to grant him conjugal rights, it was always with excessive reservations and with her in a full-length night-gown that was never allowed to be raised. Beneath the nightgown was an artfully-placed apron which covered and obscured the entrance to the temple of Venus. The express clauses set out by Madame de Sernenval were that there was to be no clandestine touching and no carnal conjunction, both of which made any connubial enjoyment impossible. Madame de Sernenval would have been infuriated if her husband had attempted to cross the limits imposed by her modesty, and her husband, had he tried it, would have run the risk of never regaining the good graces of this wise, chaste, and virtuous woman.

But as he adored his wife, Monsieur de Sernenval humored her and deigned to respect her interdicts and her shortcomings. Sometimes he tried to talk to her about her prudishness. At those times, he would speak calmly to her, pointing out in the clearest way possible that spending most of one's life in churches or with priests is not the way an honest woman really fulfills her wifely duties which, first and foremost, are to her husband and to her home. He added that these should never be neglected by a devoted wife, and that she would honor the wishes of the Lord Almighty more by living honestly in the world with her husband, whom she had married in God's sight, than she would by burying herself in a gloomy cloister, where she was in constant danger of being misled by one or more of Mary's exemplars, whereas she would be respected & protected by his friends, the company of whom she ridiculously refused to keep.

— It's because I know you & love you as much as I do, added Monsieur de Sernenval, that I sometimes worry about you during your frequent religious devotions. Can you assure me that when you're not kneeling at the Lord's altar, you do not sometimes abandon yourselves on some Levites' soft cushions? There is nothing as dangerous as a lustful priest. They use their talk of God as a way of seducing our wives and daughters, and it is always in his name that they dishonor or deceive us. Believe me, my dear, one can be honest everywhere. Virtue does not build its temple in the cell of the Buddhist priest, nor in the niche of some idol — it builds it in the heart of an honest woman. There is no reason that you cannot socialize with any of my friends and acquaintances. They are all honest and decent people. Meeting them will not interfere with nor taint your worship of virtue. You are considered by many to be Virtue's most faithful disciple and I truly believe that you are. But what proof do I have that you really deserve this reputation? I would be more convinced of it if I had seen you resist the artful seductions of renowned Lotharios. A woman does not establish her virtue by avoiding would-be seducers, but rather by being sufficiently self-confident enough to know she can easily resist any attempts to make her stray from her husband.

As was usual, Madame de Sernenval did not say anything in response to her husband's words, for, in fact, the points he made were unanswerable. She did, however, begin to cry quite piteously, itself a common enough strategy used by weak, false, or fallen women and, because of her tears, her husband took pity on her and did not care to push the lesson home any further.

This is how things stood between the good Monsieur and his wife when an old friend of Sernenval's, a man named Desportes, arrived from Nancy to see him, having come to the capital to conclude some business there. Desportes was a bon vivant, about the same age as his friend, and he was very partial to the pleasures men habitually use to distract themselves from life's hardships and burdens.

Sernenval's offer of accommodation in his own home was graciously accepted, and Desportes was overjoyed at seeing his old friend again. He was, however, somewhat taken aback by the rudeness of his friend's wife, who, as soon as she knew there was a stranger in the house, absolutely refused to put in an appearance and no longer came down for meals.

As Desportes believed he was the cause of her embarrassment, he offered to stay elsewhere.

Sernenval insisted he stay in his home as a guest and confided in his friend, having decided to explain his dear wife's seemingly odd behavior.

— Please forgive her, said the gullible husband. She makes up for these wrongs by so many virtues that she has earned my indulgence and all I ask is that you do likewise if you can.

— All right, replied Desportes, As long as nothing is directed at me, personally, I won't pass judgment. In fact, the faults of the wife of my oldest friend will never, in my eyes, be anything other than respectable qualities.

Relieved, Sernenval embraced his friend, after which their talk turned to entertainment and pleasure.

It was due to the immense stupidity of two or three dull-witted officials (and the stupidity of one particular Spanish chaplain, who earned over one hundred thousand écus a year by organizing the type of inquisition we are talking about); two or three officials then, who were solely responsible during the past fifty years for controlling the prostitutes of Paris, and it was, I repeat, due to the trivial puritanism of those stupid individuals that they eventually came up with the idiotic notion that the most efficient method of managing the State, one of the surest methods of government, in short, one of the keys to public morality, was to pass a by-law that demanded that every professional woman provide an exact account of which part of their body best delighted the individual who had paid for their services, along with the name of that individual. Those bureaucratic fools believed that there was a difference between a man who looked at breasts, and one who preferred looking at buttocks, and for those dullards, that difference was the same as the one that existed between an honest citizen and a villain, or between being a male and a being a female, and that when a man fell into one or the other of those categories (which he did solely in order to follow the dictates of his own tastes) then that person was, out of necessity, the greatest enemy of the State. Here, I repeat again, if it were not for that disgraceful directive, then it is more than likely that those two honorable men, one with a sanctimonious wife, the other a single man with a taste for pleasure, might have spent some time in the company of two or more of those aforementioned young ladies. It was because of that infamous & absurd regulation governing the pleasures of the citizens that it did not occur to Sernenval to so much as hint to Desportes that he had that particular type of leisure activity in mind.

However, Desportes realized this, but not suspecting the reasons, asked his friend why, having already offered him all the pleasures of the capital, he had not told him about this one? Sernenval admitted he objected to the stupid regulations. Desportes joked about them and then, despite the lists compiled by brothel-keepers, the reports by commissioners, the depositions of the gendarmerie, and all of the ramifications of an onerous system established by the government to monitor the pleasures of the citizens of Paris, he told his friend that he absolutely wanted to "sup with whores."

— Listen, said Sernenval, I agree with you regarding the regulations, and I would like very much to enjoy one of those women myself, but by a delicacy of sentiment that I hope you will not criticize, by which I mean those feelings of love and honor that I have for my wife and which I am unable to ignore, I hope you'll understand why I won't share your pleasures. However, I'm happy to procure one of those women for you; I'll even introduce you to one I think you'll enjoy as proof of my philosophical way of thinking on this subject... but I'll go no further than that.

Desportes briefly tried to convince his friend to change his mind, but after seeing that Sernenval was determined not to let himself be moved on the subject, he agreed to everything, and they set off.

The famous S. J. was the high priestess of the temple in which Sernenval had decided to have his friend "sacrificed."

— We need a reliable woman for this very good friend of mine, Sernenval said to her. She needs to be a decent woman, so please take really good care choosing the right one for him. He's only staying in Paris for a few days and I'd like him to go home without taking back anything that might ruin his reputation, if you follow my meaning. Do you have such a woman? And if you do, how much will you charge for him to enjoy her for a few hours?

— You're the type of gentleman I always feel honored to be addressing, S. J. said, and you're not the type that

I enjoy fooling, so I'll speak to you as an honest business woman. I have exactly what you're looking for, so all we have to do is agree on a price. The woman I have in mind is perfect for your friend. She has some exemplary skills and he'll be delighted with her. She's what we call in the trade, "priest meat," because I only hire her out to gentlemen of the clergy. I don't allow just any woman near those men, as they're my best-paying customers. I think they deserve quality for their money. And she's quality; three days ago the Bishop of M. gave me twenty louis for her, with the Archbishop of R., she made fifty yesterday, and this morning again she earned me thirty for an hour with the Co-adjutor of —. You're obviously men of distinction so I'll let you use her for ten louis, and that in truth, gentlemen, is out of genuine respect for both of you. But you must be scrupulously punctual regarding the day and the hour of the liaison, because she has a husband who watches her every move. He's incredibly jealous, so she can only get away at certain times. Please make sure you're on time, gentlemen.

Desportes said he would like to experience that particular woman, then haggled with S. J. for a while, for he had never paid ten louis for a whore in the whole of Lorraine, but the more he sought to reduce the price, the more the procuress increased it. Finally, he agreed to her terms and they set the time for the liaison at ten o'clock sharp the following morning.

Sernenval assured his friend that, although he was not going to indulge, he would accompany his friend to the assignation in the morning. Desportes was more than happy with that arrangement, realizing that the ten o'clock appointment meant that he would have the remainder of the day for other activities, before he had to return to his home town…

The clock chimed ten o'clock in the morning as the two friends were shown in a dimly-lit anteroom. It was expensively furnished. Sernenval led Desportes to the door of the goddess's boudoir.

— Go on then, love's chosen one, Sernenval said, as he pushed him into the boudoir. Go to those arms that are held out eagerly, ready to embrace you. I'm going to wait out here, so don't forget to come and tell me all about your experience, because I will take pleasure in your pleasure; your happiness will make me happy and my joy will be all the purer as I will not be jealous of it.

The acolyte entered the temple. The three hours he spent in worship were barely long enough for his tribute. He finally came out of the room and told his friend that in all of his days he had never experienced such a delectable woman, and that only a true goddess of love could have provided him with such pleasures.

— So, she's delectable, is she? Sernenval asked, beginning to feel aroused.

— Delectable? Yes. But, in truth, I can't really find the right words to make you understand how truly extraordinary she really is. Even now, at this very moment as the beautiful illusion fades, I feel that there's no artist, or no brush that could paint the floods of pleasure into which she plunged me. She has a natural artistry that is so sensual that she could be one of the Graces. She knows how to give piquant, delectable pleasures that are so intense I'm still intoxicated by her touch. My friend, you should try her yourself. Whatever your thoughts are regarding the beauties of Paris, I am can guarantee that none of them is equal to this one.

Sernenval remained resolute, but nevertheless felt somewhat curious, so he asked S. J. to make sure the woman walked past him when she left the boudoir. She agreed, and placed the two friends where they would be able to observe her better. Eventually the Goddess left the boudoir and passed them...

Good God! Sernenval stood there, frozen in total shock when he recognized his wife. It was her! It seemed that the so-called prude, who claimed she was too shy to sit down at dinner with her husband's friend had the audacity to prostitute herself in such a place.

— You whore! he bellowed, in his fury.

He rushed across the room to strike the treacherous creature, but she was far too fast for him. She had recognized him before he had recognized her, and she had bolted from the house and was already out of the building before he could get anywhere near her.

Sernenval, now in a state that was almost impossible to describe, turned angrily on S. J., demanding she explain.

The procuress pleaded her innocence, stating that the woman had been plying her trade regularly and had received hundreds of men there during the last five years, which was long before the unfortunate Sernenval had married her.

— The cheating whore! Sernenval yelled, as his friend tried unsuccessfully to calm him.

They left the building, Sernenval raging.

— No. It's all over. I've nothing but contempt for her now and I hope she can feel it. I've learned a hard lesson; a bitter lesson, which is that a woman can never be judged by the hypocritical mask she wears.

Sernenval returned home to find that his whore had packed her belongings and had gone. He did not concern himself with where she had gone or what she was doing. His friend, far too embarrassed by what had happened to stay with Serneval, returned home the next day.

The wretched Sernenval, alone, weighed down by humiliation and grief, wrote a pamphlet denouncing hypocritical wives. It did nothing to persuade any woman to alter their behavior and no man ever read it.

Émilie de Tourville, or Fraternal Cruelty

Nothing is more sacred to a family than the honor of its members. But, if this treasure becomes tarnished, however precious it may be, should those who are interested in protecting it do so by taking on the dishonorable role of persecutor of the unfortunate creatures that offend them? Would it not be reasonable to set against them the horrors they use to torment their victim and the damage, often imaginary, they claim they have suffered? Finally, who is more guilty from the viewpoint of reason: a weak and deceived young woman or a relative who, in setting himself up as the avenger of the family, becomes the executioner of that unfortunate woman? The story that we are going to relate to you, reader, will perhaps answer that question.

It was about six o'clock in the evening at the end of November when the Comte de Luxeuil, a lieutenant-general aged about fifty-six or fifty-seven, was traveling in a post-chaise to one of his properties in Picardy. As he passed through the forest of Compiègne, he heard the cries of a woman. The cries seemed to be coming from a bend in the road, not far ahead of him. He stopped and ordered his valet, who was perched on the luggage rack of the carriage, to go and see what it was. The valet ran to investigate, then returned and said it was a young girl, no more than sixteen or seventeen years old, covered in so much of her own blood that it was impossible to see where she was injured or even what she looked like.

The Comte immediately leapt from the carriage and rushed to help the unfortunate girl. He also found that, due to the descending darkness, it was almost impossible to see where the blood she had lost came from. From her weak answers to his gentle enquiries, he was finally able to discern that all of it had poured from two hole-like wounds in her arms, very like the ones surgeons made if the patient needed to be bled.

— Mademoiselle, said the Comte, after helping the poor creature as much as he could, I'm not really in a position to ask you for the details of your misfortunes, and you're hardly in a state to tell me. If you'll let me help you into my carriage I'll do all I can to convey you to where you can get help. You can use the carriage seat to rest & calm yourself.

Monsieur de Luxeuil and his valet then carried the poor young lady in the post-chaise, & then continued their journey.

As soon as the intriguing young woman saw that she was safe, she tried to stammer a few words of thanks.

The Comte quickly implored her not to speak:

— Tomorrow, mademoiselle, tomorrow. Then if you wish, you can tell me everything that has happened to you. Today, however, by the authority of my age & the good fortune I have to be of service to you, I must insist you stay still & remain silent, in order to conserve your strength and to try and calm yourself.

They arrived at the Comte's château. In order to avoid explanations, arguments, or any hint of a scandal, the Comte had his protégé wrapped in a man's coat and ordered his valet to take her to a suitable apartment in a far wing of his château without letting anyone else witness this.

The Comte went to see how she was after he had greeted and embraced his wife and his son, both of whom were waiting to have supper with him that evening.

When the Comte went to see his guest, he took a surgeon with him. The surgeon examined the young woman and found her to be in a state of extreme exhaustion. The pallor of her skin suggested that she had only a few moments left to live, although she had no obvious wounds other than some quite common small cuts that indicated she had been bled. Her physical weakness, she said, came from the enormous quantity of blood she had been losing every day for three months, and as she was about to tell the Comte the unnatural cause of that prodigious loss, she fainted from her weakness. The surgeon tended to her, then declared that she should be left to rest properly, after which he gave instructions that she have cordials & restoratives administered regularly.

The unfortunate young woman had a fairly restful night, but for the next six days she was still too weak to inform her benefactor of the misfortunes that had befallen her.

Everyone in the Comte's household, with the exception of the Comte and his valet, remained unaware that the young woman was concealed there. On the evening of the seventh day, the young woman, not knowing where she was due to the precautions the Comte had taken, begged him to hear what she had to say, & above all to grant her his understanding regarding whatever grievous faults she confessed.

Monsieur de Luxeuil took a seat and assured his protégé that he would be sympathetic and not lose interest in what she told him, because her situation was a clear indication it would be inspiring.

Reassured by the Comte's words, our beautiful adventuress began the account of her misfortunes.

Mademoiselle de Tourville's Story

I am the daughter, Monsieur, of Judge de Tourville, a man too well known and too distinguished in his profession to be unknown to you. Two years ago I left the convent & returned to my father's house, which I have not left since then. I lost my mother when I was very young, so he alone took care of my education and I can say categorically that he neglected nothing in order to give me all the graces & charms of my sex.

The attention he paid me, the plans that he announced regarding having me marry as advantageously as possible, perhaps even a degree of favoritism on his part, soon aroused the jealousy of my brothers. One had been a magistrate for three years, and he had just reached the age of twenty-six and the other, who was nearly twenty-four, had recently been made a councilor.

I did not know and could never have imagined that I was as deeply hated by them as I now have good reason to know that I was. Having done nothing to deserve those feelings from them, I was under the sweet illusion that they returned the same feelings for me that my heart innocently held for them.

Oh, merciful Heaven, how mistaken I was!

Except for the time given to my education, I enjoyed the greatest possible freedom in my father's house. Making me solely responsible for my own conduct, he did not restrict me in any way.

And in the last eighteen months he had granted me permission to walk in the mornings with my maid, named Julie, either on the terrace of the Tuileries, or on the rampart near to where we lived. He had also allowed me, if accompanied by her, to go out walking, or to go in one of my father's carriages and visit my friends or my relatives, provided that it was not at a time when a young person cannot be alone with a group of older people.

The whole cause of my misfortunes comes from this fatal freedom, which is why I am mentioning it to you, Monsieur. I now wish to God that I had never been granted it.

A year ago, I was out walking without my maid. As I have just told you, I had a penchant for walking through a somewhat secluded part of the Tuileries, where I thought I would achieve more solitude than I would on the terrace and where, it seemed to me, the air was cleaner. Six young, rather uncouth louts suddenly surrounded & accosted me, and I quickly understood from the crudity of their suggestions that they took me for... what is referred to as... a *prostitute!*

I was horribly embarrassed by the crassness of their propositions, and not knowing how to escape this cruel predicament, I was about to seek salvation in flight, when a young man, whom I often saw walking alone there, often at the same time as myself, and whose appearance, manner, and general demeanor indicated his honesty & integrity, happened to be passing by at that moment.

— Monsieur! I cried out, calling him over to me, I don't have the honor of knowing you, but we see each other here almost every morning. I walk here habitually with my maid and, I flatter myself, what you have seen of me has convinced you that I am not a... not the kind of woman these men think I am. If you believe me, I ask you in all sincerity to give me your hand and accompany me home and to deliver me from these... *men!*

Monsieur de..., you will allow me to keep his name a secret; many reasons oblige me to do so, rushed over immediately, and having convinced them of their mistake by the air of politeness and respect with which he greeted me, he quickly sent away the young rabble that had surrounded me, took my arm, and immediately led me from the garden.

— Mademoiselle, he said to me shortly before we reached my home, I think it wise to leave you here; if I take you to your home, it will be necessary to explain why. That could result in your being forbidden to go for walks alone anymore; therefore simply conceal what has just happened by making no reference to it. Continue to walk there as is your habit, after all it entertains you and your parents allow you to do so. For my part, I'll continue to walk there daily, always at the same time as you, and you'll always find me ready to offer my life, if necessary, to oppose any disturbance to your tranquility.

Such thoughtfulness and such an obliging offer made me appraise this young man with a little more interest than I had thought to do previously.

He was two or three years older than I and exceedingly handsome.

I blushed as I thanked him, and the fiery arrows of that divine young seducer, who is the cause of all of my present misfortunes, penetrated right to my heart before I had time to resist.

We separated, but I thought I could see in the way that Monsieur de ... left me that I had made on him the same impression that he had just made on me. I returned to my father's house, where I was careful not to say anything about what had happened. I returned the next day at the same time to the same place, driven to do so by a feeling that was stronger than myself.

That feeling made me feel I could face any danger that I could have encountered... What I'm saying is that perhaps I would have deliberately sought out those young louts, simply to have the pleasure of being rescued again by that same man.

I'm describing my soul to you, Monsieur, perhaps a little naïvely but you promised you would be sympathetic, and every new development in my story will make you see that I need it. This is not the only reckless thing you will hear me admit to & this is not the only occasion that I shall need your pity.

Monsieur de ... appeared on the pathway six minutes after me, and came up to me as soon as he saw me.

— Dare I ask you, mademoiselle, he said. Has yesterday's incident caused you any scandal or personal loss or upset?

I assured him that it had not and told him that I had taken advantage of his advice, which I thanked him for, flattering myself by saying that nothing would disturb the pleasure I took in going there to breathe in the morning air.

— If you find pleasure in it, mademoiselle, Monsieur de ... replied, then those who have the pleasant good fortune to meet you here no doubt enjoy it all the more. If I took the liberty of advising you yesterday not to risk anything that might disturb your walks, you owe me no thanks. I can assure you, mademoiselle, that I said it less for you than for me.

And as he said this, he looked into my eyes with such an expression... oh Monsieur, how could I have known that that softly-spoken, considerate man would be responsible for all of my later misfortunes?

I responded lightly to his remark and our conversation began as we walked round the gardens twice together and M. de ... did not leave me without asking me whom he had had the honor of accompanying home the day before. I could think of no reason to hide my name from him. I told him my name and he told me his and we separated.

For nearly a month, Monsieur, we saw each other there almost every day. This month, as you can easily imagine, we each confessed to the other what we felt and we promised each other that we would feel that way forever. Finally Monsieur de ... begged me to allow us to meet somewhere that was less restrictive than a public garden.

— I dare not present myself at your father's house, my beautiful Émilie, he said to me. I have never had the honor of being introduced to him, so he would soon suspect and then question the motive that attracted me to his home. Instead of that direct approach furthering our plans, it could prove disastrous to them. However, if you really are as good-hearted and as compassionate as I know you are, and you're not prepared to let me die of sorrow at no longer being granted that which I request of you, I will tell you of certain ways and means.

At first, I categorically refused to hear what his "ways and means" were, but soon I weakened & I asked him. These means, Monsieur, were that we met three times a week at the home of a Madame Berceil, a milliner in the Rue des Arcis, a woman who, Monsieur de … assured me, was as prudent and as honest as his own mother.

— Since you are allowed to see your aunt, he said, who lives, so you told me, quite close to there, you must simply pretend to visit this aunt. You should actually pay her short visits, and come and spend the rest of the time you would have given to her at the house of the good woman I mentioned to you. Your aunt, if ever questioned, will state that you do visit her on those days you say you visit. Therefore, it is only a matter of measuring the length of the visits, and you can be sure that no one would ever think to do that, once they verify you spoke truthfully about the days of your visits.

I shall not list for you, Monsieur, all of the objections I made to Monsieur de … in order to discourage him from implementing his plan and to make him aware of the disadvantages. What would be the point of my telling you of my resistance, since I succumbed eventually? I promised Monsieur de … I would do everything he wanted.

There was also the matter of the twenty louis which he gave to my maid, Julie. I was unaware of that transaction at the time, but once she'd accepted it, it put that girl entirely in his power, and from then on they, and I, worked toward my total ruin.

In order to make things more complete, so that I would have the time and the leisure to become intoxicated on the sweet poison that flowed into my heart, I pretended to confide in my aunt. I concocted a story. I told her that a young lady friend of mine wanted to do me the kindness of taking me three times a week to her box in the Comédie Française, and that I did not dare tell my father for fear that he would oppose it, but that I would say that I was coming to see her. I begged her to corroborate this. After a heated discussion, my aunt capitulated. She had her objections, but she had always found it difficult to refuse me anything. I explained my plot to her. Instead of my visiting my aunt, Julie, my maid, would visit her in my place. On the way back from the "show," I would simply join Julie there & we would walk back home together. I kissed my aunt a thousand times in gratitude. With the fatal blindness of the passions, I thanked her for being a party to my destruction. Without being overly dramatic, Monsieur, I was unaware that she had opened the door to a series of errors that would lead me to the edge of my grave.

Our liaisons finally began at the Berceil's house; her shop was superb, her house very respectable, and she herself was a woman of about forty whom I thought I could trust with every confidence. Trust, alas; I had too much of it in her and in my lover... the traitor.

It is time to confess to you, Monsieur... on the sixth occasion that I saw him in that fatal house, he had gained such a hold over me that he succeeded in seducing me. He used seduction to take advantage of my weakness and naïvety and, as I lay in his arms, I became the idol of his passion and the victim of my own. Cruel pleasures have already cost me thousands of tears; remorse will tear at my soul until the very last moment of my life.

A year passed in this state of fatal illusion, Monsieur. I had just reached my seventeenth year. My father spoke to me every day about a marriage that would be of benefit to myself and our family. You may judge for yourself how much I shuddered at these proposals.

And then there occurred a fatal event that finally tipped me into the eternal abyss in which I had so eagerly plunged. Grim Providence had arranged for me to be severely punished for something that I had not done wrong. I think Providence gave its permission for this punishment to be meted out in order to make it clear to me that we never can escape it, that it relentlessly pursues those who stray, and that it is the incident that we least suspect that leads imperceptibly to the one that delivers the punishment.

Monsieur de ... had forewarned me that one day some business affair would deprive him of the pleasure of the three hours of unadulterated pleasure that we had together. He promised that he would come for a few minutes before the end of our liaison. In order not to disturb our usual arrangements, he said, I should go to Madame Berceil's house for the same amount of time

I usually spent there and, I would in fact, for an hour or two, find more enjoyment with the milliner and her girls than I would if I were alone at my father's house. I thought I could rely on this woman enough for there to be no obstacle to what my lover suggested; I promised that I would do as he asked and begged him not to be too long. He assured me that he would free himself of his business obligations as soon as he possibly could, and I duly arrived.

Oh, what a terrible day it turned out to be for me!

Madame Berceil met me at the entrance of her shop, but she would not allow me to go up to her apartment as she usually did.

— Mademoiselle, she said to me as soon as she saw me, I am delighted that Monsieur de … cannot be here until later. I have something to tell you that I dare not tell him, something that means we must both go outside at once for a few moments, which we could not have done if he had been here.

— What's this all about, madam? I asked, a little alarmed by her request and her manner.

— Nothing much, Mademoiselle, Madame Berceil answered. Nothing at all. For a start, please calm yourself. It's the simplest thing in the world; my mother has noticed your affair and thinks you'll drag me into trouble. She's an old meddler, but she's as honest as a confessor. I have to handle her very carefully because she has money. She has insisted that I no longer allow you to use my

apartment for your liaisons. I dare not tell Monsieur de ...,
but here is what I have thought of. I think it best that I
take you immediately to the home of one of my friends, a
woman of my age who's as discrete as I am. I'll introduce
you to her. If you like her, you can tell Monsieur de ... that
I took you there, that she's an honest woman and that
you're happy for your liaisons to take place there. If you
don't like her, which I think is unlikely, then we'll have
been gone for a moment and there'll be no need for you
to say anything, because I'll simply inform Monsieur de
... myself that I can no longer lend him my apartment.
You will both then need to make new arrangements for
your meetings.

What this woman told me was so simple, the air and
tone she used so natural, my confidence in her so complete and my innocence so perfect, that I did not have
the slightest concern about agreeing to what she asked.

I told her I was sorry that she found it impossible, as
she'd stated, to continue to lend us her apartment, and
how much I appreciated her efforts on my behalf, & we
set off. The house I was taken to was on the same street, a
mere sixty or eighty steps away at the most from Madame
Berceil's home. There was nothing about the outside of
the house that gave me pause; a neat carriage entrance,
fine casement windows that looked out onto the street,
a general air of cleanliness and respectability about the
place. And yet a secret voice seemed to cry out from

the depths of my heart that some singular event awaited me in that ill-fated house; I felt a kind of revulsion with every step I climbed, everything around me seemed to be whispering to me: *Where are you going, you foolish girl? Get away from this dangerous place.*

On entering, however, we found we were in a rather fine antechamber where we found nobody. From there, we went into a drawing-room and the door was immediately closed behind us, as though someone had been hiding behind it. I shuddered. It was very dark in that drawing-room, so dark that I could barely see to cross it. I had taken no more than three steps when I was seized by two women. The door of a small adjoining room opened and a naked man aged about fifty stood in the doorway, flanked by two more women. The man called out to the two women who held me:

— Undress her, undress her, and bring her over here when she's completely naked.

Having quickly recovered from the shock of being seized by the two women, I realized that any chance of salvation depended on my shouts of outrage rather than on my being frightened into silence. And so I shrieked repeatedly, filling the room with a terrible noise.

Madame Berceil did everything she could to calm me down.

— It'll only take a moment, mademoiselle, she said. Please try and be a little compliant, I beg you, and you'll have helped me earn fifty louis.

— You foul harridan! I yelled at her. Don't you dare try to besmirch my honor. If you don't help me to leave here now, I'll throw myself out of a window into the street.

— If you did, one of the vile women holding me said, you'd only land in our courtyard and we'd soon bring you back, my child. It's best you just do as you're told.

As she spoke, she started pulling off my clothes. Her companion did likewise.

Oh Monsieur, spare my telling you the rest of these horrible details. Oh, no matter. I shall continue. I was naked in an instant, and my cries were stifled. I was dragged naked and thrashing across the room toward that disgustingly aroused man, who laughed at my tears and my feeble attempts at resistance. The two women continued to hold me down as though they were offering me to that monster, whose main concern seemed to be breaking my heart and making me his unfortunate victim.

He stepped forward and knelt down between... knelt in a position where he could do whatever he wanted. He was fully inflamed with ardor and sought his satisfaction with several impure caresses and a number of intimate kisses. I closed my eyes and endured his foul touch. He did not try to do anything to me other than touch and kiss certain parts of my body as he also touched himself. He continued to do this until he... until his body responded...

That seemed to be his objective, because he then stood up, went back into the room and closed the door. The women released me and helped me to get dressed, after which, they handed me back to Madame Berceil.

Dazed, confused, ashamed and filled with a kind of dark and bitter pain that froze my tears deep within my heart, I stared malevolently at that vile woman, furious at what she'd done...

— Mademoiselle, she said to me, terribly agitated, while we were still in the antechamber of that ill-fated house, I realize the full horror of what I have just done to you, but I beg you to forgive me... or if you cannot, then to at least think things over before you decide to make a scandal. If you tell Monsieur de ... what has happened here, no matter how much you protest you were forced into it, it's the kind of conduct he will never be able to forgive. It will result in you constantly arguing with, and perhaps even losing, the one man in the world whose good opinion you most desire. You have no way of ever repairing the honor he has already stolen from you, except by persuading him to marry you. You can be sure that he would never agree to that if you decided to tell him what just happened.

— Then why, you wretched woman, have you deliberately thrown me into this abyss? Why put me in a situation where I must either deceive my lover, or else lose my honor and him too?

— Please calm yourself, Mademoiselle. Let's no longer talk about what *has* been done; there's no time for recriminations. Let's concern ourselves, with some urgency, with what needs to *be* done. If you tell the truth, you're lost; if you say nothing, my house will always be open to you, you will never be betrayed by anyone, and you will stay with your lover. Revenge, however, would bring you very little in the way of satisfaction and in reality it means nothing to me because I know your shameful secret and I won't hesitate to tell Monsieur de ... if he should ever try to cause me harm. So you see, the small pleasure of revenge outweighs the huge amount of sorrow it would cause...

It was then that I fully realized what a truly despicable type of woman I was dealing with. I was also aware of the full force of her reasoned threats, and how terrible they were.

— Let's go, Madame, I said to her. Let's get out of here. Don't leave me in this house any longer. I shall not say a word to anyone, as long as you do the same. And yes, I'll continue to make use of you since I cannot break off our bond without revealing the shameful things that are important for me to keep quiet, but at least I will have the satisfaction in my heart of hating you and despising you as much as you deserve.

We returned to Madame Berceil's house... And good heavens, a whole new cause for anxiety awaited me there. We were told that Monsieur de ... had been there and that he had been informed that Madame had gone out on urgent business, and that Mademoiselle had not yet arrived. One of the girls in the house handed me a note that he had hastily written. It was addressed to me and contained only these words: *I cannot find you. I imagine that you have not been able to come at the usual time.*

I will not be able to see you this evening, it is impossible for me to wait, so I will see you the day after tomorrow without fail.

His note did nothing to calm me; its cold detachment seemed to be bad sign: *I cannot find you... not be able to see you... impossible for me to wait,* so much impatience... it all agitated me to an extent that's impossible for me to describe. Could he not have seen us leaving Madame Berceil's and followed us? And if he had, then I was surely now lost and dishonored.

Madame Berceil, as worried by this as I, questioned everyone. She was told that Monsieur de ... had arrived three minutes after we had left, that he had seemed very concerned, that he had left immediately but had then returned about half an hour later and written the note to me. Even more alarmed by this information, I sent for a carriage... but would you believe, Monsieur, the absolutely disgusting suggestion that that despicable woman dared voice?

— Mademoiselle, she said to me, when she saw that I was about to leave, it would be best if you said nothing about this matter to anyone. I cannot stress enough the importance of remaining silent. Should you have the misfortune to break off with Monsieur de ..., then, believe me, you should take full advantage of your freedom to enjoy pleasurable liaisons with other parties. It would be so much better for you than simply having one lover. You're very respectable, but you're also very young.

Your family may be wealthy, but you yourself have very little money. Since you are so attractive, you could earn as much as you want. You would not be the only one to have chosen such a course. There are many refined ladies in the best circles of society who are married to Comtes or Marquises, just as you may do one day, who, either of their own accord, or though arrangements by their governesses, have passed through our hands, just as you could. We have customers who would pay exceedingly well for a young doll-like girl like you. You experienced one such earlier. Like him, they would consider you a beautiful rose and breathe in your fragrance, but they would not bruise your flowers. Anyway, I must say farewell to you now, my beauty. Let's not shy away from each other anymore. As you can see, I may still be of use to you.

I looked at that creature in absolute horror and left at once without replying. I met Julie at my aunt's house, as was my usual arrangement, and I went home.

I no longer had any means of communicating with Monsieur de ..., for although we met in person three times a week, we were not in the habit of writing to each other. Therefore, I would have to wait until our next liaison before I could speak to him. What would he say to me? What would I say to him? Should I conceal what had happened? If I did, there was the attendant danger that it could be discovered, so should I not simply confess everything to him?...

All of these different possibilities kept me in an indescribable state of anxiety. Finally I decided to follow Madame Berceil's advice and say nothing. I knew that that woman would benefit greatly from my silence, but I felt secrecy was best regarding this shameful matter.

Ultimately, all of my schemes turned out to be worth nothing, since I would not see my lover again and the storm that was going to break over my head was already building up on all sides.

The day after this incident, my elder brother asked me why I allowed myself to go out on my own several times a week and at such times.

— I spend the afternoons with our aunt, I said.

— That is not quite true, is it, Émilie? You have not set foot there for over a month.

— Well, my dear brother, I replied, trembling, I shall tell you everything. One of my friends, whom you know well, Madame de Saint-Clair, has been kind enough to invite me three times a week into her box at the Comédie Française. I did not dare mention it, in case father disapproved and forbade it, but our aunt knows all about it.

— So you go to see shows, do you? my brother remarked. You could have told me, I would have accompanied you, and then the whole business would have been so much simpler… But going alone with a woman who is not related to you and who is almost as young as you are…

— Come, come, said my other brother, who had joined us during the conversation, Mademoiselle has her distractions. We should not be concerned… If she's looking for a husband, they'll certainly appear in droves with that sort of conduct…

And they both rather rudely turned their backs on me.

The conversation frightened me; however, as my elder brother seemed to be convinced by my story of going to the theater, I thought I had succeeded in deceiving him and that would be the end of it. Moreover, even if they had said more, short of locking me up, nothing in the world could have prevented me from going to our next arranged liaison. It had become far too important to clarify everything with my lover, and nothing was going to stop me from going to see him.

As for my father, he was still the same, idolizing me, suspecting nothing of my faults, and never interfering with my freedom. How cruel it is to have to deceive such parents, and how the remorse that arises from such deceit sets thorns amongst the pleasures that one buys at the expense of betrayals of that kind!

May this terrible example of a cruel passion be an example to any young woman who finds herself in the same predicament as me, and hopefully stop her from making my mistakes. And should they ever hear my pitiful story, then may the suffering that my guilty pleasures have cost me stop them in their tracks long before they reach the brink of the abyss.

The fatal day finally arrived. Taking Julie, I slipped out as usual. I left her at my aunt's house and quickly made my way in my carriage to Madame Berceil's home. I got out… the silence, the darkness that permeated the house greatly alarmed me at first… Inside, no familiar face showed itself to me. The only person I saw was an old woman I had never seen before, but who I was, to my cost, going to see much of. She approached me and said I should wait in one of the ante-rooms, as Monsieur de …, yes, she gave his name, would be joining me there almost immediately. An overwhelming chill suddenly made me feel quite weak and I collapsed into an arm-chair. I had hardly had time to sit down when my two brothers, both armed with pistols, entered the room and stood in front of me.

— You wretched girl! the eldest yelled. So this is how you try and trick us, is it? If you show the slightest resistance, if you so much as cry out for help, you are dead. Follow us! We are going to teach you what happens if you betray the family that you have so dishonored, and the lover with whom you have indulged your depravities.

As he uttered those last words, I lost consciousness completely. I regained my senses to find myself in the back of a carriage that seemed to me to be going very fast. I was seated between my two brothers and opposite me was the old woman I have just mentioned. My legs were tied together, and both hands were tied tightly at the wrists with a handkerchief.

The tears that had so far been kept back by my excess of despair now flowed abundantly, and I spent an hour in a state which, however guilty I might have been, would have moved anyone to sympathy, anyone, that is, other than the two tormentors who had me in their power. They did not speak to me for the entire journey. I imitated their silence and remained sunk in my suffering.

We finally arrived the next day at eleven o'clock in the morning at a château set deep in a wood between Courcy and Noyon. It belonged to my elder brother. The carriage entered the courtyard, and was ordered to remain there until the horses and servants had gone; then my elder brother came for me.

— Follow me, he said to me brutally, after he had released me...

I obeyed, trembling... God, I grew very scared on seeing the horrifying place they had chosen to be my place of detention. It was a low, dark, and damp room, with iron bars on its door and its one window. Hardly any daylight penetrated the room, and the window itself looked out onto a wide ditch full of water.

— This is to be your residence, mademoiselle, my elder brother told me. Any girl who dishonors her family in the way you have deserves such a home. Your food will be proportionate to the rest of your treatment. This is what you will be given, he continued, holding up a piece of bread of the rough type that is thrown to animals. We do not want to make you suffer for a long time; on the other hand, we want to make it impossible for you to escape from here. Therefore, these two women, he said, showing me the old woman and another who looked not dissimilar to her, who we found in the château, these two women have been ordered that you are to be bled from both arms as many times a week as you used to meet Monsieur de … at Madame Berceil's house. Inevitably, or so we hope, this regime will send you to an early grave and we will only be truly happy when we learn that the family is rid of the monster that you are.

Having made his disgusting speech, he ordered the two women to seize me, and in front of them, my brothers, both cruel villains, Monsieur, forgive me for this expression, bled me from both arms at once and did not stop this cruel treatment until I had lost consciousness…

When I came to, I found them each applauding the other's barbarity. It was as if they had wanted all of fate's blows to be inflicted on me at once, as if they enjoyed rending my heart at the same moment as they shed my blood.

The eldest brother, I hesitate to use that word, took a letter from his pocket, and handed it to me, saying:

— Read, mademoiselle, and learn to whom you owe your suffering…

I opened the letter, trembling.

My eyes barely had the strength to read those fatal words. Oh, great God… it was from my lover himself; it was he who had betrayed me. This is what his cruel letter said, the words are still imprinted on my heart in letters of blood:

I have been foolish enough to love your sister, Monsieur, and imprudent enough to dishonor her. I intended to put everything to rights; consumed by remorse, I was going to fall at your father's feet, confess my guilt, and ask him for his daughter's hand. I would have confessed my own culpability, and I was ready to be linked in marriage to your sister. However, just as I was forming these resolutions... my eyes, my own eyes convinced me that I was dealing with nothing less than a common whore, who under cover of a liaison governed by honorable and respectable feelings, opted to go to an establishment and satisfy the twisted desires of the most disgusting of men. Do not expect further reparation from me, Monsieur. I no longer owe you anything other than abandonment, and her the most inviolable hatred and the most utter contempt. I am sending you the address of the house where your sister used to go for her own corrupt reasons so that you can verify for yourself that I am not deceiving you in this matter.

No sooner had I read those fatal words than I fell back into a state of abject despair.

No, I thought to myself, as I tore at my hair in a frenzy. *No, you cruel man, you never loved me; if the slightest feeling for me had ever touched your heart you would not have condemned me without hearing me, you would not have judged me guilty of such crimes when it was you I adored… You treacherous man, it is you that has betrayed me; it is you that has pushed me into the hands of these executioners, these siblings of mine who intend to let me die a little every day… to die without being defended by you… to die despised by you, the only man I ever loved. Yet I have never deliberately offended you, and it is I alone who has been duped and victimized. Oh no, no, this situation is too cruel, it's beyond my strength to bear it!*

Sobbing, I threw myself at my brothers' feet and begged them to either listen to me or stop spilling my blood drop by drop and simply open my veins and kill me outright.

They agreed to listen to me. I told them my story, but they did not believe me. It was clear that they wanted me out of the way, preferably dead. They began to treat me abominably. Finally, once they had ceased swearing at me and spitting on me, they ordered the two women, on pain of death, to carry out their instructions to the letter and then they left me, coldly telling me in parting that they hoped they would never see me alive again.

As soon as they were gone, my two guardians left me bread and water, and locked me in the room. As soon as I was alone, I surrendered to the excesses of my despair and after a while I found I became less unhappy. During the first wave of despair, I considered unbandaging my arms in order to let myself die from loss of blood. But the horrible thought of dying without being vindicated by my lover tore at me with such violence that I found I could not bring myself to carry it out.

A little calm brings hope, Monsieur… Hope is a comforting feeling that is born in the midst of sorrow: a divine gift that nature bestows upon us to compensate for its harshness…

No, I said to myself, *I will not die without seeing him. I shall work only for that end. I have to concern myself only with that. If he persists in believing me guilty, then it will be time to die and I shall at least do so without regret, since it is impossible for life to hold any attraction for me when I have lost his love.*

Once I had made this decision, I resolved not to neglect any means of freeing myself from that hateful place. I had been consoling myself with that thought for four days, when my two jailers reappeared to renew my provisions and make me lose a little more of my strength; they bled me again from both arms and then left me on the rough bed, weak and unable to move. On the eighth day they reappeared, and this time, I threw myself at their feet and begged them to show me a little mercy. My entreaties affected them and they bled me from one arm only. Two months passed, during which time I was bled alternately from both arms, every four days.

The strength of my constitution sustained me, as did my youth. I believe that the single-minded desire I had to escape that terrible situation, as well as the amount of bread I ate to counteract my exhaustion and carry out my resolutions, contributed to my success, because at the beginning of the third month, I had managed to dig a hole through a wall and I crawled through into an adjoining room that was not locked. From there, I ran from the château and, on reaching the road, set off in the direction of Paris. I'd walked a fair way before my strength finally gave out.

That was where you found me, Monsieur, and so kindly and generously helped me to escape and then to recover. I am eternally grateful for all you have done, Monsieur. I must now ask if you could assist me by restoring me to my father, who I am sure has been deceived by my brothers, for he would never be so barbaric as to condemn me without giving me the opportunity to prove my innocence to him. I shall endeavor to convince him that I have been weak, and I'm sure he'll see that I have not been as guilty as appearances seem to prove. If you would help me, Monsieur, then you will not only have saved an unfortunate creature who will never cease thanking you, but you will even have restored honor to a family that thinks they have been unjustly deprived of it.

— Mademoiselle, said the Comte de Luxeuil after having given his full attention to Émilie's account. It would have been impossible for anyone to listen to you and to look at you without being greatly concerned. It is evident that you have not been as guilty as one might have reason to think, but there is imprudence in your conduct that must be very difficult for you to ignore.

— Oh, Monsieur!

— Please hear me out, Mademoiselle. All I ask is that you listen to me as a man of the world, one who wants nothing more than to give you as much help as I can. Your lover's conduct was terrible, not only was it deeply unjust, for he should have done all he could to inform himself better and to see you. Instead, what he did was cruel, for when he reached the point of no return and abandoned you, he then compounded his behavior by denouncing you to your family, by dishonoring you, and by handing you over to those who wanted to destroy you. So, I find the conduct of the man you cherished to be beyond reprehensible, something any decent person simply would not do.

— But the behavior of your brothers is even more unworthy. It is atrocious in all respects, for only murderers behave in such a way. Wrongs of this kind do not deserve such punishments; restraint has never served any useful purpose. It is best if one stays silent about such things, but one should never shed the blood nor take away the freedom of the guilty party, for those odious methods bring more dishonor to those who employ them than to the person who is the victim. They deserve that person's hatred; they cause a great deal of scandal and they never set anything to rights.

— However much we value a sister's virtue, her life must have an infinitely higher value in our eyes. Honor can be restored, but not blood that has been shed;

their conduct is therefore so horrible, that it would certainly be punished by law if we lodged a complaint with the authorities. However, this would mean stooping to use the same methods as your persecutors, which would then make public that which we need to keep private, so they are not the methods we should use.

— I will therefore need to act in a very different way in order to assist you, Mademoiselle. I must warn you, however, that I can only provide proper help on the following conditions: my first stipulation is that you write down for me the exact addresses of your father, your aunt, the Berceil woman, and the house of the man that Berceil took you to. My second stipulation, mademoiselle, is that you give me, without any hesitation or prevarication, the name of the man who interests you. This clause is absolutely essential and I will not conceal from you that it is absolutely impossible for me to serve you in any way whatsoever if you persist in keeping from me the name that I demand.

Émilie, confused, began by fulfilling exactly the first condition and gave all of the addresses to the Comte:

— Are you demanding, Monsieur, she then said blushingly, that I give you the name of my seducer?

— Absolutely, mademoiselle, I can do nothing without it.

— Very well, Monsieur. The man is… the Marquis de Luxeuil.

— The Marquis de Luxeuil! the Comte said, startled.

He stood up, unable to disguise the powerful emotions that his son's name had stirred within him. What? Is he capable of such things? He… He stopped and quickly composed himself: He will atone for this, mademoiselle… he will make it all good and you will be avenged… you have my word on it. Farewell.

The degree of agitation into which Émilie's last revelation had thrown the Comte de Luxeuil perturbed the unfortunate young woman greatly; she feared that she may have been reckless; however, the Comte's words as he left reassured her. Without understanding anything regarding the connection between the facts, all of which were impossible for her to unravel, and not knowing where she was, she decided to wait patiently for the result of her benefactor's actions. The care that was still taken of her by the valet, while the Comte's actions were being undertaken, finally calmed her, and convinced her that he was working solely in the interests of her happiness.

She had every reason to be entirely convinced of this when, four days after the explanations she had given, the Comte entered her room leading the Marquis de Luxeuil by the arm.

— Mademoiselle, said the Comte, I bring you both the cause of your misfortunes and the one who has come here to put everything right; a man who will now beg you, on bended knee not to refuse his hand in marriage.

At those words, the Marquis threw himself at the feet of the woman he adored. The surprise of it was too great for Émilie; she was not strong enough to bear it and she fainted. When she recovered her senses, she found that she was in the arms of her lover.

— You cruel man, she said, weeping a deluge of tears. What misery you have caused me; the one you said you loved. Could you truly believe me capable of the disgusting things you have dared suspect me of? In loving you, I, Émilie, have become the victim of my own weakness and of the deceit of others, but I could never be unfaithful.

— Oh, you whom I adore, cried the Marquis. Please forgive my horrible jealousy based on false appearances. We now know all of the details, of course, but you must acknowledge that those appearances regarding your conduct were very much against you.

— You should have valued me, Luxeuil, and you would not have believed that I could ever deceive you. You should have listened less to your despair than to the feelings I flattered myself I inspired in you. Let this example teach my sex that it's almost always through too much love… almost always by giving in too quickly that we lose the esteem of our lovers. Oh, Luxeuil, you would have loved me better if I had loved you less quickly. You punished me for my weakness, and what was supposed to strengthen your love is what made you suspect mine.

— May everything be forgotten on both sides, interrupted the Comte. Luxeuil, your conduct has been reprehensible and if you had not offered to make amends, if I had not known that in your heart that was what you wanted, I would have refused to acknowledge you for the remainder of my life. As our ancient troubadours used to say: *When you are truly in love and hear or see something about your lover when apart, don't believe your ears or eyes, but listen only to your heart.*

— Mademoiselle, the Comte said, turning his attention to Émilie, I look forward to your recovery with some impatience. I want to take you back to your parents only as my son's wife, and I flatter myself that they will not refuse to ally themselves with me to make good your misfortunes. If they do refuse, then I offer you my house, mademoiselle, so that your marriage can be celebrated here. Until my dying breath I will never cease regarding you as a cherished daughter-in-law by whom I shall always be honored, whether your marriage is approved or not.

Luxeuil threw himself into his father's arms, Mademoiselle de Tourville burst into tears as she seized her benefactor's hands, and she was then allowed to rest for a few hours to recover from a scene that, if it had lasted much longer, would have delayed her recovery that was so eagerly desired on all sides.

Two weeks after her return to Paris, Mademoiselle de Tourville was declared well enough to get up and ride in a carriage. The Comte had her dressed in a white dress that symbolized the innocence of her heart, nothing was neglected to enhance her charms, which her lingering pallor and general weakness made even more attractive.

Then Émilie, the Comte, and Luxeuil went to see Judge de Tourville, who had not been forewarned and who was extremely surprised when he saw his daughter enter. He was with his two sons, whose faces twisted with anger and rage at this unexpected sight; they knew their sister had escaped, but they believed she had died in some part of the forest and they had managed to console themselves over their loss without any difficulty at all.

— Monsieur, said the Comte, presenting Émilie to her father. Here is Innocence herself that I now return to your care.

Émilie rushed forward.

— I ask forgiveness of her, Monsieur, the Comte continued, and I would not ask you for it if I did not fully believe that she deserves it. Besides, Monsieur, he continued quickly, the best proof I can give you of the high esteem I have for your daughter is that I ask for her hand in marriage on behalf of my son. Our ranks are suitable for an alliance, Monsieur, and if there were any disproportion on my part regarding property, I would sell all that I have to provide my son with a fortune worthy of being offered to your daughter. Please make your decision, Monsieur, and allow me not to leave until I have your promise.

Old Judge de Tourville had always adored his dear Émilie. Ultimately, he was kindness personified; a man who, because of his excellent character, had not exercised his profession for more than twenty years. The old

Judge began shedding tears of joy all over his beloved daughter. Finally, he composed himself enough to inform the Comte that he was very happy with the proposed match and would give it his blessing. His only concern was that his dear Émilie was not worthy of it.

On hearing this, the Marquis de Luxeuil threw himself onto his knees in front of the Judge and entreated him to forgive him for his wrong-doings and to allow him to atone for them.

Promises, pledges, and agreements were then made; everything was settled, and everything grew calm on both sides. Only the two brothers of our attractive heroine refused to share the general happiness and pushed her away when she went over and tried to embrace them.

The Comte, furious at such disgraceful behavior, stepped in the way of one of the brothers who was trying to leave the room.

— Leave them, Monsieur, leave them, the Judge called to the Comte. They have deceived me horribly. If this dear child had been as guilty as they told me, would you consent to have her marry your son? They have marred my happiness by depriving me of my Émilie… Let them go!…

And those wretched men left the room, fuming with rage.

Then the Comte informed Monsieur de Tourville of the horrors that his sons had inflicted on his daughter. He then told him everything his daughter had done wrong.

The judge, seeing the lack of proportion between the errors and the indignity of the punishment, swore that he would never set eyes on his sons again. The Comte managed to calm him and made him promise that he would try to forget the terrible things that had happened, and instead celebrate everything that was good & joyful.

One week later, the marriage was celebrated without the brothers attending.

Monsieur de Tourville contented himself with urging them to maintain total silence about the entire incident, with a promise that if they ever spoke of any part of it, he would use his not inconsiderable powers to have them imprisoned for attempting to murder his daughter. Aware that he would do such a thing without a single qualm, the two brothers promised, and they remained silent — up to a point. They were, of course, able to discuss the matter between themselves, so they did. They ended up congratulating each other and feeling no small amount of pride regarding their outrageous behavior. They also criticized their father's indulgence regarding Émilie, and every once in a while, someone would overhear them and learn of the incident and some of the atrocious details that characterize it. Then they would wonder about the hypocrisy of those two men who could grant themselves the right to behave as they had and so barbarically punish the crimes of others, but who would then criticize everyone who conducted themselves less murderously…

It is quite right to say that such disgusting behavior is reserved for those frenzied & inept followers of Themis who have been raised on a diet of rigid inflexibility, who have been hardened from childhood by the cries of unhappiness, have had blood-stained hands since leaving the cradle, and who blame everything on everyone else whilst indulging in everything illicit themselves. They imagine that the only way to cover up their own secret vices and their own public prevarications is to make a huge show of unyielding, unbending, rigorous severity. This is a public display; an act which gives them the outer appearance of being a goose, and the inner appearance of being a tiger. The only purpose of this charade, which marks them with crimes, is to fool the gullible, which in turn makes the wise hate their abhorrent principles, their bloodthirsty laws, & their despicable personalities.

Augustine de Villeblanche, or A Strategy for Love[1]

One day, Mademoiselle de Villeblanche, of whom we are going to have the opportunity to talk more about shortly, said to one of her best friends:

— Of all the peculiarities of nature, the one that seems to be discussed the most, the one which seems the strangest to those pseudo-philosophers who want to analyze everything without ever understanding anything, is the unusual taste that women of a certain constitution or temperament have for persons of their own sex. Long before the immortal Sappho and obviously since her time, there has not been a city, nor one single country anywhere in the world, which has not provided us with examples of women of that particular type, with those desires. According to the evidence, which seems irrefutable, it would seem far more reasonable to accuse nature of eccentricity than it would to reproach those women of committing a crime against nature.

— However, the beautiful Augustine de Villeblanche continued, those women have constantly been judged harshly, and if it were not for the superior and enduring power of our sex, who knows if some Cujas, some Bartole, some Louis IX would not have implemented laws that would have resulted in those sensitive and unfortunate creatures being burned.[2] In the same way, they have accused and oppressed those men who were built along similar lines, men who for equally good reasons no doubt thought they could be self-sufficient, and imagined that the mingling of the sexes, although very useful for the procreation of the species, was not of the same importance when it came to sexual pleasures.

— God forbid that we take sides in this, my dear friend, Mademoiselle de Villeblanche said to her friend, blowing kisses that seemed a little suspect. But don't you agree that instead of the burnings, the contempt, the sarcasm, all of which nowadays are blunted and quite useless as weapons, it would be infinitely simpler, regarding this issue — which does not affect society in any way, and is not of the slightest interest to God, although it is perhaps more useful to nature than is generally believed — if everyone were left to do exactly as they pleased. What is there to fear from such depravity? According to received wisdom, committing small improprieties can prevent the committing of greater ones, but I have never seen one shred of proof that doing so leads anyone to dangerous excesses... Well, by the heavens, is there anyone who truly believes that the inclinations of these individuals of both sexes will cause the world to end? Does anyone think that they have no regard for our precious human species, and that their alleged crime will cause its extinction simply because they did not go forth & multiply?

If you think about it carefully, you'll see that all these imaginary population losses are a matter of complete indifference to Nature. Not only does Nature not disapprove, but instead shows us in a thousand ways that it wants and desires them. If the prevention of life really angered Nature, why would it tolerate it over and over, thousands of times? If the production of offspring were so essential to Nature, why would it have arranged it so that a woman could only procreate for a third of her life? Why do half of the creatures a woman produces have tastes, desires, inclinations, whatever one likes to call them, that are contrary to the procreation that she is so devoted to?

Let's put it another way: Nature allows all species to multiply, but it does not require that they do so. It's likely that Nature, knowing that there will always be many more individuals than it needs for its purpose, has no interest in thwarting the inclinations of anyone for whom propagation of the race is not their driving motive, and who is unwilling to be party to it. Oh! Let's acknowledge that Nature knows best. Let's tell ourselves that Nature's powers are immense, that nothing we do causes offence or outrage, and that the tools necessary to threaten Nature's laws are far beyond the reach of human hands.

Mademoiselle Augustine de Villeblanche, whose thoughts on nature we have just heard, was very much the mistress of her own thoughts and actions. She was twenty years old and had an annual income of thirty thousand livres. As her words may have indicated, she was not married, nor did she wish to be. She was born into a good, but not illustrious, family. She was an only child, the daughter of a man who had made his fortune in India, and he died without ever being able to persuade her to marry.

We have no wish to mislead you, reader. It must be stated clearly that Augustine was reluctant to marry due in part to her warm affinity for the unconventional individuals she had just spoken so heatedly in defense of. The repugnance that she showed for marriage was either due to advice she had been given, her education, her personality, her hot-blooded temperament (she was born in Madras), or due to encouragement from nature, or because of any of the other countless reasons one could choose. Whichever reason one finally decided upon, one thing was certain: Mademoiselle de Villeblanche hated men, and having totally devoted herself to what chaste ears will understand by the word Sapphism, she found voluptuousness, enjoyment, and complete satisfaction only with her own sex & was compensated by the Graces for what she had lost because of her rejection of Eros.

Augustine's choices meant she was a real loss to men: tall, pretty as a picture, with the most beautiful brown hair, a slightly aquiline nose, superb teeth, & expressive, vivacious eyes, and skin that was oh so delicate, and oh so white. In brief, she had the kind of voluptuousness so piquant that when men encountered her, they immediately saw that although she was made to give love, she was equally determined not to receive it.

Some of those men, unable as many men are, to accept that they are not the perfect companion for all women, directed sarcastic comments and hurtful words at the woman whose tastes, although unassuming enough, nevertheless deprived the altars of Paphos of one of the universe's most eligible hand-maidens, which consequently angered the sectarists of the temples of Venus.[3] Mademoiselle de Villeblanche laughed heartily whenever she heard those criticisms and hurtful words, and simply continued to indulge in her desires.

— The greatest of all follies, she said, is to feel ashamed of the inclinations Nature has given us. To mock any individual who has specific tastes is as barbaric as it would be to ridicule a man or woman born blind or lame. But it would be easier to halt the course of the stars than it would to persuade those barbaric fools to accept a sensible opinion. Some people derive a sense of pleasure from mocking defects in others that they themselves do not have. This pleasure is so enjoyable to those people, especially the most stupid of them, that it is rare they give it up. Ultimately, it leads to them making wicked comments, hateful witticisms, and pathetic puns. In society, which is simply a collection of human beings brought together by boredom and held together by collective stupidity, it's very entertaining to some if they speak for two or three hours without saying anything and very delicious for them if they can shine at the expense of others. They are the sort of people who seem to think that if they censure a vice in a loud voice, they are implying that they do not indulge in that particular vice, whereas we know from history that the reverse is generally true. It is an indirect way of one bestowing praise upon oneself, and with such an implied reward available, it's not really surprising that some people agree to unite with others and form a mob that then crushes any individual whose so-called crime is to think differently from everyone else. Afterwards, they return home full of righteousness regarding what they have stated, when all they have really demonstrated by their behavior is their own prudishness and stupidity.

Those were Mademoiselle de Villeblanche's thoughts, and as she was wealthy enough to do things her own way, she was absolutely determined to never bow to constraint, nor to pay any attention to mockery or criticism. She decided she would live her life with no thought for her reputation, and would instead live as an epicure, devoting her life to sensual pleasures instead of heavenly salvation, which she did not really believe in, considering it to be illusory. Surrounded by a small circle of like-minded women, our dear Augustine innocently indulged in every pleasure that took her fancy. She had had many suitors, but they had all been so badly mistreated by her that most had stopped considering her as suitable material for marriage.

A young man named Franville, who was almost as well-born and as independently wealthy as Augustine, had fallen madly in love with her. He was completely undeterred by her inflexible hostility toward men, and he was determined to win her as his bride. He set about this task with grim resolution, vowing to either succeed or die in the attempt. He outlined his intentions to his friends and they mocked him mercilessly. Undeterred, he insisted he would succeed. A wager was suggested. He accepted.

Franville was two years younger than Mademoiselle de Villeblanche. He was still too young to have a full beard. He was slender and had very delicate features, as well as the most beautiful hair in the world. When he was dressed as a woman, he looked so convincing in women's clothes that he always deceived members of both sexes. Some were taken in by his disguise, others of course were not. But whenever he was dressed in that way, he received a host of declarations so clear in their meaning that one day alone he could have become the Antinous of Hadrian, or the Adonis of Psyche. It was in women's clothing that Franville planned on seducing Mademoiselle de Villeblanche.

We shall now see how he did it.

During Carnival time, one of Augustine's greatest pleasures was to dress as a man and attend all of the social gatherings dressed that way, which mirrored her tastes so perfectly.

Franville, who had been having her followed and who had taken the precaution of not letting himself be seen by her, knew that the woman he loved was that evening going to a ball given by the Friends of the Opera, which anyone in a mask could freely attend. As was the custom of this charming woman, she would be going to the ball dressed as a Captain of Dragoons. That evening, he put on his woman's disguise. He carefully put on jewelry and accouterments, applied quite a lot of rouge, and decided he would not wear a mask.

Followed by one of his sisters who was a lot less attractive than he, he set off to the ball, where the lovely Augustine went only to find suitable conquests.

By the time Franville had circled the room three times, he could tell that he had attracted Augustine's connoisseur's eye.

— Who is that beautiful girl? Mademoiselle de Villeblanche asked the friend who accompanied her. I'm sure I would remember her if I'd seen her anywhere before today. How could such a delightful creature have escaped my notice?

Augustine then tried every method of seduction at her disposal to start a preliminary conversation with "Mademoiselle de Franville," which is how the counterfeit woman was introduced. Franville excused himself & went to another part of the room. Augustine followed. As she walked toward him, Franville turned away and was able to avoid her, thereby enflaming Augustine's ardor. Finally, Franville allowed "herself" to be cornered and an acceptably banal conversation, which gradually became more interesting, was started.

— It's very hot in this ballroom, said Mademoiselle de Villeblanche. Let's leave our companions in here and get some fresh air. We could then have a look in some of the other rooms. They'll be a lot cooler and I've heard there's gambling and drinks being served.

— Ah! Monsieur, Franville said to Mademoiselle de Villeblanche, continuing to pretend he thought she was a man. To be honest, I dare not. I'm here with my sister, but I know that my mother is due to arrive here very soon with the man she has arranged for me to marry. If either of them sees me with you, it would ruin everything that's been agreed.

— Well, you must learn to ignore childish fears. How old are you, you beautiful creature?

— I'm eighteen, Monsieur.

— Then let me tell you something you should know; at the age of eighteen you are entitled to do whatever you like. Come on, follow me — and don't be afraid.

And Franville let Augustine lead him away.

— So, you charming creature, Augustine continued, leading the individual she still believed was a young woman to one of the adjoining rooms. Are you really going to get married by arrangement? If so, I pity you. And who is the man destined to be your husband? Some bore, I'll wager. I envy that man, you're a heavenly creature. He's very fortunate. I would love to change places with him. Would you agree to marry someone else, me for example? Answer honestly, my angel.

— As you know very well, Monsieur, when we're young, we can't always follow our heart.

— Well, just refuse to marry him then. He sounds terrible. He'd be no loss to you. And then we could get better acquainted & if we found each other agreeable… we could make our own arrangements, ones that we decide. I don't need anyone's permission for anything, and although I'm only twenty years old, I'm the master of my own estate & my own fortune. If you could persuade your parents to look favorably on me, then before next week, it's possible we could be bound together with love's eternal knots.

While conversing, they had left the ballroom, and the cunning Augustine, who had not separated her prey from the others just to talk about love, had taken care to lead Franville to a very isolated room that she had hired for the night from the owners of the ballroom.

— Oh my God! said Franville, when he saw Augustine locking the room door behind them. She advanced on him and took him in her arms, her embrace strong with passion. What do you want with me? Why have you locked us in? What are you planning, Monsieur? A tête-à-tête? In this secluded place? Let go of me, right now, or I'll shout for help.

— I'm not going to let go of you, you gorgeous creature, so shout all you like, if you can! Your rose-scented breath will make my heart ignite with passion. Having spoken, Augustine pressed her beautiful mouth firmly, but gently on Franville's lips.

Franville defended himself rather half-heartedly: he found that it was very difficult to be angry whilst being kissed very tenderly for the first time by the person he was in love with.

Encouraged, Augustine resumed her advances with more force; she did so with an enthusiasm peculiar to all those delightful women of her persuasion.

Soon her hands started to explore his body. Franville, playing the role of a woman who has capitulated, also let his own hands wander. Clothes were flung off and fingers went almost simultaneously in search of those places that both parties hoped to find…

— Oh, by Heaven, Franville suddenly exclaimed. You're a woman…

Augustine put her hands on something… that was now in such a condition that it left no room for any doubt.

— And what about you, you horrible creature? Augustine demanded. Have I really gone to all this trouble just to end up with a man? Now I'm truly unhappy.

— No more unhappy than I, said Franville, putting his clothes back on and feigning an attitude of the deepest contempt. I use this disguise to attract men. I love men, I seek them out, and now, after all my efforts, I have ended up in a rented room with a whore.

— A whore? Oh no, I'm not a whore, Augustine responded sharply. I've never been one in my life. No one who detests men as much as I do could be called a whore.

— What? You're a woman and you hate men?

— Yes, and for the same reason that you're a man &
you hate women.

— It has to be said; this situation is quite unique.

— This is all very upsetting for me, said Augustine,
with all the signs of an imminent bad mood.

— In all honesty, Mademoiselle, Franville said bitterly,
it's even more tedious for me. Because of this, I've now
been dishonored for three weeks. You may not know,
but in our Order, we vow to never touch a woman.

— I'd have thought a man like you could touch a
woman like me without ever besmirching your honor.

— I can't see any particular reason to make an exception for you, Franville said. And I don't understand how
admitting a vice makes you think your case should be
exempt on merit.

— It's not "a vice." Anyway, you've no right to reproach
me for my tastes… not when your own tastes are just
as depraved as mine.

— Look, said Franville. Let's not argue. Let's just stop
all this right now. The best thing we could do now is to
go our separate ways and never see each other again.

Franville turned & walked to the door, reaching out
to turn the key and leave.

— One moment, said Augustine, preventing him from
leaving. I'll wager you intend to tell everyone about this,
don't you?

— I may do so, if I think it will amuse my friends.

— Fine. Say whatever you like. It doesn't matter to me. Thank God I don't have to worry about what people do or don't think of me. But I'll tell you something, she said, stopping him again. This whole situation is quite extraordinary. We were both completely fooled.

— Ah! said Franville. But the mistake is far more cruel & painful to someone with my tastes than it could ever be to someone with yours. Your lack of… well, it's really quite repugnant to me.

— Oh, please. You don't really believe that what you have to offer us nauseates us any less, do you? All I'm saying is that our misadventure, although unpleasant for both of us, was quite an amusing little interlude. We can agree on that, can't we? Are you going back to the ball?

— I don't know.

— Well, I'm not going back, said Augustine. You've made me feel quite angry, so I'm going to bed.

— And not before time.

— But perhaps you would be gallant enough to escort me to my home, good Monsieur? I live not far away, but I do not have my carriage here. You can leave me at my door.

— Yes, I will gladly accompany you, said Franville. After all, our different tastes do not mean we cannot be civil. Will you take my hand? Here.

— I shall take it — but only because there's no one else available.

— And I can assure you that I only offered it out of politeness, nothing more.

They walked and soon arrived at the door of Augustine's house. Franville turned to go.

— Honestly, said Mademoiselle de Villeblanche in exasperation. You are less than charming. Are you simply going to abandon me here, out in the street?

— I'm truly sorry, said Franville. I didn't like to …

— You men who don't like women are quite churlish, aren't you?

— You see, Mademoiselle, said Franville, holding Mademoiselle de Villeblanche's hand as he escorted her to her apartment, I would very much like to go back to the ball and try to redeem my earlier foolishness.

— Your foolishness? Are you saying you're upset that you met me?

— I am not saying that. But isn't it true that we both could have done infinitely better?

— Yes, you're right, Augustine said finally, as she entered her home. You're absolutely right, Monsieur. I certainly could have. For some reason, I think this fateful meeting of ours will cost me my happiness for the rest of my life.

— Why? Are you saying that you're not sure of your feelings?

— I was yesterday.

— Ah! So you're not bound by your principles then?

— I'm not bound by anything. I'm really starting to run out of patience with you.

— Very well, then I shall go now, Mademoiselle. God forbid I detain you any longer.

— No, stay. I command you. Could you, for once in your life, take it upon yourself to obey a woman?

— There's nothing I cannot do, Franville said, sitting down compliantly. You see, I told you I could be civil.

— It's really quite awful that you have such perverse tastes at your age, you know.

— Do you think it's in any way respectable for you to have such unusual predilections?

— Oh, it's quite different for us. We think of it as restraint, or modesty… it's also pride if you like. Also fear, possibly, which then becomes reluctance. Many women are reluctant to indulge in sex with men because men use seduction as a strategy for dominating women. However, our desires cannot be denied, so we take care of each others' needs. And as most of us are discreet, we manage to create a veneer of respectability that deceives almost everyone. As a result, nature is content, decency is observed, and morality is not outraged.

— Those are what I would call a series of beautiful fallacies. By using similar lines of thought, anyone could justify anything. Also, you've said nothing that we cannot also say in our own favor.

— Not at all. You think differently from me. You do not fear the same things I do. Victory for you is defeat for me. The more you multiply your conquests, the more you add to your glory, and you can only reject the feelings that we cause you to feel deliberately, either from vice or depravity.

— I think you could convert me.

— I would like to.

— And what would you gain from converting me, especially while you yourself continue to believe all of your own misconceptions?

— My sex would be obliged to be grateful to me, & since I love women, I'll be very happy to do whatever I can for them.

— If that miracle were to happen, its effects would not be quite as general as you seem to believe.

— I would not want to be converted just for one woman at most… in order that she might try me.

— But it's an honorable principle.

— Yes, but making up one's mind without having tasted every possibility does seem a little like stubbornness.

— What? Have you never been with a woman?

— Never! And you… are you by any chance as virginal as I am?

— Oh, well, I wouldn't say virginal exactly. No, the women I have… been with are very skillful and so thorough that they leave nothing intact… but I have never been with a man in my entire life.

— Do you swear that that's the truth?

— Yes. And I never want to see or know one with tastes that are as bizarre as my own.

— I'm sorry that I didn't make the same promise myself.

— I don't think it's possible to be more insolent.

At these words, Mademoiselle de Villeblanche stood up and told Franville he was to leave.

Our young lover, always cool under pressure, bowed low and turned to leave.

— So, are you going back to the ball? Mademoiselle de Villeblanche asked dryly, looking at him with a mixture of contempt and the most ardent love.

— Yes, of course. I'm fairly sure I told you I was.

— So you're not capable of making the same sacrifice for me that I'm making for you.

— I beg your pardon! What sacrifice have you made for me?

— I only came home because I had no wish to stay there any longer after having had the misfortune of meeting you.

— Misfortune?

— It is you who is forcing me to use that word. I could use a very different one. That would be up to you.

— And how would you reconcile that with your tastes?

— When a person is in love, they can sometimes give up something they love for the other person.

— Yes, that's very true. But wouldn't you find it impossible to love me.

— I would only find it impossible if you continued to indulge in those disgusting habits I've discovered you enjoy so much.

— What if I gave them up?

— Then I would immediately immolate my own on the altars of love. Oh! You treacherous creature. Do you know how much this confession hurts me? How much it wounds my pride? Have you any idea what you've just forced me to say? Augustine asked, collapsing into a chair in floods of tears.

— I have obtained the most flattering admission I could ever hear from the most beautiful lips in the whole universe, said Franville, hurling himself at Augustine's feet.

— Oh, you dear woman. My most tender love. I admit it was all an act. I'm here on my knees and I'll stay on them until you forgive me. I beg you to show me mercy. Please say you won't punish me for my deception. You see me kneeling before you, Mademoiselle, as your most constant and passionate lover. I believed that my strategy was necessary to win your heart, which I knew would be resistant to any other attempt to woo you. Have I succeeded, beautiful Augustine? Will you love without the vices that you have declared to your guilty lover… but not guilty of what you believed? Could you really believe that any impure passions could exist in the soul of someone who has never been inflamed by love except by love for you?

— You deceitful, conniving… You tricked me. But, yes, I forgive you. However, it means that you will have nothing to sacrifice for me, so my pride is hurt by that. Oh well, no matter, I shall sacrifice everything to you.

To please you, I will give up all of the mistakes into which we are led by vanity as well as by our tastes. I feel that nature prevails. I have suffocated the strange desires that I now abhor with all my soul. We cannot resist nature's power. Nature created women for men and men for women. I will obey that law of nature. It is through love that nature inspires me today, and those laws will become more sacred to me. This is my hand, Monsieur. I believe you are a man of honor, and as such, I accept you as my suitor. If I deserved to lose your esteem for me momentarily, perhaps I can make up for it with my devotion to you and my tenderness and love. My conduct will convince you that a perverse imagination does not always debase a well-born soul.

Franville, having won his bride, dripped tears of joy onto the hands he still had his lips pressed to. He stood up and rushed into her arms; arms that were spread to receive him warmly.

— Oh, this is truly the happiest day of my life, he said. There's nothing comparable to my victory. I have returned a strayed heart to the path of virtue and I shall cherish that heart forever.

Franville kissed his divine love a thousand times and more. Eventually they parted to give everyone their news. He let his friends know and they shared his happiness.

Mademoiselle de Villeblanche was too good a match for his parents to refuse her, so he married her within the week.

Tenderness, trust, reserve, and modesty were the watch-words of his marriage and, in making himself the happiest of men, he was adept enough to make the most libertine of young ladies into the wisest and most virtuous of women.

Done As You Require[4]

— My daughter, said the Baroness de Fréval to the eldest of her children who was going to be married the next day, You have just turned thirteen and you're like an angel. It would be impossible for you to be any more innocent or adorable. It's as though Cupid himself has deigned to draw your features. And yet, tomorrow, you are being forced to become the wife of an old roué whose predilections are, at best, very suspect… It's an arrangement that I very much dislike, but it's one your father wants. I would have preferred you to have been a woman of status in your own right, but instead you are destined to be known for the rest of your life by the rather cumbersome title of Magistrate's wife.

— What causes me the most despair though is that it is likely that the consummation will never… That you'll never be more than half a wife to him. Modesty prevents me from explaining this to you in more detail, you innocent young thing. All I *can* say is that these old rascals make a profession of judging others without knowing how to judge themselves. All of them have very depraved fantasies and they're accustomed to living their lives in shockingly indolent ways. These scoundrels corrupt themselves as soon as they are born; they plunge themselves into dissolution and crawl through impure mires, living by the laws of Justinian and enjoying the obscenities of the capital. Just like the snake that raises its head from time to time to swallow prey, we see them come out of the city only to do the same.

— So listen to me, daughter, and stand up straight... for if you bow your head in that way, you will please the Magistrate very much. I have no doubt that he will often make you turn and face the wall while he... In a word, my child, this is what we are talking about. On your wedding night, refuse your husband the first thing he requests of you. You can be sure that this first thing will surely be very disgusting & very unconventional...

— I have heard rumors regarding his jaded tastes; for forty-five years he has held ridiculous principles. Unfortunately this unruly rogue has a habit of never taking things the way nature intended. You will therefore refuse, my dear daughter. He will make his depraved request, you will listen attentively, and then you must say: *No, Monsieur, you may have access to everywhere else as much as you like, but not there. Most definitely not.*

That having been said, Mademoiselle de Fréval was duly married and that night, she prepared herself for her first night with her husband. She undressed, she bathed & she perfumed herself.

The Magistrate arrived, his neatly curled and powdered wig falling to his shoulders. He looked powerful and glamorous. He gave off an air of authority; he was a man used to reciting laws and regulating the state.

Thanks to his wig, his well-cut clothes, and his trim figure, he could have been forty years old, although he was nearly sixty.

He feasted his eyes on his young bride and lavished praise on her, commenting on the beauty of her face and waxing rhapsodic about her young body. The inexperienced bride could easily read in the roué's eyes all the depravity in his heart.

Finally, the time to consummate the marriage was upon them.

The Magistrate undressed and climbed into bed with his bride. Gazing on her delicate beauty and her lithe innocence the Magistrate, for the first time in his life, decided that he would like to take the time to educate his wife properly in her wifely duties. He may have decided this because he was worried that sarcasm could become the first fruit of his wife's indiscretions, but whatever the reason for his decision, the Magistrate, as I have said, for the first time in his life made the decision to choose and enjoy authentic hymenal pleasures, and so made his request to his bride.

Because of her mother's words of advice to her on the day before her wedding, Mademoiselle de Fréval was, she believed, very well-educated in this matter. She recalled that her mother had instructed her to firmly refuse the first request that her depraved husband would make, and with that lesson in mind, she said firmly to the Magistrate:

— No, Monsieur, you may have access to everywhere else as much as you like, but not there. Most definitely not.

The Magistrate was bewildered.

— Madame, he said. I must protest. Please grant me my request. I accept it's unusual for me to ask a woman for such a prize, but I believe you'll find it most enjoyable. Besides, in all honesty, between a husband and a wife, it's considered a virtue.

— No Monsieur, no matter how much you protest, you will never change my mind on this matter.

The Magistrate eagerly held *&* stroked the cherished attractions.

— Well, Madame, said the roué, I hope you will achieve satisfaction. Obviously, I'll be very upset and quite angry if I displease you, especially on the first night of our wedding. Be warned though, Madame, once I begin, I will be overcome with lust *&* you will be unable to make me change course.

— I understand perfectly, Monsieur, said the girl, confident of her mother's advice. She then positioned herself so as to provide her husband with the best view and the most convenient access to her body in the way she insisted upon. Please proceed without concern. It is I that demand this.

— Very well then, the good man said, remembering the stories of Ganymede *&* Socrates as he moved into position behind his wife. He gazed lovingly at the pale globes that awaited him. As this is what you want, he said, thrusting his length between his wife's buttocks, let it be done as you require.

The Duped Judge[5]

Oh, believe me when I say I want to praise them so much…
that for twenty years they will not dare show themselves.

It was with the utmost regret that the Marquis d'Olincourt, a Colonel of the Dragoons, a man of wit, grace, and
vivacity, saw his sister-in-law, Mademoiselle de Téroze,
become engaged to be married to one of the most appalling men to have ever existed on the face of the earth.
This charming young lady was eighteen years old, as fresh
as Flora and formed like the Graces themselves.[6] She
had, for four years, loved, and been loved by, the young
Comte d'Elbène, a Second Colonel in d'Olincourt's
regiment. She was unable to contemplate her impend-
ing marriage to the sullen and severe man her father
had chosen to be her husband without shuddering, as
from that ill-fated moment she would be separated forever from the only man who was truly worthy of her.
But how could she avoid it?

Mademoiselle de Téroze's father was a stubborn
old hypochondriac whose only genuine ailment was
gout. He was, unfortunately, a man who believed that a
young woman's feeling regarding a husband should not
be governed by considerations of love, propriety, or virtue,
but should instead be decided by reason, maturity and,
most importantly, social position.

He also believed that what a man wore in relation to his position in society was of the utmost importance. According to him, anyone who wore a long robe was someone of importance in the world, and short of marrying his daughter to royalty, which seemed unlikely, the most esteemed, most revered of all positions under the monarchy, a judge, was the one he admired most in the world. From this it followed inevitably that his daughter could only be happy if she was married to a man of the judiciary.

In spite of his beliefs, the old Baron de Téroze had nonetheless given his eldest daughter to a soldier, and one who was, unfortunately, a colonel of dragoons. That this daughter was extremely happy in every respect, that she had no reason to regret her father's choice, did nothing to alter the Baron's opinion; if the marriage of the eldest daughter had been successful, it was by pure chance, for the facts were simple enough; only a man dressed in a judicial robe could make a girl completely happy.

That having been said, it had become a matter of necessity to find a judge for his youngest daughter. Of all the possible & available judges, the most suitable in the eyes of the old baron was a certain Monsieur de Fontanis, the presiding judge of the Court of Aix. The judge was an old Provençal friend of the Baron's, so without any hesitation, deliberation, or conversation, it was Monsieur de Fontanis who was chosen to become Mademoiselle de Téroze's husband.

Few people can imagine a presiding judge in the Court of Aix; it is a species of beast of which much has been said but little understood. A strict moralist by profession, meticulous, stubborn, imprudent, vain, cowardly, talkative and stupid by nature, its face is stretched like a goose, it's as greasy-looking as Punch, and is tall, thin, and gaunt and stinks like a corpse. It's as though all the bile and inflexibility of the kingdom's magistrature has chosen to take refuge in this Provençal temple of Themis, in order to go from there whenever a French court needed to admonish or hang one of its citizens.[7]

But the above sketch by one of Monsieur de Fontanis' compatriots does not really do full justice to the creature being described.

Above his spindly body, which was a little stooped as we have just mentioned, one could see that Monsieur de Fontanis had a head that was low at the back and which sloped upwards dramatically to a very high forehead, the overall impression being that of a wedge on a stick. He had a yellow forehead that was masterfully covered by a wig that he had fashioned himself; the likes of which had yet to been seen in Paris.

His two legs readily supported the diminutive torso of this walking bell tower, from whose chest there emanated, not without some inconvenience to anyone nearby, a shrill voice emphatically uttering idle chatter, half in French, half in Provençal.[8] It was idle chatter which he never failed to laugh at with his mouth so wide open that it was possible, at such moments, to see a blackish chasm that went all the way back to the uvula. It was a mouth bereft of teeth, excoriated in various places, and which most closely resembled another of the body's orifices, one that is common to kings & peasants alike.

Additional to these physical attractions, Monsieur de Fontanis also believed himself to be in possession of a fine mind.

After dreaming one night that he had ascended to the third heaven with Saint Paul, he considered himself the greatest astronomer in France. He argued about legislation like Farinacius and Cujas and he was often heard to say, in accord with those great men, and with his colleagues who were not great men, that the life of a citizen, his fortune, his honor, his family, in short, all that society ultimately regards as sacred, was as nothing when it came to the discovery and punishment of a crime, and that it was a hundred times better to risk the lives of fifteen innocent people than to let a single guilty person go free.[9] Because Heaven is just, even though the courts are not, the punishment of an innocent person has no other disadvantage than to send a soul to Heaven, whereas to let a guilty person go free risks multiplying crime on earth.

The only type of people with any influence at all over the armored soul of Monsieur de Fontanis were whores. Not that he had much use of them in general, for although he had an ardent temperament, his voluptuous faculties were limited in both scope and size, and as he was also lacking in stamina, his desires always greatly exceeded his abilities to satisfy them.

Monsieur de Fontanis simply wanted the glory of transmitting his illustrious name to posterity, and that was all, but what compelled that famous magistrate to show indulgence toward those priestesses of Venus, was that he claimed that there were few citizens more useful to the State. Due to their lies, their deceptions, and their gossip, a whole host of secret crimes managed to be uncovered. Monsieur de Fontanis had one thing right: he was a sworn enemy of what philosophers call human weaknesses.

This somewhat grotesque combination of a physical Ostrogothic and Justinian morality left the city of Aix for the first time in his life in April 1779 and came, at the behest of Baron de Téroze (whom he had known for a very long time, for reasons of little interest to the reader).[10] He opted to stay at the Hôtel de Danemark, not far from the Baron's home.

As it was the time of year of the Saint-Germain fair,[11] everyone in the hotel thought that that extraordinary-looking creature was there as part of the fair. One of those semi-official beings, who are always offering their services in these public places, even suggested to him that he go and ask the impresario Nicolet, who would be delighted to include him in the line-up of evening entertainment.[12] Unless, of course, he would prefer to register with the rival impresario, Audinot.[13]

To this, the judge said:

— When I was a child, my maid warned me that Parisians were a very caustic & facetious bunch; the sort of people who could never appreciate my many virtues. Recently, one of my staff informed me that my glorious hairpiece would make quite an impression on them. The general populace are wont to make jokes as they die of hunger, just as they sing when they are crushed by life… oh! I have always believed that what these people really need is an inquisition like the one in Madrid or a scaffold ready and always waiting to be used unsparingly, like the one in Aix.

Monsieur de Fontanis then spent some time in freshening up a little, which could only have helped to emphasize the full glory of his sexagenarian charms. After a few squirts of rosewater and lavender, which were not, as Horace says, ambitious ornaments, after all this, I say, and perhaps after one or two other precautions, which have not yet come to our attention, the judge presented himself at the home of his old friend, the Baron; the doors were opened, his name was announced, and the judge entered.[14]

Unfortunately for him, the two sisters and the Marquis d'Olinccurt were all playing an amusing, but slightly childish game in one corner of the sitting-room, when this highly original figure of a man appeared. No matter how much effort they made, it proved impossible for them to refrain from bursting out laughing, which resulted in the Provençal judge's solemn expression being thoroughly disturbed. He had practiced his entry bow for a long time in the mirror, perfecting its sweep, for it was the bow he intended to make in order to impress his future bride, and he had executed it perfectly when that accursed laughter from the three young friends froze him to the spot, so that he was in mid-bow, very much in the shape of an arc; a position he stayed in for much longer than he had anticipated. When he finally stood up, a stern look from the Baron brought his three children back within the bounds of respect, and the conversation began.

The Baron, whose mind was already made up and who wanted to make sure everything was clear to everyone, stated his case so well that by the time that first meeting had ended, he had informed Mademoiselle de Téroze that the judge was the husband he intended for her and that she was to give him her hand by the end of the week at the latest. Mademoiselle de Téroze remained silent, the judge withdrew, and the Baron repeated that he expected to be obeyed.

The situation was a cruel one: not only did that beautiful young lady adore the Comte d'Elbène, not only did he idolize her, but she was also as weak as she was kind-hearted. Unfortunately, she had already let her charming lover pluck her flower; the one that is very different from the rose, although it is sometimes compared to it, despite not having the rose's ability to be reborn every spring.

So, regarding this important matter, what would Monsieur de Fontanis, a presiding judge of the Court of Aix, have thought upon discovering that his nuptial duty had already been accomplished by another? A Provençal judge may have many ridiculous qualities; they are in fact a well-known trait of this class, but the fact remains that the judge was fully aware of matters pertaining to wedding nights and to first fruit and would understandably expect to find them, at least once in his life, in his wife.

That was what had given Mademoiselle de Téroze pause. Although she was a very vivacious & very mischievous young lady, she nevertheless possessed all of the delicacy and sensitivity that befits a woman in that situation. Therefore, she understood perfectly well that her husband would have a considerably low opinion of her if she were to provide him with proof that she had been disrespectful to him before they had met. There is nothing equal to a man's prejudices on this matter: not only must the unfortunate young woman sacrifice all her heart's affections to the husband that her parents have arranged for her, but she will be found guilty if, before knowing the tyrant who was going to enslave her, she had listened to nature and indulged for a moment in its urgings.

With some urgency, Mademoiselle de Téroze spoke in confidence about the matter to her sister. The sister, more playful than prudish, and far more hedonistic than devout, reacted to her sister's secret by laughing like a madwoman and then immediately sharing the confidence with her husband. Her husband, the Marquis, was a thoughtful man who declared that with his sister-in-law's hymen being in such a broken and sorry state it could not, under any circumstances, be offered to someone such as Monsieur de Fontanis, a renowned priest of Themis. A gentleman such as the judge, the Marquis pointed out, would never treat a matter of such importance lightly. He added that he was very concerned that his poor little sister would also be in a city where the scaffold was always standing ready to be used, and that she would perhaps be made to climb it and be used as an example of what would happen to anyone who deliberately abandoned modesty and decency.

The Marquis expounded. His erudition, particularly after dinner, had a tendency to reveal itself. This mealtime was no exception; he set about proving that the Provençals were descendants of an Egyptian colony, and that the Egyptians often sacrificed young girls, and that a presiding judge in the Court of Aix, whose ancestors were Egyptian colonists, could without any hesitation have even the prettiest neck in the world cut, even Mademoiselle's…

— They're all head-choppers, those colonial judges, d'Olincourt continued. They'll cut off your head faster than a crow pecks at carrion, and they don't care about the right or the wrong of it. Inflexibility, like Themis, wears a blindfold over its eyes, and in a town like Aix, philosophy never seems able to remove it…

The Comte, the Marquis, Madame d'Olincourt and her charming sister decided to hold a meeting to determine what exactly could be done. The meeting was held at a small house in the Bois de Boulogne owned by the Marquis. There, the stern Areopagus decided, in an enigmatic style that was similar to the answers given the Cumaean Sibyl, or to judgments made by the Court of Aix, which because of its Egyptian heritage has a right to use hieroglyphics, that it would be best all round if the judge were "to be married, but not married."

The sentence was passed unanimously, & the actors rehearsed their various roles until they had completely mastered them. Then the group returned to the Baron's house, where the young lady offered no opposition to her father's decision. D'Olincourt & his wife are, they assured everyone, delighted with a marriage between two such well-suited people. They ingratiated themselves with the judge to an astonishing degree, so much so that they very quickly found themselves in his good graces. As they were very careful not to laugh whenever he appeared, they also soon won the approval of the son-in-law & the father-in-law. Everyone then agreed it would be a fine thing indeed to celebrate the wedding nuptials at the Château d'Olincourt near Melun, a superb estate belonging to the Marquis. The Baron apologized for being unable to attend such a wonderful celebration in such a beautiful location, but he would, he said, call in if his duties allowed him to.

The day finally arrived; the happy couple were joined in holy matrimony at Saint-Sulpice Church. Due to the bride's request for a very intimate wedding, the ceremony was attended by the couple, the priest, & two witnesses. The service was early in the morning and was performed without the slightest hitch. From the church, the newly-married couple set off for the d'Olincourt estate.

Following the specifics of the agreed plan, the Comte d'Elbène was disguised as La Brie, the Marquis's *valet de chambre*. Wearing the appropriate clothing for such a position, he effusively welcomed the wedding party when they arrived. Once supper was over he escorted the newlyweds to the bridal chamber, the decorations and machinery of which had been arranged personally by him and installed according to his precise directions. He would be fully responsible for operating them.

— In truth, my dearest, said the amorous Provençal native, as soon as he found himself alone with his wife-to-be, you have the charms of Venus herself, *capistal*.[15] I do not know where you got them, but one could search all of Provence without finding anything that matched them.

He then ran his lascivious hands all over the skirts of poor Mademoiselle Téroze, who did not know whether to laugh or be afraid.

— Oh, my, my, this here, and oh, this here too, all for me, he murmured, as his hands stroked Mademoiselle's slender body beneath her many petticoats. May the good Lord see that I never again judge whores, not if these are the true forms of love hidden beneath these infernal petticoats, which you no doubt borrowed from your mother.

It was at that moment that La Brie, carrying two gold goblets, entered the room. He bowed and presented one to the young wife, then bowed again and presented the other to Monsieur de Fontanis.

— Drink, chaste couple, he said, and may you find both find the presents of love and the gifts of marriage in this drink.

When the judge inquired about the drink and the reason for it being so formally served, La Brie answered in the following way:

— Your Honor, this is a Parisian custom that dates back to the baptism of Clovis.[16] It is a custom among us that, before celebrating the mysteries that will very soon be occupying you both, you should drink this potion that has been blessed and purified by the Bishop himself, thereby providing you with the… strength necessary for the enterprise.

— Ah, I shall certainly observe that particular custom, said the man of the law enthusiastically. So hand me that goblet, my friend, hand it to me and I'll drink willingly. But be aware, if you light the touchpaper, let your young mistress understand what is likely to occur; I am already very aroused, and if you push me past the point of no return, there's no knowing what will happen. I will not be held responsible.

The judge drank, his young wife did as he did, the valet left the room, and the couple got into bed. But no sooner were they in bed than the judge was overcome by such acute bowel pains, such a pressing need to relieve himself in a way that was the very opposite to the way a newly-married man should relieve himself, that without any regard for the beautifully-appointed room he was in, without any respect for the lovely woman he was with, he flooded the bed and the surrounding area with a deluge of liquid excrement so considerable that the terrified Mademoiselle de Téroze barely had time to throw herself out of bed to avoid it. From the safety of the landing, she called out for help.

Help arrived immediately. Monsieur and Madame d'Olincourt, who had deliberately not gone to bed, dashed into the room. The judge, dismayed and ashamed, wrapped the sheets around himself so as not to reveal his excrement-covered state to anyone, not realizing that the more he moved the sheets in his attempt to conceal what he had done, the filthier he became, until at last he was the object of such horror and disgust that his young wife, and the other people present, left the room with repeated sympathetic comments regarding his condition. The Marquis assured him that the Baron would be informed of the matter without a minute to lose, so that he could send one of the best Parisian doctors immediately to the château to tend the judge.

— O merciful Heaven! the distraught judge said to himself as soon as he was alone. What a terrible situation this is. I thought that it was only in the royal palace, and only on the fleurs-de-lis itself, that one could let flow in that manner, but to do so on one's own wedding night, in bed with one's new bride, about to consummate the marriage, well, it's inconceivable.[17]

A Lieutenant in d'Olincourt's regiment, whose name was Delgatz, had, in order to take care of the regiment's horses, taken two or three courses at the veterinary school. He arrived at the château punctually, disguised as one of the most famous disciples of Asclepius.[18]

Monsieur de Fontanis had been advised to appear only in his most casual clothing, and Madame de Fontanis, to whom, theoretically, we should not yet give this name, made sure that she told her husband how very attractive she found him in that particular outfit: he was wearing a pale yellow dressing gown with red stripes that ended at the waist and which was adorned with facings and lapels, beneath which he wore a rough brown muslin waistcoat with sailor's breeches of the same color and a red wool cap; all of this, enhanced by the interesting pallor caused by his accident the day before, inspired such a wave of increased love and devotion in Mademoiselle de Téroze that she refused to leave his side for over a quarter of an hour.

Once she had left, the judge, as was his habit, spoke aloud to himself.

— Even though I erred terribly, she truly loves me. This is indeed the woman Heaven intends for me so that I may have the happiness I deserve. I behaved without decorum last night, but it's not every day that one has an attack of diarrhea.

When the doctor arrived, he felt his patient's pulse and expressed his surprise at how weak the judge was. Then, by judicious use of a few aphorisms of Hippocrates and a commentary of Galen's, the "doctor" proved that unless the judge restored himself at dinner that evening with half a dozen bottles of Spanish and Madeira wine, it would be impossible for him to succeed with the proposed deflowering.[19] And with regard to the attack of indigestion the previous day, he assured the patient that it was nothing.

— It happened, Monsieur, he told him, because the ordure was not properly filtered by the liver's ducts.

— But, the Marquis asked, my accident was not dangerous in itself, surely?

— Forgive me, Monsieur, the disciple of the Epidaurus temple replied gravely, but that is most definitely not the case.[20] In medicine we have no minor causes that cannot become major unless they are halted immediately by the profundity of our science. That "minor" accident could have very easily caused a considerable change in Monsieur's organism. If that unfiltered effluvium was carried along the base of the aorta into the subclavian artery, then dispersed from there by the brain's delicate membranes to the carotids, thereby altering the circulation of the animal spirits and suspending their natural activity, it might very well have induced madness.

— Oh heavens, Mademoiselle de Téroze wailed. My husband is mad! Did you hear, dear sister? My husband is mad!

— Please don't alarm yourself, Madame. Thanks to the thoroughness of my care there is no longer any need for concern. I'm now taking full responsibility for the patient; he will, and I can state this quite categorically, make a full recovery — just as long as he follows my instructions to the letter. He is already far better than he was yesterday. Tomorrow he'll be even better.

At these words, everyone was greatly relieved; cries of joy were uttered & there were smiles all round. Everyone seemed lighter in their hearts. The Marquis d'Olincourt warmly embraced his brother-in-law showing, in his lively and provincial manner, the profound interest he took in him, and informing him that pleasure and enjoyment were the order of the day.

The Marquis had invited everyone on a tour of his estate, during which they would all visit his neighbors and tenants. On hearing the day's plan, the judge wanted to go and change into his finery. However, he was advised not to and everyone reveled in the pleasure they got from introducing him to everyone in the region, while wearing the same bizarre outfit his wife loved to see him in.

— But he looks so charming dressed like that, said the wicked Marquise at every opportunity. Truly, if I had known before I knew you, Monsieur d'Olincourt, that the sovereign magistracy of Aix included such agreeable gentlemen as my dear brother-in-law, I swear to you that I would never have chosen a husband except from among the members of that highly-respected group.

And bowing low, the judge thanked her, his hollow laugh ringing out. Throughout that day, he was observed on several occasions glancing at himself in a mirror and saying to himself in a low voice:

— It's true, you're not too bad at all.

Finally, the evening meal was announced.

The quasi-doctor, who was a very enthusiastic drinker, was at the table on the pretext of having to observe his patient. He therefore had no trouble persuading his patient to do as he did. The conspirators had been very careful to place an assortment of particularly strong wines within close reach of the two men, wines which quickly befuddled their senses and very quickly put the judge in the state they wanted him in.

The guests rose from the table. The Lieutenant, who had played his faux-doctor role to perfection, retired to his bed and disappeared the next day. As for our hero, his dear wife took him by the hand and led him to the bridal bed, escorted by everyone there in a triumphant procession.

The Marquise, who was always charming, but even more so when she had imbibed a little champagne, told the judge that she was certain he had indulged too much, and that she feared that, overheated by the fumes of Bacchus, he would most likely have no choice but to forego the joys of Eros for yet another night.

— It's nothing to be concerned about, Madame Marquise, the judge replied. Those seductive gods when gathered together become all the more formidable. As for reason, which many seem to manage without, what does it matter whether one loses it in wine or in the flames of love? What does it matter if I've sacrificed it to one or the other of those two deities? As for reason itself, it's the one thing in the world that we judges know best how to do without; we have banished it from our courtrooms as well as from our heads, we make a sport of trampling it underfoot, and this is what makes our judgments masterpieces, for although they are devoid of common sense, they are carried out as resolutely as though we knew precisely what they meant.

The judge stumbled a little, and then stooped to pick up his red cap, which a moment's lost balance had caused to fall from his bald head. He then continued.

— As you may know, Madame Marquise, yes, most truly, as you may be aware, I am one of the best legal minds in my court building. It was I who last year persuaded my learned colleagues to exile from the province for a period of ten years, and thereby ruin forever, a nobleman who had always served the king faithfully and well. As I recall, it was all over a party of delightful young women.[21] My colleagues resisted, but I pushed for the nobleman to be punished severely. In the end they gave in and saw things from my perspective… You see, my good lady, I love morality, I love temperance and sobriety, and everything that offends those two virtues revolts me, and angers me. I deal with it severely. One has to be severe; severity is the daughter of justice… and justice is the mother of… I beg your pardon, madame, there are times when sometimes the memory fails…

— Yes, yes, that's right, the Marquise replied. But please ensure that there isn't a lapse of anything else tonight, apart from your memory, for, as you well know, the union must be consummated to be legal, and my little sister, who adores you, cannot be expected to be content with such abstinence forever.

— Your fears are unfounded, Madame, the judge said, uttering his reassurances as he attempted to keep step with his bride despite his very unsteady gait. You may rest assured that I will return her to you tomorrow morning as Madame de Fontanis, as surely as I am a man of honor.

At this point, the Marquise withdrew, taking everyone else with her.

— Isn't that true, my dear lady? the man of the bench continued, turning to his betrothed. Don't you agree that tonight our objective will be successfully achieved? As you can see, it's what everyone wishes for us; there is not a single member of your family who is not honored to be united with me by our marriage: nothing flatters a household more than having a judge as one of its members.

— No one doubts it, Monsieur, the young bride replied. And I can assure you, speaking for myself alone, that I have never felt as proud as I did when I heard someone refer to me as "the judge's wife."

— I can easily believe it. Come on, undress, my young dove. I can feel myself growing a little weary, and I would like, if it's possible, to finish our little matter before sleep comes and carries me away completely.

But Mademoiselle de Téroze, as is usual for newly-wed brides, took an inordinate amount of time over her careful preparations for the nuptial bed; she was unable to find everything she needed, she was constantly calling for and sending away maids, and she could never seem to finish those extravagant preparations.

The judge, who by this time was beyond impatience, decided he could wait no longer and climbed into bed, from where he continued calling to her for over a quarter of an hour:

— Come along, for God's sake! Do hurry, dearest. I simply cannot understand what's taking you so long. What are you doing? Come along now, or it'll be too late.

However, no matter how much he cajoled, begged, swore, or promised, nothing happened. And, considering the state of drunkenness that our modern Lycurgus was in, he found it rather difficult to rest one's head on a pillow without falling asleep upon it.[22] The judge therefore yielded to the moment's most urgent need, and was already snoring, as though he had just finished sentencing some Marseilles whore, before Mademoiselle de Téroze had taken off her undergarments.

— He's asleep! the Comte d'Elbène said as he crept quietly into the room. Come, my love, let's share more of our happy moments together, the ones we enjoy when you give me what this coarse animal would like to steal from us and delight in.

He then led the beloved object of his affections out of the room. Once they were gone, the lights went out in the bridal chamber, and the parquet floor was immediately strewn with mattresses. Another signal was given and the part of the bed occupied by our man of law separated from the rest and, by means of a sophisticated pulley system, was so very carefully raised twenty feet above the ground that our legislator, due to his inebriated state, noticed nothing.

At about three o'clock in the morning, awakened by the pressure of a full bladder, the judge remembered seeing a bedside table, beneath which was the chamber pot necessary to relieve himself. He reached out for it, amazed at first to find only emptiness all around him. He groped further, leaning forward over the side of the bed to facilitate his search for the much-needed item. The bed, which was suspended only by the ropes, conformed to the movement of the person leaning over, and finally reaching tipping point, upended completely, spilling its load into the middle of the room.

The judge fell and landed safely enough on the mattresses that had been prepared for him, however his surprise was so great that he began to bellow like a calf being butchered.

— What the devil's all this? he said aloud. Madame, you are no doubt nearby, so could you please explain the reason for my fall? Yesterday, when I went to bed I was four feet from the floor, and now, while reaching for my chamber pot, I fell more than twenty.

But no one responded to his questions, so the judge, assuming his wife was asleep, and not being at all uncomfortable where he was lying, gave up trying to find out what had happened and spent the rest of the night where he had larded, as though he were in his own Provençal bed.

Great care was taken, after the judge had fallen asleep, to very quietly lower the bed section so that it slotted back into its housing perfectly, once more giving the impression that the bed was a single item of furniture.

At nine o'clock in the morning, Mademoiselle de Téroze crept silently into the room. As soon as she was inside she opened all of the windows and rang for her maids.

— Let me say, in all honesty, Monsieur, she said to the judge, your company is not exactly enjoyable, and I'm hereby giving you notice that I intend to complain in no uncertain terms to my family about your attitude to me and about the way you treat me.

What's going on? the judge asked sleepily, as he rubbed his eyes and tried to understand the accident that caused him to land on the floor.

— What do you mean, what's going on? the young woman demanded, as she continued, to the best of her ability, to act the part of the neglected wife. Last night, driven by the feelings and needs that rightly bind me to you, I came over to you, wanting to receive assurances of the same feelings from you. But you pushed me away so angrily and with so much force that I fell onto the floor...

— Oh, merciful Heaven, said the judge. Listen, my dear, I think I'm beginning to understand something about what happened last night... I offer you my sincerest apologies. Last night, awoken by an urgent need, I was reaching for the means to relieve myself, and because my movements were so hurried, I tipped myself out of bed, and landed on the floor. Without realizing it, I must have tipped you out of bed too. I feel I should be forgiven, because I was most definitely dreaming. I thought I had fallen from a height of twenty feet. Come now, my angel, it's nothing, nothing. We must simply postpone our sport until tonight and I promise you that I will stay sober, as sober as a judge. I'll only drink water. But at least give me a kiss, my sweetheart, let's have peace between us before appearing in public, or otherwise I will believe you have a grudge against me, and I wouldn't want that for all the world.

Mademoiselle de Téroze was prepared to offer one of her cheeks, still flushed from the flames of love, to the foul kisses of the old satyr. When the company came into the room, husband and wife took great care to make no mention of the unfortunate nocturnal disaster.

The whole day was spent in pleasurable activities, including a particularly long walk that took Monsieur de Fontanis away from the château and gave La Brie time to prepare new surprises.

The judge, determined to consummate his marriage, was so careful during meals regarding what he ate and drank that it became impossible to use those means to do anything to affect his reason. But fortunately our conspirers had more than one card to play and the worthy Fontanis had too many enemies for him to be able to escape the traps they had set for him.

Finally, the company got up to go to bed.

— Ah! Tonight, my angel, the judge said to his younger half, once he was in their room. I flatter myself that you will not get away from me tonight.

But despite his boasting and bragging, the judge knew that the weapon he would be called upon to use was far from adequate and not even in a state of readiness so, thinking of the act of consummation as a sporting event such as a joust, one for which he felt he should prepare for in order to acquit himself well, the poor Provençal began a series of the most incredible exercises in his own corner.

He lay on the floor and stretched, he made his body as stiff as possible, so that all of his nerves grew taut, he flexed his muscles, then he stood on the bed and jumped up and down on it vigorously, with two or three times more force than if he had been simply resting on it. It was this last series of actions that bounced him from the bed and onto the floor. His heavy, ungainly landing broke the beams in the floor, beams that had been very carefully sawn almost all the way through, and the unfortunate judge plummeted straight down into the pigsty that just happened to be directly below his room.

There was a lengthy discussion between those that were gathered at the Château d'Olincourt regarding who must have been the more surprised; the judge on finding himself among animals so common in his part of the country, or the animals themselves, upon seeing in their midst one of the most famous judges of the High Court of Aix. There were some who claimed that the satisfaction must have been mutual: in fact, shouldn't the judge have been elated to find himself, so to speak, in good company, and able to breathe for a moment that familiar and powerful tang of the earth?

And for their part, surely those animals denounced as unclean by the blessed Moses, should they not give thanks to Heaven for finally finding a judge in their midst, and not only that, but a judge of the Court of Aix who, accustomed from childhood to judging causes relating to these beast's favorite element, might one day arrange

& prevent any discussion tending to this element so analogous to the organization of both parties?

Be that as it may, because introductions were not made immediately, and as civilization, the mother of politeness, is not much more advanced among the members of the Court of Aix than among the animals eschewed by the children of Israel, there was a moment of stillness and shock during which the judge won no laurels: then there was a flurry of porcine fury as the judge was battered, bruised, beleaguered by trotters and snouts. He reprimanded them, but was not listened to; he promised to record their grievances, but they ignored him; he spoke of decrees, but they were not impressed at all; he threatened them with exile, and they trampled him underfoot. The hapless Fontanis, by then completely covered in blood, was about to sentence them all to be burned at the stake, no less, when help finally arrived.

It was La Brie and the Colonel of Dragoons who, armed with torches, had come to try to haul the judge out of the muck he was mired in. It was also a question of knowing how to lift him out, as he was well and truly covered from head to foot making it difficult, and very unfragrant, to get any purchase on him. La Brie went looking for a pitchfork, a stableboy was sent to fetch another, and using those two implements, they hauled him, as best they could, out of the unmentionable stinking morass into which he had fallen and been buried…

But now a new difficulty arose, and it was not an easy one to solve. Now they'd got him out, where were they to take him?

Purging the decree was discussed; the guilty had to be cleansed. The Colonel proposed letters of annulment, but the stableboy, who understood nothing of those grand words and phrases, said that it was simply a matter of depositing the judge in the horses' drinking trough for a couple of hours, and after he had been sufficiently immersed, handfuls of straw could be used to clean him up and make him presentable again.

But the Marquis was of the opinion that the coldness of the water would have a detrimental effect on his brother-in-law's health. However, once it was discovered that the kitchen boy's washhouse was still filled with hot water, the judge was carried in there by La Brie and the Colonel and put into the care of that disciple of Comus, who in no time at all made Monsieur de Fontanis as clean as a piece of fine bone china. [23]

— My suggestion is that you do not rejoin your wife tonight, said d'Olincourt as soon as he saw the freshly-scrubbed man of law. I know how fastidious you are, so La Brie will take you to a modest bachelor's apartment where you can spend the rest of the night in peace.

— Very well, my dear Marquis, the judge said. I approve of your plan... but you have to admit, I must be bewitched to have had so many strange things happen to me every night since my arrival at this accursed château.

— There is most assuredly some physical explanation for all of this, the Marquis replied. As the doctor is
coming back to see us tomorrow, might I suggest you
consult him on the matter?

— I will indeed, the judge replied, as he was led off to
his modest quarters by La Brie. The truth, my friend, he
said to La Brie as he prepared for bed, is that this night I
was closer to the goal than I have been since all of these
strange occurrences began.

— Alas, Monsieur, the clever young man replied, as
he made his way out of the room, I feel that there's an
inevitability about it all that indicates it may be being
decreed by Heaven. If that is the case, then I pity you
with all my heart.

*

Once Delgatz had taken the judge's pulse, he assured
him that the beams had broken simply due to an excess
of engorgement of the lymphatic vessels, which had
doubled the mass of the humors, and proportionally
increased the animal volume. Consequently, he said, it
was necessary to impose a strict diet, which, once it had
effectively purified the acridity of the humors, would
necessarily reduce the physical weight and contribute
to the success of the proposed course of action, besides
which...

— But, Monsieur, Fontanis said, interrupting him,
I fell and dislocated my left arm and left hip in that
terrible fall...

— I'm sure you did, the doctor said, but these second-ary accidents are not what concern me; I always try to trace everything back to their causes. It's all a matter of the blood, Monsieur. By reducing the acrimoniousness of the lymph, we relieve the vessels, and the circulation of the vessels becomes easier and we necessarily reduce the physical mass, from which it follows that floors no longer collapse under your weight, and you will be able to indulge all the sport you wish on your bed without fear of any subsequent dangers.

— And my arm, Monsieur, and my hip?

— Let us purge, Monsieur, let us purge. Let us proceed with a couple of localized bloodlettings & everything will slowly heal.

On that same day the diet began.

Delgatz, who did not leave his patient's side for the entire week, put him on a chicken broth only diet, and purged him three times running, forbidding him above all to have any thoughts about his wife.

As ignorant of medicine as Lieutenant Delgatz was, his enforced diet succeeded perfectly, and he later enter-tained the company by telling them about how, when he had worked at the veterinary school, he had once treated an ass that had fallen into a very deep hole and after a month of the same treatment as the judge was getting, the recovered animal was once again happily carrying its bags of plaster, just as it had always done.

Indeed the judge, who did have a tendency to be bilious, soon had a trace of his usual color back again, and once the bruises faded, everyone's concern turned to restoring him to perfect health, so that he would, once again, have the necessary forces to achieve what was still his to claim.

On the twelfth day of treatment, Delgatz took his patient by the hand and presented him to Mademoiselle de Téroze.

— Here he is, Madame, he said to her. Here is the man against whom the laws of Hippocrates seem to rebel. I return him to you safe and sound, and if he abandons himself unchecked to the forces I have restored to him, we will have the pleasure of seeing before six months, Delgatz continued, placing his hand lightly on the lower belly of Mademoiselle de Téroze... yes, Madame, we will all have the satisfaction of seeing this beautiful stomach rounded by the hands of Hymen.[24]

— May God hear you, Doctor, the spirited young woman replied. You must admit that it is very hard for me to be a woman when over the fortnight since I married I have remained a girl.

— It's bordering on the incredible, the judge said. One does not suffer from indigestion every night, nor is it every night that the need to urinate makes a husband fall out of his bed, or that believing he is about to fall into the arms of a beautiful woman, he is dropped into stinking pig excrement in a stinking pigsty.

— We shall see, said Mademoiselle de Téroze, sighing deeply. We shall see, Monsieur. But if you loved me as I love you, I'm certain that all these misfortunes would not have happened to you.

Supper was a very cheerful affair; the Marquise was both very gracious and very wicked, she wagered against her husband in favor of her brother-in-law's nuptial success, and then everyone retired.

The couple prepared hastily. Out of modesty, Mademoiselle de Téroze begged her husband not to allow any light at all in the bedchamber. The judge, too dispirited by previous events to refuse, agreed to everything his bride requested. The room was plunged into total darkness and the couple got into bed.

There were no further obstacles, and finally, the intrepid judge triumphed! He plucked, or thought he plucked, that precious flower to which mankind foolishly attaches so much value. He consummated his marriage five times in succession.

In the morning, when the curtains were drawn back and the rays of the sun that shone through the windows finally revealed to the eyes of the pursuer the quarry that he had finally caught and made his own…

Merciful Heaven, imagine what he must have felt when he saw in bed beside him an old black woman instead of his wife; when he saw a face that was so dark it was almost black, instead of the delicate & beautiful attractions which he had thought he had been repeatedly possessing.

He recoiled and cried out that he was bewitched. At that moment, his wife entered the room and found him in bed with that divine creature from Tenares and demanded, with extreme bitterness in her tone, what it was she had done to him that deserved such a cruel betrayal.[25]

— But, Madame, wasn't it with you last night that I—

— Monsieur, I may be totally humiliated and embarrassed, but I can assure you I have been nothing but a dutiful wife to you since you were chosen to be my husband. You, on the other hand, when I sent this woman in to turn down my bed covers, so I could join you for that happy & longed-for moment, you grabbed hold of her and pulled her to you. When I tried to intervene, you ignored me completely and instead, positioned *her* in my place in our bed, after which you proceeded to treat her as though she was your wife. I could not stand to see my husband enjoying himself with another woman after denying me for so long, so I ran from the room, hurt and confused, with only my tears to keep me company.

— Please tell me, my angel, are you quite sure that all of these allegations are in fact true?

By now, the heated words had drawn several people to the bedchamber. Mademoiselle de Téroze turned to them.

— Oh, the monster! No matter the outrages he has perpetrated against me by defiling our bed, he now wants to insult me with sarcasm. Is this to be my reward, when I expected an apology & an attempt at amends... Oh, dear sister, please go and fetch the rest of our family, so they can all see the unworthy object for whom I have been sacrificed... And look... Look at her lying there! That's my rival! the young wife shouted before bursting into floods of tears. And now he even dares to hold her in his arms, despite repeatedly denying me my conjugal rights. O my friends, Mademoiselle de Téroze continued despairingly, gathering everyone around her. Please help me. Please lend me the right weapons to take on this perjurer. Should I really have expected this, adoring him as I did...

It is unlikely that there was anything more comical than Fontanis's face when he heard those bewildering words. Occasionally he would glance at his black bed companion, and then he would shift his gaze to his wife and stare at her with a fixed, foolish, obsessive look in his eyes, a look that could very well have indicated that there was something wrong with his mind.

By one of those rather peculiar twists of fate, since the judge had been at the Château d'Olincourt, La Brie, his disguised rival, the man he should have feared the most, had become the person in whom he confided everything.

He sent for him.

— My friend, he said to him, you have always seemed to me to be a perfectly reasonable sort of chap. Would you please tell me if you have noticed any changes in my mind?

— Well, Your Honor, La Brie replied, his expression both sad and confused, I would never have dared to say anything to you, but since you have done me the honor of asking my opinion, I feel I must say that since your fall into the pigsty, the ideas that have emanated from the membranes of your cerebellum have not been totally pure. But don't let that worry you, Monsieur, the doctor who has already treated you is one of the greatest medical men we have ever had in this region…

— In fact, he continued, we once had here a judge from the Marquis's home town who had become so deranged that no young libertine from the region could have so much as a bit of fun with a woman, without this rascal immediately pressing charges and putting him on trial, with decrees and sentences and exiles and all the other platitudes that are always on the lips of fools like that.[26] Well, Monsieur, our doctor, that skilled physician who has already had the honor of attending to you with eighteen bloodlettings and thirty-two different types of medicines, made that judge's head as healthy as if he had never judged anyone in his life. But what a coincidence, La Brie added, turning toward a sound he had just heard. Doesn't it prove how that old saying, "Speak of the devil and he will appear," is absolutely correct, for here he is in person.

— Good morning, Doctor, said the Marquise, seeing Delgatz arrive. I have to say, I don't think we have ever needed your ministrations quite so much as we do now.

Last night our dear friend the judge had a slight aberration of the mind, which caused him, in spite of everyone's efforts to stop him, to go to bed with this black woman instead of his wife.

— In spite of everyone's efforts to stop me, the judge said, surprised. Did someone try to stop me? Who?

— Me, for one, said La Brie. I tried with all my strength to pull you off, but you were going at it so vigorously that I thought I'd better let you get on with it rather than risk being manhandled by you.

On hearing this, the judge began to scratch his head in consternation, no longer sure what to believe. The doctor went to him and took his pulse.

— This is more serious than the last accident, says Delgatz, lowering his eyes. This is some unnoticed vestige of your last affliction, like a shielded fire that escapes the intelligent eye of the observer and then bursts into flame the moment one least expects it. There is a definite obstruction in the diaphragm and a prodigious erethicism in the organism.

— Hereticism! the furious judge bellowed. What does this imbecile mean by hereticism? You need to know, you scoundrel, that I have never been a heretic. You're a damned dimwit without so much as a basic understanding of the history of France. Are you totally unaware that it's we who burn heretics? Go and visit our part of the country, you forgotten bastard from Salerno; go, my friend, go and see Mérindol and Cabrières still smoking from the fires that we lit there, or walk on the rivers of blood that the upstanding members of our court use to water the soil of the province.[27] Listen & you'll still hear the screams of the poor wretches we have sacrificed in our rage, or the sobs of the women whom we've torn from their husband's arms, the cry of the children whom we crushed inside their mother's wombs, finally, take a close look at all the holy horrors we have committed, & then after observing our conduct, tell me whether or not a fool like you has any right to accuse us of being heretics.

The judge, who was still in bed next to the black woman, had grown so incensed during his narration that, in the heat of the moment, he punched the unfortunate woman on the nose so hard that she ran from the room yelping like a bitch from whom her puppies have been taken.

— My, what is all of this sound and fury my friend? d'Olincourt asked, as he approached the patient. My dear judge, is this any way for a man of distinction to behave? Surely it must be obvious to you now that your health is getting worse and that it is essential that we think about your care and your recovery.

— At last, some courtesy, said the judge. You see, Marquis, when I am spoken to in that way, I am only too happy to listen, but to hear myself accused of being a heretic by this road-sweeper from Saint-Côme is something, you must admit, is far more than I should be expected to tolerate.

— My dear brother-in-law, the Marquise said, with her customary grace, he did not intend insulting you. Erethicism is a medical synonym for profound inflammation. At no point did he mention the word "heretical."

— Ah! In that case, my dear Marquise, I apologize. I misunderstood because I am sometimes a little hard of hearing. Let that worthy disciple of Averroës come over here and give me his diagnosis.[28] I'll listen to him… in fact, I'll do more than listen; I'll follow whatever advice he gives me.

Delgatz, who had retreated to the far side of the room during the judge's angry tirade out of fear he would be assaulted in the same way as the black woman, moved back to the side of the bed.

— As I was saying, Monsieur, said the latter-day Galen, taking his patient's pulse, there is a very serious erethicism in the organism.

— Heretic…

— Erethicism, Monsieur, the doctor said hastily, leaning away from the bed in case his patient launched a punch at him. It's a condition about which I conclude we should proceed with a quick phlebotomization of the jugular vein, followed by a series of ice baths.

— I am not sure I agree with you regarding the bloodletting, d'Olincourt said. His Honor, the judge is no longer of an age to withstand that kind of assault, unless there is a very urgent need for such a procedure. Following the examples of Themis and Asclepius, I am most assuredly not a disciple of the bloodletting mania.

My own personal theory is that there are as few illnesses that are worth the trouble of letting the blood flow out of the body as there are crimes that deserve to be punished by the shedding of blood. And so, my dear judge, I hope you will approve of what I say about sparing your own blood; perhaps I would not be as sure of you agreeing if you had less of a personal interest in the matter.

— Monsieur, the judge replied, I agree with the first part of what you said, but I hope you will not take offence if I disagree with you on your second point. Crime can only be erased by the shedding of blood. It is by blood alone that crime is purged and prevented. I simply ask you, Monsieur, to compare all the evils that crime creates on earth with the inconsequential misfortune of a dozen or so ill-fated individuals executed each year to prevent it.

— Your paradox is not based on common sense, my friend, d'Olincourt said. Also, it appears to be dictated by total inflexibility and by stupidity. Within you is a very definite preoccupation for the state and for shedding blood in its name. You should repudiate both of these forever immediately. If you think about it for a moment, you will see that your ridiculously harsh sentencing has not yet stopped crime, not even the sort of crimes you punished the most harshly. Therefore, your punishments are not a deterrent. It is utterly absurd to insist that one crime can pay for another and that the death of a second person can in any way atone for another. You and your colleagues should be ashamed of such methods, which are far from proving your integrity, but instead they provide evidence for your all-consuming predilection for despotism. It is absolutely right that you are referred to as the torturers and executioners of the human race: you destroy more men, by yourselves, than all of nature's disasters put together.

— Gentlemen, said the Marquise, it seems to me that this is neither the place nor the time for such a discussion. Instead of calming my dear brother-in-law, Monsieur, she continued, addressing her husband, you are instead inflaming his blood all the more and if you continue, you may very well cause his illness to become incurable.

— The Marquise is right, the doctor said. Please allow me, Monsieur, to order La Brie to fetch forty pounds of ice and have it put into the bathtub, which will then be filled with well water. While the bath is being prepared, I'll attend to the patient and get him ready.

Everyone immediately withdrew. The judge got up and remonstrated for a while about the ice bath, which, he said, was going to make him fit for nothing for at least six weeks. But Delgatz stayed resolute. They made their way downstairs and the judge was plunged into the ice bath. The doctor insisted the judge stay immersed in the icy water for ten to twelve minutes, which he did, in full view of the entire company, who had discretely placed themselves into every nook and cranny of the room in order to view the judge's discomfort and to be fully entertained by the spectacle. And once the patient had been well-dried, he dressed and rejoined the company as though nothing had happened.

Once dinner was over, the Marquise suggested they all go for a walk.

— The exercise will be good to the judge, won't it, doctor? she asked Delgatz.

— Most assuredly, he replied. Madame no doubt recalls that even the most rudimentary of hospitals provides its inmates with a courtyard in which they can get some fresh air.

— But I flatter myself, said the judge, that you don't consider me totally bereft of my wits.

— Not far off, Monsieur, Delgatz responded. But this is a slight abnormality that will have no consequence if we have caught it in time. But, in order for it to be totally reversed, it will be necessary for you to have total calm and tranquility.

— What do you mean by that, Doctor? Do you think that tonight I will be able to claim my prize?

— No, not tonight, Monsieur! The very thought of it makes me shudder; if I were to impose the same stern measures to you, as you do with others, I would prohibit you from having anything to do with women for three or four months.

— Three or four months, good heavens… and he turned to his wife. Three or four months, my lovely. Will you be able to wait that long, my angel? Can you wait for me to recover?

— Oh, I'm sure Monsieur Delgatz will reconsider very soon, the young Téroze said with feigned naïvety. He will at least take pity on me, even if he does not have any for you.

And with those words, everyone set off on the walk.

Their walk followed a route that took them to a ferry. The ferry was due to stop off at the home of a neighboring nobleman who, having been briefed on everything that was happening regarding the judge and his new bride, had invited the company to his home for tea. Once on the ferryboat, our young friends began to party, and Fontanis attempted to imitate them in order to please his wife.

— Judge, said the Marquis, indicating a rope hanging over the ferry. I'm willing to wager that you can't hang from this rope for several minutes, like I just did.

— Nothing could be easier, the judge said, extinguishing his pipe and standing on tiptoe to give himself the advantage of having a higher grip on the rope.

— Well, that's infinitely better than you were able to manage, my dear brother, said Mademoiselle de Téroze as soon as she saw her husband dangling from the rope.

But while the judge, thus suspended, called to the company to admire his grace and his skill, the ferryman, who had been briefed as to the company's plan regarding the judge, began to double his oar strokes, and the ferryboat moved away, leaving the unfortunate judge dangling there, suspended between the sky and the water…

He shouted, he called for help; the ferry was about halfway across the river, with more than fifteen toises to go before the boat reached the bank.[29]

— Do the best you can! someone shouted. Use your hands to swing yourself toward us! You can see that the wind is carrying us away; it's impossible for us to come back for you!

The judge took the shouted advice and, slipping, sliding, struggling, and grunting from the exertion, he did everything he could to use the rope to try and catch up with the boat that the ferryman was very skillfully keeping just ahead of the swinging judge.

If there was ever an amusing sight to behold, it certainly must have been that of one of the most distinguished judges of the High Court of Aix in his long wig & black coat, suspended by a rope over a flowing river as the boat he was supposed to be on with his young and beautiful wife sailed away without him.

— Judge, the Marquis shouted at him, suppressing his amusement. The truth of all this is that it's simply an act of Providence. It's what you would call *lex talionis*, my friend, an eye for an eye, the favorite law of your courts.[30] Why are you complaining about being dangled from a rope? Haven't you often condemned poor wretches to the same fate; wretches who didn't deserve it any more than you do?

But the judge was past hearing. Terribly tired from the violent exertions he had been forced to make, his hands slipped from the rope and he plummeted into the water like a stone. Immediately, two divers, who had been kept ready, swam to help him and he was quickly brought onboard, soaking wet and swearing like a drayman. He began by rebuking them for their practical joke that he insisted was totally appropriate… They swore to him that they had not played a joke on him at all, that a gust of wind had made the boat move away. They took him to the ferryman's cabin, which was heated. There his dear wife hugged him and made a fuss of him and helped him get changed into dry clothes. In short, she did everything she could to make him forget his little accident, and Fontanis, who was quite weak and very much in love, soon began to laugh along with everyone at the spectacle he had just made of himself.

After a while, the ferry docked and the company arrived at the nobleman's house, where they were given a very warm welcome. A sumptuous high tea was served, and great care was taken to serve the judge a pistachio cream cake that had no sooner made its way into his intestines than he was suddenly and alarmingly obliged to inquire where the toilet was.

He quickly made his way to where he'd been directed, finding himself a room that was in total darkness, with neither light nor window. In a terrible hurry, he sat down and proceeded to relieve himself with something akin to alacrity. Once he was finished, the judge found he was unable to get up off the seat.

— Now what on earth's this? he said in exasperation, shaking his bottom in an attempt to get loose from the seat. But it was no use; no matter how much he tried to move he was unable to pull himself free, short of leaving some of his skin behind.

It wasn't long before his prolonged absence was noticed, causing consternation and quite a lot of general concern. The party began to wonder what could have happened to him until, attracted by his loud cries for help, they were finally drawn to the closed door of the ill-fated toilet.

— What on earth is keeping you in there for so long, my friend? said d'Olincourt. Are you afflicted with some new type of colic?

— Oh, for God's sake, the poor devil said, redoubling his efforts to free himself. Can't you see that I'm stuck...?

But in order to give the company a little more entertainment, and in order to make the judge even more uncomfortable as he tried to pry himself loose from the seat he was inexplicably stuck to, the group had made sure there was someone positioned beneath the privy who lit a spirit-soaked candle and began to run the flame over the judge's buttocks, singeing hairs and sometimes scorching his skin, causing him to jump and jerk wildly and to grimace horribly.

The more people laughed, the more furious the judge became; he insulted the ladies and he threatened the men and the more irritated he became, the more comical his flushed face was to behold. Because of the violent movements he made, his wig had become separated from his head, and his bare skull helped to make his facial contortions even more comical.

At last their host arrived. He was deeply embarrassed and he apologized profusely. He begged the judge's pardon a thousand times for not warning him that that particular water closet was not in a fit condition to be used by anyone, let alone a man of the judge's standing.

The nobleman and his servants managed to pry loose the hapless judge as best they could, but not without causing him to leave behind a circular layer of skin which remained attached to the seat. This was because the painters had sized the seat with strong glue in preparation for the paint they intended to decorate it with.

— The truth is, said Fontanis, reappearing amongst the company with tenacious boldness, you're happy to have me amongst you as long as I serve as the butt of your jokes.

— You are an unjust friend, said d'Olincourt. Why must you always blame us for the misfortunes that are visited on you by fate alone? I thought that when one put on Themis's halter, justice become a natural virtue, but I can see that I was wrong.[31]

— It's because your ideas on what is called justice are not clear, the judge said. We of the bar acknowledge several kinds of justice. There is what is called relative justice and personal justice...

— Is that really so? the Marquis asked. I have never noticed that this virtue, which is so frequently analyzed, is very often practiced. What *I* call justice, my friend, is quite simply the law of nature. One is always just and honest when one follows it; one only becomes unjust when one deviates from it. Tell me, Judge, if you had indulged in some whim of your imagination in the privacy of your own home, and a troop of inquisitors came into your family home carrying torches and resorting to a whole range of inquisitorial tricks and ruses, and using bought information in an effort to find some old excusable mistake you may have made when you were twenty or thirty years old, would you find it very just? And if they tried to use those atrocious methods to ruin you, to exile you, to destroy your honorable name, to dishonor your children, and to plunder your property, tell me, my friend, tell me honestly, would you describe those scoundrels as just? And if you believed in a Supreme Being, would you be willing to worship Him if He exercised *that* type of justice over you — and wouldn't you always be trembling in abject fear at the very notion of being, at any time, subjected to the whims of His tyranny?

— Is that your understanding of Law? Do you blame us for looking diligently for crime? It's our sworn duty.

— That is not true! Your duty consists only of punishing crime when it has been uncovered. Leave the barbaric and disgusting task of finding criminals like vile spies or disreputable informers to the stupid and vicious maxims of the Inquisition. What citizen can feel safe when, surrounded by servants who have been bribed by the likes of you, his honor or his life will be in the hands of people who, embittered by their servitude, think they can escape it, or perhaps simply alleviate their burden, by selling you the man who imposes servitude upon them? And what will you have achieved? You will have increased the number of criminals in the state, you will have made women treacherous, servants slanderers, and children ungrateful: you will have doubled the sum of vices without having given birth to one single virtue.

— It is not a matter of creating virtues; it is only a matter of eradicating crime.

— But the methods you use multiplies it.

— Yes, you're absolutely right. But that is the law, and we must follow it. We are not legislators, my dear marquis, we are merely *implementers.*

— I have a better term, Judge, a far better term, d'Olincourt replied, warming to his topic. I'd say that you, by which I mean the judiciary, are the *torturers*, or rather, the *executioners.* I'd also say that you are quite obviously a very dangerous enemy of the State, and you derive your only enjoyment from opposing its prosperity, from placing obstacles in the path to its happiness, from sullying its glory, and from shedding the precious blood of its subjects for no reason.

Despite the two ice-cold baths that Fontanis had taken in his day, bile is such a difficult thing to destroy in a man of the judiciary that the poor judge shook with rage to hear a profession that he considered utterly respectable denigrated in such a way. He was unable to believe that the judiciary could have such accusations leveled at it, and he was perhaps about to respond to the attack in the language of a sailor from Marseilles, when the ladies approached and requested that they set off home.

The Marquise asked the judge whether he needed to pay a visit to the water closet before he left.

— No, no, Madame, said the Marquis. This respectable judge does not always suffer from colic. You'll have to forgive him for taking his recent attack a little too seriously. It's considered an illness of some consequence in Marseilles or Aix, this minor movement of bowels. Ever since we heard a troop of rogues, colleagues of this fellow here, judge that a few whores who were suffering from colic were *poisoned*, it should come as no surprise that colic is considered a very serious matter indeed to a Provençal judge.

Fontanis was one of the severest judges in the case to which the Marquis referred. It was a case that had brought long-lasting and immense shame to the entire judiciary of Provence. The judge was, at that moment, in a state difficult to describe; he stammered, he twitched, he frothed at the mouth, very much resembling one of those mastiffs in a bullfight that is unable to bite the bull.

D'Olincourt took full advantage of the judge's reaction.

— Look at him, ladies. Just look at him and tell me, I implore you, if you would feel confident about the fate of an unfortunate nobleman who, trusting in his innocence and good faith, should see fifteen mastiffs such as this one snapping at the seat of his breeches.

Before the judge could retort angrily to the remark, the Marquis, who was biding his time and did not want to create any scandal, at least at that moment, went out to his carriage, leaving Mademoiselle de Téroze to soothe the wounds he had just inflicted. She had great difficulty in placating the furious judge, but she finally succeeded.

There were no further incidents as the party boarded the ferry and it crossed the river. The judge gave no indication that he had any interest in hanging onto any of the dangling ropes that the ferry passed on its way back to the quay. Everyone arrived safely back at the château.

They had dinner, during which, the doctor was careful to remind Fontanis of the need to observe his abstinence.

— Your advice is totally useless, the judge said. How do you expect a man who has spent the night with a black woman; who has been accused of being a heretic in the morning; who was made to take an ice bath for his lunch; who shortly after that fell into the river; who on finding himself stuck fast to a toilet seat, like a creature in a trap, had his buttocks burned while he was moving his bowels, and who has been told to his face that judges who go looking for crime are despicable rogues, and that whores who have colic are not whores who've been poisoned, how, I ask you, do you expect such a man to even consider deflowering a virgin?

— I am very pleased to see you being so reasonable, said Delgatz, as he accompanied Fontanis to the bachelor's quarters he occupied when he had no designs on his wife. I urge you to continue being so. If you do, you will soon feel resulting benefits.

The next day the ice baths were repeated. For the duration of the treatment, the judge did not need to be reminded of the necessity of restricting his pleasurable activities. Consequently, the delectable Mademoiselle de Téroze was able to take advantage of the interval of several days to enjoy every pleasure of love in the arms of her charming d'Elbène.

Finally after a fortnight, Fontanis, as reinvigorated as he could ever be, began to make his desires known to his wife.

— Oh really, Monsieur, said the young lady, when she saw that further delay was virtually impossible. I now have many quite pressing matters other than love on my mind, Monsieur. Read what is written in this letter that I have just received. I am ruined!

She handed her husband a letter in which he read that the Château de Téroze, part of Mademoiselle de Téroze's dowry, located four leagues away from the one in which they were staying, in a neglected and seldom-visited area of Fontainebleau Forest, had, for the last six months, been haunted. According to the letter, several ghosts had driven everyone away, including the local farmer, and the land was now so neglected and the soil degraded that the once-considerable value of the property was decreasing daily, and unless something was done to resolve the problem immediately, it was likely that the judge and his wife would never receive so much as a sou from it.

— This is terrible news indeed, said the judge, handing back the letter. But could we not ask your father to give us something other than this wretched château?

— And what do you suggest he give us, Monsieur? Must I remind you that I am the youngest daughter? My father gave my older sister a huge dowry when she got married. He gave me the château and its land as my dowry. It is not an inconsiderable property. It would be ungrateful of me to ask him for something else. We must be satisfied with what we have and try to put things right.

— But your father must have been aware of this issue when he gave you to me in marriage.

— Yes, but it was not something he believed at the time. Besides, the property is worth a lot. There is merely a slight delay in us reaping the benefits of it.

— And does the Marquis know about this?

— Yes, but he does not dare talk to you about it.

— He is wrong. We must discuss this matter together.

D'Olincourt was sent for and when asked about the Château de Téroze, he admitted that he had heard about the ghosts. Finally, the two men agreed that the best thing to do, despite the inherent dangers, was to go to the château, spend two or three days there, put an end to any ghostly disruption, reinstate the tenants, & then determine exactly how much revenue could be recovered from the property.

— Do you have a modicum of courage, Judge? the Marquis asked.

— Courage is a virtue of little use in my profession, Fontanis replied.

— I'm fully aware of that, the Marquis said. All you need is ferocity. I suppose it's more or less the same for that virtue as for all the others; you know exactly how to legally rob a man so thoroughly that you never take anything except that which ruins him.

— There you go again with your sarcasm, Marquis. Let's talk like reasonable men, please, and leave malice for some other time.

— Very well, here's what you need to do: you have to go and spend a few days in the Château de Téroze, destroy the ghosts, straighten out the property's finances, and then come back here and sleep with your wife.

— Wait, Monsieur. Just a moment, please. Let's not be quite so hasty. Have you considered the dangers involved if we go into the midst of such creatures? Proper legal proceedings, followed by a decree would be a far more effective way of resolving this entire issue.

— There *you* go again with your proceedings and decrees… Why don't you also excommunicate, like priests do? Atrocious weapons of tyranny and stupidity! When will all those cockroaches in their robes, all those clowns in their morning coats, all those advocates of Themis and the Virgin Mary, stop thinking that their insultingly empty monologues and their ridiculous papers have the slightest effect on the world? Haven't you learned, brother-in-law, that it is not with scraps of papers such as the ones you propose that you can put a stop to any determined villains, but with swords, powder, and bullets? You must decide, therefore, whether you intend to starve to death or to muster up the courage to fight them in that way.

— My dear Marquis, you reason like a Colonel of Dragoons. Allow me to look at things with the eye of an expert in law. As a person of importance to the State, I should never have to expose myself to danger of any sort without proper consideration of the facts.

— Did you just refer to yourself as "a person of importance to the State," Judge? It's been a long time since I've had a good laugh, but since you've decided to use humor on me, then I must congratulate you on your wonderful joke. But please tell me how on earth you arrived at the idea that someone generally of humble birth, an individual who is always in revolt against all the good that his master may desire, neither serving his purse nor his person, in constant opposition to all his good intentions, whose sole task is to encourage division among individual citizens, to feed the dissent that rears its head from time to time in the kingdom, and to harass & upset its citizens... how, I ask again, can you imagine that such an individual can ever be "a person of importance to the State"?

— I refuse to take part in a conversation in which the other party merely wishes to be insulting and to vent his spleen.

— Very well, my friend, I agree. Let's instead look at the facts: even if you spent a month thinking about this situation, and if you then rather pathetically asked your aged colleagues to give their opinion of it, I can tell you categorically that there is no other way of resolving this issue but to go and take up residence in the very place that someone or something is trying to deprive you of.

The judge again began to haggle, to defend his position and his vaunted opinion of himself. He used a thousand paradoxes, each more absurd and more arrogant than the other, until he finally came to the same conclusion as the Marquis, namely that they would both leave the next day, taking only two valets from the Château d'Olincourt with them. The judge asked for La Brie. We do not know why he asked for him, but as we have already mentioned, he did seem to confide in the young man a great deal. D'Olincourt, only too aware of the important affairs that were going to keep La Brie at the château during their absence, replied that it was impossible to take him, and the following day at dawn, they prepared to leave.

The ladies, who had risen early in order to see them off, had dressed the judge in an old suit of armor that they had found in the château. The judge's young wife personally placed the helmet on his head after wishing him all kinds of success, and urged him to return promptly to receive in abundance the laurels he was going to pluck. He embraced her tenderly, mounted his horse, and followed the Marquis.

In spite of the fact that the people of the region had been forewarned regarding the bizarre parade that was due to pass by, the gaunt judge in his decidedly outlandish and ancient military accouterments looked so ridiculous that he was followed from one château to another accompanied by jeers and bursts of laughter. His sole consolation was the Colonel, who occasionally came over to him and offered him words of encouragement. On one occasion, the Colonel, with an expression of the utmost seriousness, said to him:

— You see, my friend, the world we live in is nothing but a farce. Sometimes we're actors, sometimes we're the audience, and we either observe what is taking place onstage, or we appear on it ourselves.

— That's all very well and good, said the judge. But on this occasion, we're being jeered at.

— Is that so? the Marquis responded, impassively.

— I'm not mistaken, Fontanis stated. Surely you must admit that you're finding it as hard to take as I am.

— What! said d'Olincourt. Surely you're accustomed to these minor disasters. You must realize that in your courtroom, you are mocked for every stupidity you commit from your bench, which is so beautifully-decorated with the fleur-de-lis. Of course, you, in your profession, are clearly made to be ridiculed, dressed as you are in that grotesque manner that makes everyone laugh the moment they see you. How can you imagine that with so many unfavorable things on one side, you'll be forgiven for your stupidities on the other?

— You don't like judges, do you, Marquis?

— I haven't hidden it from you, Judge. I value only what is useful. Any person who has no other talent other than for making gods or killing men seems to me to be an individual who deserves nothing but public contempt, and ought to be either lambasted or forced into hard labor. Don't you think, my friend, that with those two strong arms that nature has given you, you would be of infinitely more use behind a plough than on a bench in a courtroom? In the first instance you would be honoring the faculties given to you by Heaven... whereas, in the second instance, you are discrediting them.

— But there have to be judges.

— It would be better to have only virtues, they could be acquired without the need for judges; all judges could then be trampled underfoot.

— And how do you expect a State to be governed?...

— By three or four simple laws filed in the sovereign's palace, and upheld in each class by the elderly of that class. In this way each class would have its peers, and any young gentleman who is accused would no longer have to suffer the awful shame of being judged & condemned by a villain like you, someone who is so prodigiously far from being that man's equal.

— Oh! This is something that requires a long discussion…

— A discussion that will have to be very short, said the Marquis, for we're here at the Château de Téroze.

They entered the château; the tenant-farmer, Pierre, appeared and took the gentlemen's horses. He then led them to a large room, where they sat and listened to him as he described the unusual things that were going on in the château.

Every night, terrible sounds, screams, moans, shouts of anguish and pain, bellows of anger, were heard throughout the château, without anyone being able to ascertain where they were coming from. Several peasants employed by the tenant-farmer had spent a few nights in the château, watching and waiting, initially to no avail. Then the ghosts had appeared. The peasants had been, it was said, severely beaten and none of them was any longer inclined to expose themselves to danger or injury. But what it was they suspected was impossible to say. The rumor going around was that there were several ghosts, led by one particular ghost that was believed to be the spirit of a former tenant-farmer of the château. He had lost his life by being unjustly hanged, and he had sworn to return every night to drive everyone away with his infernal screams, vowing only to stop once he'd had the satisfaction of wringing the neck of a judge within the château.

— My dear Marquis, the judge said, as he got up and headed for the door, it seems to me that my presence here is actually quite pointless. We are quite unaccustomed to this kind of revenge and we, like the doctors, prefer to kill whoever we choose indiscriminately and without a single thought for the deceased, or the deceased's family.

— Just a moment, brother-in-law, just one moment, said d'Olincourt, stopping the judge who was on the point of leaving. Let's listen to the rest of this man's explanation before we decide on anything. He turned to address the tenant-farmer. Is that all, Master Pierre? Are there any other details you wish to share with us regarding this unusual situation? And does this head ghost have a problem with all judges in general?

— No, Monsieur, Pierre replied. The other day, he left a written message on this very table. The message stated that no judge with any integrity is at risk from him. He went on to state that it was only dishonest judges he resented, and that he would be unsparing with any judge who entered the château who was motivated by despotism, stupidity, or revenge, or who, due to the baseness of their own passions, had deliberately sacrificed any of their fellow men.

— Well, as you can see, I have no choice but to leave, the judge said, with dismay. There is nowhere inside this building where I will be able to feel safe.

— Ah! Then you most certainly are a villain, the Marquis said. If you are not a "judge with any integrity," then it's your crimes that are causing you to tremble with fear. All the people you've disgraced, or sent into exile for ten years over a party of well-paid young women, all your vile conniving with families, all the bribes you've paid out, all the payments you've received in order to ruin a young nobleman, and all the other unfortunate wretches you have sacrificed to your rage or ineptitude, these are the ghosts that have now come to disturb your conscience, aren't they? How much would you give now to have been an honest man all your life! Hopefully this cruel situation will one day serve to teach you something; may you realize beforehand what a terrible weight guilt is, and that there is not a single worldly happiness no matter how great it may have seemed to us, which compares to the tranquility of the soul and the enjoyments of virtue.

— My dear Marquis, the judge said, with tears in his eyes. I ask your forgiveness. I am a ruined man. Do not sacrifice me to these evil spirits, I implore you. Let me return to your beloved sister, who is anxiously awaiting my return. She will never forgive you if you deliver me to whatever haunts this accursed place.

— Coward! They are right to say that cowardice always accompanies falsehood and betrayal… No, you shall not leave; it's too late to run away. This château is my sister's only dowry; if you want to profit from it, you have to purge it of whoever defiles it. Defeat them or die: there is no middle ground.

— I beg to differ on this point, my dear brother-in-law, but there *is* a middle ground. All I need to do is beat a hasty retreat and give up any idea of being able to live on the profits from this property.

— You vile coward, so that's how you show how much you love my sister, is it? You'd rather see her languish in poverty than fight to free her inheritance from the ghostly ties strangling it… Do you want me to tell her, when we get back, that those are your true feelings toward her, feelings you were only too happy to share with me?

— Good heavens! What a terrible state I've been reduced to!

— Come now, the Marquis said. Where's your courage, man? Let's have dinner, then get yourself prepared for battle and be ready for the first sign of attack.

Dinner was served. The Marquis insisted that the judge dine in full armour. Master Pierre joined them at the table. He informed them that there was absolutely nothing to fear until eleven o'clock at night, but from then on until dawn, the ghosts made the château un-inhabitable.

— No matter what, the Marquis vowed, we will not abandon it. Here with me is a brave comrade on whom I can rely almost as much as I can rely on myself. I am certain he will not desert me.

— Let's not answer for anything until after the event, Fontanis said. I admit, I am a bit like Cæsar, courage is very seldom with me.

Meanwhile, the interval was spent in a walking re-connoiter of the surrounding area, and in going through the tenant-farmer's accounts. When night came, the Marquis, the judge, and their two valets retired to their rooms in the château.

The judge had a large room that looked directly out onto two gloomy-looking towers, the mere sight of which made him shudder violently. It was from those towers, it was said, that the ghosts began their haunting so the judge knew he was most likely going to come into contact with the ghosts before his companions. A brave man would have been delighted at a chance to prove his love, loyalty, and courage, but the judge, like all the world's judges, and particularly Provençal judges, was the opposite of brave.

On hearing this piece of news, the judge indulged in such a cowardly reaction that he was, with the reluctant assistance of one of the valets, obliged to change every item of clothing he was wearing; no medicine had ever had a prompter effect. He was washed and dressed in clean clothes, then put back into his suit of armor. Two pistols were put on a table in his room, a lance that was at least fifteen feet long was placed in his hands, three or four candles were lit and the valet left him to his own devices.

— Oh, poor, unfortunate Fontanis, the judge said aloud, as soon as he was alone. What evil spirit has led you into this dire situation? Couldn't you have found, in your own province, a young woman as good as this Téroze one, and one who would not have given you quite so much grief? But it was her you wanted, wasn't it? — which makes you a poor judge. You wanted her, didn't you, my friend? You're here because you were tempted by the grand idea of a wedding in Paris. But look at the results… *Pechaire*, you may die here like a dog without ever having had the chance to consummate your marriage with that delectable creature.[32] Or you may very well die here without a priest administering the last rites… These damned unbelievers with their laws of nature, their ideas regarding justice and their benevolence. They seem to think that paradise ought to be open to them as soon as they say those three great words… Let's have less nature, less justice, and less benevolence. Instead, let's issue warrants for their arrest, let's banish and exile them, let's burn them at the stake, let's hang them, let's break them on a wheel and then let's go to Mass and be forgiven — that's a far better way of doing things than all this nonsense.

— This d'Olincourt, the judge continued, he seems almost obsessively interested in the trial of that nobleman I… that *we* sentenced last year; there must be some connection there that I was unaware of… But, if I recall, it was quite a scandalous affair. A thirteen-year-old valet we bribed came and told us, because we had paid him to tell us, that that particular nobleman was killing whores in his château. The valet told us a tale reminiscent of

Bluebeard, and his confession was so like a fairy tale, and so far-fetched *&* unlikely that a nanny would refuse to tell it to her charges.[33] When dealing with a crime as momentous as the murder of a prostitute, a crime can be proven beyond any doubt if its details are included in the written deposition, the purchased written deposition no less, of a thirteen-year-old valet. Eventually, we had to have him whipped because he did not want to say what we wanted him to say. After a hundred lashes his deposition was word-perfect, even if I do say so myself, and the nobleman was then clearly guilty of murder. It seems to me that what we did was absolutely necessary. I don't think we were too harsh, as some suggested... Do we really need a hundred witnesses to make certain a crime has been committed? Surely one informer encouraged to provide one damning deposition is enough. And what about our learned colleagues from Toulouse: did they carefully scrutinize all of the evidence before they executed Calas on the wheel in the cathedral square?[34] If we were to punish only those crimes that we were completely certain were crimes, we would have the pleasure of dragging our fellow human beings to the gallows only four times a century, and it is only our judicious use of the gallows that keeps everyone respectful of our power. I would like someone to tell me what kind of a court we would be if our funds were constantly available for the needs of the State; a court which would never issue reprimands; one which would carefully register and record every edict, and one which would never kill anyone... it would be an assembly of fools; a court which would have no use existing because no one would need it...

— Don't be discouraged, the judge went on, greatly enjoying the sound of his own words. You've done your duty to the best of your abilities, my friend. Let the sworn enemies of the judiciary shout as much as they like. They will never destroy it. Our power is built on the weakness of kings and it will last for as long as the empire endures. God's will, as far as kings are concerned, is that their power does not end up dethroning them. It will only take one or two more misfortunes like those that marked the reign of Charles VII to lead to the ultimate destruction of the monarchy and its replacement by a republican form of government. It's what we in the judiciary have been secretly aiming for, for so long, and if it happens, it will place us at the pinnacle, just like the Senate of Venice and, if it occurs, it will deliver into our hands the chains which we will then use with impunity to crush the people.

The judge was about to continue with the next part of his impassioned monologue when a terrible noise was heard simultaneously in all of the rooms and in all the corridors of the château... The judge began to tremble uncontrollably; he clung to his chair & closed his eyes.

— I must have completely lost my mind! he shouted. What business is this of mine? What business does a Presiding Judge of the High Court of Aix have in fighting ghosts? Oh, tell me, you ghosts, what have you and the High Court of Aix ever had in common?

However, the intensity of the noise redoubled, the doors of the two towers burst open, followed by the door to the judge's chamber as several terrifying figures entered the room… Fontanis dropped to his knees and begged the ghosts to show him mercy; that he not be harmed and that his life be spared.

— You despicable villain! one of the ghosts said in a terrifying voice. Did *you* have any mercy in *your* heart when you unjustly condemned all of those unfortunate people that appeared before you in your court? Did their terrible fate touch you in any way? Were you any less vain, less proud, less greedy, or less immoral the day your unjust sentences plunged the victims of your ridiculous inflexibility into misfortune, or into the grave? And where did you get the dangerous idea that your legal power placed you above the law, as well as the illusory notion that you had some sort of legislative omnipotence and could act with impunity? Was it from the kind of public opinion that philosophy destroys in an instant? We will now act in accordance with the same principles you believe in and which you use when making a judgment in court. You are about to be judged by our authority. Court is in session.

With those words, four of those physical spirits roughly seized Fontanis, and in an instant stripped him totally naked, without eliciting from him anything other than tears, a few screams, & a fetid layer of sweat that drenched him from head to toe.

— Now what do we do with him? one of the ghosts asked.

— Wait, the ghost who appeared to be in charge replied. I have here the list of the four principal murders that *this villain* has legally committed. Let's read them to him:

— In 1750 this villain sentenced to the wheel an unfortunate man whose only crime had been to refuse him his daughter whom this villain wanted to abuse.

— In 1754 this villain offered to save a man's life in return for that man paying this villain two thousand écus; the man could not afford nor borrow the sum so this villain had him hanged.

— In 1760, on learning that a man in his town had made a few derogatory remarks about him, this villain sentenced him to be burned at the stake the following year as a sodomite, although this unfortunate man had a wife and several children, and was completely innocent of the crime.

— In 1772, a young man of distinction, a native of the province, wanted to exact his revenge on a whore who had given him an unwanted and unwelcome present. The young nobleman gave the whore an aphrodisiac and lightly whipped her. This villain, this unworthy and bitter villain, turned that practical joke into a serious crime and treated the matter as a poisoning and an attempted murder. This villain then talked all of his colleagues into agreeing with his ridiculous opinion, after which, he quickly disgraced the young man, then ruined him, then had him sentenced to death *in absentia* because this villain had been unable to bring that young nobleman to trial in person.[35]

— These are his main crimes, the ghost said. It's for you to decide his punishment, my friends.

Immediately, another of the ghosts said:

— The law of retaliation, Monsieurs. Because he has unjustly sentenced people to the wheel, I vote that he be broken on the wheel.

— I vote that he be hanged, another ghost said. For the same reason that was just given.

— He should be burned at the stake, the fourth ghost said. I vote for this for two reasons: because he dared to use this method of torture and killing when it was undeserved and because he himself has deserved it many times.

— Let us show him an example of mercy and moderation, comrades, said the first ghost, and let's use his fourth crime as the basis for our judgment. A whipped whore is a crime worthy of death, according to this foolish incompetent, so let this villain's punishment be a sound whipping.

The four ghosts seized the frightened judge and lay him face-down on a narrow bench, to which they tied him securely by his wrists and ankles. The four ghosts, cackling wildly, each took a five-foot-long leather strap, and choosing a one-two-three-four cadence, proceeded to thrash Fontanis's bare body using the full strength of their arms. After three quarters of an hour of constant whipping, the judge's education was deemed complete. His body was lacerated and looked like one huge welt, from which blood poured profusely.

— That's enough, said the first ghost. As I said, let's give him an example of pity and charity; if this villain had us at his mercy he'd have us drawn and quartered. We have him at our mercy, but I say we should let this fraternal punishment be enough. We can only hope that this lesson he has learned in our school will teach him that it is not always by murdering men that we manage to make them better. He has had no more than five hundred lashes, but I would be willing to wager that those five hundred lashes will have convinced him to change his mind completely about injustice, and that he will in the future be one of the most honest judges in his profession. Let us release him and be on our way.

Once the judge was sure his tormentors had gone, he sobbed uncontrollably from the pain of his whipping. Finally, he stopped crying and went to his bed, where he tried to lie down. In the end, he perched uncomfortably in a chair and thought about what had happened. As was his habit, he began, again, talking aloud to himself.

— Well, I can see that if we hold up a torch to the actions of others, if we seek to trick them in order to punish them, then yes, I can clearly see how that gets immediately returned to us — but multiplied. Now, who on earth could have told these people everything I've done? How is it that they're so well informed regarding my conduct?

Not having immediate answers to those questions, Fontanis busied himself with trying to make himself presentable. He had only just, and very gingerly, put his coat back on when he heard several terrible screams coming from the side of the château which the ghosts had set off toward after they had left his room. He listened intently and thought he recognized the Marquis's voice shouting for him to help.

— To hell with him, the exhausted judge muttered. I can barely move. Even if those ghosts were thrashing him to within an inch of his life, as they did to me, I'd still refuse to interfere. We each have our own problems and we shouldn't really interfere in the affairs of others.

However, the shouts and screams grew louder, until finally the Marquis d'Olincourt burst into Fontanis's room. He was followed by his two valets. All three of them were screaming and yelling in anguish as though they were being slaughtered. All three of them were covered in blood. One had his arm in a sling, the other had a bandage around his head, and if anyone had seen the pale, disheveled, & bloody state they were in would have assumed that they had just been battling a whole legion of devils escaped from hell.

— Oh, my friend, d'Olincourt said, what an assault! I thought they were going to flay the three of us alive and then strangle us.

— I can assure you that whatever's happened, you've not been as badly mistreated as I have, the Judge said, showing his lacerated buttocks and bloody back. Look what they've done to me!

— Oh, my word! the Marquis said. What you have here, my friend, is a very powerful case for lodging a legal complaint. You're aware, I'm sure, of the great interest throughout the ages that your colleagues have taken in whipped backsides. Call a judicial assembly at once, my friend; find yourself a famous lawyer who will be willing to exercise his eloquence in defense of your ill-treated buttocks. There was, in ancient times, an ingenious expedient whereby an orator would emotionally move the members of the Areopagus by uncovering, in full view of the court, the superb breasts of the beauty whose case he was defending.[36] Utilizing the same principle, you should let your Demosthenes choose the most heart-breaking moment of his address to expose your bloodied, wealed, welted and much-maligned buttocks to the entire court, thereby invoking great pity in everyone present.[37]

— Above all, when you are obliged to appear before those Paris judges, you might consider reminding them of that infamous incident that took place in 1769, when their hearts were filled with more compassion for the flogged backside of a common prostitute than for the people they professed they paternalistically protected; people they nevertheless let die of hunger.[38] They were, if you recall, determined to put on trial, as a criminal, a young soldier who had given the best years of his youth in the service of his king. On his return home, there were no laurels waiting for him, instead, there was nothing but the humiliation prepared by the hands of the greatest enemies of the very State he had just defended… Come along, my dear fellow-unfortunate, let's hurry, let's leave this accursed château. We're not safe staying here. Let's get our revenge. We'll appeal directly to the protectors of public order, the defenders of the oppressed, the pillars of the State. They'll help us.

— I can barely support myself, the judge said. And if those damned ghosts were to return and peel me again like an apple, I beg you, just find me a bed and leave me to sleep for at least twenty-four hours.

— Don't joke about something like that, my friend. You'll be strangled to death.

— Then so be it. It will simply be payment for one of the many things I've done wrong. There's so much remorse in my heart right now that I'll look on all further misfortunes that might befall me as having been ordered by Heaven.

As the commotion had completely ceased, and as d'Olincourt saw that the poor Provençal native was really in need of a little rest, he summoned Master Pierre and asked him if there was reason to think that the ghosts would return again the following night.

— No, Monsieur, Pierre replied. After they have attacked someone, they are usually quiet for eight to ten days. You may all rest safely for the next few days.

The judge was taken to a comfortable room, where he gratefully removed his clothes and then carefully got into bed, positioning himself as comfortably as he could. He then rested for a good twelve hours. He was sleeping soundly when he suddenly felt something wet splashing onto him and onto the bed. He looked up and saw that the ceiling was perforated with thousands of holes and that water was pouring out of each hole, drenching him and the bed. He realized that he ran the risk of being drowned by the veritable fountain unless he decamped as quickly as possible. Stark naked, he ran out of the room and dashed, as fast as his thrashed back and buttocks allowed, down the stairs and into one of the rooms, where he found d'Olincourt and good Master Pierre seated at a table bearing a dish of pâté & a cask of Burgundy wine, with which they were drowning their sorrows.

On seeing Fontanis run into the room in such a state of undress their first reaction was to laugh heartily. Once the judge began to recount to them the latest indignity inflicted upon him, they made him sit down at the table, although they gave him no time to put on his breeches, which he clutched under his arm very much in the manner of the natives of Pégu.[39] The judge began to drink and he found consolation for all his woes at the bottom of the third bottle of wine. As there were only two hours remaining before their scheduled departure for the Château d'Olincourt, they decided to have their horses saddled and to set off.

— That was a hard lesson you had me learn there, Marquis, said the Provençal judge, as soon as they were in the saddle.

— I'm certain it will not be the last, my friend, d'Olincourt replied. Man was born to learn lessons, and men of law most of all, for it's beneath the ermine-collared robe of the judge that stupidity has erected its temple and it's only in your courts that it can breathe freely and in total peace. However, whatever else you may say, you did very well to stay at the château in order to clarify what was happening there.

— But now knowing that, what good does it do us?

— Because we now have the reason for what happened, so we can now lodge our complaints with authority behind our case.

— Complaints! To the devil with complaints. I don't intend to make any. I fully intend to keep what happened in that infernal château to myself and I'd be grateful if you'd do likewise.

— My friend, you are not at all consistent. If you find it ridiculous to lodge complaints when one has been mistreated, why do you constantly look for them, why do you constantly provoke them? What you say makes no sense! Why do you, one of crime's greatest enemies, want to leave a crime unpunished when it is so clearly established and has so many witnesses? It's one of the most sublime axioms of jurisprudence, is it not, that even assuming that the injured party withdraws his claim, justice must still take its course and demand its due? Are you not, judge, quite clearly violating the course of justice when you refuse to press your claims and lodge your complaints regarding what has happened to you? Are you refusing justice the legitimate homage that it requires?

— You are quite possibly correct regarding everything you say on the matter, but I don't intend to say a word about it to anyone.

— And what about your wife's dowry?

— I am going to count on the Baron's sense of fair-mindedness, and I will entreat him to take responsibility for clearing up this matter.

— He will not involve himself in your affairs.

— Then we'll be paupers and we'll have to eat crusts.

— Oh, what a gallant fellow you are! You will be the cause of your wife cursing the very day she met you, and of her regretting for the rest of her life that she ever linked herself to a coward like you.

— Oh, as far as regrets are concerned, I think we shall both have our share. But tell me, Marquis, why are you now so insistent that I lodge a complaint, when earlier, you criticized me for suggesting the very same thing? It seems a little inconsistent.

— Because I did not know what the issue was then. And as long as I believed we could resolve the situation without recourse to outside help, then I was prepared to follow that route. However, now that I am aware of what's happening to your property, I firmly believe that it is necessary for us to get the full support of the law. So tell me, in what way is that inconsistent?

— Wonderfully countered, Fontanis said, as they arrived at the Château d'Olincourt. The judge looked at d'Olincourt as he dismounted. However, let's say nothing regarding what happened back there. That's the one favor I ask of you.

Although they had been gone for only two days much had transpired at the Marquise's.

Mademoiselle de Téroze was in her bed, a feigned indisposition, caused by the anxiety and the sorrow of knowing that her husband was exposed to danger, had kept her in bed for the past forty-eight hours. An attractive attendant was by her bedside, her face and neck swathed in twenty aunes of gauze...[40] A very touching pallor made Mademoiselle look a hundred times more beautiful than ever, which only served to arouse the desires and the ardor of the judge, whose body was further inflamed by the impassioned flogging he had recently received.

Delgatz was at the patient's bedside, and he took Fontanis aside for a whispered conversation. He warned him against manifesting, expressing, or mentioning any of his desires, given the dire condition of his wife. The critical moment had occurred during her menstrual cycle & there was still, the pseudo-doctor said, a very great danger of losing her.

— Oh, for God's sake! the judge said. I must have been born beneath an unlucky star. I have just been severely thrashed on account of this woman, and I don't mean just mildly thrashed either, but thrashed within an inch of my life, and yet it seems I am still to be deprived of the pleasure of consummating my marriage.

Also, the number of guests at the château had increased by three, and it is essential to introduce these characters now.

Monsieur and Madame de Totteville, a wealthy couple, were neighbors of the d'Olincourts, and they had just arrived at the château with their daughter, Lucile, a vivacious, petite brunette girl of almost eighteen whose features were equal in loveliness to those of Mademoiselle de Téroze.

And, in order not to leave you, dear reader, in suspense any longer, we shall immediately inform you of the identity of the three newcomers that we have seen fit to introduce at this late stage of our narrative, either for the purpose of delaying the outcome, or because they will help to lead the story to a more fitting conclusion.

De Totteville was one of those impoverished knights of Saint-Louis and as such he was not above dragging his title through the mire in exchange for a few dinners or a few écus, and he accepted indiscriminately whichever roles that he was asked to play.

His supposed wife was an old adventuress of another sort. Now of an age at which she was no longer able to trade on her own physical attractions, she compensated for this by trading the attractions of others. As for their beautiful princess, who they successfully passed off as being their daughter, it was easy to imagine, from her alliance with such a couple, from what class she had come. A pupil of Paphos from childhood, she had already ruined three or four farmers-general, and it was because of her artfulness and her beauty that the couple had specifically taken her in.[41]

And so, each of those characters, chosen from the best of what their class had to offer, had been instructed, schooled, and rehearsed to perfection regarding what was expected of them. Also, each was in possession of a façade of good breeding and comportment that was so convincing that it would have been difficult, seeing them mingle with men and women of the aristocracy, not to believe that they too were of noble birth.

No sooner had the judge entered the château, than the Marquise and her sister asked him for news of his adventure.

— It was nothing to speak of, said the Marquis, respecting his brother-in-law's request for silence on the matter, merely a gang of villains that will be chased off sooner or later. It's simply a question of knowing what the judge wants to do regarding this matter. I'll be happy to comply with his wishes.

And as d'Olincourt had already forewarned them of the judge's success, as well his desire that the events at the château should remain unremarked on, the subject was immediately changed and there was no further mention of the ghosts of the Château de Téroze.

The judge expressed his grave concern regarding his dear wife's condition. He also mentioned the extreme sorrow he felt that her accursed illness had forced a further postponement of their moment of nuptial happiness. Since it was late they dined & went to bed that day without any further incidents.

Monsieur de Fontanis was a worthy judge who, in addition to his many other excellent qualities, had an excessive proclivity for young ladies, and he immediately noticed the introduction of young Lucile into the Marquise d'Olincourt's circle. Interested, he began by asking his confidant, La Brie, who the young lady was; the latter answered the query in such a way as to encourage the burgeoning seeds of lust he could see were planted in the judge's heart, and he readily persuaded Fontanis to proceed with his wooing of the young lady in question.

— She is a young lady from a very well-respected family, the deceitful confidant replied. But that does not mean she would be immune to a proposal of love from a man of your standing. Your honor, continued the untrustworthy young man, you are the concern of fathers

and the terror of husbands, and no matter what vows
of chastity and fidelity a young female may have made,
most would find it very difficult to resist your interest
and your declarations of love. Putting your fine figure
aside for a moment, there's your respectable position in
society; what woman can resist the attractions of a man
of justice: that long black robe, the square cap, do you
honestly think that all that is not seductive?

— Yes, well, it's true that a great many women do
find us difficult to resist… I remember a certain judge in
our court who was a veritable terror to every virtuous…
but tell me honestly, La Brie, do you really think that if
I were to let her know…

— She would immediately give herself to you, I am
certain.

— But you would need to keep silent, La Brie. I'd
need to rely on your discretion. You know the situation
I find myself in. It's important for me not to start my
relationship with my wife with my infidelity.

— Oh, Monsieur, you would drive her to despair if
she ever found out; she loves you so much.

— Really? Do you think she loves me, even just a little?

— She absolutely adores you, Monsieur, and it would
be tantamount to murder to deceive her.

— However, if you look at things from my point of
view, you really believe?…

— …that your affair will bloom and reach its inevitable conclusion, if that is what you want. Yes. It is only
a question of letting the young lady know your desires.

— Oh, my dear La Brie, your words fill me with immense joy. What a pleasure to conduct two affairs simultaneously and to deceive two women at once! To deceive, my friend, to be unfaithful, what an absolute delight for a man of law!

As a result of this encouragement, Fontanis made his preparations, then dressed himself in his finest clothes, forgetting all about the lashes that had lacerated his back and buttocks, and all the while keeping his wife simmering on a back burner with kind words although she was still too unwell to share their bed. Instead, he directed his energies at the cunning Lucile who listened to him at first with great modesty and very slowly began to reciprocate his advances.

This delightful little game went on for about four days without anyone appearing to notice. During that time, news sheets and gazettes were received at the château, inviting all astronomers to observe, on the following night, *"the passage of Venus under Capricorn."*

— Ah, yes, said the judge as soon as he heard the news, and acting as though he were an authority. It is a most singular event and I must say, I did not expect this phenomenon to occur. As you may know, ladies, I am considered by some to be a leading authority on this particular science. I have even written a six-volume work entitled *On the Satellites of Mars.*

— *On the Satellites of Mars*, said the Marquise with a smile. An interesting title. However, I am very surprised that you chose that subject, Judge, since Mars has not been particularly favorable to you.

— Always joking, my dear Marquise, and always charming. I can see that my little secret has not been kept. However, I am most curious to witness the astronomical event that will occur tonight. Do you have a place here, Marquis, from where we can observe the trajectory of this planet?

— Certainly, the Marquis replied. At the top of one of my towers is a very well-appointed observatory. There you will find some excellent telescopes, quadrants, and compasses, in fact everything that is needed in an astronomer's observatory.

— So you also have some knowledge of the subject?

— Not at all, but I have eyes just like everyone else. I also enjoy meeting men of science and I'm obviously delighted to learn from them.

— Well, in that case, I'll be happy to give you a few lessons; within six weeks you'll know the skies better than Descartes or Copernicus.[42]

However, when the time came for him to make his way up to the observatory, the judge was disappointed that his wife's illness was going to deprive him of the pleasure of playing the astronomer in front of her, completely unaware, the poor devil, that she was going to play the leading role in the singular comedy that had been arranged.

Although gas-filled balloons had not at that time become a matter of public knowledge, one had been constructed in 1779.[43] The skilled physicist, who intended to launch the one that we will shortly be mentioning, was far more learned in aeronautics than any of the other physicists who came after him. An inventive man, he was also a man of great sense, which was why he said nothing when he discovered that intruders had stolen his invention. Later, as he stood at a distance and watched it ascend, he marveled at it along with everyone else.

Mademoiselle de Téroze, beautiful in the arms of the handsome Comte d'Elbène, was reclined in the very center of a perfectly constructed aerostat, and as the balloon rose, the couple would celebrate their deep love for each other with a warm embrace and a loving kiss. This beautiful conjunction would be lighted by a subtle artificial light, one which was cleverly designed to shed enough light on the tableau for the benefit of those who knew, but would easily dupe a complete fool like the judge, who had never so much as looked inside the kind of book he claimed to have written and so had not the least idea of what a passing star looked like.

The whole company arrived at the top of the tower; everyone furnished themselves with telescopes & the balloon ascended.

— Do you see anything yet? someone asked.

— Not yet.

— Yes, I see it.

— No, that's not it.

— I beg your pardon? Look, over there, to the left. Look toward the east.

— Ah! I have it! the judge yelled, suddenly excited. Yes, I have it, my friends. Look where I'm looking. Follow my telescope… a little closer to Mercury, not as far as Mars, far below Saturn's orbit. There. Ah, great God, that is a beautiful sight!

— I see it too now, Judge, the Marquis said. You're right. It truly is a most beautiful sight to behold. Do you see that wonderful conjunction?

— I'm looking at it right now. It's very clear through this telescope…

And just as he said those words, the balloon passed directly over the tower.

— I believe the notices we received were wrong, the Marquis said, for didn't we all just witness *Venus over Capricorn?*

— You are absolutely right, the judge said. That has to be, without doubt, one of the most beautiful spectacles I have ever seen in my life.

— Who knows, said the Marquis, whether you will always have to ascend so high to see it so clearly.

— Ah! Marquis, your joke is ill-timed for such a beautiful moment…

And as the balloon was by then disappearing into the darkness everyone descended from the tower, very pleased with the allegorical phenomenon that art had just lent to nature.

On his return to the château, Monsieur de Fontanis had found his wife in bed looking feverish and disheveled and slightly the worse for wear, which he took to be a sure sign of the persistence & the seriousness of her illness.

— The truth of the matter is that I am sorry that you could not come with us to share our pleasure in witnessing that unique event, he said to his wife. It would be difficult to conceive of anything as beautiful.

— I'm sure that you are absolutely right, the young woman said, but I was informed that there were some quite immodest things about that rather curious event, & if that were the case, then I'm not upset that I missed it.

— Immodest! the judge said, with a derisive laugh which only served to emphasize his innate charm. Not at all. It was a very lovely conjunction. Is there anything more beautiful in nature? It's exactly what I should like to finally happen between us, and it's what will happen whenever you say the word. But tell me, in all good conscience, sovereign mistress of all my thoughts... haven't you made your slave languish for long enough? Will you soon grant me the due reward for all my efforts?

— Alas, my angel, his young wife said lovingly, I hope you know that I am just as eager as you for our marriage to be exquisitely consummated, but you can see my condition... and I think you see it without feeling sorry for me, you cruel man. After all, my ailment continues to keep me in bed because I constantly worry about you and the risks you take on my behalf. If I didn't have to worry so much about the things that concern you, I'd be a lot better off.

The judge was overjoyed to hear himself spoken of in such a way; he strutted, he straightened up, he preened, and he stood there stiff and at attention. Never had any judge, not even one who had just sentenced someone to be hanged, been quite so firm and upstanding.

But despite this sweet talk from Mademoiselle de Téroze, the obstacles that stood in the way of the judge effecting a conjunction multiplied daily. The same could not be said for the situation between the judge and Lucile, for the young girl gave many indications that she was ready to play the most beautiful game in the world. Once he knew she was ready to be picked, Fontanis did not hesitate to choose the flowery myrtles of love rather than the late roses of marriage.

— One cannot escape me, he said to himself. I'll always be able to have her whenever I want her. But the other may only be here for a fleeting moment so I should take advantage of the opportunity as quickly as possible.

It was according to those principles that Fontanis lost no opportunity in making further advances.

— Alas, Monsieur, the young lady said to him one day with the feigned innocence of a seventeen-year-old girl. Will I not become a most unhappy creature if I grant you what you demand… Bound in marriage as you are, will you ever be able to repair the damage you will do to my reputation?

— What do mean by "repair"? There is nothing to repair in such a case. Neither of us will have anything to repair. This would be a complete waste of our time. There is never anything to fear from a married man because he is concerned primarily with keeping his affairs secret, and that secrecy will not prevent you from finding a husband.

— And what about religion, Monsieur, and honor?

— Mere nothings, that's all they are, my dear. You should have been named Agnes. I think you should enroll in my school for a few lessons. Ah! I would very quickly make all of your childish prejudices disappear.

— But I thought that your profession committed you to respecting and protecting them.

— Well, yes, that's true, but that's only a façade. All we have is that façade, without substance or philosophy, so we must use that façade in order to inspire respect. But once stripped of that vain decorum which obliges us to show a certain respect, we merely resemble the rest of humanity. How could you expect us not to indulge in their vices? Our passions, much more heated by the recital or the perpetual portrayal of theirs, make no distinction between theirs and ours except by the excesses that they fail to recognize and which we make our daily delights. Almost always protected from those laws with which we make others tremble, this impunity excites us and we become even greater villains...

Lucile listened to this long-winded nonsense, and although she was repulsed by the judge's physical appearance, & horrified by his morality, she continued to offer him her charms, because the reward that she had been promised was hers only on those conditions.

The closer the judge came to achieving his amorous goals, the more his fatuousness made him unbearable. There is nothing as amusing on the face of the earth than a judge in love; it is the perfect picture of awkwardness, impertinence, and clumsiness. If the reader has ever seen a turkey about to multiply its species, that is the image that we feel offers the idea we wish to convey.

No matter how carefully he disguised his intentions, one day his insolence made it obvious what he was up to, so the Marquis decided to humiliate him in front of his goddess.

— Judge, he said, I have just received some very distressing news for you.

— What news is that?

— It has just been confirmed that the High Court of Aix is going to be abolished. The public complains that it serves no useful purpose. Aix needs a court far less than Lyon needs one, and that city, much too far from Paris to be dependent on it, will be responsible for all of Provence. Lyon dominates Provence, just as it always has, and it is ideally situated, which it needs to be so that the judges of that very important region can reside there.

— It's an arrangement that makes no sense.

— It's a very wise move. Aix is at the end of the world. It doesn't matter which part of the region a Provençal native may live in, everyone prefers to go to Lyon for their business, rather than trek all the way to that pigsty, Aix. Terrible roads, no bridge over the Durance River which, like your intelligence, is totally unused for nine months of the year. And then there are some very specific short-comings that I will not even try to hide from you; first of all, they have found fault with the organization of your court as there is not, they say, a single member of the Aix court who is able to write his own name... fishmongers, sailors, smugglers — in short, a troop of despicable rogues that the noble families of the region want nothing to do with; a very unsavory bunch of buffoons and fools who harass and insult the people to compensate for the discredit into which it has fallen... they are idiots, fools... My apologies, Judge, I'm only telling you what was written to me. I'll let you read the letter after dinner... in short, villains of the lowest order; the type who have carried fanaticism and scandal to such lengths that they have a working gallows standing in their city square, always there as a proof of their lack of humanity and integrity; gallows that they are always ready to use on the slightest pretext, and which is nothing more than a monument to their rigid inflexibility.

— The people should tear down that monument and use its broken foundations to stone to death those disgusting executive notaries who, in their insolence, dare to leave the gallows in working order and on public display as a constant reminder of the punishment they will willingly inflict. It's surprising that the people haven't risen up and done exactly that, although it seems that the day is not that far off and it won't be much longer before they do...[44] A whole host of unjust judgments and warrants, an affectation of severity, the sole purpose of which conceal the many legislative crimes that the members of the court choose to commit; finally, a few more serious charges to bring all this to a conclusion... unequivocal enemies of the state, not only now, but also throughout each decade; that is what people are daring to say quite openly.

— The horror felt by the public after your defilement of Meredol still lives on in people's hearts.[45] You must realize on that day you offered the most horrible spectacle that it is possible in this day and age to depict. Can anyone imagine, without shuddering, the guardians of law and order, peace and equanimity, running wildly through the province like madmen; a flaming torch in one hand, a dagger in the other, burning, killing, raping, and massacring anyone or anything that is in their way, like a pack of rabid tigers that had escaped from the jungle. Is this any way for judges to behave?

— There were also several instances when you quite stubbornly refused to offer to help your king when he needed it most. You were, at various times, ready to incite the province to revolt rather than agree to pay the taxes that had been assessed and demanded of you. Do you think that everyone has forgotten that unfortunate time, when, without being threatened by any danger, you led the citizens of your town and brought the keys of the city to the Constable of Bourbon who had betrayed his king?[46] Or perhaps you remember that time when, trembling with fear at the approach of Charles V, you hurried to pay homage to him and welcome him into your town?[47] Do you think no one knows that the first seeds of the Catholic League were fomented in the Aix courtrooms?[48] So, in short, in every era, throughout history, the members of the Court of Aix have been either seditionists, rebels, murderers or traitors.

— You Provençal judges know better than anyone that when you want to ruin someone, you simply seek out everything they may have done wrong in the past, and then you very carefully bring those past mistakes to light in order to imply that the person has not changed and cannot be trusted and will continue to make those same mistakes to the detriment of everyone around them. Do not be surprised, therefore, when others use those very same methods on you; methods that you used on all the unfortunate victims you have sacrificed to your pedantry. Remember this, my dear judge, it is no longer legal for an individual, or for a body of men, to slander, libel, or attack in any way, a peaceful & honest citizen. If anyone tries to act in such an outrageous way, then it should come as no surprise to hear many voices raised in disapproval, demanding the rights of the weak and insisting on virtue instead of despotism & immorality.

The judge was so incensed by the Marquis's words that he was unable to answer or respond to these accusations. He left the table in a blind fury, swearing that he was going to leave the château. Next to the spectacle of a judge in love, there is nothing more laughable than a judge in a rage; when his face muscles, naturally arranged by hypocrisy, are suddenly forced to move from their usual serene state to the contortions of rage, they can only do so by violent gradations, the sight of which is very comical to behold.

The company had, of course, derived an enormous amount of amusement from the manner in which the judge had stormed furiously out of the room, but as they had not yet reached the stage when, if things went as planned, they would be rid of him forever, they did their best to calm him down so that he would then be ready for his next humiliation. Someone followed him, talked to him placatingly, then took him back to the dining room and by the end of the meal, the torments he had been beset by during the day had obviously been forgotten because Fontanis seemed to have reverted to his former self.

Mademoiselle de Téroze was gradually improving, although she still looked exhausted. She started to sit at the table at mealtimes and even walked around a little with the company, despite her wan pallor and her obvious lack of energy.

The judge began to spend less time with his wife than he had done previously, because his thoughts were primarily occupied with his seduction of Lucile. Nonetheless, he could see quite clearly that the time would come when he would have to devote all of his attention solely to his wife. Consequently, he resolved to press on with the other affair, as the time for its culmination had arrived. Mademoiselle de Totteville no longer offered any objections; she informed the judge she was ready to give herself to him.

All that remained was to find a safe place for the liaison.

The judge suggested his bachelor's quarters. Lucile, who did not sleep in the same bedchamber as her parents, eagerly concurred. The time was agreed for the following night and, once everything was arranged, Lucile immediately reported every detail to the Marquis. The company diligently rehearsed her role with her and the rest of the day passed quietly.

At about eleven o'clock, Lucile excused herself from the assembled company, claiming a headache. The judge had given her a key to his quarters and had instructed her to leave before him and to wait in readiness for him in his bed.

A quarter of an hour later, the eager Fontanis also excused himself, but the Marquise stopped him by stating that, by way of apology for his earlier discomfort and to honor his position in society, she and her husband would like to accompany the judge and light the way to his quarters. The whole company immediately joined in with the joke; Mademoiselle de Téroze foremost amongst among them. They ignored the judge's protestations and picked up candles. The judge, on tenterhooks, racked his brains for a way to extricate himself from this ridiculous display of manners, or at least to prevent the company from discovering the young lady, stark naked and in the position he had instructed her to assume, in his bed.

Carrying the lighted candles, the men led the way and the women surrounded Fontanis. They all took his hands and this exuberant procession inexorably made its way to the door of the judge's quarters…

Our unfortunate gallant could barely breathe:

— I will not be held accountable for anything, the judge mumbled. Think how imprudent you are acting. What if it transpires that the object of my love is at this very moment awaiting me in my bed? And if that is the case, have you thought carefully about all of the resulting ramifications of your lack of discretion?

— In that case, I shall call out a warning, the Marquise said, opening the door. Come on, you beauty, who, we hear, awaits the judge in his bed! Don't be shy! Show yourself. Don't be afraid!

But imagine everyone's surprise when the candles cast their light on an enormous donkey, lying quite comfortably in the sheets, and which, by a happy coincidence, and no doubt delighted with the role it was being made to play, was peacefully asleep in the judicial bed, snoring voluptuously.

— Ah! Wonderful! d'Olincourt said, trying to hold in his laughter. Consider for a moment, Judge, this creature's composure and happiness. Doesn't it remind you of one of your colleagues in the courtroom?

Everyone laughed.

The judge began to laugh along with everyone else. He was very pleased at the outcome of the practical joke, for he felt that it would serve to cover up the fact of his planned liaison. He imagined that Lucile, having discovered the creature first, had done whatever was necessary to guarantee that their intrigue was not suspected by anyone. The judge, as I said, began to laugh along with the others.

They extricated the poor donkey from the bed as best they could. It was very distressed at having its nap interrupted. The bed was remade with clean sheets and Fontanis got into bed, replacing, with the utmost dignity, the most superb donkey the region had to offer.

— It was truly very difficult to tell the difference, the Marquise said, after she had seen the judge lying there in the newly-made bed. I would never have believed that a donkey and a judge of the High Court of Aix could have so many similarities. They looked so much alike.

— That is where you are mistaken, Madame, the Marquis replied. Are you sure you had no idea that it was from among the best of those splendid creatures the

Court of Aix has always chosen its members? In fact, I would be willing to wager that the one we saw being led from the room was its first presiding judge.

The next day, at the first opportunity, Fontanis asked Lucile how she had managed to avoid being caught in a potentially awkward situation.

Again, her answers had been very well-rehearsed. She told the judge that, as soon as she saw the beast, she realized someone was playing a joke on the judge. She immediately realized the danger of them being caught if she stayed anywhere near his quarters, so she made her way to her room and got into bed where she remained the entire night. She had, she said, been unable to sleep due to her concern that she had been betrayed, and she was eager to find out if that were the case.

The judge put the young lady's mind at ease by re-assuring her that she had not been betrayed or com-promised at all; that he had simply been the victim of someone's rather simple-minded practical joke and that they should proceed with their planned liaison as soon as possible. Lucile put on a slight show of modesty and resistance as befitted a young girl, which caused Fontanis to become even more ardent. He quickly made sure everything was arranged in accordance with his desires.

But if their initial assignation had been interrupted by a little broad comedy, the second one was going to turn into a veritable disaster.

The day passed by fairly uneventfully. That evening, on cue, Lucile was the first to leave the company, saying she intended to go to bed. The judge followed her shortly afterwards; this time no one challenged him. In his quarters, he found Lucile on his bed, stark naked, in the position he had instructed her to assume. Inflamed with desire at the delectable sight of the young girl, so submissive to his desires, so erotically positioned, and so obviously ready to receive him, the judge quickly undressed and hurried to join her on the bed. Moving into the most advantageous position and taking hold of the young woman, he was just about to give her the unequivocal proof of his passion… when suddenly the door burst open, revealing Monsieur and Madame de Totteville, the Marquise, and Mademoiselle de Téroze herself.

— You monster! she screamed furiously at her husband. So this is how you laugh at the tenderness I show you, is it?…

— You ungrateful child! Monsieur de Totteville said sternly to Lucile, who rushed over to her father in tears. So this is how you abuse the freedom we've allowed you, is it?…

For their part, the Marquise & Madame de Totteville were staring in incredulous horror at the two culprits, Madame d'Olincourt's accusatory glare was abruptly interrupted by her need to catch her sister who, as the judge clambered off the bed & scrabbled for his clothes, fainted.

It would be difficult to describe the expression on Fontanis's face during all of this: surprise, shame, dismay, terror, anxiety, embarrassment, annoyance; all of these different emotions crossed his face simultaneously, as he stood there as still as a statue, his hands holding his clothes and his eyes on his wife who was slumped in her sister's arms.

The Marquis arrived at the door and took in the scene. He asked his wife what had happened and she informed him. The Marquis became visibly angry and indignant with each word.

Lucile's father looked steadily at the Marquis.

— Monsieur, he said, I would never have expected that a young lady from an honorable family would have to fear affronts of this kind in your home. I trust you will understand why I cannot tolerate such an insult under any circumstances and that I will be leaving immediately with my wife and my young daughter in order to seek legal redress from those who have wronged us.

— Really, Monsieur, the Marquis said curtly to the judge, you must admit that such behavior is hardly the sort I have a right to expect from a guest in my home. Did you seek to marry into my family in order to dishonor my sister-in-law and to tarnish our family name?

He turned to address Totteville.

— The legal redress you seek is just, Monsieur. But may I respectfully request that you make every effort to avoid a scandal? I do not ask this lightly, and I do not ask it in order to save this insufferable fool, for he is beneath contempt and deserves to be severely punished. No, I make my request for my family's sake, Monsieur, and mostly for the sake of my poor father-in-law who unfortunately placed his full trust in this contemptible buffoon and will surely die of grief upon realizing how severely mistaken he was to choose this creature to be my sister-in-law's husband.

— I would like to oblige you, Monsieur de Totteville said haughtily to the Marquis, as he ushered his wife and daughter out of the room. But I have to place my own and my family's honor above these considerations. You and your family will not be compromised in any way, Monsieur, by the complaint I am going to lodge. He pointed at Fontanis, then added: The only person who will be implicated will be this dishonest creature here. And now, I have heard enough and must leave, for vengeance calls.

With those words, the three of them left the room with such determination that no one could have stopped them. It was clear to everyone present that they intended to go to Paris as fast as they could and present a petition to the court against Judge Fontanis for the outrages he would have committed against their young and innocent daughter, had he not been stopped...

However, once they had departed, there was further distress and despair in that disharmonious château. Mademoiselle de Téroze, who had been making very good progress in her recovery, had taken to her bed again with a fever that was, according to the physician, at a very dangerous point.

Monsieur and Madame d'Olincourt hurled a barrage of insults and indictments at the judge who, as he had no other sanctuary than their home, and given the awkward and embarrassing position he now found himself in, did not dare to respond to their reprimands, all of which were rightly directed at him.

Things remained in that state for three days, then the Marquis received a letter from de Totteville informing him that the matter was being treated by the court as so serious that it was being dealt with as a criminal case. The court had issued a warrant and constables were about to be sent to detain Fontanis.

— What? the terrified judge said. Without hearing my side of the story?

— That's the law, isn't it? d'Olincourt replied. Surely, as a High Court Judge, you know that the court does not allow the person for whom a warrant has been issued any means of defense? One of your own personal customs is to sully a defendant's name prior to his being heard in court. You have done this many times. The court seems only to be doing what you have been doing for over thirty years. Are you suggesting the court is being unjust? If so, then you must have also been unjust. If you acted rightly, then it is only reasonable that you have become, at least once in your life, a victim of legal proceedings.

— But why make all this fuss over a young woman?

— Cases like this one, which involve young ladies, are usually the most dangerous cases of all. You've tried enough cases involving young women to know this. That wretched affair from a few years back, the one which was referred to as you received five hundred lashes in the haunted château, that was over a few young women, wasn't it? And didn't you once judge that an incident involving a few young women was sufficient cause for you to set about ruining a young nobleman's reputation? An eye for an eye, Judge, an eye for an eye. That's been your guiding compass, therefore have the courage to submit to it.

— Merciful Heaven! Fontanis said. In the name of God, my dear brother-in-law, do not abandon me.

— We will do all we can to help you, d'Olincourt replied. No matter what dishonor you have brought upon us, and no matter what cause for complaint we may have against you, you can rely on us to stand by you throughout this. But the means are not easy... you of all people know what they are...

— What are they?

— The King's favor. A *lettre de cachet*.[49] That seems to be your only way out of this.

— What a terrible situation I'm in!

— I agree, but what other choices do you have? Would you prefer to leave France and be ruined forever or serve a few years in prison, which will perhaps expiate this whole affair? I can see you find the idea distasteful, but haven't you used the exact same method yourself? Wasn't it by such barbaric advice that you finally succeeded in crushing that nobleman that those ghosts avenged with their whips? Didn't you have the audacity to force that young officer to make a choice between prison or disgrace? Didn't you agree to suspend your despicable legal wrath only on the conditions that he would be crushed by those of his king? There can't be anything surprising about what I'm suggesting, my friend. Not only is this a path you've used often, but it's one you that you should now be welcoming.

— Oh, these are dreadful memories, the judge said, tears running down his face. Who would have believed that Heaven's vengeance would burst on my head almost at the moment when my crimes were being committed? What I have done is being paid back, and all I can do is suffer, suffer and keep silent.

However, as his assistance was most urgently required, the Marquise urged her husband to leave for Fontainebleau, where the court was then in residence.

Mademoiselle de Téroze did not take part in the family council; shame and sorrow outside, and the Comte d'Elbène inside, kept her constantly confined to her bedchamber, the door of which was locked to the judge. He had gone to her door several times & knocked and he had even tried using tears and remorse, but he had never succeeded. Her door remained closed to him.

The Marquis departed. He rode fast and the journey was not a long one. He was back two days later, escorted by two officers and in receipt of a so-called warrant; the mere sight of which caused the judge to tremble from head to toe.

— You've come at a most appropriate time, said the Marquise, who pretended to have received news from Paris while her husband was away at court. The court case is proceeding with astonishing speed, & my friends have written to me urging me to help the judge escape as quickly as possible. My father has been informed of the matter; he is in a state of despair. He requests that we serve his friend faithfully, & explain to him the amount of pain this has caused him… his health does not allow him to offer any help other than his best wishes. They would have been more sincere if his friend had been a little less foolish… Here's the letter.

The Marquis read it quickly, and after berating Fontanis for his appalling behavior, he handed the judge, who was having great difficulty in reconciling himself to the thought of going to prison, over to the two court officers who were none other than two sergeants from the Marquis's own regiment. He then urged Fontanis to console himself with the fact that he fully intended to keep in constant contact with the judge.

— I have managed, the Marquis told the judge, to obtain with great difficulty, a château located about five or six leagues from here. Once there, you'll be under the care and protection of one of my old friends who will treat you as if you were me. I am sending a personal message to him with these guards, requesting that they treat you with respect and deference. Therefore, you may put your mind at rest.

The judge wept like a child, for no tears are as bitter as those of a remorseful criminal who sees himself overwhelmed by all the scourges that he himself has used… but nonetheless, when it was time for the judge to depart, he asked for permission to kiss his wife goodbye.

— Your wife, the Marquise said brusquely. She's not that yet, fortunately. In the midst of all our calamities, that's the only consolation we have.

— Very well, the judge said. I'll try to find the courage to bear this new wound. And, escorted by his guards, he climbed into the carriage.

The château to which the wretched man was taken was part of Mademoiselle d'Olincourt's dowry, and everything there was made ready to receive him. A Captain of d'Olincourt's regiment, a strict, harsh man, had been chosen to play the role of prison governor. He received Fontanis, dismissed the guards, and then assigned his prisoner to a small, bare cell. He told Fontanis that he had received further orders that overrode his first orders; those orders compelled him to treat the judge with the utmost severity, and he did not dare ignore those orders.

The judge was left in this cruel situation for almost a month. Not a single visitor came to see him. He was served only soup, bread, and water. His bed was a few handfuls of loose straw and his room was constantly humid.

The only time he ever saw anyone was — as is the custom in the Bastille; that is to say, the way they treat the beasts of the zoo — when he was brought food. During this period of incarceration, the judge was not disturbed and he had time for some serious reflection.

Eventually, the bogus prison governor appeared and, after offering a few inconsequential words of consolation, he spoke to the judge in the following manner:

— You should have realized, Monsieur, he said to him, that your first mistake was wishing to marry into a family so far above you in every respect. Baron de Téroze and the Marquis d'Olincourt are people from the highest ranks of nobility; aristocrats who care about the welfare of the whole of France, and you are only a poor Provençal judge, without station or name, without accolades or estates.

— If you had taken a little time to think seriously about yourself, you would have realized that you should have told Baron de Téroze — who was blind to your faults — that you were not at all the right match for his daughter. Moreover, how could you have imagined, even for a moment, that that beautiful young lady, as beautiful as love itself, could ever wish to become the wife of an old and ugly ape like you? It is permissible to be blind to one's faults but not to that extent.

— The reflections you must have made during your stay here, Monsieur, must have surely convinced you that during the four months that you have spent at the Marquis d'Olincourt's château, you have been a laughing-stock for everyone; only that and nothing more. A person of your station and appearance, of your profession and stupidity, of your wickedness and deceit, should expect nothing but treatment of that kind. By a thousand tricks, each one more amusing than the next, you were prevented from enjoying the young lady you claimed as your wife. You were made to foul your marriage bed on your wedding night; you were dressed in outlandish clothes and paraded throughout the region for the amusement of the locals; you were bled and given unnecessary daily ice baths by a man pretending to be a doctor; you were given wine until you were too drunk to consummate your marriage; you were tipped out of bed onto the floor while your wife spent the night with her lover; you were dropped into a pigsty and covered from head to toe in pig excrement; you were tricked into going to bed with a black woman; you have been insulted daily: called a heretic, a fool, an idiot, amongst many other names; you were dangled at the end of a ship's rope, then dunked into the river; you were fed a laxative and then stuck to a privy seat, after which you had your buttocks burned; you were tricked into going to a "haunted" château wearing an old suit of armor, & you were again paraded through the region for everyone's amusement; you were made to receive five hundred lashes from a supposed group of ghosts, which you believed were real; you were drenched while asleep and then made to sit naked at a table while your hosts drank wine and ate pâté; you were made to watch a balloon in which your wife was being embraced and kissed by the man she adores, which due to your ignorance and arrogance you foolishly mistook for an astronomical or celestial phenomenon; you had a donkey put in your bed instead of a young girl; you were caught in bed with a well-paid and very experienced young whore who has subsequently told everyone she knows that she found you utterly repulsive; she also mocked your manhood, which she described as "pathetic." In the eyes of everyone, you are a fool and now you have been locked away in this château, where the Marquis d'Olincourt, the Colonel of my regiment, will keep you for the rest of your life, something he will most certainly do if you refuse to sign the document that I have here.

— Before reading it, Monsieur, the so-called governor continued, be aware that you are merely one man, one man amongst several suitors, who wanted to marry Mademoiselle de Téroze, but you are not, and you never will be, her husband. Your marriage was performed in secret; the two witnesses have agreed to swear they know nothing about it and they themselves now have witnesses to say they were elsewhere at the time; the priest who performed the ceremony has returned the marriage certificate, which I have here; the notary has returned the marriage contract, which you see here before your very own eyes; you have never slept with your wife — your marriage is unconsummated, therefore null & void. It is tacitly annulled with the full consent of all parties, which gives it the validity of all civil and religious laws. Here is the Baron de Téroze's statement of withdrawal, and here is his daughter's. All that is missing is your signature. So here is your moment, Monsieur; you must now choose between amicably putting your signature on this paper, or of facing the certainty that you will end your days here… That is all I have to say. I will now let you read, decide and answer.

The judge, after a moment of thought, took the paper and read these words:

I attest and confirm to all those who will read this that I have never been Mademoiselle de Téroze's husband. With this document I give back to her all the rights that for a short period of time were thought to have been given to me with respect to her and I hereby promise I shall not attempt to reclaim them during my lifetime. I have nothing but praise and gratitude for the hospitality given and the kindness shown to me by her and her family during the summer that I spent in their home. It is by mutual agreement, by our own free will, that we renounce any plans for marriage that may have been planned for us, and we give each

*other back the freedom to dispose of our persons as
if there had never been any intention in joining us.
And it is of my own volition, and in good health in
both body & mind, that I sign this at the Château
de Valnord, belonging to The Marquise d'Olincourt.*

— You explained to me, Monsieur, the judge said, after
reading these lines, what awaited me if I did not sign this
document, but you did not tell me what would happen
to me if I consented to everything.

— Your reward will be your immediate release, the
false governor said. This jewel, worth two hundred louis,
is from the Marquise d'Olincourt, and it is a parting
gift which she begs you to accept. At the château gate
you will find a valet tending two excellent horses, one
for you; one carrying the belongings you brought here
with you. The horse will take you back to Aix. You may
keep both horses.

— I will sign and leave, Monsieur. I am keen to be away
from these people. I have no desire to delay my departure.

— That's a very wise decision, Judge, the Captain said,
taking the signed document from the judge & handing
him the jewel. But be aware of your future conduct; once
outside, if you grow tempted by an obsessive desire for
revenge, please keep in mind, before you begin doing
anything, that you would be dealing with a truly formidable enemy; this is one of France's most powerful
families that you would be offending by your actions.

In that situation, they would have no choice but to have the country's top doctors declare you a madman and you would, without doubt, spend the rest of your life in an insane asylum.

— You do not need to worry, Monsieur, the judge said. My only interest is in having nothing more to do with such people. I will make every effort to avoid them.

— I suggest you do exactly that, Judge, the Captain said, finally unlocking the judge's cell door. Leave here in peace and may we never see you in this part of the country again.

— You have my word, the judge said as he climbed onto his horse. This little adventure has cured me of all my vices. If I lived another thousand years, I would never come to Paris, looking for a wife. I understood the sorrow of being cuckolded during marriage but I did not know that it was possible to become one before… My judgments will now be governed by wisdom and discretion. I'll no longer set myself up as a mediator between whores and men who are better than I. It costs too much to take the side of those young ladies and I no longer want to deal with people who are only intent on revenge.

The judge departed and, having become wise at his own expense, was never heard from again. The Provençal whores complained that they were no longer given any judicial support, the result of which was that virtue triumphed, because the young ladies, on seeing they could no longer count on that corrupt support, preferred the path of virtue to the dangers that awaited them on the road of vice, when the magistrates became wise enough to realize the terrible disadvantages of providing them with protection.

The reader may be able to imagine how, during the judge's incarceration, the Marquis d'Olincourt, after having persuaded Baron de Téroze to look less favorably on Fontanis, made every effort to ensure that all of the arrangements that we have just read about were carried out faultlessly. Thanks to his skill and influence, he succeeded so well that three months later Mademoiselle de Téroze was married in a public ceremony to Comte d'Elbène, with whom she lived in perfect happiness.

— I sometimes have a few pangs of regret at having so badly mistreated that unpleasant man, the Marquis said one day to his dear sister-in-law. But when on the one hand I see the happiness that has resulted from my efforts, and on the other I realize that the person I persecuted was merely a socially useless buffoon, essentially an enemy of the State, a disruptor of public peace, and the tormentor of an honest and respectable family; a creature who slandered and ruined a distinguished nobleman whom I have the highest regard for, and to whose family I have the honor of belonging, that's when I find consolation in the words of the well-known philosopher: O sovereign Providence, why are the ways of man so limited that good can never be achieved without a touch of evil?

This tale was finished on 16 July 1787, at 10 o'clock in the evening.[50]

The Marquise de Télème, or the Effects of Libertinism[51]

The Marquis de Telême, a man from a noble but somewhat impoverished family, who lived in his home town of Poitiers, had been married for about eighteen months to one of the richest, youngest, and most beautiful heiresses in the province.

No couple was more devoted. The obvious affection, harmony, refinement, reciprocal trust, esteem and tender love they had for each other tightened the emotional ties of these newly-weds: those who saw them could not help but admire them, anyone who met them immediately treated them with the utmost respect.

But it is not without reason that Zeus has been painted seated between two enormous urns, one of which is filled with evils, the other with blessings. It is said that he always pours out the blessings from the former urn first, and then mixes in a little evil from the second urn. Different people receive a drop of this mixture daily. Zeus always mixes it from both urns, never from one urn only.

Six weeks after their wedding, a plague caused the young Marquise to lose her parents. Within a few days, an unknown man appeared at their home; he claimed he was Madame de Telême's elder brother.

It was true that Madame de Telême had indeed once had a brother, but he had been killed in a duel, and so could certainly not make a sudden reappearance.

When challenged, the imposter recounted the story of the duel accurately enough. He went on to assure the Telêmes that he had been badly wounded & not, as the reports had said, killed in the duel and his body quickly removed by his friends so as to avoid any scandal. He went on to state that it was the seriousness of the wound, as well as his fear of legal reprisals, that had caused him to shun his family for all of these years. It was only after he had learned of the death of his father that he had reappeared in order to collect his inheritance and to manage the estate that was now rightfully his.

The man had legal papers to prove who he was; he also had a lawyer, a large retinue of servants, and a lot of friends. He moved into the family home and took the best rooms for himself. Before long, the Marquis de Telême's fortune, which almost entirely consisted of his wife's dowry, was taken control of and frozen by the usurper's lawyers. Within a short space of time, what had been the most beautiful château in the entire province was reduced to a squalid-looking, uncared for building.

The usurper's story was clearly absurd and he told it with a lot of effrontery. Despite this, Madame de Telême had no choice but to surrender her fortune to his lawyers.

On receiving the first sum of his inheritance at the end of the month, the man immediately set off for Paris, no doubt intending to spend Madame de Telême's money on consolidating his position.

What can one do in such cruel circumstances?

Nothing could be simpler than to contest such appalling and unjust behavior; it was merely a matter of soliciting the correct legal advice and taking the offending party to court.

Monsieur de Telême did not hesitate. He gathered together every note and every coin of all the money that he could put his hands on; money that belonged to him, not to Madame de Telême, and made a decision: he decided that his wife would go by herself to the Paris High Court and seek legal redress for this dreadful wrong. It would be an important case. He assured the Marquise that nothing would convince a Paris judge to rule in her favor so much as the honest solicitations of a young and pretty woman from a noble family.

That shy and naïve young woman was very unwilling to take charge of such an important undertaking because she greatly feared failure. On her return, what would become of her if, once in Paris, she had to spend all of their little remaining money on bringing the imposter to justice, and then the case was unsuccessful? Would she dare then look into the eyes of the husband she adored, whom she would have robbed through no fault of her own; a man she would see die of grief simply because he had taken her as his wife? She very delicately suggested several different alternatives for raising money to the one her husband had suggested: she would sell the little she had left and the money would go directly to her husband as compensation, and she would lock herself away in a cloister where she would live devoutly for the rest of her life. Or she would simply disappear and no one would ever see her again or, if he preferred, she would work to earn a living and pass her earnings on to her husband so he could use his abilities and skills to increase their fortune.

None of these ideas, dictated more by despair than by wisdom, pleased Monsieur de Telême: he informed his wife that she must leave for Paris, that she must go and seek recourse to the law, and he added in a firm tone that not only must her case be fought for but that it must, out of dire necessity, be won.

Defeated by such serious interdicts and by prayers that too closely resembled orders for the young Marquise to be in any doubt, she set off for Paris accompanied by her maid, Flavie, a pretty, vivacious, and spirited creature about twenty years old.

It often happens that a provincial gentleman who has avoided military service due to being assured of a pleasant existence on an estate in the country, and who has held on to his good name and his property, visits Paris without contacts or without knowledge of the city, and then, because he expects to be treated with the same consideration he is accustomed to receiving from his friends and acquaintances who cherish and respect him, ends up suffering from a lack of civility, recognition, or consideration.

One could regard this longing for consideration as a fantasy, for it is an insistence that others must give the one demanding it their full attention, as well as their time and their care. It is a selfish requirement, one that is usually acquired in the antechamber of ministers. It is not something that is present in the mores of the nation, nor is it present in the history of the last century or two. It could be considered a fashion, or more accurately, a fad. One should regard it in the same light as one regards a top hat: the narrow cycle of luxury items varies from one season to the next, as do the situations, and all the different ways of life. The great customs have been around a little too long to go through all the points of the circumference, but they eventually change too, and the revolution that this nation's penchant for agromania is already heralding is perhaps not as far away as we believe.

The owner of huge estates in Versailles will eventually see that he is not really all that powerful when he is in Paris; he will end up being confused by his social inferiors who will often overwhelm him with their wealth and their ostentatious extravagance, or else he will be used by his social superiors who will dine and party as much as they can at his expense so that, in the end, he finds that there he is regarded as nothing more than a servant, whereas he was a sovereign at home.

Be that as it may, the Marquis de Telême, who knew no one in the capital, and did not want the humiliation of having to beg the province's Intendant for letters of introduction, was convinced that his wife, with her youth, her slender figure, her beauty, her noble name and, of course, her money and her estates, had everything necessary to succeed, and so it was, exactly as we have described that the young Marquise arrived in the capital.

The next day she went out in search of a lawyer. She found a law firm near to the hotel in which she was staying. She sat in a neat and well-appointed office and told the lawyer, Monsieur Saint-Vérac, all that had transpired and how her husband had sent her to Paris to obtain legal advice and representation in her case against the man who was pretending to be her brother. She mentioned the fact of her straitened circumstances, but promised the lawyer she would pay him handsomely if he could help her win such an important case; one in which she was clearly in the right.

Saint-Vérac asked her to call back the following day and by then, he affirmed, he would have information for her regarding her case. When she returned the next day, the lawyer informed Madame de Telême that her adversary was no longer in Paris. Happy at having been so successful in his fraudulent activities, he had left for Poitou and was already planning his return to the property he claimed belonged to him. Saint-Vérac then agreed to represent Madame de Telême.

The wealthiest of Parisian libertines was never without agents in all districts. Some of those agents were, by necessity, lawyers. When a wealthy libertine and a lawyer worked together, it was not long before a crowd of widows and orphans inevitably fell daily into their nets. The pairing of a wealthy debauchee and a mercurial legal mind was an advantageous alliance, almost a brotherhood.

By a very singular inevitability, Saint-Vérac, Madame de Telême's lawyer, was also the legal adviser of Monsieur de Fondor, one of the richest traders in the capital.

As soon as the lawyer had seen that the young woman was about seventeen years old and had a very slender and beautiful figure, with a fresh-looking mouth, two very expressive eyes, very lustrous hair, a beautiful throat, the softest & whitest skin, the most delicate features in the world, in short, the most beautiful and desirable woman he had ever seen, he had hurried to inform his employer that Venus herself had arrived from Kythera to visit her son's estates.

Or, to abandon the metaphor, the lawyer informed Fondor that he would very quickly place the young, beautiful, naïve provincial in dire straits, so that she would be more than receptive to receiving financial help from Fondor within a week. He added that she was delicious prey that fate had brought to Paris solely for them both to use and divest of everything. With regards to her claims, he had investigated them fully, and on having read all of the relevant documents, he was in no doubt that she was correct in her conviction that the man making a claim on her estate and her fortune was an obvious impostor, therefore it was only a matter of enlightening the court of this fact so that within the month Madame de Telême would find herself the rightful owner of what had been left to her by her parents.

— You have done very well regarding this Telême woman, Fondor said. But you must now proceed with the utmost care. The best thing to do now, it seems to me, is to start relieving the young woman of all the écus that she has left in her purse. Once you have done that, make her think that her case is not as easily winnable as you first thought. Let her believe her legal hearing might go against her if she proceeds without significant financial resources to ease the case's movement toward success. Ensure that she realizes she may be forced to leave Paris with the dagger of failure in her heart. Once she is at that point, you must carefully mention my name to her. Tell her I am a man of significant credit and one who considers it a duty to help noble families with legal troubles. A few days later, you will introduce me and I will make my offer, or rather, my proposition. If the beauty rebuffs my proposition, we will return her with neither money nor estate to her husband and we will soon recoup our expenses with someone else. If, on the contrary, she agrees to my demands, the funds that I will advance to her if she is insolvent will compensate her for what is needed regarding your inflated legal fees, and we will take the final steps to make her win her case, by which I mean her fortune, from which we will then deduct and obtain our significant legal costs. So, my dear Saint-Vérac, you must begin immediately to prepare the way for me to succeed. There is nothing to be done with a woman who has money, except try to relieve her of it. The virtue of all ladies is usually settled by her financial status: no sooner is a woman without money than she is found to be more docile than a lamb and willing to surrender to every demand made by a benefactor.

Those were the principles of that evil man. It was his wealth that no doubt made him possess such traits. Fondor's success with women was due entirely to his gold in all its pristine ugliness; he could only hold a woman because of his money, whereas a sensitive man holds a woman because of his affection and his love.

Fondor was already an old, despicable figure; a short, squat man who smelled of old bank notes. He himself could smell money from a league away. His desires were still very lively and he neglected nothing to immediately satisfy them. Fondor judged all women according to the cruel position to which he reduced them. He had never been within reach of knowing their hearts because he was never delicate enough nor kind enough to inflame any woman's heart. And so he took his revenge on the adorable sex because he had never been able to appear to them as anything other than an object of hatred and contempt.

Everything was settled. The plan that had just been drawn up by the two men was agreed on, and the next day Saint-Vérac began to act. He began by making sure that Madame de Telême fully understood the very real & very expensive difficulties of such a trial…

— This young man who claims to be your brother has interested the whole court and the whole city. His claims seem unassailable. Are you certain you can successfully challenge his claims?

He continued:

— This trial could ruin you, Madame de Telême. Moreover, you will have to spend whatever remains of your money, and if you lose your case, you may well end up being forced to return home on foot to a husband who may start to treat you very badly, seeing in you only a woman who has ruined him. Perhaps, he concluded, it would be better if you saved the little money you have left and returned to Poitiers, thereby avoiding starting a legal battle which requires immense sums to fund the inevitably protracted legal proceedings.

Our beautiful heroine's answer to this was to shed copious tears…

But does a man who has the misfortune to wear a black court robe and make a living from public dissension ever heed a woman's tears? If he did, the most beautiful women of France would drown him with their laments. Not that he would care for anything except making sure he hid from public sight his criminal activities, his greed, and his lasciviousness… his comical outfit is a suit of armor. It is more likely that manna from heaven would rain down than an honest soul could be found in any of those unfortunate individuals who have the misfortune to wear court robes, whatever title they may be decorated with.

— However, Madame, continued Saint-Vérac, if you insist on proceeding, we shall challenge the man, but I am not promising you anything. But first, tell me the state of your funds.

— Unfortunately, Monsieur, replied the Marquise, all we have left is five hundred louis. My husband, who has no fortune of his own, is ruined if I am, and this sum that is from his savings is all that we were able to accumulate at the moment our income was seized & frozen by that usurper.

— Five hundred louis, said Saint-Vérac, rising and opening the door. Look out here at our clerks, Madame, and see if there is someone there who wants to undertake such a case for a mere five hundred louis. I am not sure that such an amount would even get your case heard. It is probably best if I do not represent you.

— But, Monsieur, I have some jewelry.

— How much is it worth?

— Perhaps an equal sum.

— Yes, perhaps if one were buying, but if one is selling, then it's half the value at best. However, in order to be certain, please place your trinkets on this desk, so that I may have them valued. Perhaps the whole amount together will be enough to cover the expense of a few days in court making sure your case is heard.

After some deliberation and not without some feelings of disquiet, the Marquise consented and divested herself of her jewelry. She placed each piece on the lawyer's desk, whereupon it was agreed that a jeweler would come to the lawyer's office the following day to value Madame's jewels.

What legal challenges was Madame prepared to use to counter the claims of her opponent? the lawyer asked. And how could she afford lengthy court case costs if she lost the case?

Seeing Madame de Telême's discomfort at the mention of costs, Saint-Vérac casually mentioned Monsieur de Fondor, the benefactor of several noble families that had faced legal issues in Paris. Perhaps the Marquise had heard of him? She had not, but she eagerly asked for more information. What business was he in?

— He has many businesses, Saint-Vérac said. He is a very successful businessman & also a brilliant horseman.

Saint-Vérac went on to explain how he had become acquainted with Monsieur de Fondor because of his business success in Paris, and that they had developed a friendship through the courts after Monsieur de Fondor had successfully helped several noble families keep their estates and their fortunes.

— That is someone I would be interested in meeting, the Marquise de Telême said, trying to maintain a degree of composure and dignity in the face of possible financial ruin.

— With that agreed, said the prosecutor, I would now like you to start following my legal advice. It is now necessary that you leave the accommodation you are currently residing in because it is much too expensive for your situation.

He led her to his office window and indicated a small, nondescript hotel. Coincidentally, it stood directly in front of one of Fondor's town houses.

— There, he said to her, is where you should stay while I prepare for the court case. There are a number of reasons for this: I will be within easy reach if I need to talk to you about specific details; it will be less expensive for you, and it is anonymous and private; all of these things are necessary in your current position. Also, it is essential that during the days before your case that you see absolutely no one; that you talk to no one, not about the case nor about yourself. If you must speak to anyone, speak only to me or to those that are important to your case. As to Monsieur de Fondor, I will bring him to you and make the introductions myself. As for these, he said, indicating the jewels, I will use them to heat the irons in the judicial fire.

And having made these recommendations, Saint-Vérac stood up. He escorted the Marquise out of the office and had one of his clerks escort Madame back to her hotel.

Madame de Telême had agreed to give her husband an accurate daily report of her progress, so she wrote to him that evening to inform him of everything that had happened that day. Although she had been given carte blanche regarding everything pertaining to their case & could, if she chose, continue to act as she pleased, she had decided to conform to the suggestions of the one who represented her.

The next day she left the beautiful hotel in which she had been staying, and then booked herself and her maid into the one that Saint-Vérac had suggested. Everything there had been prepared for her. She was given a very spartan suite of rooms, the bedroom of which had its windows directly in front of one of Fondor's rooms.

On entering her rooms, it was impossible, unless the curtains were closed, for Madame de Telême to hide her actions from anyone who cared to be looking out from behind the seemingly-closed shutters of the business-man's office. It was from there, from the first day she had moved into the hotel, that the libertine ogled the young beauty at his leisure. As he watched the Marquise de Telême during moments she thought were completely private, his obscene heart ignited with the most illicit passion he had ever felt in his life. These effervescences of debauchery ignore the delicacy of the feeling that is necessary to appreciate true beauty. Fondor's praise was fleeting, used by him in order to gain a hold over the object he temporarily adored. Power was his god and he sacrificed everything to that one deity. He believed that constancy was a crime.

Fondor's pursuit of power over the Marquise led him to realize that the attractive maid, Flavie, was most likely his best method of recourse to the unfortunate Marquise. He decided he would seduce Flavie, and then use her to gain access to Madame de Telême.

Flavie, a vivacious woman, warmed the intemperance of that ugly creature. He believed that not only would he be satisfied by her without any danger of Madame knowing of her seduction, but that that creature, once she had been seduced by him, would help to hasten the defeat of the noble-born woman.

The next day Fondor mentioned his plan to Saint-Vérac and as the latter could find no flaw with the enterprise, Fondor immediately set about obtaining Flavie's obedience. He used his usual method of seduction; he offered her money.

Flavie, despite her misgivings, had no intention of refusing a hundred écus, and immediately agreed to his demands. Once in his rooms, she greatly satisfied every desire of the financier as soon as he expressed it. From that moment, Flavie became one of Fondor's most faithful slaves, always willing to use her young body to gratify his many desires.

As soon as he saw she was won over, the libertine thought he would entrust her with his false project and elicit her help in achieving his aims. The maid agreed and promised to serve him faithfully.

— I need an introduction to your mistress, Fondor said to the maid. Arrange it.

The poor woman was so taken in by Fondor's machinations that she promised Fondor that if he and the lawyer did not quickly succeed in rescuing her mistress from her current state of misery and dependency then she, Flavie, would do everything she could in order to have the pleasure of seeing her mistress win her case and triumphantly leave the poorly-furnished hotel she currently resided in.

— Do not think I would not do more, she added, as she left to make the appointment.

She duly returned with a time, and informed Fondor that Madame was eager to meet him to discuss business matters.

The next day, Flavie opened the door to Fondor's knock and led him in to Madame's sitting room. After introductions, Flavie left the libertine and her mistress alone.

Fondor came to the point. He told the Marquise what he wanted and what she would get in return. He also explained that if she refused him, he would guarantee that the man claiming to be her brother would win his case and claim legal expenses from her as part of his settlement.

— I'll give you back your five hundred louis and your jewels, he said mockingly. They may last you half a year if you are frugal.

The Marquise considered her options, and then, in a voice that she barely recognized as her own, agreed to Fondor's terms.

He bowed, ordered her to be ready to receive him at eleven the next morning. She was to make no appointments for that day and she was to give her maid the day off. He then left.

On his way home, Fondor heard several people mentioning the imminent revolution and the possible fate of the aristocracy. He paid no attention to such trifles normally, but now he listened with great care to what was being said. He made a few enquiries, then went home to ruminate.

It was true then. Things were changing. People were demanding change. There was a violent charge in the air over the capital. Paris felt dangerous.

Fondor thought about his prospective victim. Finally, he reached a conclusion and made a decision.

The next morning, he set off for the hotel. He knocked and the Marquise admitted him to her quarters.

Fondor gave his instructions.

The Marquise slowly removed her clothing.

Fondor sat on the room's only good chair and watched his victim reveal her perfect form to his lascivious eyes.

The libertine then gave further instructions, & although the Marquise blanched at his orders, she moved to comply. Further instructions were given; the Marquise obeyed. Finally, fully satisfied, Fondor stood up and got dressed.

He looked down at the Marquise, sprawled on the hotel room floor. He did not offer to help her to her feet.

He reached into his coat and pulled out a leather purse. He dropped it onto the table.

— Here is your payment: five hundred louis *&* your jewels, he said. He turned to leave.

The Marquise was on her feet in an instance. She looked inside the purse. She looked questioningly at Fondor.

— What is this, Monsieur? You told me that you would bring me funds, and that you would support the cost of my trial?

— Things have changed, Fondor said, looking out of the hotel window at the city beyond. Things that have affected the terms of our transaction. In truth, I said several things without having seen what I was purchasing, and once I had seen what I had purchased, I can tell you in all honesty I had to use a lot of effort and imagination to deliver my promise. Tell me, is it right that I should pay you more than you are worth?

Those cruel words caused a black and awful despair to seize Madame de Telême in its merciless grip.

— But you gave your word. You said —

— Madame, there are always things that are said before one takes one's pleasure. You are a woman of the world. You took your pleasure, just as I took mine. We are both far from regretting our actions. We know only too well that the treacherous hand of enjoyment frequently tears off the veil of prestige and leaves the object in a state of truth that can be unsettling or dangerous, sometimes even fatal. But we take our pleasures where we can. If it's any consolation, you are worth five hundred louis and a handful of jewels…

Once she was alone, the Marquise called for Flavie to pack her belongings, possibly for a final time.

The maid, aware of what had happened, confessed her part in bringing the libertine to Madame. She admitted that she had been deceived regarding the service she had believed Fondor would render to her mistress. She then sat at her mistress's feet sobbing with remorse at having so horribly betrayed the noble woman she was employed by.

An hour later, in the cheapest carriage available, the two women set off for Madame's family home. In an apartment in a part of the château that was seldom used, the Marquise embraced her husband and admitted she had failed.

He held her close to him and tried to reassure her.

— You tried, my angel, you tried.

It was his love for her that gave her the strength to do what she did next. Steeling her resolve, she confessed that she had allowed herself to be tricked & seduced, and her confession was seasoned with bitter tears. She spared no detail, wanting the man she loved to be fully aware of the vile depths she had been pulled down to.

The Marquis listened to her confession and realized the part he had inadvertently played in all of it.

He calmed his wife.

— What has just happened to you, he said to her, must have been extremely unpleasant and distasteful. It no doubt also seems shocking and extraordinary. Unfortunately, it is one of the commonest things in the world. It was entirely my fault: I sent you to Paris without credit, without resources, without connections, without any introductions, without friends. You are barely seventeen years old, you are very beautiful, you have a slender, perfect figure, and you are imbued with nobility and grace. Of course you were duped and seduced. But it is not your fault. It is my fault. I am sorry.

— What are we to do? the Marquise de Telême asked.

— I know very well that your fortune has been taken from you, the Marquis answered, and I am certain we will be asked to leave here very soon, so that the thief can continue with his pretense of being the Marquis de Telême. All I can now do is hope that our relatives will show us a little consideration, at least until we can replenish our funds. But, I will say this; no matter what our situation may turn out to be, I feel we should again try legal methods against this thief who would rob us of what is rightfully ours. It is true that it will take us a while to raise the money for a court case, but I firmly believe we should try again as soon as we can. Our evidence is good; our case would be strong. If we tried again, we would most likely succeed…

Retaliation [52]

He was a respectable citizen of Picardy, possibly the descendant of one of those illustrious troubadours from the banks of the Oise or the Somme, one of those dragged from the shadows — after ten or twelve years of dull existence — by a great writer of this century. He was, as I say, a respectable and honest citizen who lived in the city of Saint-Quentin, itself famous for the great men it has given to literature. He lived there respectably with his wife and a three-times-removed cousin, a nun who had an administrative position at one of the city's convents.

The three-times-removed cousin was a small brunette with mischievous eyes, a pretty face, a turned-up nose and a slender figure; she was twenty-two years old and had been a nun for four of those years. Her name was Sister Pétronille, and she had a pretty voice. She was by nature more inclined to loving than to praying.

As for Monsieur d'Esclaponville, which was the name of our model citizen, he was a personable man, aged about twenty-eight, very much enamored of his beautiful cousin & not quite so enamored of Madame d'Esclaponville, given that he had already been sleeping with her for ten years, and a ten-year habit is fatal to any fire lit by lust.

Madame d'Esclaponville — for I have to describe her; a writer would be despised if he did not "paint" his characters during this age in which pictures are demanded;

where even a tragedy would be rejected if art dealers were unable to find at least six subjects for painters in it — Madame d'Esclaponville, as I was saying, was a somewhat insipid blonde, with a very pale, washed-out look about her, with fairly pretty eyes. She was quite voluptuous, & possessed attributes that are commonly referred to by many as *a good handful.*

She was as virtuous as her mother, a woman who had lived with the same man for eighty-three years without ever being unfaithful to him, yet she was still naïve enough, still innocent enough, to not so much as suspect her husband of this awful crime that dilettantes have named adultery, and that the liberals have simply labeled "gallantry." But a deceived wife is soon goaded by her resentment to seek revenge, and as no one likes to be labeled the guilty party, there was nothing she would not do as soon as she could to ensure that no one ever blamed her for her husband's behavior.

Madame d'Esclaponville finally noticed that her husband frequently visited the three-times-removed cousin and jealousy took hold of her soul. She watched him closely; she sought out information, and finally discovered that there were very few citizens in Saint-Quentin that did not know about the affair between her husband and Sister Pétronille.

Finally, and only after she was certain she was in possession of all of the facts, Madame d'Esclaponville went to her husband and informed him that his affair was causing her immense pain, that it pierced her very soul. She concluded by saying that she did not deserve to be treated so abysmally by him and asked him to end the sordid affair.

— Sordid affair! the accused husband said calmly, remaining cool under fire. Oh no, my dear, there's nothing sordid about it at all. In fact, it's the exact opposite of what you say, because the only reason I have repeated sexual liaisons with my cousin is because I'm working on my salvation. Remember, she's a nun. My soul is cleansed every time we have a sacred union. Don't you know that there's no sin in having an intimate relationship with a person who has consecrated themselves to God? Such individuals purify every thought and action, so to engage in intimacy with such a person is a way to identify with the Supreme Being, a way to incorporate the Holy Spirit into oneself: and to associate with them, in short, is to unlock the gates to heavenly bliss.

Although Madame d'Esclaponville was very unsatisfied with the outcome of her confrontation, she remained silent, although she promised herself she would find a way to achieve her ends that was more eloquent and totally unanswerable.

Interestingly, women generally have ways of asserting themselves, even the less attractive of them. They generally only have to say "Yes" and a whole host of avengers or defenders will appear from all directions. Until that moment, Madame d'Esclaponville had been unaware that there were a number of ways available to a woman for exacting revenge on an unfaithful husband.

In the same city, there was a parish priest known as the Abbé du Bosquet. He was a lecherous man in his thirties and he seduced every woman he met. He was the reason that most of the husbands living in Saint-Quentin were cuckolds.

Madame d'Esclaponville got to know the Abbé; very delicately, the Abbé also got to know Madame d'Esclaponville, until finally they both knew each other so intimately that they each could have painted a full-length nude portrait of the other in such detail that there would have been no mistaking either.

After about a month, people started making veiled comments to d'Esclaponville, for he was prone to regularly boasting that he, and he alone, had a wife who was impervious to the Abbé's formidable amorous advances, adding that his was the only forehead in the whole of Saint-Quentin that was free of cuckold's horns.

— You're very much mistaken, d'Esclaponville said to anyone who spoke to him on the matter. My wife is as pure and as faithful as Lucretia, and you may say differently until you're blue in the face, but I simply won't believe you.

— Come with me, then, said one of his friends. Come with me now and I'll give your eyes the proof of all you've heard. Perhaps you'll believe your own eyes. We'll see afterwards if you still have doubts.

D'Esclaponville allowed himself to be led away by his friend, who took him to the city limits, then half a mile beyond, until they reached an isolated place where the Somme, bordered by two fresh, flower-bedecked hedges, formed a natural pool, a delightful bathing-place for the inhabitants of the city.

The time of the liaison had been arranged for an early hour, a time when no one normally bathed. The hapless husband was upset to see his virtuous wife arrive quite early, followed a few minutes later by the Abbé du Bosquet. The early hour of their liaison meant that they would be unlikely to be interrupted by anyone for some time.

— Well, the friend asked d'Esclaponville, is your forehead beginning to itch where your cuckold's horns are growing?

— Not yet, said the husband, involuntarily rubbing his forehead. She's probably met him here so he can hear her confession.

— Then let's stay a little longer, said the friend. It wasn't much longer.

The moment he saw his lover arrive, Bosquet stood by the side of the river and removed his clothes. Madame d'Esclaponville stood near a sweet-scented hedge and did likewise. There was now nothing to impede the sensual contact that the Abbé and the married woman desired and naked, they embraced, then moved into their favorite positions. Then the Abbé du Bosquet, for perhaps the thirtieth time, very piously set about making sure that the respectable and honest citizen, Monsieur d'Esclaponville, was placed firmly in the ranks of Saint-Quentin's cuckolded husbands.

— Do you believe me now? the friend asked.

— Let's get away from here, said d'Esclaponville angrily. Yes, I believe you. And I would cheerfully throttle that damned priest if it weren't for the too-high price I'd have to pay for ridding the world of him. So, let's leave here, my friend, and please don't mention what you've seen here to anyone, I beg you.

D'Esclaponville returned home in a very agitated state. Shortly afterwards, his wife arrived and took her seat at their breakfast table.

— Just a moment, my dear, said the furious husband. When I was a young man, I promised my father I would never share a table with a whore.

— With a whore, Madame d'Esclaponville said, her tone calm and mild. Your insinuation shocks me, my dear husband. What do you accuse me of, if indeed, you are accusing me?

— Accusing you? Yes, I'm accusing you, you bitch! You know what you were doing earlier this morning in the bathing-place with the Abbé du Bosquet!

— Oh, for Heaven's sake, said d'Esclaponville's wife, gently. Is that all? Is that all you wanted to say?...

— My God! *All!* Is that all! What do you mean by *is that all?*

— But, my dear husband, I really don't understand you. I took your advice. Didn't you tell me that we have sexual unions with holy people in order to earn our salvation? Didn't you say that we risk nothing through intimacy with members of the church? Didn't you tell me that the soul is cleansed by any sacred union? Didn't you tell me there's no sin in having an intimate relationship with a person who has consecrated themselves to God? Don't you remember telling me that such individuals purify every thought and action, so to engage in intimacy with such a person is a way to identify with the Supreme Being, a way to incorporate the Holy Spirit into oneself: and to associate with them, in short, is to unlock the gates to heavenly bliss? Please understand, my dear, I have simply done exactly what you told me to do, and therefore you should be praising me for my devotion, not insulting me by referring to me as a whore and a bitch. And I can assure you that if any of those blessed servants of God have the means of unlocking the gates that lead to heavenly bliss, then it is certainly the Abbé du Bosquet, for I have never seen such an enormous key.

The Self-Made Cuckold, or the Unexpected Reconciliation

One of the greatest deficiencies of ill-bred people is that they constantly utter a host of indiscretions, slanders, or defamations on everyone that breathes, very often in the presence of people they do not really know. One cannot imagine the number of problems that this sort of idle chatter causes: what honest man can stand by and hear evil spoken about someone he cares for without reprimanding the fool who said it?

Unfortunately, the current education of young people does not include the principle of wise restraint; they are not taught anything about the world, nor the names, attributes, and the qualities of the people with whom they live amongst; instead, they are taught a thousand frivolous subjects, all of which are quickly trampled underfoot as soon as they reach the age of maturity.

The general impression is that everyone is brought up by capuchins and is therefore taught bigotry and uselessness, but no sound moral maxims.

Delve deeper and ask any young man about his duties to society, or ask him to explain his duties to himself and what he owes to others, or enquire how he must conduct himself in order to live a happy life: he will tell you that he does not understand what it is you are asking him, because he was taught to go to Mass and to recite litanies, and that he was taught how to dance and how to sing, but not how to get along with other men.

The specific incident that was the result of the deficiencies we have just begun to describe was not a serious matter; no blood was spilled, but its result was reasonably entertaining, so in order to recount it, we request a few minutes of your time, patient reader.

Monsieur de Raneville was about fifty years old. He was one of those self-possessed characters that everyone finds amusing. He did not laugh much himself, but he seemed to be able to make others laugh quite easily with his witty comments and his dry delivery, or sometimes simply by remaining silent, or by deploying comical facial expressions or gestures. He was far more amusing at the social events he was invited to than the boring and monotonous talkers who always have a tale to tell, usually one that they themselves laugh at for an hour in advance, but which is never really amusing enough to make their scowling listeners laugh or even smile.

He had a fairly important job as a tax collector. In order to console himself for a very bad marriage that he walked out on in Orléans, abandoning his unfaithful wife, he lived quietly in Paris on twenty or twenty-five thousand livres a year, with a very pretty woman whom he kept and with a small circle of friends, all as amiable as he was.

Monsieur de Raneville's kept woman was not a prostitute; she was a married woman, & therefore all the more desirable, for it is a well-known adage that a small pinch of adultery often adds a lot of spice to an affair. She was very pretty; thirty years old, with the most beautiful body imaginable. Separated from a dull and boring husband, she had come from the provinces to seek her fortune in Paris, and had not taken long to find it.

Raneville was a natural libertine and, as such, he was always on the lookout for a tasty morsel. He had employed every strategy he knew in order to not let this one get away. For three years he had treated her with the utmost respect and dignity; he regularly exercised his wit and humor to entertain her and he spent a lot of money on her. Consequently, he made the young woman forget all the sorrows that she had endured after she'd gone along the path to her unhappy marriage.

Since they shared more or less the same fate they consoled each other and confirmed a great truth which, unfortunately, reforms no one: that there are so many unhappy marriages and consequently so much misfortune in the world because miserly or stupid parents marry their offspring into fortunes rather than into happiness.

— It is quite obvious, Raneville often said to his mistress, that if fate had united the two of us instead of giving you a ridiculous tyrant of a husband and giving me a whore for a wife, then roses would have sprung up under our feet instead of the thorns that we have had to endure.

One day, an event that was far too inconsequential to be mentioned led Monsieur de Raneville to the filthy and corrupt city named Versailles. Versailles was where kings, who were meant to be revered in their capitals, fled to in order to avoid the presence of their subjects, many of whom desired them to be permanently available for an audience. Versailles was also where ambition, avarice, revenge, & pride daily brought together a crowd of unfortunate people who flew there on the wings of boredom in order to make their sacrifice to the idol of the day. Versailles was where the elite of the French nobility, who could have played a far more important role by staying on their estates, had instead consented to humiliate themselves in antechambers by groveling to lowly door-keepers and humbly begging for dinners that were inferior to the ones they could have had at home. Some of those individuals were ones whom fortune had raised briefly from the mists of obscurity only to plunge them back into it shortly afterwards.

His business concluded, Monsieur de Raneville climbed into one of those court carriages known as a *pot-de-chambre* and by chance found himself seated next to a certain Monsieur Dutour, a very talkative, very fat, very dull-witted, and very self-righteous man, employed, like Monsieur de Raneville, in the Orléans department of tax collection; Orléans being his home town, just as it had, as we have already stated, once been the home town of Monsieur de Raneville.

They began a conversation, and Raneville, as laconic as always, gave nothing away about himself, but quickly got to learn his fellow traveler's first name, surname, place of birth, and job, without having said a single word about himself.

Having told his travelling companion those details, Monsieur Dutour expounded a little more on matters of society.

— You have been to Orléans before, Monsieur, said Dutour. I believe that you told me so earlier.

— I lived there for a few months a long time ago.

— Then let me ask you: have you ever met a Madame de Raneville, one of the most skilled and versatile prostitutes to have ever lived in Orléans?

— This Madame de Raneville, is she a very pretty woman?

— Yes, that's the one.

— Yes, I think I've met her socially.

— Well, I can tell you in confidence, I've had her multiple times. In every way, over three days. We did everything. If ever there was a cuckolded husband, I think it's fair to say that this poor Raneville is one.

— Do you know him?

— Not personally, but I've heard he's a bad sort, ruining himself in Paris by partying with whores and others who are just as debauched as he is.

— I can't tell you anything about him, I've never met him, but I feel pity for any cuckolded husband. You're not one yourself, are you?

— Which of the two do you mean, a cuckold or a husband?

— I mean both, of course. These days, the two are so closely linked that it is really almost impossible to tell the difference between them.

— I am a married man, Monsieur. I had the misfortune to marry a woman who never made any attempt to accept my ways. I never really cared that much for her character, either. We separated amicably enough. She decided to move to Paris to share her solitude with one of her relatives, a nun, at the convent of Sainte-Aure. She lives in the convent and from time to time she writes to me to tell me her news, such as it is, but I don't see her.

— Is she very devout?

— No. Perhaps I'd like her better if she were.

— Ah! I see. And even though your business is causing you to stay for a while in Paris, have you never been curious enough to enquire after her health?

— No. To tell you the truth, I don't really like convents. They're dark, depressing places. I enjoy pleasure and excitement. It suits my temperament. Socially, I'm in demand. I have no intention of rushing off to some airless convent parlor and risking having to put up with my lady's gamut of moods, upsets, and agitations for the next six months at least, probably longer.

— But a woman...

— ... is simply an individual who interests us while we have a use for her, but from whom we must be ready to detach ourselves quickly and firmly when serious reasons start to put distance between us.

— What you're saying is incredibly harsh.

— Not at all… it's philosophically realistic. It's the attitude of today. It's the language of reason. One must either adopt it or be labeled a fool.

— But that implies some fault on the part of your wife. Please explain this to me: do you mean a defect of nature, a shirking of responsibilities, or poor conduct?

— A little of each of those… a little of each, Monsieur. However, let's drop this particular subject, please, & return to the delightful Madame de Raneville. By God, I simply cannot understand how you were in Orléans yet never amused yourself with that promiscuous creature… Everyone has her.

— Not everyone has, no, for, as you now know, I never did. I don't care for sport with married women.

— Please excuse my curiosity, Monsieur, but with whom do you spend your time?

— My business associates mostly, and then a pretty creature with whom I dine from time to time.

— You're not married, Monsieur?

— I am.

— And your wife?

— She lives in the provinces, which is where I leave her, just as you leave yours in Sainte-Aure.

— Married, Monsieur. You're married. And are you one of the horned brotherhood? Please tell me.

— Did I not say that husband *&* cuckold are synony-
mous? The current era's moral depravity, an uninformed
taste for luxury… there are so many things to bring about
a woman's downfall.

— That, Monsieur, is true. Very true.

— You answer like a man who has experience of such
a situation.

— Not at all, Monsieur. Am I to understand that it's
a very pretty woman who consoles you for the absence
of a neglectful, and neglected, wife?

— Yes. I can honestly say she's a very pretty woman.
In fact, I'd like you to meet her.

— Monsieur, that would be a great honor for me.

— Oh, please. Let's have less of the formality, shall
we? We're both men of the world. I'll leave you free this
evening because you have business matters to take care
of, but I'm inviting you to supper tomorrow evening,
when I'll introduce you to the beautiful woman. I'll be
at the address written on here.

Raneville very carefully wrote a false name and his
real home address on a blank card and handed it to
Monsieur Dutour. When he got home, he alerted his
staff to the false name he had used and instructed them
to show in to him anyone who arrived asking for him
by that name.

The next day Monsieur Dutour arrived punctually,
as had been arranged. Raneville was at home. Monsieur
Dutour asked for him by the false name written on the
card, and he was duly admitted *&* taken to Raneville.

Once the introductions were made, it was easy to see that Dutour was disconcerted by not having so much as a glimpse of the beautiful woman.

— You're an impatient man, Raneville chided. I can see what you're looking for, even from here. You've been promised a pretty woman, and you'd love to have your eyes — and probably a lot more — alight on her. You're accustomed to deceiving the husbands of Orléans, and I'm sure you'd enjoy treating the husbands of Paris in the same way. I'll wager that you'd be more than happy to demote me to the same rank as the unfortunate Monsieur de Raneville, of whom we spoke yesterday.

Dutour responded just as a man who was an inveterate womanizer would respond; that is, arrogantly and foolishly. Consequently, the conversation brightened for a moment and Raneville, after taking his guest by the sleeve, said:

— Come with me to the temple in which the beautiful goddess is waiting for you.

Having spoken, he then led Dutour into a sumptuously-furnished boudoir, in which Raneville's mistress, having been briefed as to the deception and eager to take part in it, was reclining wantonly on a velvet ottoman, naked except for several strategically-placed muslin veils, none of which hid the sheer grace and beauty of her body. One of the veils obscured her face.

— What an absolutely beautiful woman, Dutour said, in admiration. But why deprive me of the pleasure of admiring her face? Are we in the harem of some foreign prince?

— No, but keep your voice down, please. It's a matter of protecting her modesty.

— Her modesty?

— Of course.

— Surely you don't think I want to confine myself to showing you only my mistress's veiled body, do you? My triumph must be complete and the only way that it can be is if I remove all those veils, thereby convincing you of how happy I am to have sole access to this beautiful woman's charms. However, this young woman is incredibly modest, & she would be utterly embarrassed by my actions if her face were to be uncovered. So, she has consented to this solely on the understanding that her face remains veiled the entire time the rest of her body is being unveiled to you. You know what women are like when it comes to modesty & decorum? Monsieur Dutour, you're a man of taste and fashion, so surely this woman's modesty will not halt the proceedings, will it?

— Not at all. But what precisely is it you're going to let me look at?

— Everything, as I have told you. No one has less jealousy in him than me. The happiness that one tastes alone seems tasteless to me, I find delight only in pleasures that are shared.

And in order to convince his guest of the truth of his word, Raneville removed one of the veils, thereby revealing the most beautiful pair of breasts imaginable.

Dutour grew visibly excited.

— Well, Raneville prompted. What is your opinion?

— These are the breasts of Venus herself.

— Believe me, such white and firm breasts are made to inflame desire. Go ahead, touch them, my friend. See how they feel. Sometimes our eyes deceive us. My view is that when it comes to pleasure, we must use all the senses.

Dutour approached the woman and reached out, his hands trembling. He ecstatically fondled the exquisite breasts, unable to fully believe the generosity of his host.

— Let's look further down, said Raneville, raising the next veil to the woman's waist and slowly parting her thighs, thereby giving his guest an unobstructed view of the woman's most intimate charms.

— Well, what do you have to say about these parted thighs? Have you ever seen such perfect alabaster columns supporting such a beautiful temple of love?

And the good Monsieur Dutour ran feverish hands over the alabaster columns that Raneville had described.

— I can read your mind, you lecherous rogue, the complacent host continued. Look at this delicate temple that the Graces themselves have covered with the wispiest down… You're burning with desire to spread those portals, aren't you? And I'd wager you'd like nothing more than to kiss it, wouldn't you?

And Dutour, overwhelmed and reduced to stammering incoherently, was able to reply with actions only. Everything he saw fed his senses. He trembled violently as Raneville offered further encouragement. Dutour's libertine fingers caressed the portico of the temple that voluptuously opened in response to his touch. He leaned forward to bestow the kiss he had been granted. He planted and savored the kiss for a long time.

— My friend, he said finally, reluctantly ending the kiss. I can stand this no more! Either throw me out of your house, or permit me to go further.

— What do you mean, go further? Where on earth do you want to go?

— Oh, you don't understand my meaning. I mean that I am so aroused that I can no longer restrain myself.

— I see. But what if you find this woman to be ugly?

— It is impossible for a woman with such perfect attributes to be ugly.

— But if she is…?

— Let her be whatever she is. I tell you sincerely, I can no longer control myself.

— In that case, my hot-blooded friend, you must satisfy your desires. Take your pleasure. But before you do, I want you to acknowledge your gratitude for my generosity and my kindness to you.

— I do acknowledge it. Without a doubt.

And having spoken, Dutour began to gently push his host away, as though intimating that Raneville should leave him alone with the woman.

— Oh, no! said Raneville. I'm not going to leave. I promised I would not. But tell me, are you so scrupulous that you will be unable to achieve satisfaction if I remain here? Between men like us, surely such niceties are of no consequence. Besides, these are my conditions; either with me present, or not at all.

— I'd do it in front of the Devil himself, said Dutour, unable to contain himself any longer, and making a lunge for the sanctuary where his incense was to be burned. But as they're your conditions, I consent to everything...

— But, said Raneville phlegmatically, have appearances deceived you? Are the sensual delights that are promised by so many charms illusory or real? Ah! I never saw anything so erotic.

— Oh, but this damned veil, my friend. Might I be allowed to remove it?

— Yes, but only at the very last moment; only during that delectable moment when all your senses are seduced by the rapture of the gods; in the instant that a woman makes a man feel like a god, and often far more powerful than any of them. The surprise of it will double your ecstasy: to the delight of enjoying the body of Venus herself, you will add the inexpressible joy of contemplating the face of Flora, with everything coming together to increase your pleasure. You will plunge more deeply into an ocean of erotic pleasure that for a man is consolation for his existence. When you signal that moment to me, I'll remove the veil...

— Oh! I'll signal, Dutour gasped. I'm nearly at that point now...

— Yes, so I see, said Raneville, taking hold of the veil.

— Oh, my friend, the heavenly moment approaches now. Go on. Remove the veil. Take it off. Let me look on the very vision of heaven.

— There you are, said Raneville, quickly pulling off the veil. But take care you don't find your heaven is perhaps a little too close to your hell.

— Oh, good God! Dutour exclaimed, immediately recognizing his wife. What's this… *You*, Madame. What's this, Monsieur, some sort of bizarre joke? You deserve to be… *Not this whore!*

— Now just a minute, you hypocrite. You deserve everything that's happened to you and you know it. Listen and learn, my friend. You need to be a little more circumspect with people you do not know, far more than you were yesterday with me. The unfortunate Raneville, whom you admitted you treated so badly in Orléans, well, Monsieur, that's me. I'm Raneville. I am returning your wrongdoing to you in Paris. Besides, you are much more successful than you thought; you imagined that you were going to make me into a cuckold, when, in fact, you have just made yourself into one.

To his credit, Dutour accepted the reprimand and understood the lesson. He and his host shook hands, as though sealing an agreement. Dutour admitted that he had only got what he deserved.

— But as for this treacherous whore…

— Doesn't she simply do as you do? What barbaric law constrains her sex with inhuman chains, while granting us men total freedom? Is that a fair law? By what right do you shun your wife and make cuckolds of the husbands of Paris and Orléans? My friend, this is clearly neither equitable nor just. This charming woman, whose worth you have never known nor appreciated, came here to seek other conquests. She was absolutely right to do so. She found me and I make her very happy. You may try and do the same for Madame de Raneville; I give my consent. Let the four of us live happily, & let's not allow the victims of fate to become the victims of men also.

Dutour could see that Raneville was absolutely right, but inconceivably, although possibly inevitably, he fell madly in love with his wife all over again. Raneville, even as caustic as he was, had a soul too noble to resist Dutour's pleas to be reunited with his wife. The young woman consented, and in this unique situation, we no doubt have a very singular example of the unpredictability of fate and of the vagaries of love.

Room for Two [53]

There was a very attractive woman about town who lived on the Rue St. Honoré and was aged about twenty-two. Her body was extremely fresh and appetizing and well-formed, although some may have said it was somewhat full in its contours, or perhaps tending to voluptuousness. She was also intelligent, witty, and vivacious with a healthy taste for many of the pleasures that were denied her by the conventions of marriage.

To this end, the demanding woman, named Dolmène, had recruited two young men to supplement the unpleasant, unskillful, and increasingly rare attempts to satisfy her by her ugly and old husband, who, if he had attempted to develop his skills might have provided his wife with a modicum of satisfaction and made her alternative arrangements unnecessary.

Nothing was better arranged than the daily appointments she had made with her two lovers. Des-Roues, a young, energetic soldier, spent the time between three-thirty and five in the afternoon with her, and Dolbreuse, an incredibly handsome young businessman, spent the time between five-thirty and seven with her. Other times were impossible to arrange, as Madame Dolmène had matters relating to the shop she owned to attend to in the morning — and sometimes in the evenings too. At other times her husband was at home with her and he insisted she sit and listen to his tales of high finance.

Moreover, Madame Dolmène had confided in one of her female friends that she was very partial to having the second bout of pleasure follow the first one in very close succession, so that the fires of pleasure remained stoked high and did not die down. In fact, she maintained that there was nothing so delightful as to go directly from one pleasure to the other, as one did not have to exert oneself to get under way again; one was already at the peak of one's appreciation.

Madame Dolmène was a charming creature who had worked out how to achieve all of the pleasures and sensations of love; very few women had studied the subject as much as she had, and it was due to her considerable talents that she was able to acknowledge, without any hesitation, that having two lovers was far better than having only one. She felt the same regarding her reputation; one protected the other; people could be mistaken, it could be the same man, a servant, who came and went several times during the day. As far as pleasure was concerned, what a difference it made!

One of Madame Dolmène's major concerns was pregnancy. She had arranged things in such a way as to guarantee that her husband never made the mistake of ruining her figure, just as she calculated that having two lovers created less risk regarding what she feared with one; namely that, thinking the way a good anatomist would think, two competing seeds of love would mutually destroy one another.

On one particular day, the smooth transition between appointments was upset and the two lovers, neither of which was aware of the other, became acquainted, as we shall see, under curious and amusing circumstances. Des-Roues had arrived first, as was his custom, but he had been late and had delayed his leaving because of it. Dolbreuse, who was second, had arrived far too early.

The intelligent reader will immediately deduce that these two normally insignificant mistakes led to the inevitable encounter that did indeed take place. I will now describe how this occurred and, if I can, I will tell it deploying all of the decency and restraint demanded by such events, events which are already very licentious in themselves.

Due to a series of decisions and coincidences, of which one can find many taking place amongst humanity, the young soldier was growing weary and offered to lie on the bed in a more passive position than was usual for him. Madame concurred and instead of being held in her lover's arms, she waited until he had positioned himself with his prized part proudly pointing upwards, then she, her back to the bedchamber door, moved above him until she found the optimum position, after which she lowered herself onto the object of desire in a manner that suggested a sacrifice taking place on an altar.

Madame Dolmène was as naked as the statue known as the Callipygian Venus, and the particular part of the body for which that statue is worshipped with devotion by the Greeks, the part of female anatomy which is particularly admired in Paris, and which all men find beautiful, was facing the door of the bedchamber where the rites were being performed.

Such was her position when Dolbreuse, accustomed to entering the house freely, arrived, humming a cheerful tune. Opening the bedchamber door, he was greeted with the sight of that particular part of the lovely lady's anatomy moving in delightful circles.

The sight, which would have delighted most, caused Dolbreuse to take a step back.

— What is this I see? he demanded angrily. You traitress! Is this the "place" you've reserved for me?

Madame Dolmène was, at that moment, experiencing the type of crisis during which a woman acts infinitely better than she reasons. Because of this, her response was as audacious as her lover's pretended hurt feelings.

— What's the matter with you? she demanded of her second lover, as she continued to derive pleasure from her other lover. I've given you a view to admire. Are you upset by it? If so, leave us. If not, then don't pretend you are. Instead, take your place in the place reserved for you. I'm sure you can see there's room for two.

Dolbreuse couldn't help but admire his mistress' sangfroid and, having come to the conclusion that the most sensible thing was to follow her advice, he disrobed and joined his mistress and her lover on the bed.

So successful was Madame Dolmène's impromptu innovation that the three of them continued to enjoy themselves in that particular way for a very long time.

The Punished Husband

A man who was already middle-aged decided to get married, even though he had lived without a wife until then. What he did that was perhaps most foolish, especially in view of his predilections, was to marry an eighteen-year-old girl, blessed with the most gorgeous body and the most beautiful face in the entire world. Monsieur de Bernac was this husband's name, and he compounded his foolishness by taking a wife, when he himself had no interest in the many erotic pleasures that the hymen can, on a loving and devoted wife, give a man. His tastes ran to other obsessions; obsessions he had substituted for the chaste and delicate pleasures of the conjugal knot, and which were far from the desires of a sensual young woman like Mademoiselle de Lurcie, the unfortunate woman whom Bernac had just linked to his own fate.

The first night of the wedding, after having made his young wife swear not to reveal anything to her parents, he declared his tastes to her. His pleasure was in administering, as Montesquieu famously says, "the most humiliating of chastisements that takes one back to one's childhood." His young wife was to assume the posture and attitude of a little girl who deserves punishment. She was to avail herself for fifteen or twenty minutes, more or less, to the brutish whims of her older husband, and it was in the illusion created by this scene that he managed to taste that delicious delirium of pleasure that any man with less unconventional desires would certainly have experienced only in delightful and passionate embrace of Mademoiselle de Lurcie.

The procedure seemed extremely harsh to the sensitive, pretty girl, brought up in comfortable circumstances and far removed from pedantry. However, since she had been instructed to be submissive, she believed that all husbands behaved as hers did; it is quite possible that Bernac encouraged her to believe it to be so, and so she gave herself in the sincerest and most devoted way she could to the depravity of her satyr-like husband; it was the same every day and often twice rather than once.

After two years, Mademoiselle de Lurcie, whom we shall continue to call by this name, since she was still as virginal as on her wedding day, lost her father and her mother, and with them any hope of their providing help to ease her suffering, which was something she had been pinning her hopes on for some time.

Her loss only made Bernac more enterprising, and although he had shown a degree of self-restraint during the lifetime of his wife's parents, as soon she lost them and she was unable to implore anyone to assist or avenge her, he lost every shred of self-control.

What at first seemed to be nothing more than a harmless joke gradually became real torment; Mademoiselle de Lurcie could not bear it; she grew embittered and thought only of revenge. She saw very few people, as her husband isolated her as much as possible. However, her cousin, the Chevalier d'Aldour, despite all of Bernac's efforts to keep him at a distance, had not ceased calling to see his relative.

The Chevalier was a very handsome young man, and it was not without some purpose that he persisted in regularly visiting his cousin; as he was very well-regarded in society, the jealous husband, afraid of how he would be perceived if he showed any hostility toward the young man, did not dare turn him away from the house too often...

Finally, Mademoiselle de Lurcie decided to confide in this particular relative and to plead with him to liberate her from the slavery in which she lived. After she had become used to his regular visits and appreciated his careful, thoughtful way of speaking, she finally opened up to him and confessed everything.

— Avenge me on this man, she said to him, and avenge me in a way that is so powerful that he would never dare divulge it. The day when you succeed in this will be the day of your triumph. I shall be yours only at this price.

D'Aldour was enraged by his cousin's treatment at the hands of her tyrannical husband, but delighted to be invited to avenge her. He promised to do everything he could to liberate her. He then spent the next few days concentrating on a plan that would succeed, and ensure him some very pleasurable moments with a beautiful woman. When his preparations were complete, he went to Bernac.

— Monsieur, he said to him one morning. As I have the honor of being so closely related to you, and since I have complete confidence in your discretion, I must tell you of a secret marriage that I have just been contracted to.

— A secret marriage, said Bernac, delighted to be rid of the rival who he feared.

— Yes, Monsieur. I have just united myself to a very charming woman & tomorrow she is going to make me a very happy man by becoming my wife. It's true she's a woman with no property, but what do such things matter to me? I have enough for both of us. I will be marrying, it's true, a whole family, as there are four sisters all living together, but their company is very enjoyable so it's all the more happiness for me… I really hope, Monsieur, the young Chevalier continued, that you and my cousin will do me the honor tomorrow of coming to the wedding breakfast.

— Monsieur, I go out very little and my wife even less. We both live a life of quiet seclusion. She likes it. I do not place any restrictions on her in any way.

— I know your tastes, Monsieur, d'Aldour replied. I can guarantee that everything will be exactly to your taste… I love solitude as much as you do. I also wish to keep this marriage ceremony a private affair; a secret for now, as I have already told you. It is in the countryside, the weather is fine, no one else is invited, and I give you my word of honor that we will be absolutely alone.

Mademoiselle de Lurcie in fact hinted that she desired to attend her cousin's wedding breakfast and her husband did not care to refuse her request in front of d'Aldour, and so the wedding party was arranged.

— Why must you insist on attending such a thing? Bernac complained, as soon as he was alone with his wife. You know very well that I don't care for any of this. I will forbid all similar outings in the future. And I warn you now that, in due course, I intend to send you to one of my remotest estates, where you will never see anyone but me.

His threat, whether real or not, had the desired effect. Mademoiselle de Lurcie became docile & submissive to her husband. She lowered her head in a way he enjoyed. His ardor increased.

— Do as you please, Monsieur, his wife said, humbly. You have granted my request. I owe you my sincere gratitude.

He seized the opportunity and made Mademoiselle de Lurcie go into the bedchamber and assume her position, ready for him.

— We will go to the damned wedding, he said, as he entered the room. Yes, I promised it, but you will now pay dearly for your desire to attend…

The poor, unfortunate woman, believing herself to be very near to the end of her slavery, tolerated everything her husband did to her without complaint.

Such sweetness & such resignation would have disarmed anyone else, but not the libertine Bernac. His heart was full of vice, so nothing stopped him. He took his pleasure and then they went quietly to bed.

The next day d'Aldour, as had been agreed, came in his carriage to pick up husband and wife and convey them to the place where the wedding was to be celebrated.

— You see, Mademoiselle de Lurcie's young cousin said as he led the husband and wife into an extremely isolated house, you see that this does not look too much like a public celebration. No carriages, no servants. As I told you, we are absolutely alone.

At this point, four women all aged about thirty; all strong, vigorous, and nearly six feet tall, came up the steps to welcome Monsieur and Madame de Bernac.

— This is my wife, Monsieur, d'Aldour said, drawing one of the women forward and introducing her to Bernac and Mademoiselle de Lurcie. And these other three women are her sisters. We were married early this morning in Paris, and we are waiting for you so that we may celebrate with the nuptial breakfast. Will you please join us?

Everything proceeded with mutual politeness all round. After relaxing with refreshments in the drawing-room, Bernac convinced himself to his great satisfaction that he was as alone as he could have wished.

The commencement of the wedding breakfast was announced & everyone adjourned to the dining room and sat at the table. It was a cheerful, happy repast.

The four so-called sisters, each accustomed to sharing witticisms, brought a liveliness and spontaneous joy to the table that could not help but affect the other diners accordingly. Decorum was not neglected for an instant and Bernac, thoroughly deceived, believed himself to be in the best company in the world.

Mademoiselle de Lurcie, for her part, was delighted to watch her tyrant of a husband as he fell into the carefully-designed trap. She laughed with her husband and silently decided to reject her imposed celibacy, for it had so far brought her nothing but sorrow and tears. Hiding her true feelings, she quaffed champagne with him and overwhelmed him with many tender glances.

The four women, who would need all of their strength very soon, ate well but drank sparingly, although each gave a very credible impression of drinking liberally. They also made Bernac the focus of their attention.

Bernac, enjoying himself immensely, still suspecting only simple pleasures in such circumstances, did not abstain from drinking any more than any of the others in the party. But as it was necessary for a few of them to keep a reign on their reason, d'Aldour interrupted the proceedings after a while and invited them all to have coffee.

Once the coffee was finished, the Chevalier said to Bernac:

— And now, my honored guest, could I prevail upon you to come and see my house? You're a man of impeccable taste. I bought it and furnished it on the occasion of my marriage, but I fear that I have made a mistake regarding its value. Would you have a look at it and give me your opinion, please?

— Willingly, said Bernac. No one understands these matters the way I do. I'll estimate its value to the nearest ten louis.

D'Aldour took his pretty cousin's hand and led her to a staircase. They descended together. Bernac followed them and, as he walked along, he found himself surrounded by the four sisters. It was in that formation that they entered a very dark and very isolated apartment, right at the far end of the house.

— This is the bridal chamber, d'Aldour said to the jealous older man. Do you see this bed? This is where the bride will cease to be a virgin. Isn't it time that this happened? After all, she's been languishing as a virgin for such a long *time!*

The last word uttered by the Chevalier was his signal: as soon as he uttered it, the four women took hold of Bernac and pinned him to the floor. He struggled, but they were far too strong and easily held him in place. One of the women went to a bundle of birch rods and selected four of them. She gave one to each woman and kept one for herself. The women then stripped Bernac & in turn beat him mercilessly with the birches. He screeched, he howled, he tried, to no avail, to break free but the women worked in pairs; two holding him down as the other two thrashed him.

At a signal from d'Aldour, the beating was halted.

— My dear Bernac, the Chevalier said, I told you yesterday everything would be exactly to your taste. I couldn't think of a better way to please you than to let you experience what you make this charming wife of yours experience every day. I trust you are not barbaric enough to do anything to her that you would not enjoy being done to you, so I feel I can congratulate myself on the way I have organized this method of you receiving so much pleasure. However, there is one aspect of this ceremony that needs to be addressed, namely, your wife, my cousin. She is still, it is claimed, as virginal as the day she met you, although she has been with you for such a long time. It's as if you had only married yesterday; such neglect on your part can only be due to ignorance. I am willing to wager you don't know how to go about it, my friend, so I will now demonstrate the correct method.

And having spoken, the cousins undressed and got on the bed in plain sight of Bernac. D'Aldour positioned himself between Mademoiselle de Lurcie's smooth thighs. He thrust his prodigious member into the willing and eager bride, making her a woman in front of her unworthy husband. The four women commenced beating Bernac again, timing their strokes to coincide with d'Aldour's thrusts. When the couple reached their joyful, noisy, ecstatic conclusion, the ceremony ceased. D'Aldour withdrew and descended from the altar.

— Monsieur, you will no doubt find the lesson a little harsh, but the outrage needed to be more powerful than your own. I am not, nor do I want to be, your wife's lover. So, here she is. I am returning her to you, but I advise you in the future to behave in a more gentle and thoughtful manner with her; otherwise you will find I am a far less merciful avenger should there be a second time.

— Madame, said Bernac, furiously. This whole situation…

— … Is one you very much deserved, Mademoiselle de Lurcie replied. But if you don't like it, you are perfectly at liberty, as is each of us, to let everyone in society know about it. If we each explain our reasons for what has happened here and why it happened, we will soon see which of us becomes the capital's laughing stock.

Deeply ashamed and embarrassed by the truth she spoke, Bernac acknowledged his faults. He no longer tried to find excuses for his cruelty. He threw himself at his wife's feet and begged her to forgive him. Mademoiselle de Lurcie, by nature a sweet and generous woman, held out her hand and helped her husband to his feet. She embraced him and kissed him passionately, and then the two of them returned to their home.

I do not know how Bernac managed it but from that moment on, Paris never saw a more intimate household, nor a married couple as tender, as loving, or as virtuous.

The Husband Who Said Mass, A Provençal Tale

Between the town of Menerbe in the Avignon region and Apt in Provence there is a small, isolated Carmelite monastery called Saint-Hilaire, sitting on the side of a hill so arid that even goats have trouble grazing on it. This modest building is more or less a dumping-ground for all the neighboring Carmelite communities, each one relegating to it those Brothers who have brought shame or dishonor to the order. From this, it is easy to judge the notoriety of the society in such a dwelling: drunkards, lechers, sodomites, gamblers, such is more or less the noble company that are housed there, recluses who in this depraved asylum, offer to God, as best they can, hearts that the world no longer wants.

The town of Menerbe was only a league from Saint-Hilaire, & there were one or two châteaux visible from the monastery's highest tower. However, the monks of Saint-Hilaire, despite their cassocks & their religious calling, were nevertheless far from finding all the doors of the region open to them.

For quite a while Father Gabriel, one of the saints of this hermitage, had coveted a certain woman of Menerbe, whose husband, Monsieur Rodin, was one of life's natural cuckolds if ever there was one.

Madame Rodin was twenty-eight years old, petite, brunette, with a wandering eye and a round bottom. She was also the kind of woman who had every intention of letting her body be used as a delicious treat for a monk.

As for Monsieur Rodin, he was a good man, tending to his business & his property without saying much: he had once sold cloth, he had once been a viguier,[54] so he was considered by the majority to be an honest citizen.

Not totally sure of the faithfulness of his other half, he was nevertheless philosophical enough to realize that the best way to negate the rapid sprouting of cuckold's horns was to give the impression of not suspecting that he had sprouted any at all. He had studied for the priesthood, he spoke Latin better than Cicero, and very often played the draughts with Father Gabriel, who, as a skillful and consummate womanizer, knew that one must always flatter the husband a little if one wants to seduce his wife.

Among the sons of Elijah, Father Gabriel was an absolute stallion. One only had to look at him to see that the entire human race could confidently rely on him for its propagation. He was a child-maker if ever there was one: wide shoulders, a back as broad as a table-top, a dark, swarthy face, a brow like Jupiter, six feet tall and (which characterizes many Carmelites) as well-endowed, it was said, as the finest prize-winning mule in the region.

What woman could resist being drawn to such a lusty specimen?

So, unsurprisingly, he was considered to be both appealing and attractive to Madame Rodin, who was unable to find such sublime faculties in the good man that her parents had chosen for her as a husband. Monsieur Rodin appeared to close his eyes to everything, as we have said, but this does not mean that he was not a jealous man. He said nothing, but he was always there, and he stayed there at times when others would have liked him to have been far away; the fruit was ripe for plucking.

The naïve Madame Rodin had once quite brazenly declared to her would-be-lover that she was only waiting for the opportunity to respond to desires that seemed much too ardent to her to resist any longer, and on his side Father Gabriel had made sure that Madame Rodin was in no doubt that he was fully ready & very eager to satisfy her... During a very brief moment when Monsieur Rodin had been obliged to go out, Gabriel had even shown his delectable mistress-to-be his impressive credentials; credentials calculated to persuade any woman who perhaps had a residual inclination to hesitate... And all that then remained necessary was an opportunity.

One day, Monsieur Rodin called on his friend at Saint-Hilaire and invited him to dinner, with the idea of suggesting the two of them go hunting together. After having emptied a couple of bottles of Lanerte wine, Father Gabriel realized that circumstances were at that moment fully conducive to him fulfilling his desires.

— Oh, God, Monsieur Viguier, said the monk to his friend. I am really pleased to see you today. You've come to see me at a most opportune time. I have a matter of the greatest importance to attend to and you can be of the utmost help in the matter.

— What is it, Father?

— Do you know a man in town named Renoult?

— Renoult the hat-maker?

— That's the man.

— What of him?

— Well, the man's a rogue; a rogue who owes me a hundred écus and I have just learned that he's on the verge of bankruptcy. Perhaps, as I sit here talking to you, he is already making his way across the border... I absolutely have to go there right now, but I can't.

— What's stopping you?

— My Mass, for God's sake, I have to say my Mass. If I had the hundred écus in my pocket, the Mass could go to hell.

— Can't you be excused?

— Excused! If only I could be! There are three of us here who are responsible for the Mass and if we don't each deliver it daily as we're supposed to, one in the morning, one in the afternoon, and one (me) in the evening, then the Superior, who somehow never seems to deliver any Masses at all, would report us to Rome. But there is a way you can help me, my dear friend. Should I tell you how, so you can decide if you want to or not?

— Certainly, I'll help. What's on your mind?

— I'm alone here with the sexton; the first two Masses have been said, and all of our monks are already out and about, preaching, assisting, and so on. No one would ever know. The congregation will be tiny, no more than one or two peasants, and possibly that very devout lady who lives in Château Le — about half a league from here. She's an angelic creature who imagines that her austere observances will somehow be reparation for the promiscuity of her philandering husband. I believe you once mentioned you studied to be a priest.

— That's right.

— Which means you must have learned how to say Mass.

— I can say Mass like an archbishop.

— My dear old friend, Gabriel continued, throwing his arms around Rodin's neck, then for God's sake, put my cassock on, wait until it strikes eleven o'clock — it's ten now — and when it does, say my Mass for me, please. The Brother who's the sexton is a decent sort; he'll never betray us. If any of the congregation say they didn't think it was me, we'll just say it was a new Brother who'd just arrived. As for the others, they don't need to be told anything. While you do that, I'll dash round and catch that swindler Renoult, and either get my money back or make him wish he were dead. Either way, I'll be back here within two hours. So, wait for me, grill the sole, poach the eggs, uncork the wine. When I return we'll have dinner, and then we'll go hunting. Yes, my friend, hunting, and I think it'll be good hunting this time. We've heard reports that there's a creature with antlers in this vicinity, and I certainly want my chance to bring it down, even if means we end up with twenty summonses from the lord of the manor!

— Your plan is good, said Rodin. And as for doing you that favor, there's nothing I wouldn't do to help. But tell me, if I do say Mass for you, isn't it a sin?

— Sin isn't the right word in this case. It might, possibly, have been a sin if the Mass was said carelessly or incorrectly, but even that's doubtful as novices often fluff their lines and they're not consigned to hell because of that. If someone who is not ordained says Mass, then everything that is said means nothing, because it's as though nothing has been said at all. Believe me, I am a casuist, and there's nothing in this procedure that might be called a venial sin.

— But is it necessary for me to say the words?

— And why not? These words have power only if they are uttered by the ordained. You see, my friend, I only have to say those words over your wife's belly in order to transform the temple where you perform your sacrifice into the body of Christ. No, my dear friend, only we have the power of transubstantiation. You could utter the words twenty thousand times and the words that you uttered would never cause the Holy Ghost to descend. And even with us the ritual doesn't always work. Faith is everything. With a grain of faith we can move mountains, you know, Jesus Christ Himself said that, but he who has no faith can move nothing... Take me, for example. Sometimes during Mass, I'm thinking more about the girls or the women in the congregation rather than that damned piece of bread I'm about to break & distribute. Do you think that I have the power to make anything descend then? I would rather believe in the Koran than believe something like that. It means that your Mass will therefore be almost as valid as mine. Therefore, my dear friend, be resolute, and above all, good luck.

— By God, Rodin exclaimed. I have an all-consuming appetite, and there's another two hours before dinner!

— What's to prevent you from eating something while you're waiting for me? Help yourself.

— And what about fasting before the Mass that I have to deliver?

— By Heavens, what difference does it make? Do you think God is more defiled if He ends up in a full stomach rather than in an empty stomach, or that it matters if the food is on top of Him or underneath Him? I'll be damned if I can see any difference. Listen, my dear friend, if I had to report to Rome and confess every time I had lunch before saying Mass, I would spend my entire life on the road. Anyway, you're not a priest, so our rules don't apply to you. You'll only be giving the ritual the appearance of being a Mass; you won't be delivering an actual Mass. Therefore you can do whatever you want before or after.

You could even pleasure your wife if she were there. It's simply a matter of doing exactly as I would do; it's not a question of celebrating Mass, nor of consummating the sacrifice.

— Very well, said Rodin, I'll do it. Don't worry.

— Good, said Gabriel. He quickly introduced his friend to the sexton and explained his role in the upcoming Mass.

— You can rely on me, Rodin said.

— In that case, I'll be back in two hours, the overjoyed priest said, before hurrying away.

One can easily imagine how quickly he got to the viguier's wife's house. Surprised to see him, as she thought he was her husband, she asked him the reason for his unexpected visit.

— Let's be quick, my dear, said the breathless monk. Let's be quick as we have only a few moments to ourselves. Let's have a glass of wine and then let's go to bed.

— But my husband?

— He's saying Mass.

— He's saying Mass?

— Yes, by God, saying Mass, my sweet, the Carmelite replied, as he led Madame Rodin to her bed. Yes, you precious soul, I have made a priest of your husband and while the fool celebrates a divine mystery, let us consummate our secular desire...

The monk was incredibly vigorous, and he was difficult to resist, particularly once the woman was pinned, squirming and moaning beneath him. He demonstrated his case so conclusively that he soon fully persuaded Madame Rodin of his abilities, and as he was more than happy to continue convincing the playful twenty-eight-year-old with the Provençal temperament, he repeated his demonstration more than once.

— Oh, you're a real angel, said the lovely woman, by now perfectly convinced. Look how the time has passed. We must part. If our pleasures are to last only as long as it takes to say Mass, then he must be saying *Ite, missa est* right now.

— Not at all, my sweet, said the Carmelite, who had one further argument to put to Madame Rodin. We still have lots of time, so once more, my dear, once more. Novices don't rush through Mass as we do, believe me, so we've time to indulge one more time. I'm happy to wager that he has not yet got to the blessing of the bread.

However, time was short and they had to part, although not before they had promised each other they would see each other again, and had outlined several strategies for doing so.

And then Gabriel went and found Rodin, who claimed he had said Mass better than any Archbishop.

— I only embarrassed myself at one point, he said. It was when I got to the *quod aures*. I started with the bread, not the wine, but the sexton put me right. Did you get you hundred écus, Father?

— I have them, my son. At first, the fool refused to pay me, so I grabbed a pitchfork and, although he put up a fight, I knocked him around the head and body with it until he paid up.

Once they had eaten, the two men went hunting. When he got home, Rodin told his wife about the help he had given Father Gabriel.

— I celebrated Mass, the cuckold announced, laughing happily. Yes, that's right. I performed Mass like a real parish priest, while our friend went and got his money back from Renoult... He said he found a pitchfork and used it threateningly in order to extract the money from the thief. What do you think of that, my love? It wouldn't surprise me if Renoult has a few bumps and bruises tomorrow. Anyway, it's an amusing little story. Now, what about you, my dear, what were you doing while I was conducting Mass?

— Ah! my dear husband, said the viguier's wife. It seems that Heaven has inspired us both today. Don't you see how the Heavenly Host has filled us both to overflowing today, without the other knowing it? While you were saying Mass, I was reciting the beautiful prayer that the Virgin offered to Gabriel when he came to her & announced that she would be with child by the intervention of the Holy Spirit. If we go on doing such things, we'll earn our salvation for sure. Let us both continue, each in our separate ways, to perform such wonderful deeds as we performed today.

The Lady of the Château de Longeville, or A Woman's Revenge

In the days when aristocrats lived on their estates like despots; in those glorious days when France had within its borders innumerable sovereign lords, instead of thirty thousand slaves groveling in front of a single ruler, the Lord of the Château de Longeville, the owner of a rather large fief near Fismes in Champagne, lived with his wife on his large estate.

Madame de Longeville was a petite woman with brown hair. She was mischievous and very vivacious. Although she was not conventionally pretty, she was quite brazen, and was a passionate lover of pleasure in all its forms. She was perhaps twenty-five or twenty-six years old, and Monsieur de Longeville was thirty at most; they had been married for ten years, and because they were both old enough to enjoy any distractions from the tedium of their married life, each tried to satisfy their needs using the best of what the region had to offer.

The town, or rather the hamlet, of Longeville did not have much to offer. However, a petite eighteen-year-old farmer's wife, very attractive and still with the bloom of youth on her, had found she could keep Monsieur de Longeville satisfied, and for two years their arrangement was satisfactory for all concerned.

Louison, as his Lordship's cherished dove was called, came every night to her master's bed via a secret staircase that had been built into one of the towers containing de Longeville's apartment. Every morning, she decamped before Madame, as was her habit, entered her husband's rooms so they could breakfast together.

Madame de Longeville was by no means unaware of her husband's unbecoming little *dalliance*, but as she was not averse to being pleasured similarly herself, she said nothing. There is nothing so sweet-natured as an unfaithful wife; they have so much interest in hiding their own actions that they do not bother to look at the behavior of others, whereas the more prudish, who want to be outraged, are always inclined to pry.

Colas was a local miller. He was a young man of eighteen or twenty years of age, with skin as white as his flour. He was very muscular and as well-equipped as his mule. He was as handsome as the roses that grew in his little garden. Every evening, he entered the room that adjoined Madame's apartment and then waited until everything was quiet in the château before joining Madame in her bed.

There was never a more tranquil sight than when these twin liaisons were underway. If something devilish had not got involved, I am sure the couple would have been heralded throughout the entire Champagne region as the ideal example; one to not only be envied, but also imitated.

Do not smile, gentle reader, no, do not laugh at the word *example*; in the absence of virtue, vice that is either decent-looking or well-hidden can serve as a model. It is just as worthy as it is clever to commit an offence without scandalizing one's social circle. How can anything offensive be evil if it is not known?

So, reader, in order to decide for yourself, it is time for you to look at this couple's conduct and ask yourself this: however irregular it may appear, is it not preferable to the spectacles of depravity that current social mores offer?

Do you not prefer his Lordship, Monsieur de Longeville, stretched out and entwined in the arms of his pretty farmer's wife, and his respectable wife writhing beneath a handsome and virile miller, their arrangements and their happiness known to no one but those involved, rather than one of those Parisian Duchesses publicly changing lovers every month, or indulging in lewd acts with servants, while her husband spends two hundred thousand écus a year on one of those despicable creatures that use money to over-paint their faces, are base-born, and are riddled with the pox?

I say again: until some devilish discord poisoned these four favorites of the God of Love, there was nothing sweeter and more exemplary than their charming little arrangement.

But the Lord of Longeville, like many unjust husbands, cruelly believed that while he had every right to be happy, his wife did not deserve the same. The Lord of Longeville, who imagined that, like the ostrich, if he kept his head buried, he would not be noticed, discovered his wife's arrangements and decided to bring her happiness to an end. Despite his own conduct being equal to the conduct he was censuring, he proceeded to vilify that very conduct and was determined to eradicate it.

From discovery to revenge is a short distance for a jealous mind. Monsieur de Longeville therefore resolved to say nothing, but to get rid of the horns that had sprouted from his forehead.

To be cuckolded by a man of my own rank is one thing, he said to himself, *but to be humiliated by a miller is unacceptable. Oh Monsieur Colas, you will be kind enough to go and do your grinding in another mill. I will not have it said by anyone that my wife spreads herself wide open for you and begs for your seed.*

The intense hatred of these feudal despots always manifested itself as cruelty, and they often abused the power of life and death that feudal laws granted them over their vassals.

Monsieur de Longeville resolved to have poor Colas thrown into the moat water that surrounded his château and drowned.

— Clodomir, he said one day to his master butcher, you and your staff must rid me of a villain who is defiling Madame's bed.

— It will be done, Monsieur, Clodomir replied. We'll slit his throat if you like, and serve him up to you trussed like a suckling pig.

— No, my friend, Monsieur de Longeville replied. It'll be enough to tie him in a sack with some rocks in it, and simply let him sink to the bottom of the moat.

— It will be done.

— Yes, but first of all, he has to be caught and we haven't caught him yet.

— We will, your Lordship. He'll need be very smart to get away from us. We'll catch him, I promise you.

— He'll be here at nine o'clock tonight, said the offended husband. He'll creep through the garden and go directly into one of the ground-floor rooms next to Madame's. It'll be the room nearest the chapel and he'll hide in there until Madame thinks I'm asleep. Then she'll signal him and he'll creep into her apartment. You must let him do all his usual preliminary maneuvers and just be content to watch him. As soon as he thinks he's safe in that room, that's when you can grab him. Not before. I'll make up a drink that'll put out his fire. If you force him to drink it, he'll be a lot more manageable.

No one could have thought of a better plan and poor Colas was certainly going to end up being eaten by fish if everyone had kept quiet. But his Lordship had confided in too many people, and he was betrayed.

A young kitchen lad who was enamored of Madame, and who perhaps aspired to one day savor her charms in the same way the miller regularly did, decided to ingratiate himself with the lady by telling her all he had heard. If he had given it some thought, he would have possibly been glad that his potential rival was going to be removed as an obstacle, but this did not occur to him, so he told Madame of the plot that was being hatched. He was rewarded with a kiss and two gold écus. He walked away, valuing the écus less than the kiss.

— What is certain, said Madame de Longeville, as soon as she was alone with her most trusted maid, is that his Lordship is a very unjust man; he does whatever he likes, and even though I never say a word, he considers me wayward if I compensate myself for each day of abstinence he forces upon me. Well, I won't have it! I won't put up with it anymore! Listen, Jeannette, are you willing to help me with my plan to save Colas and teach his Lordship a lesson?

— Of course, Madame. You only have to give me your instructions. I'll follow them to the letter. Colas is such a pleasant young man. He's so strong and handsome too. Of course I'll help, Madame. What is it you want me to do?

— I want you to go right now and warn Colas not to come to the château until I send for him. He is not to come here at all. Make sure he understands. Then ask him to lend me a complete set of clothes he wears when he… visits me. As soon as he gives you the clothes, Jeannette, I want you to take them to Louison, my treacherous husband's lover. Tell her that you have been sent by his Lordship, who wants her to dress in the clothes that you will then hand to her. Tell her not to go to his Lordship by her usual route, but that she must go through the garden and then hide in the room adjacent to mine, the one next to the chapel. Tell her that his Lordship will meet her there and take her to his apartment. If she questions you on any of these changes, or challenges you in any way, tell her it's because Madame has found out everything and is furiously jealous. Say that Louison's usual route is being watched. If she seems worried, reassure her and give her something as a gift and tell her that it is vital that she meets his Lordship tonight as he wishes to discuss something of the utmost importance with her, something to do with why Madame is so jealous.

Jeannette left and performed both errands exactly as she had been instructed.

At nine o'clock that evening, the unfortunate Louison, wearing Colas's clothes, entered the room next to Madame's apartment; the room in which Madame's lover was about to be caught and severely dealt with.

— Now! said Monsieur de Longeville to his men, who had seen the villain creep into the room they were watching. Get him. You all saw him as plain as I did, didn't you?

— Yes, your Lordship. He's a handsome lad. Strong-looking too.

— So open the door slightly, throw those drapes over his head to confuse him. Pin him down, then push him into the sack, carry him out of here quickly and drown him without further ado.

The men moved forward & carried out their instructions perfectly.

The unfortunate captive's mouth was gagged before she could identify herself. Then she was sealed inside the sack so that it was impossible for her to be recognized. Large stones had been placed in the bottom of the sack. The men carried their victim to the window & heaved her out and dropped her into the moat. They watched the sack sink to the bottom & turned & left, dispersing quickly.

Monsieur de Longeville returned to his apartment, for he was very eager to welcome the lover he believed would not be long in coming, a lover he would never imagine for one moment was now lying in a cold, wet bed.

Half the night passed and no one came.

As it was a very beautiful moonlit night, the worried lover decided to walk over to his lover's house and ascertain for himself her reason for not coming to see him.

During his absence, Madame de Longeville, who was aware of his every move, got into her husband's bed & extinguished his light.

At Louison's house, Monsieur de Longeville learned that she had left the house as usual & was most certainly at the château. No one spoke of the disguise because Louison had not said anything about it to anyone. She had left without being seen.

His Lordship returned to his château and found the candle that he had left burning in his room had been extinguished. He took the taper to relight it; as he approached the bed he heard breathing & simply assumed that his dear Louison had arrived while he was out, and, impatient at not finding him in his apartment, had simply got into bed to await him.

He did not hesitate. He was between the sheets in an instant, stroking his wife's body, whispering the words of love and tender expressions that he used with Louison.

— Why did you make me wait, my love? Where were you, my dearest Louison?

— You hypocrite, Madame de Longeville sneered, uncovering the light of a small lantern that she had kept hidden. I no longer have any doubts regarding your conduct. Look at me! I'm your wife, not some whore to whom you give what belongs solely to me.

— Madame, said the husband, while remaining totally calm, I think I am master of my own actions, especially as you are trying to dupe me.

— Dupe you! In what way?

— I am fully aware of your dalliance with Colas, one of the vilest peasants to set foot on my estate.

— I, Monsieur? the lady of the château replied haughtily. I? Do you honestly think that I would demean myself in such a way? You are imagining things. There's not a word of truth in anything you say and I challenge you to provide proof of any of it.

— It would, in all honesty, Madame, be very difficult to provide any evidence at the moment because I have just had the villain who has dishonored me thrown into the moat. You'll never see him again.

— Monsieur, Madame de Longeville responded, with even more effrontery, if you have had that unfortunate man thrown into the water on such suspicions, you are certainly guilty of a great injustice, but if, as you say, he is punished only because he came into the château, I am afraid you are mistaken, for he has never set foot here in his life.

— Madame, your words make me fear for my sanity.

— Let us clear up this mystery, then. Let us look into this matter. Nothing could be easier. Give the order for Jeannette here to fetch the peasant of whom you are so mistakenly and so ridiculously jealous *&* we shall soon see who is mistaken.

His Lordship agreed.

Jeannette was sent to fetch Colas. She returned with him, having comprehensively briefed him on the manner in which he was to act *&* behave.

Monsieur de Longeville rubbed his eyes in disbelief when he saw Colas. He immediately ordered all of his servants out of bed and demanded that they waste no time in finding out exactly who it was that had been thrown into the moat. They hurried off, but all they brought back was the sodden corpse of the unfortunate Louison, which they placed carefully on the ground for his Lordship to see.

— Oh, by Heavens, his Lordship muttered. An unknown hand has acted in all this, but it has been guided by Providence. I will not complain of the blows I have been struck. Whether it is you or someone else, Madame, who has caused this unfortunate and deeply unpleasant occurrence, I shall refrain from asking. You are now rid of the one who gave you cause for concern. Do the same and get rid of the one who causes me concern; ensure that Colas leaves this region forever. Do you agree to that, Madame?

— I shall do much more than that, Monsieur. I will join you in ordering him to leave immediately. Let peace be restored between us. Let love and mutual esteem return to their rightful place in each of us. Let us both guarantee that nothing will cause them to be excluded in the future.

Colas left the region and was not seen again. Louison was buried and ever since then there has not been a couple in all of the Champagne province more devoted to each other than the Lord and the Lady of the Château de Longeville.

The Confidence Tricksters

In Paris, there has always been a group of people who spread throughout society, their sole business being to live off the money & possessions they inveigle from others.

There is nothing more skillful nor sophisticated than the many maneuvers of these scheming confidence tricksters; there are no limits to the inventiveness they bring to the craft of relieving innocents of their money and possessions. There is nothing that they will not pretend, there is nothing that they will not do; no strategy nor deceit of any sort that they will not deploy in order to lure their victims into their ready traps.

While the main group of thieves worked in the city, smaller units worked in the wings, scattered throughout the countryside and traveling mainly in public carriages.

With these grim facts firmly established, let us now turn to the young, inexperienced woman for whom we will shed tears when we see her fall into one of the confidence trickster's evil traps.

Rosette de Flarville, the daughter of an honest Rouen citizen, had, by continued pleading, finally received permission from her father to go and visit the carnival in Paris under the care of her rich uncle, Monsieur Mathieu, a money-lender who lived on the Rue Quincampoix. Rosette, though a little naïve, had just reached eighteen years of age. She was blonde with pretty blue eyes, alabaster skin, and a graceful figure. Encased in a thin dress, it was possible to see that her breasts and buttocks were so beautifully-shaped that they alerted connoisseurs to the fact that what she kept barely concealed beneath her thin clothing was far more rewarding that any visible part of her.

As always, there were a few tears during the leave-taking. It would be the first time that the diligent father had not had his daughter at home. She was good, she was well-mannered, she was reasonably confident, and, although a little too trusting, she was able to take care of herself. She would be staying with a respectable and responsible relative and she would be back home for Easter, all of which were reassuring points. But Rosette was very pretty, Rosette was very innocent, and she was going to a city, parts of which were very dangerous for the fairer sex, especially attractive young women from the provinces who arrived there full of innocence and virtue.

Rosette was taken to the coach stop and her fare was paid. Her trunk was stowed by the coachman as her father gave her a final embrace. Then the coachman cracked his whip, and everyone said their farewells and waved as the coach moved forward.

And so it was that the beautiful creature set off, equipped with everything she needed to sparkle in her small Parisian circle. She carried with her a fairly large amount of jewelry and presents for her Uncle Mathieu and his daughters, her cousins.

But, as everyone knows, the love that children have for their fathers is not as tender as the love their fathers have for them: nature has allowed daughters to discover pleasures that leave their young heads spinning, debauched diversions which cause them to involuntarily distance themselves from their parents & which cause the feelings of tenderness to cool in their hearts, feelings that are more one-sided, more ardent, and more sincere in the hearts of most fathers & mothers.

All parents are fully aware of their offspring's fatal indifference; an indifference that makes them insensitive to the pleasures of their youth, and makes them regard their parents as no more, so to speak, than sacred objects that gave them life.

Rosette was no exception to this general rule. Her tears dried as she thought of the pleasure she would get in seeing Paris.

Wanting to get to know the gentleman she was sharing the carriage with, especially if he knew the city better than she did, she asked if he knew where the Rue Quincampoix was.

— That's where I live, Mademoiselle, he replied. He was a tall, well-built man who, because of his uniform of sorts, and because of the preponderance of his tone, naturally held the attention.

— Oh, so you live on the Rue Quincampoix, Monsieur?

— I have lived there for more than twenty years.

— Oh! Well, in that case, said Rosette, you must know my uncle Mathieu.

— Monsieur Mathieu is your uncle, Mademoiselle?

— Yes, Monsieur. I'm his niece; I'm on my way to see him now. I'm going to spend the winter with him and his daughters, my cousins, Adelaïde and Sophie. I expect you know them too.

— Oh! Of course I know them, Mademoiselle. I know them well. Monsieur Mathieu and his two young daughters are my closest neighbors. Incidentally, I have been in love with one of them for more than five years.

— You're in love with one of my cousins? I'll wager it's Sophie.

— Then you'd lose the wager. It's Adelaïde. She has such a beautiful face.

— That's what everyone in Rouen says. I can't comment because I have never met her. They've never visited Rouen and this is my first visit to Paris.

— Ah! So you do not know your cousins, Mademoiselle? Nor do you know Monsieur Mathieu.

— Well, no. My uncle left Rouen the year my mother gave birth to me, and he has never returned.

— Your uncle is a very honest man and he will be delighted to receive you.

— Tell me, monsieur, is it a very big house?

— Yes, it is very big. But your uncle rents out part of it. He and his daughters occupy only the first-floor apartment.

— And all of the ground floor too.

— Of course. I believe he also has the use of a room at the top of the house.

— Oh, I know he's a very wealthy man, but I'm determined that I will not let my poor means make him feel ashamed of me. My father has given me a hundred double louis, so that I can dress in fashionable clothes and not embarrass anyone. I also have some lovely presents for them. I have some silver earrings, they're worth at least a hundred louis. They're for Adelaïde, or should I say, for the woman you love. I have a necklace that cost the same. That's for Sophie. And that's not all: I've a portrait of my mother in a gold picture frame. We've had the frame valued and it's worth just over fifty louis. That's for my uncle Mathieu; it's a present from my father. So, I'm sure that in presents, clothes, money and jewelry, I have more than five hundred louis with me. That should make my uncle welcome me, the poor relation, into his home, without reservation.

— You really don't need all of those trinkets in order to gain your uncle's approval, Mademoiselle, said the confidence trickster, eyeing the beautiful young woman and making plans to relieve her of her louis. He will of course be more than pleased to see you, even if you arrived without any gifts.

— That's not really the point, Rosette said. My father is a man who does things properly, and he doesn't want us to be looked down on, simply because we live in the country.

— In truth, Mademoiselle, everyone will no doubt find your company so delightful that no one will want you to leave Paris. In fact, I predict the Monsieur Mathieu plans to have his son marry you.

— His son! Uncle Mathieu doesn't have a son.

— His nephew, I meant to say. A pleasant, friendly young man...

— Do you mean Charles?

— Yes, I mean Charles. My best friend, no less, by God!

— Really? So you knew Charles too, did you, monsieur?

— *Knew* him, Mademoiselle? I still *know* him. As I said, he's my best friend. He's the reason I'm traveling to Paris. I'm on my way to see him now.

— Oh, no. You're very much mistaken, Monsieur. Charles is dead. My father always planned on Charles marrying me. He often spoke of it. Although I had never got to meet Charles, I heard how polite, pleasant, and handsome he was. Then he enlisted in the army. When the war started, he was sent to fight and was killed in battle.

— Ah, now I understand, Mademoiselle. It all comes clear. Based on what you have just said, I now believe that everything you have wished for is going to come true. Perhaps I had better explain my thoughts on this matter. I think it is likely that they, your relatives, have arranged a surprise for you; Charles is not dead. Everyone thought he was, but the army had made a mistake; he arrived home safely six months ago. Recently, he wrote to me and informed me that he was getting married;

married to someone he'd been promised to for several years. He asked me to stay with him for a week or so, and then attend the wedding as the best man. And now you tell me you have been summoned to Paris to stay with your uncle. My conjecture is that during your sojourn in Paris, Charles will propose to you. Perhaps your gifts are, in fact, wedding presents. There simply can't be any other explanation.

— What you say sounds very likely, Monsieur. Some of the comments my father has made over the past few weeks now make perfect sense when combined with what you have just told me. Your predictions seem more than likely. So, I am to be married in Paris, am I? I'll be a Parisian lady. This is all very wonderful, Monsieur. If all of it is true, then I will most certainly do what I can to make sure your relationship with Adelaïde blossoms. I shall speak to her on your behalf. I won't stop until I've persuaded her to marry you. In time, we can go out together as a foursome.

Such was the conversation between the sweet and naïve Rosette and the villain who gently quizzed her. The trickster promised himself he would take full advantage of this naïve young thing who had willingly divulged so much to him about herself. Five hundred louis and a pretty young thing was a tidy haul for him and his gang of crooks.

Reader, do you find that you are a little intrigued by this prospect?

As they approached Pontoise, the last coach stop before Paris, the villain said:

— Mademoiselle, I have an idea. I shall alight here and ride a fast horse to the capital, therefore getting ahead of the coach and arriving at your uncle's house before you. I'll announce your imminent arrival and then we'll all come & meet you at the coach stop, so that you will have family with you when you arrive in that great city.

The plan was agreed upon, so the devious one quickly hired a horse and galloped off to alert his cohorts to the charade he had devised. He briefed the gang on what Rosette had told him and gave them all very precise instructions regarding the subterfuge they were to carry out.

Two cabs then conveyed a bogus family to an inn in Saint-Denis, which was the last stop the carriage made before entering the city center. Everyone got out, checked their appearances, and took up their positions. When the carriage from Rouen pulled to a halt, Rosette alighted and was met by her Uncle Mathieu, her two charming cousins, and Charles, tall and handsome and recently discharged with full honors from the army.

Everyone hugged each other. Rosette handed over the letters she had brought from home, and the good Monsieur Mathieu shed tears of joy on reading that his brother was in excellent health.

In Paris, people do not wait politely for presents to be distributed. Rosette was no exception to this. Eager to assert the largesse of her father, she immediately gave out the gifts she had brought for everyone. There were more hugs, and more thank yous.

The pretend family then led the beautiful young woman to their hide-out, having told the unsuspecting dupe they were going to the family home in the rue Quincampoix.

They arrived at a very elegant-looking house. Mademoiselle de Flarville was installed, and her trunk was carried up to her room. Then the chief confidence trickster's thoughts turned to preparing the dinner table. Great care was taken to ensure that everything appeared "normal." The plan was that Rosette should be given enough to drink to cloud her senses.

Accustomed to drinking only tiny glasses of cider, she was persuaded that champagne was made from the juice of Parisienne apples, after which, drinking one, then two, then more glasses, the compliant Rosette answered everything she was asked. Finally, she succumbed to the alcohol's effects. Once the gang perceived she was totally helpless, they opened her trunk and shared out her possessions. Then they stripped her, leaving her totally naked. They took their time inspecting her young, bare body, which was now bereft of everything except the beautiful attributes that nature had blessed it with.

Exchanging meaningful glances, the gang tacitly agreed that they would not leave unspoiled any of those bounteous gifts from nature; they would use them all entirely for their own gratification. And so the entire gang gleefully used that young woman's ripe body exactly as they liked, deriving a range of pleasures and delights from her firm flesh repeatedly throughout the night.

Finally, satisfied that they had got out of the poor girl all that it was possible to get, & content with having taken away her possessions, her money, her virginity and most likely, her reason, they draped her in a filthy, old, ragged coat and just before dawn they took her and dumped her on the top steps of the church of Saint-Roch.

The unfortunate woman opened her eyes just as the sun rose. Upset, confused, and deeply troubled by the appalling state in which she found herself, she momentarily wondered if she was dead or alive.

Before long, a motley group of tramps, street-walkers, and beggars crowded around her & proceeded to have their own lewd fun with her.

Eventually, a passer-by took pity on her and led her to the captain of the watch, where, between bouts of sobbing, she recounted her sad story. She begged the captain to write to her father and ask him to come & take her home, and also to help her find somewhere safe to stay while she waited for him to get to Paris from Rouen.

The captain could immediately see such naïvety, such innocence, and such honesty in the wretched young woman that he decided he would spare her further harm by putting her up in his own home.

When Monsieur de Flarville finally arrived in Paris, many tears were shed on both sides. The doting father took his emotionally-damaged daughter back home and, it is said, that for the rest of her life, she never wanted to see the cosmopolitan & civilized capital of France again.

Dorci,
or The Unpredictability of Fate

Of all the virtues that nature has allowed us to exercise on earth, charity is undoubtedly the sweetest. Is there a greater pleasure, in fact, than in helping another person? It is at the moment of giving that our soul surrenders and assumes the divine qualities of the Being who created us. Misfortune, we are told, is sometimes attached to acts of charity, but no matter; we have derived pleasure from it, others have derived pleasure from it, so isn't that reward enough?

The Comte and the Marquis de Dorci were brothers. They were close in age, one being thirty and the other thirty-two. They were both officers in the same regiment. They were very close friends as well as being brothers; in fact, over the years, it would be difficult to find an example of a stronger friendship. Nothing had ever come between them. Since the death of their father, they had inherited a considerable fortune & an estate. In order to strengthen the bond that was so precious to them, they shared the same house, employed the same staff, and had resolved only to marry two women whose qualities were equal to their own and who would consent to continue living the communal life that the brothers enjoyed and wanted to continue enjoying for the rest of their days.

The tastes of these two brothers were not, however, absolutely alike. The Comte de Dorci, the eldest of the two, enjoyed tranquility, solitude, walks and books; his somewhat somber nature was nonetheless gentle, sensitive, honest, and he got genuine pleasure from being able to help others. Not someone who particularly enjoyed company, he was never happier than when his duties permitted him to spend a few months a year at a rather charming property that the two brothers owned near Aigle, in the Forest of Perche.

The Marquis de Dorci, infinitely more lively than his brother, infinitely more a man of the world, did not share his brother's love for the countryside. Blessed with a handsome face and the sort of wit that most women find irresistible, he was a little too much a slave to sartorial elegance and these defects, which he could never suppress, coupled with a fiery temper, became the cause of his undoing.

A very pretty young woman from the region we have just described had a romantic hold over the Marquis that was so strong that he was no longer, so to speak, his own master. He had failed to join his regiment that year, and the Comte had not seen him in their home for some time, for the Marquis had decided instead to stay in the small village where the object of his affections lived, and there, preoccupied with his cherished one, he forgot to ensure that his feet remained firmly on the ground.

It is said that love increases when jealousy spurs it on; that was certainly the case with the Marquis. But fate had presented him with a rival; a man, it was rumored, who was as dangerous as he was cowardly.

These reasons — to please his mistress, to be at hand to prevent any plots being hatched by his cunning rival, to surrender blindly to his passion — were what kept that young man there that summer; reasons that kept him far from the brother who idolized him, and who had quickly become bitterly upset over his brother's absence and seeming indifference. The Comte barely received any news from the Marquis; when the Comte wrote to ask for news, there was either no reply from the Marquis, or else a note that was so terse that it succeeded in convincing the Comte even more that his brother was distracted and was gradually distancing himself from him.

Meanwhile, the Comte continued to enjoy his life in the country. He occupied himself with his customary reading, reflection, walking and the occasional act of charity and in living in such a way found a great deal of happiness, whereas his brother, who lived in a state of constant agitation, barely had time for a single moment of reflection.

That was the general state of things when one day the Comte, preoccupied by what he was reading and seduced by the beautiful weather, wandered so far from his home that, by the time he considered retracing his steps, he found himself more than two leagues beyond the boundaries of his land and more than six leagues from his château, in a remote part of the forest, unable to determine which path would lead him back home.

Confused, he looked around and saw a tiny peasant's cottage about a hundred yards away. He decided to rest for a moment, then go there and ask for directions.

He rested… he reached the cottage… he opened the door… he entered a small, dark kitchen, the largest room in the cottage — and in that room his sensitive soul was presented with an interesting tableau.

A young girl of sixteen, as beautiful as a rose, was holding in her arms a woman of about forty who looked like her mother, and who had clearly fainted. The young girl was crying bitterly.

— Whoever you are, she said, when she saw the Comte standing there, I hope you are not here to take my mother from me too. I would rather you took my life than you took her. Leave her alone!

And as she said this, the young girl threw herself at the Comte's feet, and, as she implored him, she raised her arms above her head as though forming a barrier between the Comte and her mother.

— In truth, my child, said the Comte, as touched by her actions as he was surprised, your fear is misplaced and unnecessary. I don't know what has alarmed you, my friends, but what I do know for certain is whatever your troubles are, I am here, by heavens, not as your enemy, but as your protector.

— A protector! said the young girl, getting up and hurrying over to her mother who, having recovered from her faint, had taken refuge in a corner of the room, where she cowered fearfully.

— Mother! Did you hear? A protector! This gentleman says he will protect us and that he has been sent by Heaven in answer to your prayers.

And turning to the Comte, she said:

— Ah, Monsieur! what a noble deed it would be if you helped us. There are not two creatures on Earth to be pitied more. Help us, Monsieur… help us. This poor woman has not eaten for three days. We have no food, so what would I feed her even if she was in a condition to eat? There's nothing in the house, not even a crust of bread. Everyone has abandoned us. No doubt we'll die quite soon and yet God knows we're innocent! Alas! my poor father. The most honest and the most unfortunate of men. He's no more guilty of a crime than we are… and yet, tomorrow, perhaps… Oh, Monsieur! you have never entered a more miserable house than this one… God never abandons those who suffer misfortune, or so they say.

The Comte was able to determine from the girl's wild-sounding words and her behavior, as well as the frightened state of the mother, that some appalling catastrophe had happened to them in that house. Due to his altruistic nature he wondered if he had stumbled across a perfect opportunity to demonstrate an act of charity.

He immediately begged the two women to calm themselves, and repeated several times his offer of protection,
which he did in order to reassure them. He then insisted
that they tell him in full the story of their misfortunes.

After further tears caused by their unexpected good
fortune, the girl, introducing herself as Annette Alain,
begged the Comte to sit down. Once he was seated, she
began to tell him about the dreadful misfortunes of her
family, although she often interrupted her account with
sobs & tears.

— My father is one of the poorest and most honest
men in the region, Monsieur. His name is Christophe
Alain and he is a woodcutter by trade. He has two children by this poor woman here: a boy of nineteen and
myself, who has just turned sixteen. Despite his poverty,
he did everything he could to bring us up well. My brother
and I have been boarding at a school in Aigle for over
three years, and we both can read and write. During
those three years, our parents ate nothing but bread in
order to be able to give us an education. My father took
us out of school after our first communion; the cost of
our continued education was too much and it was no
longer possible for him to spend so much on us. When
we returned home, my brother was strong enough to
work with my father. I helped mother and, within a short
time, we started to do a little better. In short, Monsieur,
fortune favored us and it seemed that our hard work
earned us a blessing from Heaven. And then, one week

ago today, the greatest catastrophe that can happen to poor people like us, that is people with no credit, no money, and no protection, occurred.

— My brother was not with my father that day. My father was working alone about three leagues from here, on the Alençon side of the forest, when he saw what he thought was a dead man lying at the foot of a tree… He approached the corpse with the intention of seeing if the unfortunate man could be helped or not. He turned the body over. He poured a few drops of wine from his gourd and was rubbing it into the man's temples, when suddenly four constabulary horsemen rode up to him at a gallop, seized him, secured him, and then took him off to the prison in Rouen, where they charged him as guilty of having murdered the man he had been trying to revive.

— You can easily imagine our anxiety, Monsieur, when our father did not return home as usual. My brother, who had just got home from work, went and looked for him in the usual places and came back the next day to tell us the bad news. We immediately gave him the little money there was in the house, and he ran to Rouen to help our poor father. Three days later my brother wrote to us. We received the letter yesterday.

— Here it is, Monsieur, said Annette, sobbing loudly. Here is that fateful letter. In it, my brother warns us to be on our guard, that at any moment we may be taken off to Rouen prison to be confronted with our father who, although innocent, can no longer be helped. No one knows who the dead man is, so searches are underway for witnesses, as it seems certain that the dead man is a gentleman from the region. The accusation is that he was killed and robbed by my father, who, seeing the constabulary men coming, threw the money into the woods. The evidence for this is that there was not so much as a sou found in the deceased's pockets. But, Monsieur, this man may have been killed the day before, so he could have been robbed either by whoever murdered him, or by someone who found his body shortly after he died? Oh! believe me, Monsieur, my poor father is incapable of such an action; he would rather die than harm any living creature. Yet we are going to have the misfortune of losing him. You now know everything that happened, Monsieur. Please excuse my tears and help us if you can. We will spend the rest of our days praying for the preservation of our loved ones... You are no doubt aware, Monsieur, that the tears of the unfortunate can move the Lord to help. Our prayers will be for you too, Monsieur.

The Comte had been deeply moved by the young girl's account. Wanting to be useful to them, he first asked them the name of the owner of the land that their cottage was on. He made it clear that it would be prudent for them to seek his protection.

— Alas! Monsieur, replied Annette. This house is built on land owned by the monks. We have already spoken to them about helping us, but they have told us in no uncertain terms that they cannot assist us in any way.

If our home had been built on the other side of the hill, on the land owned by the Comte de Dorci, then we would have no fears, because he is the most charitable lord in the region and the most compassionate.

— And do you know anyone else to turn to other than him, Annette?

— No, Monsieur. No one else.

— Well, in that case, I will introduce your situation to him. I can do more; I can promise you his protection. I give you my word that he will use all his power to assist you.

— Oh, Monsieur, you are so kind, said Annette's mother. How can we ever repay you for what you're doing for us?

— By forgetting all about it as soon as I am successful.

— Forget it, Monsieur! Never! The memory of such a charitable act will live on as long as we live.

— Very well, the Comte said. I realize I must make myself known to you. I am the Comte de Dorci...

— You, Monsieur? The Comte de Dorci?

— Yes, it is I, the Comte, your friend, your helper and your protector.

— Oh, mother! Mother, we're saved! young Annette cried. Did you hear, mother? We're saved. The noble Comte has promised us his support.

— And now, my children, the Comte said, it's getting late, and I have a long walk home ahead of me. Although I have to leave you now, I promise I'll go to Rouen tomorrow evening *&* I'll send you news in a few days of the steps I've taken. Meanwhile, Annette, as you are in urgent need of funds, please accept these fifteen louis and use them in whatever way you need to take care of your father and brother.

— Oh! Monsieur, how kind you are! This is all so unexpected. Good God! Never has so much charity shone so brightly in the soul of a mortal! Monsieur, Annette continued, you cannot be a mere man; you must be a divine being descended to Earth to help the unfortunate. What can we possibly do to repay you? Just ask, Monsieur, and it's yours. Please let us know how we can be of service to you.

— I'm going to demand something right now, my dear Annette, the Comte said. I've lost my way and don't know which path I have to take to get home. If you'll be my guide for one or two leagues then you'll have fully acquitted yourself of any debt you may have; a debt on which your gentle and sensitive soul places a higher value than its true worth.

One can easily imagine how quickly Annette hurried to comply with the Comte's request. She led him along the path that led to his estate, pointing out the way & constantly thanking him and singing his praises as they walked along. Every so often, her emotions overcame her and she cried softly. The Comte basked in the sweet sensation of being loved and appreciated, which gave him a foretaste of heavenly happiness, and made him feel like a god on earth.

Oh, glorious Humanity! If you are truly the daughter of heaven and the queen of men, why would you allow a source of remorse and sorrow to be the reward of your followers, while those who incessantly offend you triumph by insulting you with their debris on your altars?

About two leagues from Christophe's house, the Comte recognized several landmarks.

— It is late, little one, he said to Annette. I now recognize where I am, so you should turn back and go home. Your mother will be worried. When you get back, please reassure her of my services, and tell her that I shall not return from Rouen without her husband.

Annette grew upset at the idea of leaving the Comte; she would have followed him to the ends of the earth. She asked his permission to embrace him.

— No, Annette, it is I who shall embrace you, the Comte said, taking her chastely in his arms, embracing her.

The Comte was thirty-two years old, he owned the land he stood on, he was in the middle of a forest, in his arms he held a beautiful young girl who was totally beholden to him… and he wept over the misfortunes that had befallen her and was only concerned with helping her.

Citizens of this century! Whoever is reading this, I would ask that you take careful note of the dominion that virtue has over a beautiful soul, and if you are incapable of imitating that man, then allow his example to reach you, touch you, and affect you positively.

— Go home, my child, the Comte said, releasing her. Continue to serve God, your parents, & your neighbors. Always be honest & the blessings of Heaven will never forsake you.

Annette clutched the Comte's hands, she was close to tears again, so she held them back, which prevented her from expressing what her sensitive soul was feeling.

Dorci, deeply moved, embraced Annette a final time, then gently pushed her away and walked on.

As soon as the Comte arrived back at his château, he arranged everything for his departure to Rouen. It was a presentiment of disaster, the inner voice of nature, which we should never ignore, that compelled him to speak in confidence to one of his friends who helped him manage his estates. He told the friend all that had happened and then he confessed that it was impossible for him to ignore an impenetrable emotion which seemed to be advising him not to become involved in the Alain affair... But his charitable nature prevailed. Nothing could compare with the pleasure Dorci felt when doing good and he set off for Rouen knowing he had made the right choice.

When he arrived at Rouen, the Comte went to see all the judges involved in the Alain case. He told them all that he would stand as surety for the unfortunate Christophe, should that be necessary, and that he was sure of the man's innocence. He asked to see the accused man, and was allowed to do so. He questioned him and was very pleased with the answers he was given, and was soon convinced that Christophe was incapable of the crime of which he was accused.

Dorci then informed the judges that he would take on the full cost of the defense of the peasant and that if by any misfortune he was convicted, then he, Dorci, would apply to the Court of Appeals, and have a detailed report of the case written and distributed throughout France, shaming any magistrate who was unjust enough to condemn a man so obviously innocent.

The Comte de Dorci was well-known in Rouen; his birth and his rank meant that he was highly regarded in everyone's eyes. Those involved in the case soon realized that they had been perhaps a little hasty in the prosecution of Christophe; the investigation was reopened with the Comte paying all the attendant costs. Inevitably, there was not one piece of evidence against the accused. It was then that the Comte de Dorci sent Annette's brother home to his mother and sister, recommending they set their minds at rest, and assuring them that they would soon see Christophe again; a free man, fully absolved.

Everything was going exceedingly well when the Comte received an anonymous note. It contained the few words that you are about to read:

Abandon the case you are assisting with immediately. Halt all investigations into the death of the man in the forest. You are digging a grave in which you will bury yourself. Your virtues are going to cost you dearly! Cruel man, how I pity you… but it may already be too late. Farewell.

The Comte shivered violently after reading the note; he suddenly felt faint. When he thought about what the fearful note contained and then considered the presentiment of disaster he had experienced before leaving for Rouen, he saw clearly that he was being threatened by a sinister & malevolent force.

Thereafter, he remained in the town, but stopped his involvement in the processes that were unfolding around him. Merciful heavens! He had been warned, but it was already too late; he had done too much, the ill-fated steps he had taken had succeeded far too well.

At eight o'clock in the morning, fifteen days after his arrival in Rouen, a court administrator that the Comte knew asked to speak to him on a matter of some urgency.

— You must leave Rouen, my dear Comte! he said, clearly agitated. Leave immediately. You are the most unfortunate of all beings & I sincerely hope that your unfortunate situation never becomes public knowledge. If it does, it could convince people of the dangers of virtue and thereby cause them to abandon it altogether. If it were possible to believe in an unjust providence, then today would be the day on which to do so.

— You are frightening me, Monsieur! Please explain. What has happened?

— Your protégé is innocent, as you surmised. He will be released immediately. Your investigations have led to the discovery of the murderer. He is, as we speak, already in one of our cells, awaiting execution. What else do you need to know?

— Speak up, Monsieur. Go on, tell me what you know. Drive the dagger into my heart! Who is the murderer?

— It's your brother.

— Good God! No, not him!

And the Comte de Dorci fell to the floor, senseless. It was over two hours before he came round. The same friend was there to inform him what the panel of judges had determined had happened.

The murdered man was the Marquis's rival; they were returning together from Aigle. During the journey, a few misspoken words had sparked an argument. The Marquis, furious that his enemy would not agree to duel with him, called him a treacherous coward and, in a moment of blind fury, knocked him to the ground and, with his own horse, trampled him to death.

Once the deed was done, the Marquis, on seeing his rival lifeless on the ground, completely lost his head and instead of running away, he had contented himself with killing the man's horse and hiding its body by submerging it in a pond. He had then brazenly returned to the small town where his mistress lived, despite having told everyone he knew there that he would be away for at least a month. On seeing him back in the town, some of those who knew him asked the whereabouts of his rival. The Marquis said that he had only travelled with the man for about an hour, after which they had gone their separate ways.

When the news of the rival's death and the story of the wood-cutter accused of having killed him reached the town, the Marquis listened to it all without any outward sign of being distressed and, just like everyone else, he even recounted the details of what he had heard.

Meanwhile, the secret enquiries instigated by the Comte produced more exact results and suspicion fell squarely on the Marquis. It was no longer possible for the Marquis to defend himself, and he did not try to. Although he was quite capable of hot-tempered action, he was ill-equipped for crime. He confessed everything to the officers who came to question him, and allowed himself to be arrested, saying that they could do with him whatever they wanted.

The Marquis was unaware of the part his brother had played in the matter, believing him to be still living his tranquil life in their château, where he himself had thought he would be rejoining him very soon. He had requested that his disgrace, if at all possible, be kept from the brother who adored him and who would be sent to an early grave by the terrible news. Regarding the money taken from the corpse, it had no doubt been stolen by some poacher who, for obvious reasons, had remained silent. They had finally taken the Marquis to Rouen, and it was then that the Comte had been informed of everything.

Dorci, once he had recovered a little from his initial shock and despondency, did everything in his power, either on his own account or by entreating his friends, to save his wretched brother. Everyone sympathized, but they could not listen reasonably to his efforts to abort the law. He was even denied the satisfaction of visiting the Marquis, and, in a state difficult to describe, he left Rouen on the very day of the execution of the one person on earth who was most precious and sacred to him, and that he himself was sending to the scaffold. He returned briefly to his estate, but with the intention of almost immediately leaving it forever.

Annette had learned the identity of the man who was being executed in the place of her father. Quite courageously, she and her father called at Dorci's château. They both threw themselves at his feet and Christophe begged the Comte to kill him on the spot in recompense for the Marquis's life. And, he added, if the Comte could not bring himself to execute the wood-cutter, then perhaps he would let them compensate him for his loss by allowing them to serve him without pay for the rest of his days.

The Comte, as prudent in the midst of misfortune as he was charitable in prosperity, but whose heart had become hardened by his excessive suffering, was no longer able to be tolerate sentiments that had cost him so dearly. He ordered the woodcutter and his daughter to leave suggesting that they both enjoy, as long as they could, the fruits of his actions that had taken away his honor and his peace of mind forever. Those wretched people did not dare remonstrate. They left the estate quickly.

The Comte left all of his property to his closest relatives, on the condition that he receive an annual allow-
ance of one thousand écus for the rest of his life. Until
he died he spent the last fifteen years of his miserable
life in a retreat, far from the public gaze, every moment
of which was marked by acts of despair & misanthropy.

Dialogue Between a Priest and a Dying Man

PRIEST: Having arrived at this fatal moment, when the veil of illusion is torn away to let man see the cruel picture of his errors and vices, do you not repent, my son, of the multiple evils which human weakness & fragility have taken you to?

DYING MAN: Yes, my friend, I do repent.

PRIEST: Well, you should take advantage of this timely remorse to obtain from Heaven, in the short space of time that is left to you, the general absolution from your faults, and consider that it is only through the mediation of the most holy sacrament of penance that it will be possible for you to obtain it from the Eternal.

DYING MAN: I don't understand you any more than you understand me.

PRIEST: What?

DYING MAN: I told you that I repented.

PRIEST: I heard you.

DYING MAN: Yes, but without understanding.

PRIEST: What other interpretation is there?

DYING MAN: This one… I was created by nature with very keen tastes and very strong passions and placed on this earth solely to indulge and to satisfy them. These effects of my creation are nothing but necessities directly relating to nature's fundamental designs or, if you prefer, nothing but essential derivatives that come from nature's intentions regarding me, in accordance with its laws.

I regret not having recognized nature's omnipotence as fully as I should have, and my repentance relates only to the negligible use I have made of the faculties (criminal in your opinion, very ordinary in mine) that nature had given me to serve it; I sometimes resisted it, which I regret. Misled by your absurd doctrines, I used them as weapons to fight desires I had been given by a far more divine inspiration, & this I also regret. I plucked mere flowers when I could have harvested an abundance of fruits… These are the real reasons for my repentance. Do not assume that I have any others.

PRIEST: Where have your mistakes led you? Where have your fallacies led you? You ascribe to the created being all the power of the Creator, and these unfortunate inclinations have led you astray. Do you not see that they are only the products of a corrupt nature, to which you attribute omnipotence?

DYING MAN: My friend, it seems to me that your dialectic is as false as your thoughts. I would like you to either reason more clearly, or let me die in peace. What do you mean by Creator, and what do you mean by corrupt nature?

PRIEST: The Creator is the master of the universe, it is He who has done everything, created everything, and who preserves everything by a simple fact of His omnipotence.

DYING MAN: A very great being indeed. Now, tell me why this being who is so powerful has nevertheless, in your opinion, created what you referred to as corrupt nature.

PRIEST: What merit would men ever have if God had not given them free will? And what merit would they have in enjoying it if there were not on earth the possibility of doing good and avoiding evil?

DYING MAN: So your god deliberately wanted everything to be wrong in order to tempt, or to test his creature; so did he either not know or not doubt the result?

PRIEST: He undoubtedly knew, but once again, He wanted to give man the merit of the choice.

DYING MAN: What is the point of that? He already knew the course mankind would take, since it was the one he had decided they would take. As he was, as you say, all-powerful, all he had to do was make mankind choose what suited him.

PRIEST: Who can comprehend God's immense and infinite designs for man and who can grasp all that we see of His universe?

DYING MAN: Anyone who simplifies things, my friend, especially anyone who does not multiply the causes in order to confuse the effects. Why do you need a second difficulty, when you cannot explain the first? And as it is possible that nature alone has done what you attribute to your god, why do you want to regard your deity as nature's master? The cause of what you don't understand is perhaps the simplest thing in the world. Perfect your physics and you will better understand nature, refine your reason, banish your prejudices, and you will no longer need your god.

PRIEST: You wretched man! I thought you were a mere Socinian,[55] so I had a range of points ready to refute you, but I see that you are an atheist *&*, as such, your heart refuses to accept the immensity of the authentic proofs that we receive every day of the existence of the Creator. Therefore, I have nothing more to say to you. The blind man is not restored to the light.

DYING MAN: My friend, let's agree on one fact; the one who is the most blind must surely be the one who puts on a blindfold rather than the one who tears it off. You instruct, you formulate, you increase; I refute, I simplify. You add errors to mistakes; I fight them all. Which of us is blind?

PRIEST: So you do not believe in God?

DYING MAN: No. And this for a very simple reason: it is completely impossible to believe what we do not understand. Understanding and believing what is understood is the foundation of faith. If there is no understanding, then faith is dead. Those who claim to have faith without understanding, they deceive. I challenge you yourself to believe in the god you preach to me about, because you cannot prove he exists to me, because it is not in you to define him to me. Therefore you do not understand him and as soon as you do not understand him, you can no longer provide me with any reasonable argument concerning him and therefore everything that is beyond the bounds of the human mind is either illusion or futility.

Because your god cannot be one or the other of these things, I would be a fool to believe in the first of these, and an even bigger fool to believe in the second. My friend, prove to me that matter is inert, and I will grant you a creator, prove to me that nature is not sufficient to itself, and I will allow you to imagine it is ruled by a higher force; until then expect nothing from me. I only acknowledge the evidence I receive from my senses; where they stop my belief stops too. I believe in the sun because I see it; I conceive it as the center of all the flammable matter in nature. Its periodic movement pleases me but does not surprise me. It is an operation of physics, perhaps one as simple as the force of electricity, but one which we are not able to understand.

What? Do I need to say more? When you have placed your god above such phenomena, would I be any further forward in my understanding? Will it not still take me as much effort to understand the workman as to define his work? Therefore, you have done me no service by creating your illusion; you have confused me but you have not enlightened me, for which I owe you resentment instead of gratitude. Your god is a machine that you have created to serve your passions and you have manipulated it to please them. As soon as it tried to interfere with my own passions I had no choice but to reject it.

And at this moment, when I am weak and my soul needs calm & philosophy, do not come to terrify it with your delusions, which would alarm it without convincing it, which would irritate it without improving it. My soul is my best friend, which is what nature intended. That is to say, nature fashioned my soul the way it is fashioned because of nature's own ends & needs; and since nature has an equal need for vices and virtues, when it pleased nature to make me do evil, it inspired my desires, and I indulged in them. When I was made by nature to do good, I did so because nature roused in me a desire to do good. Look no further than nature's laws to know the sole cause of all human inconsistency, and you will find in nature's laws no other principles than its will and requirements.

PRIEST: So everything that in the world is needed.

DYING MAN: Precisely.

PRIEST: But if everything is necessary, then everything is regulated.

DYING MAN: I would not say otherwise.

PRIEST: And what can regulate everything except an all-powerful and all-knowing hand?

DYING MAN: Isn't it necessary for gunpowder to ignite when you put a spark to it?

PRIEST: Yes.

DYING MAN: And what wisdom do you find in that?

PRIEST: None.

DYING MAN: It is therefore possible that there are things that are necessary without them being governed by wisdom, therefore it's possible that everything derives from a primary cause, without there being any reason or wisdom in that primary cause.

PRIEST: What are you getting at?

DYING MAN: I'm trying to prove to you that everything can be what it is and as you see it, without any wise and reasoning cause directing it, and that natural effects must have natural causes, without it being necessary to invent any unnatural causes, such as your god who himself, as I have already told you, would require being explained, but would not provide an explanation of anything. Therefore, as soon as it is acknowledged that your god is no good for anything, he is perfectly useless; that what is useless is null, and that all that is null is nothing. Thus, to conclude that your god is an illusion, I need no reasoning other than that which provides me with the certainty of his uselessness.

PRIEST: On that point, I think there's no great need for me to talk to you about religion.

DYING MAN: Why not? Nothing amuses me more than evidence showing the extent to which men will take their fanaticism and their stupidity; these are such remarkable examples of folly, that the spectacle is, in my opinion, although horrible, still interesting. Answer me honestly and above all try to be objective. If I were weak enough to let myself be tricked into believing in your ridiculous theories about the existence of a fabulous being that makes religion necessary, in what form would you advise me to offer him my worship? Would you like me to adopt the thoughts of Confucius, rather than the absurdities of Brahma? Should I worship the great serpent god of the Mexicans, or the sun god of the Peruvians? Or what about the god of Moses's armies? Which of the sects of Muhammad would you like me to surrender to, or which Christian heresy would you say was preferable to all the others? Be careful how you answer.

PRIEST: Can it be doubtful?

DYING MAN: So you refuse to be objective…

PRIEST: No, it's out of love for you that I advise you embrace what I believe.

DYING MAN: And it is by believing in such huge errors that you reveal how little you love either of us.

PRIEST: But who can be blind to the miracles of our Divine Redeemer?

DYING MAN: The one who sees him and his representatives as vulgar charlatans and unmitigated swindlers.

PRIEST: O God, you hear him and yet I don't hear you thunder!

DYING MAN: No, my friend, everything is at peace because your god, either from impotence or from reason, or whatever you finally choose, is a being that I admit exists for a moment only out of consideration for you or, if you prefer, to put myself in your place so I have your sorry perspective, because this god, I say, if he were to exist, as you are mad enough to believe, would not have chosen to persuade us of his existence and laws by such ridiculous means as those supposedly uttered by your Jesus.

PRIEST: What? The prophecies, the miracles, the martyrs, are all these not evidence?

DYING MAN: How do you logically expect me to be able to accept as proof anything that needs proof itself? Before a prophecy can be offered as proof, I would first have to be completely certain that it had actually been pronounced. Prophesies that have been recorded in history are merely examples from history, and therefore have the same strengths and weaknesses as all items in historical records; three quarters of which are very dubious. To this I would add that it is more than probable that they have been transmitted to us by historians who were not always, if at all, totally objective, but simply recorded what they wanted us to believe. I am perfectly entitled to be skeptical. Who will assure me that this prophecy was not made after the fact, a combination of simple political expedience such as the prediction of a happy reign under a just king, or of frost during winter? And if all this is so, how can you expect any prophecy that needs to be proved to become evidence itself?

With regard to your miracles, they do not impress me any more than your prophesies. All confidence tricksters have performed them and every fool has believed in them. For me to believe the truth of a miracle, I would have to know of course that the event you call a miracle was absolutely contrary to the laws of nature, for only that which is outside nature can qualify as a miracle. Who is there who knows nature well enough to assert the precise point at which nature is violated? It takes only two things to accredit a supposed miracle, a charlatan and a few gullible onlookers. There is absolutely no point looking for other origins to your miracles; all the new sectarians have used them, and what is most extraordinary is that all of them have found fools who believed in them. Your Jesus did nothing that Apollonius of Tyana did not do, and yet no one thinks to take Apollonius for a god.

As for your martyrs, they are certainly the feeblest of all your arguments. It only takes enthusiasm and resistance to make a martyr, and as long as an opposed cause offers me as much as your cause, I will never believe one better than the other, but would most likely be inclined to assume them both pitiable.

My friend, if it were true that the all-powerful god you preach of existed, would he really need miracles, martyrs, and prophecies to establish his kingdom? And if, as you say, the heart of man were his creation, then would he not simply have chosen that organ to be the repository for his laws?

This equitable law, since it would emanate from a righteous god, would be engraved deeply in the hearts of every human being from one end of the world to the other, with everyone having this delicate and sensitive organ in common. They would all resemble each other through the homage they would pay to the god from whom they received it, and everyone would love, worship, and serve him in the same way. It would also be impossible for them to disregard this god as they would be unable to resist their inner impulse to worship him; an impulse that he had furnished them with.

Instead of this, what do I see throughout the world? There are as many gods as there are countries; as many ways to serve these gods as there are different minds or different imaginations, & this multiplicity of opinions, which it is physically impossible for me to choose from, would be in your opinion the work of a righteous god. You insult your god by presenting him to me in this way. Let me deny him completely for, if he exists, then I insult him far less by my disbelief than you do by your blasphemy.

Come to your senses, preacher! Your Jesus is no better than Muhammad, Muhammad is no better than Moses, and all three no better than Confucius who nevertheless uttered a few sound principles while the other three raved irrationally. In general all of these individuals were nothing but frauds; individuals who were mocked by philosophers, believed in by the mob, & who ought to have been executed by due process of law.

PRIEST: Alas, justice dealt with one of them far too harshly.

DYING MAN: He was the one who deserved it the most. He was seditious, troublesome, slanderous, deceitful, a libertine, a crude buffoon and a dangerous villain. He possessed the art of imposing his subversion on the common people and therefore became deserving of punishment in that kingdom in the state which Jerusalem was then a part of. The authorities were very wise to get rid of him, and this is perhaps the only case in

which my usually very lenient and tolerant maxims are
in accordance and agreement with the severity of the law
of Themis. I excuse all mistakes, except those that are
a threat to the government where one lives; kings and
their majesties are the only living things that I respect,
and whoever does not love his country and his king is
not fit to live.

PRIEST: But do you believe that there is something awaiting us after this life? You must have sometimes tried
piercing the darkness of the fate that awaits us. What
other theory could have satisfied your spirit better than
the one where there is a multitude of sorrows for those
who have lived wickedly and an eternity of rewards for
those who have lived a good life?

DYING MAN: Which other, my friend? That of nothingness? That has never caused me any fear. In it I see
nothing but that which is consoling and unpretentious;
all the others are the creation of pride. The theory of
nothingness is the work of reason. Besides, it's neither
terrible nor absolute, this nothingness.

Every day I see before me the example of nature's
perpetual generation and regeneration. Nothing perishes,
my friend, nothing is destroyed in the world; today a
man, tomorrow a worm, the day after tomorrow, a fly.
Isn't that to always exist? And why do you want me to
be rewarded for virtues I have in my nature through
no choice of my own, or punished for crimes of which

I cannot accept blame for as my nature compelled me to commit them? Can you align the goodness of your so-called god with this theory? Could he really have created me simply in order to give himself the pleasure of punishing me as a consequence of a choice he does not give me the freedom to determine?

PRIEST: You are free.

DYING MAN: Yes, but only in terms of your prejudices; however, reason destroys them and the theory of man's freedom was only invented to create the illusion of grace, which became so important to your contemplations.

What man on earth, seeing the scaffold next to the crime, would go ahead and commit the crime if he were free not to commit it? We are driven by an irresistible force and not for a moment are we able to do anything other than what we are inclined to do. There is not a single virtue that is not necessary to nature and, conversely, not a single crime that nature does not need, and it is in the perfect balance it maintains between the two that contains of all nature's science. So, if we go to one side or the other of the balance as nature compels us, can we be any more guilty for being on a particular side than a wasp is guilty of following its nature and planting its sting in your skin?

PRIEST: So, according to you, even the greatest crimes should not cause us any fear.

DYING MAN: That is not what I said. It's enough for the law to convict the criminal and for the sword of justice to punish him. Once a crime has been committed, we must accept the inevitable and not indulge in futile remorse; its effect is negligible, since remorse has not been able to prevent us from committing the crime and futility cannot be used to make amends. It is equally as absurd to fear being punished in the other world if we have been lucky enough to have escaped being punished in this world. God forbid that my words are construed as wanting to encourage crime, but we must learn to avoid it as much as we can through reason, and not by false fears that lead to nothing and whose effects are easily overcome by a steadfast soul.

Reason, my friend, yes; reason alone must warn us that harming our fellow men can never bring us happiness. We know in our hearts that contributing to the bliss of others is the greatest joy that nature has granted us on earth; all human morality is found in one phrase: *Make others as happy as you desire to be yourself and never to do them any more harm than you would like to receive.* This, my friend, is the only principle that we need to follow and there is no need for religion or god. To subscribe to it, all that is necessary is to have a good heart.

But I am growing weak, preacher, so put away your prejudices. Be a man, be a human without fear and without hope; forget your gods and religions too. All they do is set man against man. The mere name of these horrors has caused more blood to be spilled on earth than every other war and plague combined. Renounce the idea of another world; there isn't one, but do not renounce the pleasure of being happy & of making yourself happy in this world. This is the only way nature offers you a way of doubling your existence or extending it.

My friend, voluptuous pleasures have always been dearer to me than anything else. I have worshipped them all my life, and I want to finish my life experiencing them all one last time. The end of my life is approaching. Six very beautiful women are in the adjoining room. I reserved them for this moment; you may indulge if you wish. You could follow my example and use their naked beauty to try to forget all of the vain fallacies of superstition and all of the foolish mistakes of hypocrisy.

NOTE: The dying man rang a bell, the six women entered & in their arms the priest became a man corrupted by nature, simply because he had been unable to explain what he meant by corrupt nature.

Postscript

Our good forefathers used to say: reader, salvation, health and joy, after finishing their tale. Why be afraid to imitate their politeness and frankness? I will therefore say like them: reader, salvation, wealth & pleasure; if my words have given you any of those, then place this book on a good shelf in your bookcase; if I have annoyed you, accept my apologies and throw my words into the fire.

Non-Fiction

Some Thoughts on the Novel [1]

What we call a novel (a *roman*) is an imaginative work in which are written the most singular events in the lives of men.

But why is this kind of work called a novel?

In which countries should we look for its origins, and which are the most famous examples?

And what, finally, are the rules that must be followed in order to achieve perfection in the art of writing the novel?

These are the three questions we propose to answer. Let us start with the etymology of the word. *Why is this kind of work called a novel?*

Since there is nothing to indicate what name imaginative works were given by people of antiquity, we must, it seems to me, attempt to discover the reason it has the name (*roman*) it was first given in France.

The *Romance* language was, as we know, a mixture of Celtic and Latin, in use under the first two dynasties of our kings.

It is reasonable enough to assume that the works of the kind of which we speak, composed in this language, had that name & one could say *une romane* must have been used to describe a work in which the plot consists of amorous adventures, as the term *romance* referred to ballads or laments of the same kind.

It is pointless seeking a different etymology for this word; common sense offering no other, it seems best to simply adopt this one.

So let's move on to the second question, which is: *In which countries should we look for the novel's origins, and which are the most famous examples?*

Common opinion seems to suggest that the novel was invented by the Greeks; it went from them to the Moors, from whom the Spaniards took it, after which they passed it on to our troubadours, from whom our chivalrous novelists received it.

Although I respect this particular lineage theory — I have after all, out of convenience, sometimes used it myself — I am reluctant to accept it totally. It is a difficult theory to accept as it refers to the centuries during which travel was virtually unknown and communication was unreliable. There are also cultural fashions, customs, & tastes that cannot be transmitted. They are an inherent part of all men from birth. Wherever men exist, there are inevitable traces of these tastes, customs, & fashions.

Let us be in no doubt, it was in the lands where they first recognized the existence of gods that the novel originated; which therefore means in Egypt; the cradle of all religions. No sooner did men feel the need to claim the existence of immortal beings than they made them act and speak. From then on, there were metamorphoses, fables, myths, parables, novels; in short, works of fiction that were created as soon as fiction took hold in the minds of men. The moment it became a question of imaginary creatures, men began to create some fabulous works of the imagination.

And once these fanciful notions had taken root, books of myths began to appear. At the urging of priests, people from one nation began to slaughter people from another nation in the name of non-existent deities, and then later in the name of their king and their country. Superstition was replaced, sensibly, by heroism. Heroes replaced gods and were immortalized in poems and songs. The heroes' great deeds were embroidered & added to for effect. New heroes were created when people grew tired of the old myths and invented new heroes who resembled the old ones, but who were superior to them in a number of ways; the new heroes were more plausible and more relevant to men and men's experiences than the stories of deities & their foibles had been.

Hercules the great general who valiantly fought and defeated his enemies is a hero from history; the Hercules who destroys monsters & kills giants is a god...[2] the myth and the origin of a superstition, but a reasonable superstition, since it is solely concerned with the rewards of heroism; the gratitude paid to the liberators of a nation, whereas the superstition that invents beings that are unreal and consequently never seen has no other motive behind it other than to provoke fear and hope, and to disturb the mind.

Each culture therefore had its gods, its demigods, its heroes, its true stories, its myths and its fables. Some aspects of it, as we have just seen and as it pertains to heroes, may have had a basis in truth. But the rest of it was pure fantasy, fabulation; everything else was a work of invention, *a novel*, because the gods spoke only through the mouths of men who, because they had a lot invested in this ridiculous artifice, immediately proceeded to create the language of the spirits out of their own minds using anything they imagined would suitably influence or frighten; anything, therefore, that was mythical.

It is now common knowledge, says the scholar Huet, that the name *novel* was once given to history and that it was later applied to fiction, which is a strong indication that the one is derived from the other.[3]

Novels, then, were written in every language, in every country in the world; novels which in style and content were modeled on their nation's customs and on the nation's opinions regarding those customs.

Man is subject to two weaknesses that are related to his existence; two weaknesses which characterize it. Everywhere he must *pray* and everywhere he must *love* — and it is these two elements that are the basis for all novels. Novels were written so writers could show the beings they entreated and novels were written so writers could celebrate those they loved.

The first kind of novel, created out of terror or hope, was dark, expansive, and full of fabrications and fictions, such as the ones that Ezra created during the captivity of Babylon. The second kind of novel contained scenes of delicacy and feeling, such as *The Aethiopica* by Heliodorus.[4] But because people *prayed* & because people *loved*, novels appeared everywhere, in every inhabited part of the world. These were works of fiction, which is to say works of fiction that showed either the fabulous objects of man's belief, or the more real world of his love.

It is therefore not necessary to try and locate the origins of this kind of writing in one nation in preference to another. All we need to do is accept that all nations have used the term *novel* and have defined the word in the way that most suits their preferences for love rather than superstition, or for superstition rather than love.

Now we will briefly consider the nations that have provided us with most examples of this type of work, and also those who composed them. We shall then trace those novels to our own time in order to let our readers establish some of their own ideas regarding comparison.

Aristides of Miletus is the earliest novelist mentioned by writers of antiquity, but his works no longer exist. We only know that his tales were called *Milesian Tales*. A passage from preface to *The Golden Ass* seems to confirm that Aristide's writings were licentious: "I will write this in his style," Apuleius says, at the start of *The Golden Ass*.[5]

Antonius Diogenes, a contemporary of Alexander the Great, wrote in a more restrained style in *The Loves of Dinias and Dercyllis* (*The Incredible Wonders Beyond Thule,* a novel full of fictions, magic, journeys and extraordinary adventures, which Le Seurre copied in 1745 in a short and very curious work for, not content like Diogenes to make his heroes travel through familiar countries, he sometimes sent them to the moon and sometimes to the underworld.[6]

Then there are the adventures of Sinonis and *Rhodanes (Babylonian Stories)* by Iamblichus; the loves of *Theagenes and Chariclea,* which we have just mentioned; Xenophon's *Cyropedia*; Longus' pastoral romance, *Daphnis and Chloe*; the loves of *Ismene and Theoclymenus* and many others, some translated, some totally forgotten today.[7]

The Romans, more critically-minded and more given to depicting wickedness than love or prayer, were content to create a few works of satire, such as those by Petronius and Varron, which we should be careful not to classify as novels.[8]

The Gauls, more inclined to the two above-mentioned weaknesses, had their bards, who may be regarded as the first novelists from that part of Europe we inhabit today. According to Lucan, it was the job of those bards to write, in verse, the immortal acts of their national heroes, and to sing them to the sound of an instrument that resembled a lyre.[9] Very few of these works are known today.

Then we had the words and deeds of Charlemagne, attributed to Archbishop Turpin, and all the romances of the Round Table, Tristan, Lancelot, the lady of the lake, and Perceforest, all written with the view of immortalizing real heroes, or inventing newer ones based on them, all of whom, embroidered by imagination, surpass them by the sheer wonder of their deeds.[10] But what a distance these long, boring, superstition-filled works are from the delightful Greek novels that preceded them! It was barbarity and coarseness that followed the novels of taste and subtle invention that the Greeks had given us as models worthy of emulation. Although there may well have been others before them, they are the earliest novels known to us.

Then it was the time of the troubadours and, although they should be considered poets rather than novelists, the large number of beautiful tales they composed in prose nevertheless rightly places them among the ranks of the kind of writers of whom we speak. Anyone who needs to be convinced of this only has to look at their *fabliaux*, written in the Romance language, during the reign of Hugh Capet, and which were copied so enthusiastically in Italy.[11]

This beautiful part of Europe, still groaning beneath the Saracen yoke, still far from its status as the cradle of the Renaissance of the arts, had almost no novelists until the tenth century. They first appeared in Italy at about the same time as our troubadours (whom they imitated) appeared in France. We take pride in this: it was not the Italians who were our masters in this art, as La Harpe says (p. 242, vol. 3). On the contrary, it was in France that it was truly mastered. It was from our troubadours that Dante, Boccaccio, Tassoni, *&* possibly Petrarch, learned to craft their compositions.[12] Almost all of Boccaccio's tales were taken from *fabliaux* written in France.

The same was not true of the Spanish, who were taught the art of fiction by the Moors, who themselves learned it from the Greeks, as they possessed Arabic translations of all the Greek works of this kind. The Spaniards wrote beautiful novels that were imitated by our French writers. We will come back to them.

As gallantry grew widespread in France, the novel form developed and it was then, which is to say, at the beginning of the last century, that d'Urfé wrote his novel *L'Astrée*, which persuaded us, quite rightly, to prefer his charming shepherds from the banks of the Lignon to the cumbersome knights of the eleventh *&* twelfth centuries.[13]

A frenzy of imitation then took hold of all those to whom nature had given a taste for writing of this kind. The astonishing success of the *L'Astrée*, which was still being read in the middle of this century, had succeeded in appealing to a huge readership, and consequently, it was much imitated without ever being equaled.

Gomberville, La Calprenède, Desmarets, *&* Scudéry thought they could improve on the original by putting princes & kings in the place of the shepherds of the Lignon and, in so doing, made mistakes that their model avoided.[14]

Mademoiselle de Scudéry made the same mistake as her brother; like him, she wanted to ennoble d'Urfé's style and tone and so, like her brother, she put boring heroes in the place of pretty shepherds. Instead of utilizing the character of Cyrus to represent the kind of king that Herodotus has described, she created an *Artamène* far more insane than all the characters of *L'Astrée* combined… a lover who spends his entire day, from morning to night, weeping, and whose languid excesses end up being boring rather than interesting. The same defects appear in her novel *Célie*, in which she gives the Romans all the excesses of the models she imitated. These Romans, whom she badly misrepresents, end up being depicted by her as grotesque.[15]

Here we would ask the reader to permit us to go back for a moment, to fulfill the earlier promise we made to take a look at the novels of Spain.

Certainly, if chivalry had inspired the novelists of France, to what extent did it influence writers beyond the Pyrenees? The contents of *Don Quixote*'s library, so amusingly catalogued by Miguel Cervantes, demonstrates this perfectly.[16] Whatever the answer may be, the renowned author of the memoirs of the greatest madman to have ever come from the mind of a novelist, certainly had no rivals. His immortal work is known throughout the world, has been translated into every language, & is considered by many to be the first novel. It undoubtedly possesses, far more than any other novel, the art of storytelling, for its skillfully interwoven adventures, and in particular for its ability to entertain as it instructs. "This book," said Saint-Évremond, "is the only one I can reread without getting bored, and the only one I wish I had written." The twelve *Exemplary Tales* by the same author, full of interest, wit, & subtlety, place this famous Spanish author in the front rank of novelists. Without him, we might never have had that delightful novel of Scarron's, nor anything by Le Sage.[17]

After d'Urfé and his imitators, after the Arianes, the Cleopatras, the Pharamonds, the Polixandres, in short, all those works in which the hero, after sighing his way through nine volumes, is only too glad to find a wife in the tenth — after, I say, all this nonsense, which is mostly unreadable today, came Madame de La Fayette.[18] Although Madame de La Fayette was clearly influenced by the languorous tone of the authors who preceded her, she was nevertheless far more concise, and by being more concise, she made herself more interesting. It has been said, because she was a woman (as though her sex, naturally more delicate and more suited to writing novels, could not claim to be more successful than men at this sort of work) it was claimed, as I said, that she was given unlimited help; she wrote her novels using La Rochefoucauld's *Maxims* for her philosophical content and Segrais for her style. But that aside, no novel is as interesting as *Zaïde,* nor as beautifully-written as *La Princesse de Clèves.* An amiable and charming writer, the graces clearly directed her pen, but we cannot help but wonder why love was not allowed occasionally to direct it?[19]

Then Fenelon appeared and tried to make himself interesting by giving a poetic lesson to sovereigns, who completely ignored him. Oh, as the sensual lover of Madame Guyon, his soul needed to love, and his mind needed to write.[20] If he had abandoned pedantry, by which I mean the arrogance of trying to make kings learn lessons, we would have had masterpieces from him, instead of one book that no one reads any more.

The same cannot be said of the delightful Scarron, for until the end of the world, his immortal novel, *Roman Comique,* will make everyone laugh and his descriptions will never grow old. Fenelon's *Télémaque,* which survived for less than a hundred years, has perished under the ruins of its own century and is already no more; but those actors from Le Mans, written by Scarron, himself a dear and kindly child of folly, will amuse even the most serious of readers, for as long as there are men on earth.[21]

Toward the end of the same century, Madame de Gomez, the daughter of the famous Poisson, created works in a very different genre to the writers of her sex who had preceded her; works which, for this reason, were no less entertaining. Her *Les journées amusantes,* as well as her *Cent nouvelles nouvelles*, will always, despite several defects, be on the bookshelves of all lovers of her story-telling.[22]

Gomez knew her art, and no one should deny her this richly-deserved praise. Mademoiselle de Lussan, Mesdames de Tencin, de Graffigny, Elie de Beaumont, and Riccoboni emulated her. Their writings, so full of delicacy & taste, certainly honor their sex. Graffigny's *Lettres d'une Péruvienne* will always be a model of tenderness and feeling, just as *Les Lettres de Juliette Catesby* by Riccoboni will be of eternal use to anyone who wishes to learn grace & lightness of style.[23]

But let us go back to the century we left a while ago, for we feel compelled to praise the admirable women who gave men so many good novel-writing lessons.

The decadence of Ninon-de-Lenclos, Marion Delorme, the Marquis of Sévigné and the Marquis de La Fare, as well as the Chaulieus and the Saint-Évremonds, in short, all of the members of this charming society which had freed themselves from the languors of the god of Cythère, began to think, like Buffon, that "There is nothing good in love but the physical part." This attitude brought about a swift change of tone in novels.[24]

The writers who appeared after them felt that their bland adventures would no longer amuse a century poisoned by the decadent Regent; a century that had renounced chivalric follies, religious excesses, and the adoration of women.[25] Finding it easier to amuse or corrupt women, than to serve them or to praise them, they created events, dramatic scenes, and conversations that more accurately reflected the spirit of the times. They wrapped cynicism and immorality in a pleasing & playful, sometimes philosophical, style which at the very least delighted their readers, even if it did not instruct them.

Crébillon wrote *Le Sopha, Tanzai, Les Égarements du cœur et de l'esprit,* etc. Each of these novels flattered vice and mocked virtue but when they appeared they were great successes.[26]

Marivaux, more original in his method of depicting reality and more subtle too, provided fully-developed characters which captivated the souls of his readers and made them cry.[27] But how could a writer possess such energy and yet write in such a precious, mannered style? He is proof that nature never grants a novelist all the gifts that are necessary for the perfection of his art.

Voltaire's aim was quite different. Having no other purpose than to insert philosophy into his novels, he abandoned everything else in his determination to achieve this. And he succeeded. Despite all the criticism leveled at them, *Candide* and *Zadig* will always be masterpieces.[28]

Nature bestowed upon Rousseau a delicacy of sentiment equal to the wit it gave to Voltaire.[29] Consequently, Rousseau's approach to novel-writing was vastly different.

There is an abundance of vigor and energy in *Julie, ou la Nouvelle Héloïse.* If it was Momus who dictated *Candide* to Voltaire, then it was the god of love himself who lit up every burning page of *Julie* with his torch, and it can confidently be stated that this sublime book will never have imitators.[30] May this truth make the pens drop from the hands of the multitude of ephemeral writers who, for the last thirty years, have not stopped presenting us with their pale imitations of this original immortal. May they also understand that to reach that standard, they will need a soul of fire like Rousseau's and a mind as philosophical as his; two things that seldom occur together in nature twice in the same century.

Meanwhile Marmontel gave us the tales which he called *Contes moraux,* not (as one esteemed writer claimed) because they taught morality, but because they described our mores, although it was done in a very similar manner to Marivaux's style.[31] Besides, what are these tales? Juvenile nonsense, written for women and children; tales which no one would believe were written by the same hand that wrote *Bélisaire,* a work which alone bestows greatness upon the author.[32] How could the man who wrote chapter fifteen of *that* book be content with the lukewarm response he got for giving us those watered-down, rose-tinted tales?

Finally, it was the English novels, by which we mean the vigorous works of Richardson and Fielding, that taught the French that it is not by describing the tedious languors of love or by reporting the boring conversations of salons that one achieves success in this genre; but by creating strong male characters who, as the playthings and victims of the effervescence of the heart known as love, show both its dangers and miseries.[33] This is the only way to achieve the plot developments and the attendant passions that are both so well depicted in English novels.

It was Richardson and Fielding who taught us that it was only the profound study of the human heart, one of nature's true labyrinths, that can inspire the novelist to create work that makes us see man, not only as he is, or as he presents himself, which is the task of the historian, but as he can be, once his vices have been corrected, and once he has been subjected to all the shocks of passion. It is necessary, for any writer wanting to work in this genre, to know the passions well in order to utilize them. From them we also learned that it is not always by making virtue triumph that a writer keeps the reader's interest. While it is certainly something that should be aimed for in life, this rule, which is neither in nature nor in Aristotle, is simply one we would prefer all men to respect, although it is in no sense essential in a novel and is not even the principal that makes a novel interesting.[34] When virtue triumphs, things being as they are, our tears dry up before they have had a chance to flow. But if, after the harshest trials, we finally see virtue crushed by vice, our souls will be torn apart, and the novel, having deeply moved us and, as Diderot said, made our hearts bleed from the back, will undoubtedly create the level of interest which alone ensures success.[35]

Let us ask this: if after twelve or fifteen volumes of *Clarissa*, the immortal Richardson had ended up virtuously converting Lovelace and making him peacefully marry Clarissa, would the novel, if it had been reversed in this way, have caused as many exquisite tears to be shed by its readers as it now does?[36]

Writers working in this genre must be able to capture nature; they must be able to capture the heart of man, that most singular of nature's creations, and not virtue, because virtue, however beautiful, however necessary it may be, is nevertheless only one of the manifestations of this astounding heart; the profound study of which is essential for every novelist because the novel, if it is to be a faithful mirror of the human heart, must inevitably reflect every part of it.

Prévost is a learned translator of Richardson; one to whom we are indebted for having rendered the beauties of that famous writer into the French language.[37] He is owed a tribute and any praise he receives is utterly deserved, as he could rightly be called the French Richardson. He alone had the art of keeping the reader interested in his complex plots and intricate fables, and always sustained that interest, despite dividing it. He alone was consistently sparing enough of his episodes that they augmented and complemented the main plot, rather than detracted from it. Although it is the large number of plot events that La Harpe criticizes him for, it is *that* which enables him to produce the most sublime effects, but at the same time that which also provides the best evidence of the greatness of his mind, and the excellence of his genius.[38] Finally (to add what we think of Prévost to what others have also thought of him), *Mémoires et aventures d'un homme de qualité*; *Cléveland*; *Histoire d'une Grecque modern*; *Le Monde moral*; and particularly *Manon Lescaut* are filled with touching and terrible scenes, which strike at and irresistibly affect the reader's mind.[39] The situations in these works, so admirably arranged, culminate in moments when nature shudders with horror, etc. And that is what is called writing a novel. And that is why posterity has guaranteed Prévost a place that none of his rivals can ever attain.

Then came the writers of the middle of the century. Dorat, as mannered as Marivaux, as cold and amoral as Crébillon, but a more pleasing writer than either of the two to whom we have just compared him.[40] The frivolity of his times excuses his own, and he possessed the art of capturing it perfectly.

Will you allow me to offer the charming author of *Aline, reine de Golconde* a crown of laurels? One rarely encounters a more agreeable mind, and even the most delightful tales of the century are not worth that one story that immortalizes him. He is both more engaging and more inventive than Ovid. And since the Hero-Saviour of France summoned him back to his country of birth, he has demonstrated that he is as much a friend of Apollo as of Mars, and now strives to fulfill the hope of this great man by threading more pretty roses through the hair of your beautiful Aline.[41]

D'Arnaud, an imitator of Prévost, often claimed to surpass him; they both dipped their pens in the Styx, but D'Arnaud sometimes prettified his writing with the flowers of Elysium; Prévost, more energetic, never diluted the ink with which he wrote *Cléveland*.[42]

R… floods the public with so many of his works that he needs a printing press at his bedside; fortunately that is the only press that has to groan under the weight of his terrible productions.[43] His writing style is dull and pedestrian, his disgusting adventures are always peopled with characters of the worst kind; finally, he has no other merit than a prolixity… for which only the pepper merchants will thank him.

Perhaps, at this point, we should attempt to analyze the new novels whose merit consists, for the most part, of their reliance on sorcery and phantasmagoria. At the forefront, I would place *The Monk*, superior in all respects to the bizarre impulses coming from Mrs. Radcliffe's brilliant imagination; but to do so would make this essay too long.[44] Let us agree that this genre of novel, whatever one's view may be, is certainly not without qualities. It was the inevitable result of the revolutionary upheaval which was felt by the whole of Europe.

For those acquainted with the evil methods that the wicked use to torment good people, novels became as difficult to write as they were monotonous to read. There was no one alive who had not experienced in four or five years more misery than the most famous novelist in all of literature could have created in a century.

It was therefore necessary, in order to create interesting novels, for writers to project the history of man, and to set what was common to their own age in the realms of fantasy, in short, to describe Hell itself! But there were many disadvantages to this kind of writing. The author of *The Monk* avoided them no more successfully than Mrs. Radcliffe. The novelist therefore has to make an unavoidable choice: either develop the supernatural and risk losing the reader's interest, or never provide an explanation and descend into the most ridiculous implausibility. Should there ever be a work published in this genre that is good enough to attain this goal without breaking against one or the other of these reefs, then far from disparaging it for the means by which it has succeeded, we would offer it as a model.

Before we begin to answer our third and final question: *What are the rules of the art of writing the novel?* we must, it seems to me, respond to the perpetual objection of a few atrabilious individuals who, in order to give themselves the veneer of morality, from which their hearts are usually very distant, constantly ask: *What is the point of the novel?*

What is their point? you perverse hypocrites, for it is you alone that ask this ridiculous question. Their point is to describe you as you *are,* you arrogant individuals who wish to escape the artist's brush because you fear the consequences. The novel, if I may express myself in this way, is the picture of the mores of its era and, to the philosopher who wants to understand man, the novel is as essential as history. The historian only records details of the man in his public role, when he is not being his true self; ambition and pride cover his face with a mask that shows only those two passions, and not the man. The novelist's pen, on the contrary, captures his inner truth… catches it when he lowers his mask and the resulting sketch, which is more interesting, is also much truer: this is the point of novels.

Unemotional censors who do not like novels, you are like those legless cripples who asked: *What is the point of portraits?*

If it is therefore true that the novel is useful, let us not be afraid of setting down here some of the principles that we believe necessary to bring this genre to perfection. I feel that it is difficult to carry out this task without arming my enemies with weapons they will use against me. Won't I become doubly guilty of not *writing well,* if I prove that I know what it takes to *write well?* Ah! Let us leave these vain considerations; let us subordinate them to the love of art.

The novelist's most important requirement is an understanding of the human heart. Now, all discerning minds will no doubt be in agreement when we state that this important knowledge is acquired only through *suffering* and *travel*.

One must have encountered men of all nations to know them, and one must have suffered at their hands to know how to appreciate them. The hand of misfortune, by elevating the character of those it crushes, gives the novelist the right perspective from which to observe and to study others. He observes them from there, just as the passenger observes the waves furiously breaking against the reef on which the storm has driven his ship. But wherever nature or fate has placed him, if he wants to know men, let him speak little when he is with them; we learn nothing when we speak, we learn only by listening; and that's why most talkers are usually just fools.

You who want to follow the thorn-strewn path in pursuit of this thorny career! Do not lose sight of the fact that the novelist is a man of nature. Nature created the novelist to be its portraitist. If he does not love his mother from the moment she brings him into the world, then he must never write, for we will not read him. But if he acquires an ardent desire to paint everything; if he shudders as he looks at nature's bosom in which he seeks his art and then wants to draw models from it; if he has fire and talent and enthusiasm and genius, he should follow the hand that beckons him, for he has guessed the secret of man and he will paint it.

Governed by his imagination he must yield to it, and then embellish what he sees. Any fool can pick a rose and strip it of its petals, but the man of genius breathes in its fragrance and paints it: that is the kind of novelist we will read.

But, while I advise you to embellish, I forbid you to deviate from plausibility. The reader has every right to be angry if he suspects that the writer is trying to mislead him, or if he believes that the novelist is demanding too much of him. If he feels the novelist is trying to fool him in any way that revokes plausibility, his pride will suffer and he will simply stop believing anything the novelist says.

Since there is nothing to constrain you, you have the right to use as many stories from history as you please, even if it becomes necessary for you to abandon total authenticity for the sake of the delights you put before us. Again, you are not being asked to say what is actually true, but only to say what appears to be true in appearance. To demand too much from you would harm the pleasures we expect from your work. Do not, however, replace the true with the impossible, and let what you invent be well expressed. You will be forgiven for substituting your imagination for the truth only on the condition that it is for the express purpose of adorning and astounding. A novelist has no right to write badly when he is free to say whatever he wants. If, like R..., you wrote only what everyone already knows, & were you, like him, to give us four volumes a month, it would not be worth picking up a pen.

No one will force you to do this kind of work; but if you undertake it, do it well. Do not choose it as a way to earn a living: your work would smell of your needs. You will transmit your weakness into it and it will have the pallor of hunger. There are other professions available to you; make shoes, but do not write books. We will not think any less of you, in fact, since you will not be boring us with substandard writing, we may like you all the more.

Once your outline is set down, work hard to extend it, but do this without restricting yourself to the limitations that it seems at first to impose on you. If you adhere to those constraints, your work will be cold and slight. What we expect from you are bursts of invention, flights of creativity, not adherence to prescriptive rules. Exceed your initial draft, vary it, expand it; it is only as you work that ideas will come. Do you think that the ideas that occur to you while you compose are not as good as the ones dictated by your original outline? I only require one thing of you, and that is to sustain my interest until the last page. You will miss the mark if you disrupt your story with incidents that are repeated, or that do not add to the story. Those that you do include must be as highly-polished as the main narrative. This is how you compensate the reader for forcing him to leave something that interests him, in order to offer a secondary incident. He may well allow you to interrupt him, but he will not forgive you for boring him. Ensure that your incidents always derive from & return to the story. If you make your heroes travel, then be familiar with the countries that their travels take them to, and imbue your stories with such magic that I can identify with them. Remember that I am walking with them, no matter where you place them, and I may know more than you of that region. I will not forgive you any mistakes regarding manners, customs, or costumes, nor will I forgive any geographical errors.

As no one forces you to devise these escapades, you must either make your local descriptions authentic, or you must remain at home. This is the only area in all of your writing where invention cannot be tolerated, unless the countries to which you transport me are imaginary, and if that is the case, then I demand that it be plausible and believable.

Avoid moralizing; it is an affectation and it has no place in a novel. If your characters are sometimes forced to moralize because your plot requires it, then let them do so unaffectedly and without pretention. The novelist should never preach or moralize; it should always be the characters, and then only when forced to do so by circumstances.

With regards to your ending; let it be natural, never contrived, not forced, but always established from the circumstances. I do not want you, like the authors of the *Encyclopédie*, to write in a way that tries to predict and conform to every reader's desire, for what pleasure remains for him when he has guessed everything?[45] The outcome must be such that the events must lead up to it, as this is a matter of the requirements of plausibility. You must put your imagination to work to achieve this. If you follow these principles & instructions you mind will create works of wit and taste, and if, as a result, you do not do well, at least you will do better than I have. For, it must be admitted, in the stories you are about to read, the audacity of invention that I have allowed myself does not always adhere to the strict rules of the genre. I hope that the extreme authenticity of the characters will perhaps compensate for this.

Nature, even stranger than the moralists have described, constantly eludes the restraints and the limits that their policy would like to impose upon it. Uniform in its patterns, irregular in its effects, always agitated, nature resembles the depths of a volcano that shoots forth either precious stones to be used by men, or balls of fire to destroy them. Noble when it populates the world with the likes of Antoninus and Titus; terrible when it vomits up an Andronicus or a Nero; but always sublime, always majestic, always worthy of our studies, our pens, and our respect and our admiration, because its designs are unknown to us.[46] As slaves to nature's whims or needs, we should never base our opinion of it on the hardships it inflicts on us, but on its greatness, on its energy, no matter what the results may be.

As the minds of men become corrupted, and as a nation grows old, prejudices are eradicated because nature is more closely studied and better analyzed. All of this must be made more widely known. This is the same for the arts. It is only by advancing that art moves nearer to perfection. It reaches this state only by repeated attempts. It was no doubt unnecessary to go quite so far in those terrible times of ignorance when, bent beneath the weight of religion, the Inquisition stakes became the reward for scientific enquiry and those who attempted to understand nature were punished with death.

So, considering our present circumstances, let us start from the same principle. When man has tested his restraints; when, with a fearless glance, he steps over the barriers put there to impede him; when, following the example of the Titans, he dares to shake his fist at the heavens; and when, armed with his passions which are as hot as the lavas of Vesuvius, he is no longer afraid to declare war on those who once made him tremble; when his *wrong-doings* seem to be nothing more than *errors* legitimized by his later discoveries, then should he not be spoken to with the same energy that he himself expends in directing his own conduct?[47] In short, are the men of the eighteenth century the same as the men of the eleventh?

Let us end with a positive assurance; that the stories we are presenting to you today are absolutely new and in no way rework previously-known tales. Their original quality is perhaps of some merit in an era when everything seems to have been done, when the imagination of authors seems to be exhausted and incapable of creating anything new, and the public is offered only compilations, extracts, or translations.

However, both "The Enchanted Tower" and "The Amboise Conspiracy" have some basis in historical fact. Hopefully, the reader will see, by our sincere acknowledgement of this, how far we are from wanting to deceive anyone about this.[48] One has to be original in this genre, or not get involved. Here we indicate the sources of what is in both of these stories.

The Arab historian Abul-cæcim-terif-aben-tariq, a writer little known to our writers of the day, recounts the following, regarding "The Enchanted Tower."[49]

Rodrigue, a decadent prince, obsessed with voluptuous pleasures, summoned to the court the daughters of his vassals, and there abused them. Among them was Florinde, the daughter of Comte Julien. He raped her. Her father, who was in Africa, received this news through a coded letter from his daughter. He recruited some Moors, and returned to Spain at their head; Rodrigue did not know what to do, as there were no funds in his treasures, and there was no place to hide. He decided to go in search of the Enchanted Tower, near Toledo, because he had been told that it held vast sums of gold. He entered it and saw a statue of

Time poised to strike with a huge club. On a stone nearby was an inscription, warning Rodrigue of all the misfortunes that awaited him. The prince went on and saw a large vat of water, but no money. He retraced his steps and gave orders for the tower to be closed and locked securely. A thunderbolt struck the tower and destroyed it, leaving ruins & rubble. Despite these disastrous predictions, the prince assembled an army, fought a battle for eight days near Córdoba, and was killed. His body was never found.

This is what history has provided us with. If you, discerning reader, would care to read our story now, you will soon see whether or not the multitude of events we have added to the dry little anecdote deserves, as is our contention, to be regarded as being entirely ours.

As for "The Amboise Conspiracy," if you care to read Garnier's account, you will see just how little we have borrowed from history.[50]

There were no sources to serve as guides for the other tales. Settings, narrative style, incidents, everything is our own. If it is not of the highest quality, no matter. We have always believed, and will never cease to be persuaded, that it is better to invent, even weakly, than it is to copy or translate.

Anyone who invents or creates anything has the right to the claim of genius, and may have grounds for doing so. But what can the plagiarist claim? I cannot think of a lower profession. Nor can I conceive of a confession more humiliating than the admission such men are forced to make when they admit to themselves that they have no creative talent of their own, and are therefore obliged to borrow that of others.

With regard to translators, God forbid that we should try to take away from their merits. But they draw attention to, and give success to, our foreign rivals. And even if it were only for the honor of our own country, would it not be better to say to these proud rivals, *and we too, know how to create?*

I must finally respond to certain criticisms leveled at me when my *Aline and Valcour* was published. My brush-strokes were too forceful, it was said, and I presented vice as too odious.[51] Would you like to know the reason? I do not want people to be attracted to vice. Unlike Crébillon and Dorat, I have no intention of making women love or admire the men who deceive them; on the contrary, I want them to hate them. It is the only way to prevent them from being abused. And, in order to achieve that, I have made those of my characters who follow the path of vice so appalling that they will certainly inspire neither pity nor love. In doing this, I dare say, I am far more moral than those who embellish their villains in order to make them attractive. The pernicious works of such authors resemble those fruits common to America; fruits which, beneath their brightly-colored skins, carry death in their flesh.[52] This betrayal of nature's, the motive of which it is not for us to reveal, is not meant to be imitated by man. In conclusion, I shall never, I repeat, never, depict crime other than in the most vivid colors of hell. I want readers to see crime in all its nakedness, to fear and to hate it, and I know no of other way to achieve this than to depict its characteristic ugliness and to show it in all its horror. Woe to those who dress crime in roses! Their intentions are not pure, and I will never imitate them.

Based on this philosophy, I state now that I no longer wish to have the novel *J...* attributed to me.[53] I have never written books of that kind *&* I surely never will. There are, of course, fools and villains who, despite the truth of my denials, will continue to suspect me or accuse me of being its author. Because of this, and from this moment on, the only weapon I will use to fight their slander will be my utter contempt.

To Madame de Sade [54]

My Grand Letter

20 February 1781

Indeed, my dear friend, I rather believe that your intention would be to inculcate in me the same respect for your petty divinities that you so devoutly feel for them. And just because you grovel & crawl before that pack, you would require that I do the same, so that a ***, and a ***, and an ***, and a ***, and *** were my gods just as they are yours! If, unfortunately, you do indeed hold such a conviction in your head, then remove it forthwith, I beg you. Misfortune will never defile me:[55]

> *Despite my chains, my heart will be forever free.*
> *(Les Arsacides)*[56]

and it always will be. These despicable chains, yes, were they to drag me to my grave, you would still find me exactly the same. I have the misfortune of having received at birth a strong soul that has never bent to anyone, nor ever will. I have not the slightest fear of, nor concern for, offending anyone at all, no matter who they might be. You have given me too many proofs that the length of my sentence is determined for me to doubt it:

therefore, it is not within anyone's power to increase it or reduce it. Moreover, even were this not so, the people that hold me here would not be the ones to do it: this would be a matter for the king, and he is the only person in the entire kingdom that I respect — he, and the princes of his bloodline. Beneath them, I regard everyone else to be so utterly indistinguishable, so insignificant that, given the circumstances, I have no wish to look closely at any of them, as it would reveal a superiority that favors myself so much, it would confirm my already profound contempt.

As I am sure you will no doubt agree, it is absurd that they treat me as they do and yet demand that I do not complain about it. Let us consider this reasonably for a moment: when a term of imprisonment has to be as long as mine is, can there be a more utter evil than to try to make it more terrible by the methods your mother has implemented in order to torment me here? What! Is it not enough to be deprived of everything that makes life pleasant and agreeable; is it not enough to be deprived even of breathing clean air, to witness all one's desires endlessly shattered against four walls and to see one's days go by, each so alike that they resemble those that await us in the grave? But this hideous torture is not enough for that horrible creature: it is necessary to aggravate it further with whatever else she can conceive to double all the horror. You will admit that only a monster is capable of carrying vengeance to that extreme…

But it is all in your imagination, you are going to tell me; *they are not doing that at all; these are delusions that naturally develop in your situation*. Delusions, you say? Very well! I am going to look in my journal, where I have written no less than 56 proofs of the sort I am about to cite, and you will see, from the one solitary example I select, that it is venomous rage which is responsible for all the maneuvers that this hateful shrew has set against me, and if that proof can properly be called delusions.

You ought not doubt for an instant that a prisoner, for whatever reasons he might have for believing his release is in the far distance, will seize with incredible eagerness upon the slightest action that might appear to him to suggest an earlier release. That is exactly in accord with human nature, and as it is not wrong, it ought not be something that someone is punished for, but perhaps pitied. Therefore it is an act of patent cruelty to incite, instigate, or put into action any such plans or initiatives that will deliberately mislead him.

One should take extreme care to do the exact opposite, and basic humanity (if there were any here) should serve as a constant reminder in the core of one's soul to do nothing in any way to agitate the most painful of the poor wretch's feelings, because it is clear in the end that all the suicides originate solely from destroyed hope. Therefore, one should not encourage hope when there is no actual vestige of hope; anyone who does so is manifestly a monster. Hope is the most sensitive part of the soul of anyone who is suffering and in pain, and anyone who holds out hope only to destroy it is imitating those torturers of hell who, they say, reopen a wound and then focus their endless cruelty on its most lacerated spot, rather than anywhere else.

That is exactly what your mother has been doing to me for the past four years: a multitude of fresh hopes month after month.[57] To listen to the people here and to examine your parcels and letters, etc., it seemed that I was always on the point of imminent release. Then, when that point finally came, there was the sudden thrust of a carefully-aimed dagger, followed by *a huge laugh* at my expense. It seems that this despicable woman amuses herself by having me build châteaux of paper in order to have the pleasure of demolishing them no sooner than they are built. Putting aside the ways that this affects one's optimism, and the likelihood of it inculcating a sense of futility at feeling any hope at all for the rest of one's life, as well as the certainty of it utterly destroying one's sense of hope in its entirety, there is, you will agree, the much greater risk of the final excess of despair. I have, at this moment, no reason to doubt that this is her sole purpose, and that having failed to have me killed, and then leaving me for five years in the hideous situation I was in before I was in prison, she decided she would try and accomplish it in another five years using more certain methods. From the multitude of proofs that I just mentioned to you that I have of this vicious game she is playing with me; a game that consists of her raising me up only to knock me back down, I am going to cite a more recent one in order to convince you of what I say.

About six months ago, you sent me a curtain for my room. Although I begged the people here to hang it for me, they never wanted to. What should I conclude from that? *That it was not worth it.* So obviously this raised my hopes; they then left it like that until I had had enough time to build an entire château of paper, and only then did they come to hang it — and thus my paper château was smashed to the ground. Such are the cruel games of Madame la Présidente de Montreuil; games which have preoccupied her for the past four years, along with the lackeys she has hired to assist her in these affairs and who have all had a good laugh at her expense (at least that was what Marais, no doubt jealous at not being included, told me) as soon as they have received her gifts or her money. There are 56 maneuvers of this kind, not to mention those yet to come; not that I have had 56 different opinions concerning my release. Heaven forbid! I would have then spent my entire life counting, and that is exactly what I have refrained from doing (you have examples of my more serious occupations), but I have kept a careful eye on matters and I have noted that it is very likely that instead of the fourth paper château which I am now on, and which, however long it may take me to build, will doubtless be crushed just like the other three, instead of just four, as I said, she has schemed to try and get me to build 56.[58] I cannot help asking if this is reasonable behavior for a sensible woman, an intelligent woman, and a woman who, because of the ties that bind us, ought to be alleviating my suffering rather than increasing it?

But she is offended, you tell me. In the first place, I deny that; she has been offended only because she has chosen to be, and she should place the blame squarely on her own evil genius for whatever she takes as a personal affront. But let us assume that she has in fact been offended: does that mean she should seek to exact revenge for it? Such a pious woman, who has the *outward appearance* of fulfilling the ceremonial aspect of her religion, should she ignore the first and the most important of all its rules?[59]

Even so, let her have her vengeance, I will concede that: but a prison term as long as I have served, and as harsh, is that not revenge enough? Does she need more? *Oh! you do not understand,* you add; *all of this has been necessary; it is to rehabilitate you!* — To rehabilitate me! Honestly, suppose I were to get out of here tomorrow, would you dare say that I had been rehabilitated, without being afraid that I should accuse you of an outrageous impudence? Rehabilitate! — to put somebody in prison for four or five years because of *a party involving some girls*; the kind of party which happens eighty times a day every day in Paris![60] And then to tell him how fortunate he is to be released after five years in prison and that if those years of captivity had affected him the way they have done, that it was simply to *rehabilitate him!* No, I reject this idea outright, because it disgusts me too much, and I am quite sure that you will never have the audacity to suggest it to me again.

Let us now return to that phrase *a party involving some girls*, a phrase that I can well imagine upsets those who are distressed at not being able to convince me that all of the slanders leveled against me are true. My adventures come down to three. I will not mention the first incident, as it was entirely Madame la Présidente de Montreuil's doing, and if anyone should have been punished, it was she.[61] But in France they do not punish those with an income of one hundred thousand livres a year. Below them are *the little victims* whom they can sacrifice to the voraciousness of those monsters whose profession is to make a living from the blood of unfortunates. They require their *little victims*: others provide them, and so the debt is paid. That is why I am in prison.

The second adventure was the Marseilles incident, & I believe that it is pointless to discuss this one too.[62] It has been well established, I think, that there was nothing but libertinage involved and that everything they judged as criminal, which was pure invention, was so judged in order to slake the vengeance of my enemies in Provence and the rapacity of the chancellor who wanted my title for his son. Therefore, that one, I believe, has been fully redressed by the Vincennes imprisonment and by the banishment from Marseilles.

Let us move on to the third. I beg your forgiveness in advance for the terms I will have to employ. I will moderate them to the best of my ability by using abbreviations. Between husband *&* wife, one may, when the case requires it, express oneself rather more freely than with strangers or with ordinary friends. I beg you to forgive me for my revelations, but I would prefer that you considered me a libertine rather than a criminal. My faults will be laid bare and I shall conceal not one iota from you.

Having been reduced to spending my time alone in a very isolated château, nearly always without you, and having the minor idiosyncrasy (one must admit it) of loving women perhaps a little too much, I went to see a well-known p—— in Lyons and I told her: I want to take four or five servant girls back to my château, and I want them young and pretty; provide me with some that answer that description.[63]

This p——, named Nanon, for this Nanon was a well-known p—— in Lyons — I shall prove it when necessary — promised me those girls and in fact provided them. I took them home with me; I used them. After six months, parents came and asked for those girls, assuring me that they were their daughters. I returned them, and suddenly there was a charge of kidnaping *&* rape made against me! And there you have the greatest of all injustices. The law regarding that, as I got it from Monsieur de Sartine (he had the kindness to explain it to me himself; he should be able to recall it), is as follows: it is expressly forbidden in France for any p—— to furnish girls who are virgins, and if the girl furnished is a virgin and if she complains, it is not the man who is accused, it is the p——, who is rigorously punished on the spot. But even if the man had asked for a virgin, it is not he who is punished: he is doing only what all men do. To repeat, it is the p—— who gave her to him and who perfectly well knew that that was expressly forbidden. Therefore, in that first deposition made against me, at Lyons, for kidnapping and rape, there was no legitimate charge; I was guilty of nothing. It was the p—— that provided the girls who should have been punished, and not me. But there was no profit to be made from a w——, and the parents were hoping to extract some money from me.[64]

Let us continue. Earlier on, I had had an adventure in Arcueil, in which a lying, scheming woman, in order to get some money (which rather stupidly, she was paid), spread throughout Paris a series of untruths about me; namely that I had conducted certain "experiments" & that the garden behind my home was a cemetery in which I had buried the bodies I had used in those experiments.[65] This far-fetched fantasy was far too convenient for my enemies, who, in their rage, embellished it and used it against me at every opportunity. Consequently, one of the accusations leveled at me during the Marseilles affair was that I was again experimenting on young girls and apparently, one of those young girls disappeared, never to be seen again. Some of those girls, it is true, did not return to Lyons, however they did reappear in other parts of the country.

Let us examine the details. There were, it is generally agreed, five girls from Lyons. One, frightened by the solitude she was being kept in (not in order to perform experiments on her, but because decency required it) escaped and went to my uncle's. *So we know what happened to her.* Another one stayed on, employed as my housekeeper until she died of natural causes, as is known by the entire province, because in her final days she was very well cared for by the director of public health.[66] *There you have another who is accounted for.* Two of them have been returned to their parents, *so they are also accounted for.* As for the fifth and last, like her friend, she too threatened to run off and spread malicious gossip about me if she was kept any longer in isolation. As she had no parents, nor relatives of any sort to ask for her return, I put her into the care of a La Coste peasant, whom I will name in due course, one you know very well. She was then employed as a maid in the home of one of his relatives in Marseilles. Since I have complete proof of all of this, I confess it would give me great pleasure to present this evidence if called upon to do so. She was conducted there, put to work there, and left there, and a certificate to that effect was brought to me and I have put that document in a safe place so it can also be shown if need be. I have since learned that this creature had left that house and set herself up as a p———. And there you have the details of those five girls from Lyons clearly established in such a way that I can defy the cleverest or rather the most cunning-minded magistrate, and prove the contrary to any accusation.

Let us go one step further. Three other girls, of such age and condition that they were unlikely to be asked for by their families, lived either before or after this time, for a few weeks at the Château de La Coste.

Let me give a full account of them, so that this may be a general confession, because that is my intention, and I want, if possible, to eradicate once & for all even the slightest suspicion of all the horrors that certain people have enjoyed inventing about me and which have encouraged Madame de Montreuil to treat me as she has, both because of her extreme penchant for believing everything she hears, and because these lies have conveniently provided her with the weapons of her vengeance.

The first of these three girls was named *Du Plan;* she was a dancer at the Comédie de Marseilles. As a governess, and therefore not incognito, she lived openly at the château. When she left La Coste, she did so quite openly. More than a year later, I found her again at the Comédie de Bordeaux, and she was still living in a small provincial town that had been pointed out to me during my journey to Aix. So there is nothing to be concerned about in her case.

The second girl came from Montpellier; her name was *Rosette.* She stayed at the château for about two months, keeping mostly to herself. At the end of this period, she said that she wanted to leave, and so we both decided that she should write to a man she knew in Montpellier, and that this man, I believe by trade a carpenter and her landlord in Montpellier, would personally come to fetch her. Once he had agreed to meet her, the hour, the place, the day, the rendezvous (at the foot of the château walls) was all agreed. On the appointed day, the man arrived, and I personally handed the girl over to the said man. The girl named *Marie* (the Lyons girl who had remained in my service) carried her bag out and gave it to the man. He had brought a mule, and he put the girl and the bag on the mule then, after receiving from me six gold louis that the girl asked me to pay him — a sum which she had earned from me — they departed. That happened in June 1775.

In October 1776, I left, as you know, to spend two weeks at Montpellier and brought back the third girl, about whom I wish now to speak. The girl named *Rosette* was living at Montpellier at that time, my proof being that I saw her there; *that I saw her there in every way imaginable, or, to put it more decently, saw her in the full meaning of the term.* She was the one who convinced the third girl, named *Adelaïde,* to come and to work for me, assuring her in front of two or three other women, who perhaps will not be too confused if I ever have to speak about it, set about assuring the girl that she would have no reason, except for the loneliness there, to be concerned with working for me, and having said this, proceeded to praise me and all of my dealings with her.

It was only because of *Rosette's* personal recommendation that I got the other one to come with me. Not knowing me, she would certainly not have come otherwise. So *Adelaïde* arrived and stayed until the third of Madame de Montreuil's disgraceful acts. This was when the postmaster of Courthézon most resolutely arrived at the château and took *Adelaïde* off. So there you have the facts of what happened to the third girl clearly established.[67]

Two or three other girls, either cooks or kitchen maids, including those that we brought with us from Paris, lived at the château at different times, mostly during the time I was there avoiding my sentence, but they were there so briefly, and they came and went so openly, that I consider it pointless to even mention them. Among them was a niece [Anne Sablonnière] of Nanon,[68] the above-mentioned p——, whom we sent to a convent. Madame de Montreuil had her removed from it, so she knows what has become of her. That is everything. That is my complete confession, such as I would make before God, if I were on the point of dying.

What then are we to conclude from all this?

Are we to conclude that Monsieur de Sade, whom they doubtless accuse of all sorts of horrors, since they

are keeping him in prison for such a long time, and whom
they have every reason to fear, both because of what
he soon will reveal, and because he has already twice
suffered whatever malignant slanders the public could
bring against him, but who is, nevertheless, no more
guilty of *torture, experiments*, or *murder* in this most
recent episode than he was in any of the others.

Or are we to conclude that Monsieur de Sade has
simply done what everyone else in the world does, that
he has consorted with women who were either already
totally debauched or were supplied by a p——, and that
seduction, therefore, is not an issue in this case; and that
nevertheless Monsieur de Sade is being punished and
made to suffer as if he were guilty of the darkest crimes.

Let us now examine the evidence they brought
against him:

1st — *The testimony of a guilty p——:* Was her instinct
for self-preservation so strong that in her attempt
to exonerate herself, she tried, as much as she could,
to incriminate the one she believed to be her ac-
complice?

2nd — *The disappearance of the girls:* I would bet my life
on this not being the case and I would willingly lose
it without any regrets if I were ever shown any proof
of this.

3rd — *Human remains found in a garden:* Some bones
had been brought to the château by one of the girls,
the one named *Du Plan*. She is very much alive, *&*

they can interrogate her. She decided, as a joke, in good or bad taste (I leave it to you to decide), to decorate a small room with them. The bones were used for that specific purpose & when the joke or, to my mind, the stupid prank, was done, they were thrown into the garden. Let them count and compare what they found against the list that I have from *Du Plan's* own hand of the number and type of bones that she brought with her from Marseilles: they will see that not one additional bone was found.

All these verifications & confrontations are indeed essential in matters of this kind: but have they taken the trouble to undertake a single one? No, of course not!

In fact, it was not the truth they wanted to find: it was to put me in prison — and here I am. But one day I will get out, perhaps, and when I do, they may perhaps give me enough credit to understand that I shall clear my name and, in turn, denounce those who are treating me this way; or at least, if I am unable to succeed in that endeavor because of their wealth and their protection, I intend, at the very least, to publicly cover them with ignominy, shame, and confusion.[69] (*The Duped Judge*)

Let us continue: I wish to leave no stone unturned. What more can be added to all this evidence? *The testimony of a child*? But that child was a servant: therefore, as a child & as a servant, his evidence is inadmissible.[70] Moreover, there is another obvious motive here: this child had a very greedy mother who believed that by making him report a thousand horrors, she was going to assure herself of a guaranteed income. She knew about the one hundred louis paid at Arcueil [by Mme de Montreuil to Rose Keller].[71] Of course, someone may raise the following objection: *How do you know that the child testified against you? Since you are so afraid of his testimony, he must have seen something, or known something?* That is what I was expecting you to say, for that is precisely at the crux of the infamy. First of all, he would have been apprehensive, knowing that the same people who had caused such a fuss in Lyons were coming to take him back there. For me, this is a primary reason to suspect that he made it all up, merely following the example of those others & with the same ends in mind.

But that is not all, and here is what I learned and what I was told during my trip from Provence by someone who seemed so well-informed of the facts that I cannot suspect him of inventing any of it. I have given my word of honor that I will never compromise him and I will certainly never divulge his name. But I also give my word that this secret will not be kept forever. If he is dead when I am released from here, then I will no longer be bound, and I will be able to name him; if he is still alive, I am sure I will be able to get him to release me from my promise to keep his identity a secret, and at that point you will know who he is. I am going to write what he said in his own words, as though he were speaking directly to you, in order that the whole thing is better understood:

"You have everything to fear, Monsieur," he told me, "even if your Aix affair is settled. As soon as the young lad you had as your secretary left the château in 1775, he went with his mother immediately to testify at the Court in Aix, where he made a statement that was then used by the Chief Prosecuting Attorney. Although I was not in attendance myself, I can assure you that they were both coached in what needed to be said. Monsieur de Castillon [the Chief Prosecuting Attorney for the Court of Aix], feared that once your case was closed, you would attack his cousin, Monsieur de Mende [the King's Prosecuting Attorney at Marseilles], who had brought those unfair Marseilles charges against you.[72] The reports he was getting from Paris were not very reassuring as he was unable to know nor guess what your intentions were. However, he could see clearly enough that the said Monsieur de Mende would be completely undone if you were to bring charges against him, and so he decided to attack first, in order to protect himself against you. And so they encouraged the child and the mother to concoct a whole array of lies and horrors by giving them some money, whereupon the two of them said and wrote whatever was demanded of them. After that, Monsieur de Castillon, in order to give himself the appearance of the sort of man who, far from looking for trouble, sought only to circumvent it, informed your mother-in-law, and they both, working together, had the mother and the child sent off to Paris, so well paid, so full of hope for the future, and so well instructed, that they have probably continued to say the same things in Paris that they had been taught to say at Aix."

That is what I was told, *I give my word of honor*, by someone who surely was in a position to know. Whatever may happen, I swear I will get his permission to reveal his name someday, and then you will see that what I say here is absolutely true.

Therefore, in a matter of such importance, I have testifying against me a *p——* who once worked for me, and a child, who also once worked for me. The *p——* has the obvious motive of wanting to exonerate herself at my expense, and the child has obviously been paid off by my worst enemies. One point I would like to make, apart from all of my assertions: have you not had enough proof, all of it as clear as day, that as soon as those people in Aix decided to act, they knew exactly how to bring about my downfall? In another earlier affair in Aix you had proof of the malice of these people, which was also as clear as day, so why do you wish to deny the proof that might exist in a second affair? You will agree that this presumption is not only very strong, but also very much in my favor. Tell me this: would you willingly go into a forest where your purse had been stolen once before? And if it were stolen a second time, would you not be more than justified in thinking that the very same thieves were responsible? If I had been in Madame de

Montreuil's shoes, that alone would have been enough for me to reject all charges coming from that particular town that had been made against my son-in-law.

Let us go on; there are further points and I would like everything resolved. Three items were found, or allegedly found, in my wallet; items which were then used against me. Let me explain all three.

The first was a prescription for use by a pregnant woman who wishes to get rid of her child. I admit it was a mistake for me to have written down such a thing, and imprudent of me to have had it on my person. I have certainly never made use of it, nor did I copy it out with the intention of ever using it.

In my life I have had occasion to see two or three women or girls — no need to elaborate — who had urgent reasons to hide the result of their misconduct with their lovers and who were then compelled to commit such a crime. They revealed their situation to me and at the same time confided to me the very dangerous method that certain practitioners of the profession used on them, which, it seemed to me, was a danger to their lives. It was in Italy that I learned of the method that they discovered written on a notebook page in my wallet. Finding it extremely mild and absolutely safe, curiosity prompted me to make a note of it. I believe that in the eyes of any reasonable man, there is nothing here worth making a fuss about, and every choirboy knows that *sabine* has that very effect.[73]

The second paper was the result of an argument I had with the little doctor from Rome.[74] He claimed that the Ancients poisoned their iron blades by the method that he described; and I claimed the contrary, assuring him that I thought I had read somewhere of a very different procedure. This occurred in the context of the poisoned antique weapons we had seen together at the Château Saint-Ange arsenal.[75] As I wanted to include a few words about it in my description of Rome, I wrote down his opinion, promising him to send him mine as soon as I had rediscovered the source, and then, in my essay, to decide which view was the most plausible. In fact, I found the opinion that differed from his in one of the books that you sent me, the fourth volume of the *Histoire des Celtes*.[76] It was an herb called *linveum* and, according to Pliny *&* Aulu-Gelle, *Hellebore*, which the ancients rubbed on the weapons they wanted to poison.[77] I therefore opted for that opinion, rather than the opposing one that he had offered. And there you have the explanation of what they found. Is that another sin?

But we now come to the most important point: *a full legal investigation into matters very similar to those you were accused of* [Madame de Sade had been accused of tampering with the religious faith of her young servants at La Coste].[78] Yes, it is a damning piece of evidence, but one could say that it is very similar to the story of the mass of the magpies.[79] You doubtless know it? Well, from that story, and from the one about that business about Calas and his son, and from many others like them, you learn, you who imprison people so quickly, that one should never judge by appearances, nor punish people without a fair hearing, certainly not in a country which considers its laws & its government free of malicious prosecution.[30] In short, there is not a single citizen that you have the right to lock up without a fair hearing, or who would not afterwards have the right to avenge himself in whatever manner he may choose, in order that he may punish you for your injustice.

Yes, whoever you may be, keep this in mind, and listen to what I have to say of this most important point. This document is the confession of the errors committed by an unfortunate wretch who, like myself, was seeking asylum in Italy. He had given up thinking that he could return to France from there; and, on seeing that I was preparing to return to France via the Alps, he gave me a document he had written, and begged me to show it to a lawyer in France, and to then let him know the lawyer's response. I promised I would. Two days later, he came to me and begged me to return the document, stating that as it was in his handwriting it could become, he said, a piece of evidence to be used against him. He wanted to have it transcribed, but knew no one who could write in French. I copied out the entire document myself, thinking only of obliging him and not considering the implications, or the possible consequences of having such a document written in my handwriting.

There then is yet another fact about which *I give you my word of honor is true* and to which I will attach the most authentic proof when needed.

There you have, then, all of my so-called faults, there you have what I challenge and what I will prove, *I swear it*, with evidence and means of such authenticity that it will be absolutely impossible to refute their testimony.

I am guilty only of libertinism, pure and simple, as it is practiced by all men, to a greater or lesser degree depending on the temperament or inclination that they were given by nature. Everybody has their faults; let us not make comparisons: my torturers might not come out at all well if we made comparisons.

Yes, I am a libertine, I admit it; I have imagined everything that can be imagined in this area, but I have certainly not done everything I have imagined and surely never shall. I am a libertine, but I am neither a criminal nor a murderer, and since I am forced to place my apology next to my justification, I would therefore say that it is likely that those who condemn me unjustly are not able to balance their infamy with their good deeds in ways that are equal to those which I can compare to my own. I am a libertine, but three families living in your neighborhood have lived for the last five years on my charity, and I have saved them from the worst excesses of destitution. I am a libertine, but I saved an army deserter, abandoned by his entire regiment and his colonel, from certain death. I am a libertine, but at Évry, witnessed by your entire family, I saved (by risking my own life) a child who was about to be crushed beneath the wheels of a cart pulled by runaway horses, which I did by throwing myself in its way.[81] I am a libertine, but I have never compromised my wife's health. I have never indulged in any of the other branches of libertinism that are so often fatal to the fortunes of one's children. Have I ruined their future by gambling or by incurring debts that could have deprived them of or even made inroads into their inheritance? Have I mismanaged my possessions in any way, during the time I had control of them? Did I, in a word, ever indicate in my youth a heart capable of the depravities of which I am accused today? Didn't I always love everything that deserved my love and everything that I hold dear? Didn't I love my father? (alas, I still weep for him every day.) Did I ever treat my mother badly? And surely you recall that time when I went to be with my mother and stayed with her devotedly as she drew her last breaths, and your mother had me dragged off and locked inside this horrible prison where she has left me languishing for the last four years? Or better still, just examine my life since my earliest childhood. You have in your entourage two people who knew me well during that time, *Amblet* and *Madame de Saint-Germain*. Ask them. From there, move on to my youth, which was observed by the Marquis de Poyanne who personally watched me grow and mature.[32] From there, go forward to the age when I married, and have a good look around, consult everyone from that time and enquire whether I ever gave any signs of the ferocity that I am supposed to possess, and if I ever committed any evil acts that may have served as harbingers of the crimes that are attributed to me: there must be, for as you know, crime does not come out of nothing.

Can you then readily accept that from such an innocent childhood and youth, I have suddenly attained the absolute depths of conscious horror? No, of course you don't believe that. And you who tyrannize me so cruelly today, you do not believe it either: your revenge has confused your mind, you have acted blindly, but your heart knows mine, judges it better, and knows full well that it is innocent.

One day I will have the pleasure of seeing you admit this, but that admission will not compensate for my torments, and I will not have suffered any less… In short, I want to be vindicated, and I will be, regardless of when they finally let me out of here. If I am a murderer, I will have been in prison not long enough, and if I am not one, I will have been punished far too harshly and I would have every right to demand an explanation.

This has been a very long letter, hasn't it? But I owed it to myself, and I promised myself I would write it at the conclusion of my four years of suffering. Those four years have now expired. Here it is, written like a death-bed confession, so that if death were to claim me without me having the consolation of holding you once again,

I could, as I breathed my last, refer you to the sentiments expressed in this letter, as the last sentiments that will be addressed to you by the owner of a jealous heart whose desire is to take your esteem to the grave. You will forgive this letter's disorder; it is neither witty nor profound: you must look into it for only naturalness and truth. I have erased some names placed at the beginning, so that it may get to you, and I urge that it be given to you. I am not asking you to answer it in detail, but only to tell me that you have received my grand letter: that is what I shall call it; yes, that is what I will call it. And when I refer you to the feelings it contains, then you will read it again... Can you hear me, my dear friend? You will read it again and you will see that the one who will love you unto the grave wanted to sign it with his blood.

De Sade

The Last Will and Testament of Donatien Alphonse François Sade, Man of Letters [83]

For the execution of the clauses below, I rely upon the filial piety of my children, asking that they may act with regard to the clauses as they have done with regard to me.

First: It is my true wish to herein provide evidence regarding the esteemed lady, Marie-Constance Reinelle, wife of Monsieur Bathasar Quesnet, believed deceased; my true wish, as I say, to provide evidence regarding this lady, insofar as my limited powers permit, pertaining to my extreme gratitude for the care she has provided me and the sincere friendship she has shown me from the twenty-fifth of August, seventeen hundred and ninety, to the day of my death; succor extended by her not only with the utmost tact and lack of self-interest, but also with the most courageous energy, since, during the Reign of Terror, she saved me from the revolutionary blade which was only too assuredly suspended above my head, as everyone well knows. Therefore, in light of the explanations outlined above, I hereby legally will and leave to the said lady, Marie-Constance Reinelle, wife of Quesnet, the sum of eighty thousand *livres*, to be paid in cash from the Tours mint, in whatever currency is in use in France at the time of my passing, wishing

& understanding that this sum be deducted from the freest and most unattached portion of my inheritance, and charging that my children deposit that sum in its entirety, within the space of a month from the day of my death, with Monsieur Finot, the solicitor at Charenton-Saint-Maurice, whom for this purpose I hereby name executor of my will and whom I instruct to utilize the said sum of money in the manner which is, without doubt, the securest and most advantageous to Madame Quesnet, and in a manner guaranteed to provide her with an income sufficient for her sustenance and support; an income which shall be, without fail, forwarded to her on a quarterly basis; which shall also be not transferable and not attachable to or by any other person whatsoever. I hereby stipulate moreover, that following the demise of his worthy mother, the principal and the sale of the above-mentioned endowment be revertible only to Charles Quesnet, son of the said dame Quesnet, who shall become the proprietor of the total.

And these instructions which I here express concerning the inheritance I leave to Madame Quesnet, I implore my children, in the unlikely case that they should seek to evade or avoid their legal responsibilities, I urge them to remember that they had promised the same dame Quesnet, a sum roughly similar in recognition of the care she took of their father, and as this present document merely concurs with and anticipates their initial intentions, any doubts as to their acquiescence to my final wishes is forever banished from my mind and will never for a moment trouble it further, especially when I reflect upon the filial virtues which have never ceased to characterize them and make them fully worthy of my paternal sentiments.

Second: I further leave and bequeath to the aforementioned Madame Quesnet all the furniture, effects, linen, clothing, books and papers which are in my chambers at the time of my decease, with the exception, however, of my father's papers, which shall be indicated as such by labels placed upon the bundles; papers which shall be handed over to my children.

Third: It is equally my intention and the expression of my last will and testament that the present bequest should in no ways deprive Madame Marie-Constance Reinelle, wife of Quesnet, of any future rights, claims, or charges that she may care to make upon my estate, whatever the grounds may be.

Fourth: I leave and bequeath to Monsieur Finot, the executor of my last will and testament, a ring valued at twelve hundred *livres*, as remuneration for the trouble which the execution of this document shall have caused him.

Fifth: Finally, I absolutely forbid that my body be opened on any pretext whatsoever. I categorically insist that it be

kept a full forty-eight hours in the chamber where I shall
have died, then placed in a wooden coffin which shall
not be nailed shut until the prescribed forty-eight hours
have elapsed, at the end of which period the said coffin
shall be nailed shut; during this interval a message shall
be sent to M. Le Normand, a wood seller in Versailles,
living at number 101, Boulevard de l'Égalité, requesting
him to come alone and in person, with a cart, to fetch my
body away and to convey it under his own escort and in
the said cart to a wood upon my property at Malmaison
near Épernon, in the commune of Émancé where I would
have it laid to rest, without ceremony of any kind, in
the first copse standing to the right as the said wood is
entered from the side of the château by way of the broad
lane which divides it. The trench opened in this copse
shall be dug by the tenant farmer of Malmaison under
M. Le Normand's supervision, who shall not leave my
body until after he has placed it in the said trench; upon
this occasion he may, if he so wishes, be accompanied by
those among my relatives or friends who are averse to
displays of ceremony or spectacle of any sort whatsoever,
and who shall have been kind enough to give me this last
proof of their attachment. The trench, my grave, once
covered over, shall then have acorns strewn over it, in
order that the spot become green again, and the copse
grown back thick over it, so that any trace of my grave
will disappear from the face of the earth, just as I trust
the memory of me will fade from the minds of everyone,

save for the few who in their goodness have loved me to the last, and of whom I carry a sweet remembrance with me to the grave.

Written at Charenton-Saint-Maurice in a state of reason and good health on the thirtieth day of January, in the year one thousand, eight hundred and six.

Essays on Sade

The Divine Marquis
Guillaume Apollinaire

A biography of the Marquis de Sade. — Was the Marquis de Sade responsible for the storming of the Bastille? — The political ideas of the Marquis de Sade. — His opposition to the death penalty. — The physical portrait of the Marquis de Sade. — His moral portrait. — Letter from Mirabeau to the agent, Monsieur Boucher Le Noir. — The alleged insanity of the Marquis de Sade. — His Last Will and Testament — On the Marquis de Sade. — The opinions of Doctor Eugen Duehren, Monsieur Anatole France & Émile Chevé on the Marquis de Sade. — his works on the history of civilization & their meaning. — The social ideas of the Marquis de Sade. — An unpublished fragment of one of his tales. — The Marquis de Sade's precursors. — His ideas about women. — Analysis of Justine. *— Discovery of the original manuscript of* Justine. *— Analysis of* Juliette. *— The Marquis de Sade & medical science. — Analysis of* 120 Days of Sodom. *—* Days of Florbelle. *—* The Portfolio of a Man of Letters. *— Notes on new ideas concerning punishment. — The dramatic ideas of the Marquis de Sade. — His theater. — Letter to Monsieur Girard. — Note on* Le Ruse d'amour. *— Unpublished letters of the Marquis de Sade to the Comédie-Française. —* Oxtiern. *— The Molière Theater. — Excerpt from* Le Monitor *on the second performance of* Oxtiern.

— Letter from the Marquis de Sade concerning the production of one of his plays at Versailles and Chartres. — Letter from the Marquis de Sade on Jeanne Laisné *or* The Siege of Beauvais. *—* The Marquis de Sade as an actor. *—* The Marquis de Sade and representations of Charenton. *— Sadistic dramaturgy. — Conclusion.*

We have no intention of providing a detailed biography of the Marquis de Sade. For that I would refer readers to the books written by various Sade authorities: books by Monsieur Paul Ginisty, Doctor Eugen Duehren, Doctor Cabanès, Doctor Jacobus X, Monsieur Henri d'Alméras, etc.[1] The complete and accurate biography of the Marquis de Sade has yet to be written. No doubt it will not be too long before all of the relevant documents & records have been collected, & it may then be possible to clarify some of the still-elusive points regarding the life of a very significant man, one about whom circulated — and still circulate — a very great number of legends.

The work undertaken in recent years in France and in Germany has helped to dispel many factual errors, but there are still several that need to be rectified.

Donatien-Alphonse-François, Marquis, and later Comte, de Sade, was born in Paris, on 2 June 1740. His family was one of oldest Provence families and their coat of arms depicted "a red shield charged with a black open-beaked eagle, spread over an eight-pointed gold star." He counted amongst his ancestors Comte

Hugues de Sade III, who married Laura de Noves, the woman Petrarch immortalized in his sonnets.

The Marquis de Sade (we will continue to refer to him by the title history has ensured he is known by) often professed an admiration for the great poet, a fact always ignored by biographers. The Marquis de Sade was sensitive to poetry, and one will find in *Les Crimes de l'amour (The Crimes of Love)* clear evidence of his taste for Petrarch's poetry.

At the age of ten, Sade entered the Lycée Louis-le-Grand in Paris. Aged fourteen, he became a chevalier, after which he passed, as second lieutenant, into the King's Regiment. He became a lieutenant of police officers and then earned the rank of Colonel of a Calvary regiment on the battlefields in Germany during the Seven Years' War. According to Dulaure's *A List of the Aristocracy* (Paris, 1790), the Marquis de Sade would — at that time — have been in Constantinople. Demobbed, Sade returned to Paris & was married on 17 May 1763. The following year he had his first child, a son, Louis de Sade. In 1783, Louis de Sade was a lieutenant in the regiment of Soubise. He emigrated in 1791. On his return to France, he became a writer & published, in 1805, *A History of the French Nation*, which had merit, and in which he displayed a breadth of knowledge that included much that was new about the Celtic era. Then, having begun service again, he went to Friedland and died in Spain, 9 June 1809, assassinated by guerrillas.

The Marquis de Sade's family arranged his marriage to a woman he felt nothing for: Mademoiselle Renée-Pélagie de Montreuil. He would have preferred to have married her younger sister, Anne-Prospère. When the woman he preferred was sent to a convent, he was deeply upset and extremely angry. It was from that time that he began to live his life as a libertine. In his epistolary novel, *Aline and Valcour*, the Marquis de Sade has provided the reader with many autobiographical details regarding his childhood and his youth; he painted under the name of Valcour. Perhaps one can find the details on his stay in Germany in *Juliette*. Four months after his marriage, he was imprisoned in Vincennes. In 1768 the scandal involving Sade and Rose Keller, a widow, became news. Apparently the Marquis de Sade was less culpable than is commonly claimed. This whole affair is still not resolved. On this subject, Charles Desmaze (Châtelet of Paris, Didier and C^{le}, 1863, p. 327) states:

> Among the papers of the police chiefs of Châtelet is the report, drawn up by one of them, containing accusations made against the Marquis de Sade, that he had, in Arcueil, stripped and tied a woman to a tree, cut her with a penknife, and then poured boiling sealing wax over her bleeding wounds.

And Doctor Cabanès, who quoted this passage from Charles Desmaze's book in the *Medical Chronicle* (15 December 1902), adds:

It is a report which would be useful to find and to publish, so as to clarify the case of the divine marquis.

In any event, in 1764, in one of his reports, Police Inspector Marais said: "I very strongly recommended that Brissaut, without me explaining further, would refrain from providing him with girls that would most likely go with him into unknown houses."

Marais also wrote, in his report of 16 October 1767:

We will never hear the true facts of the *horrors* perpetrated by the Comte, Monsieur de Sade. It is impossible to determine if the young Mademoiselle Rivers of the Comédie-Française actually lived with him, or if he had in fact offered her twenty-five louis per month, provided that she would spend the days she was not in the show with him in his *petites maisons* in Arcueil. This the young lady denies.

His *petites maisons* in Arcueil, Aumónerie, according to public rumor, was allegedly the base for orgies that would no doubt have appeared frightening to some, but at which it is unlikely anyone committed any real cruelties. The Rose Keller case led to the Marquis de Sade's second term of imprisonment. He was imprisoned in the Château de Saumur, then in the château de Pierre Encise (formerly the château de Pierre Scize) in Lyon. After six weeks he was released. In June 1772 the Marseille case was heard. Initially, it appeared to be less serious than the Keller widow's case, however, the Court of Aix condemned the Marquis, *in absentia*, to death. This judgment was overturned in 1778 and on the eve of his second trial, the Marquis escaped to Italy, taking his wife's sister with him.

After staying in various large cities he decided to move back to France, and so arrived in Chambéry on 8 December 1772, where he was arrested by the Sardinian police and imprisoned in the Château de Miolans. He managed to escape with the help of his young wife during the night of May 2, 1773. After a short stay in Italy, he returned to France and lived in the château La Coste where he continued his life of debauchery. He visited Paris frequently, & it was there that he was arrested on 14 January 1777, & taken to the dungeon of Vincennes. From there, he was transferred to Aix, where a judgment on 30 June 1778, overturned his 1772 sentence. A new sentence for "acts of outrageous debauchery" was imposed. He was banned from Marseille for three years, and was fined fifty louis to benefit the victims of prisoners. He was not granted his freedom.

He served his sentence in Vincennes, in Aix, but still managed to escape with the help of his wife. He was arrested a few months later at the château de La Coste. In April 1779, he was again imprisoned in Vincennes, where he had relationship with Mademoiselle de Rousset, his wife's friend, and from where he remained until he was transferred to the Bastille.

On 29 February 1784, the Marquis de Sade was transferred to the Bastille. It was there that he wrote the majority of his works. In 1789, knowing the Revolution was fomenting, the Marquis de Sade started his acts of rebellion; he deliberately clashed with Monsieur de Launay, governor of the Bastille.

In his cell, the Marquis had a long funnel-shaped tin-plate pipe that had been given to him to empty his wastewater into the ditch outside his window, which opened on to the Rue Saint-Antoine. On 2 July he had the idea of using the pipe as a megaphone & through it he shouted several times: "They're butchering the prisoners in here! Save them! Save them!"[2] At that time there were only a few prisoners in the Bastille, and so it is rather difficult to understand precisely why the marquis was able to incite the anger of the people enough for them to mount, a few days later, an attack on an almost empty prison. It is possible that it was the Marquis de Sade's shouts — supplemented by the notes he threw from his window; notes in which he gave details of the tortures being inflicted on the prisoners in the fortress — notes that most likely exerted an influence on already excited minds, provoking the prevailing incendiary mood, and finally inciting the storming of the old fortress.

On the day of the storming, the Marquis de Sade was no longer in the Bastille. Monsieur de Launay had some serious concerns regarding his prisoner (and this will not go against the hypothesis that the Marquis de Sade caused the events of 14 July) and had requested Sade's removal from the prison. Consequently, the Marquis de Sade was transferred (by royal order, dated 3 July) at one o'clock in the morning on the following day to the Charenton Insane Asylum. A decree from the constituent Assembly annulled the *lettres de cachets* and awarded the Marquis his freedom. He left Charenton Asylum on 23 March 1790.

His wife, who no longer wanted to see him, had withdrawn to the convent of Saint-Aure, and on 9 June of that year had obtained an *Award du Châtelet* that granted her *de corps et d'habitation* after her separation from Sade. This deeply unhappy woman devoted herself to piety, and died in her château in Échauffour, on 7 July 1810.

Once free, the Marquis de Sade led a regular life, living on his writing. He published his works, put on plays in Paris, Versailles and possibly in Chartres. He had serious financial difficulties, writing a whole slew of letters requesting employment, regardless of what it was:

Good in negotiations, like his father for the past twenty years, familiar with many parts of Europe, skilled in composition and drafting, especially keen to undertake any work that there is, be it the directing of a library, an office, or a natural history museum. Sade, in short, who is not without talent, beseeches your justice and your benevolence, and begs you to employ him.

(Letter from Convention Member, Bernard (de Saint-Affrique), 8 ventôse an III (27 February, 1795).

He went assiduously to the Piques section meetings of the *Société populaire*, where he was often the spokes-man. The Marquis de Sade was a true republican and an admirer of Marat, but an enemy of the death penalty. He had political ideas that were very much his own, and he presented his theories in several of his works. In his *Ideas on the Method and Enforcement of the Law*, he indicated how the law, proposed by *Société* members, was to be voted for by the people, because it was necessary to admit "with the sanction of the laws, some people are the most maltreated by fate, and since it is them whom the law generally affects, it is therefore best for them to agree on the law they will be affected by." His control during the Terror was humane and beneficial. Suspected, un-doubtedly because of his declamations against the death penalty, he was arrested on 6 December 1793, but given his freedom by *Société* deputy Rovère, in October 1794.

During his Directorship, the Marquis ceased occu-pying himself with politics. He received many people at his home, on the Rue du Pot-de-Fer-Saint-Sulpice, to which he had been transported. A pale, melancholic and distinguished-looking woman was his housemaid. The Marquis sometimes called her his Justine, and it was said the girl was an emigrant. Monsieur d'Alméras thinks that this woman was the *Constance* to whom

Justine had been dedicated. In any event, information on this friend is completely lacking.

In July 1800, the Marquis published *Zoloé and the Two Acolytes*, a *roman à clef* which caused an enormous scandal. In it, readers could easily recognize the First Consul (d'Orsec, anagram of de Corse), Joséphine (Zoloé), Madame Tallien (Laureda), Madame Visconti (Volsange), Barras (Sabar), Tallien (Fessinot), etc. The Marquis had been obliged to publish it himself. His arrest took place on 5 March 1801; he was arrested at his publishers, Bertrandet, to whom he had given a revised manuscript of *Juliette*, which served as a pretext for the arrest. He was locked up in Sainte-Pélagie, from there transferred to the insane hospital in Bicêtre, and then finally locked up again in Charenton Insane Asylum on 27 April 1803. He died there on 2 December 1814, at the age of seventy-five, having spent twenty-seven years, fourteen of them during his mature years, in eleven different prisons.

*

No authentic or genuine portrait of the Marquis de Sade exists. There is an image of the Marquis de Sade's head which was issued on a fanciful medallion. It was made by Jules Janin and it is part of a collection owned by Monsieur La Porte.

"There is another portrait," says Monsieur Octave Uzanne (in his introduction to *Some Thoughts on the Novel*). "It presents Sade — in the company of demons

— with a young face looking toward us; this ridiculous engraving states the source of the collection is M. H. of Paris. This portrait is as false as all of the others."[3]

There is also another portrait which is just as false as the others. It had been created during the Restoration and was based on Monsieur La Porte's medallion, to which had been added fauna, a dunce's cap, a sledgehammer and, at the bottom, the Marquis in prison.

It has been said that, as a child, Sade's face was so handsome that ladies often stopped to look at him. He had an imposing physique, blue eyes, & blonde, wavy hair. His movements were perfectly graceful and his harmonious voice had inflections that touched the hearts of many women.

Some authors have suggested that Sade had an effeminate manner and that since childhood he had been a passive introvert. I have found no evidence that substantiates this assertion.

Charles Nodier, in his *Memories, Episodes and Portraits of the Revolution and the Empire*, reports that he saw him in 1803. (In reality it occurred in 1802, as stated by Monsieur d'Alméras.) He slept in the same room as him, where they were four other prisoners.

"One of the men got up very early, because he had been notified that he was going to be transferred. I immediately noticed his obesity, which hindered his movements enough to keep him from physically deploying any trace of the grace & elegance found in his manners. However, his tired eyes contained a glimmer of brilliance which revived from time to time and then died like a spark expiring on an extinct coal. He was not a conspirator and nobody could accuse him of having taken part in any political affairs. His attacks had never been aimed at anything but the two social powers of relatively high importance (i.e., religion and morality) and as the secret police cared very little for the stability of those two institutions, the authorities simply indulged him and gave him a great deal of latitude. He was relegated to the rich, deep shadows of the shores of the beautiful waters of Charenton, from where he escaped whenever he wanted. We learned a few months later, in prison, that Monsieur de Sade had run away again.

"To have a clear idea of what he wrote, I re-read his books; I returned to them and skimmed through them from front to back to see if the criminal sensibility filtered through everywhere. I have a vague impression of feelings of astonishment and horror at those monstrous depravities being described, but there is always the big question of the political right being at odds with the great interest of society, and this was being cruelly and outrageously depicted in a book whose very title became obscene. This Sade is the prototype of the victims of the *extra*-judicial justice of the high Consulate and the Empire. He did not know how to submit reasonably to the public forms and debates of the courts, for he had been accused of a despicable crime that so offended the moral decency of society as a whole that no one cared to consider him as harmless. It is true to say that the materials of this hideous procedure were used more for pushing back and exploring the bloody tatters and the battered flaps of flesh than to detect a murder. It was a non-judicial body, the Board of Érat, I believe, who arbitrarily spoke advocating the defendant's perpetual detention, and did not fail to rely, as they say today, on this *arbitrary precedent...*"

"...I said that this prisoner did nothing but pass before my eyes. I remember only that when we spoke, he was polite but not obsequiousness, gracious but not too polished, and that he spoke respectfully about the things I respected."

Louis Ange Pitou had also seen the Marquis at around the same time. His portrait of Sade seems quite accurate. Indeed, one feels that Pitou bore a certain amount of sympathy for the Marquis de Sade. It was the untested sympathy for a man that the anti-royalist Pitou did not know; a man who everyone else disparaged. It seems that in order to be like everyone else, Pitou felt obliged to present Sade as a monster, but one in which he discovered traces of benevolence.

Here is the story of Louis Ange Pitou:[4]

In the eighteen months that passed in Sainte-Pélagie, from 1802 to 1803, awaiting my letters of release, my cell was in the same corridor as that of the famous

Marquis de Sade, the author of the most execrable work that human perversity ever invented. This poor wretch was sullied with the leprosy of almost inconceivable crimes, and the authorities had confined him among the maniacs, thereby giving him less status than the tormented and the violent, for Justice did not want to dirty its files with his name. The torturer, by beating him, was able to obtain a degree of celebrity for which he was so avid. He relegated Sade to a corner of the prison, and gave permission to every prisoner to relieve himself over this burden.

The ambition of literary celebrity was the principle of the depravity of this man, who was not born malicious. Unable to elevate his imaginative flights to the level of that of the moral writers of the first order, he had resolved to open the pit of iniquity and dive into it, only to reappear as the immortalizer of evil, wrapped in the wings of genius, choking every virtue and publicly deifying all vices. However, one could still see in him traces of some virtue, such as charity. This man quivered at the idea of death and fell in a faint on seeing his white hair. Sometimes, he cried and wept at the beginning of his repentance (which he did not continue): *Why am I so dreadful and crime so charming? I immortalize it, and it is necessary if one is to reign in the world.*

A man who had a fortune and did not want for anything sometimes came to my room. I was always laughing, singing and in a good mood, eating my piece of black bread or my prison soup without disgust or sorrow. His face suffused with anger.

— Are you really happy? he asked.

— Yes, Monsieur.

— Happy!

— Yes, Monsieur.

Then cheerfully putting my hand on my heart, I told him:

— I have done nothing that troubles me, I am a lord, Monsieur Marquis. See, I have a lace-edged cravat, my handkerchief is also lace; these cuffs were quite expensive, for instead of being embroidered, they are beaded & fringe, an area of fashion which I shall lead in.

— You are quite mad, Monsieur Pitou.

— Yes, Monsieur Marquis, but in my misery, I have peace in my heart.

He approached my table, and the conversation continued:

— What are you reading?

— This is the Bible.

— Tobit is a good man, but this is Job's tale.

— A tale, Monsieur, that is a reality for you & me.

— What of reality, Monsieur, for you believe these dreams and you laugh?

— We are both fools, Monsieur Marquis, you for being afraid of your dreams, and I for laughing while believing in my realities.

— That man just died at Charenton... As for me, I am free...

There is also a reference to the Marquis de Sade in a book by P.-F.-T.-J. Giraud.[5] The note confirms what we already knew of the tenacity, the commitment, and the indomitable energy of the Marquis:

> Sade, the abominable author of the most horrible novels, spent several years in Bicêtre, in Charenton, and in Sainte-Pélagie. He contended unceasingly that he did not compose the infernal *J* ***, but M. de G ***, a young author whom he often attacked, proved it was him in this way:

> You acknowledge *The Crimes of Love* as a moral work which bears your name; and on its title page you have added: "By the author of *Aline and Valcour.*" In the foreword to that recently published work, which is far worse *than J* ***, you openly declare yourself to be the author of that infamous work; you must be resigned to having ensnared yourself.

According to the physiological reports, the mind of this portrayer of crime is one of the strangest and most monstrous that nature ever produced. The Marquis himself claims that he has himself examined several of the disordered states which he has described in such detail with such tremendous energy. It was his great rage, his own fears, *&* his odious fecundity that imposed the need for him to create something that had never been seen before. In prison, everyone wanted to stifle his infernal genius. Police inspectors had the task of frequently visiting the places that he lived & removing all the writings they found there. Sometimes he hid them, so as to impede their search. M. V..., who was often instructed to make these visits, said to several people that, in spite of the icy demeanor due to his age, there were still, due to the fires of this truly volcanic imagination, far more abominable works than those presented to the public.

"It is possible that the boardrooms of the Customs Office of the Prefecture of the Police Force are used as storerooms for these infamous progeny of a depravity beyond description; but one also wishes they could be returned to the nothingness they should never have left."

Doctor Cabanès (in the *Medical Chronicle*, 15 December 1902), after having deplored the fact that no one had a genuine image of the Marquis de Sade, added:

> We believe however that there is one, a delicious miniature, which is in the possession of an erudite collector, who, we hasten to say, was not willing to deprive themselves of it, even though it is only a reproduction.

Restif of Breton, who was very familiar with the works of the Marquis de Sade, and had even printed some of his manuscripts, was worried that he had never met him. "He is," he says in *Monsieur Nicolas*, "a man with a long white beard which he wore to celebrate the pulling down of the Bastille." It is well known that on 14 July, the Marquis de Sade was no longer in the Bastille.

From his youth, the Marquis gave lectures on a variety of subjects, reading all kinds of books but preferring the works of philosophy, history, & especially the stories of travelers which gave him information on the mores of exotic people. He observed much. He was a good musician, he danced well, was a good horseman, was a good swordsman, being in the first rank at fencing, and appreciated sculptures. He loved painting & spent long hours in art galleries. He could often be seen in the Louvre. He was knowledgeable on a range of subjects. He knew Italian, German, & Provençal (he called himself the troubadour of Provence and composed Provençal verse). He often gave evidence of his courage. Above all, he enjoyed freedom. All of his actions — and his philosophical system — testify to his impassioned taste for the freedom he was denied for so long, during the course of what Carteron, his servant, referred to as his "bitch of a life." This Carteron, in letters to his master, preserved at the *Bibliothèque de l'Arsenal*, makes it known that the Marquis de Sade smoked a pipe "like a corsair" and that he ate "like four."

The long confinements of the Marquis embittered his character, which was well bred, but naturally authoritative. There are many testimonies of his anger at his incarceration in the Bastille, Bicêtre, & Charenton.

He loved good food and creature comforts, and it is pointless to comment on his haughty and aristocratic appearance. He has given enough evidence of his humanity under the Terror so that one can affirm that he was less cruel than is implied by some of his actions. He appears exaggerated & distorted when one reads his works. We know that he was neither insane nor a maniac. The stories of Jules Janin and the anecdote reported by Victorien Sardou presenting the Marquis de Sade being taken to Bicêtre & dipped in the stinking mud of a stream (*Medical Chronicle*, 15 December 1902), seem like legends. They perhaps have a basis in reality, but may have been transformed by the imagination of those who, after reading *Justine* without any understanding of either its meaning or scope, could only imagine its author as a madman full of criminal and disgusting manias. The police force of the Consulate & the Empire, by incarcerating the Marquis at Bicêtre then Charenton, was largely the cause of this gossip and the belief in the supposed madness of a man whose misfortunes would have been enough to make him crazy, if he had had the slightest provision to become so. The *Historical Notes* of Marc-Antoine Baudot, former deputy of the Legislative Assembly, published by Mme. Edgar Quinet, mentions Sade in these terms:

> This is the author of several works of monstrous obscenity & diabolic morals. He was undoubtedly a man with perverse theories. But finally he was not insane, and had to be judged on his works.

In him were the seeds of depravity, but not of madness. Similar works involve a well-ordered brain, but the actual composition of Sade's works required a great deal of research into ancient and modern literature, and it was designed to demonstrate that large depravities had been authorized by the Greeks and Romans. Such an investigation was undoubtedly immoral, but he had the reason and the reasoning to implement it; he had the right reason to put this research into action in the form of novels which utilized facts as a kind of doctrine and system..."

The last paragraph of his will, published in *Le Livre* by Jules Janin (Paris, 1870), shows the legitimate pride, dignity, and the good sense of the Marquis de Sade, who, incidentally, had been a source of other rumors:

I absolutely forbid that my body be opened on any pretext whatsoever. I categorically insist that it be kept a full forty-eight hours in the chamber where I shall have died, then placed in a wooden coffin which shall not be nailed shut until the prescribed forty-eight hours have elapsed, at the end of which period the said coffin shall be nailed shut. During this interval a message shall be sent to M. Le Normand, a wood-seller in Versailles, living at number 101, Boulevard de l'Égalité, requesting him to come alone and in person, with a cart, to fetch my body away and to convey it under his own escort and in the said cart to a wood upon my property at Malmaison near Épernon, in the commune of Émancé where I would have it laid to rest, without ceremony of any kind, in the first copse standing to the right as the said wood is entered from the side of the château by way of the broad lane which divides it. The trench opened in this copse shall be dug by the tenant farmer of Malmaison under M. Le Normand's supervision, who shall not leave my body until after he has placed it in the said trench. Upon this occasion he may, if he so wishes, be accompanied by those among my relatives or friends who are averse to displays of ceremony or spectacle of any sort whatsoever, & who shall have been kind enough to give me this last proof of their attachment. The trench, my grave, once covered over, shall then have acorns strewn over it, in order that the spot become green again, and the copse grown back thick over it, so that any trace of my grave will disappear from the face of the earth, just as I trust the memory of me will fade from the minds of everyone, save for the few who in their goodness have loved me to the last, and of whom I carry a sweet remembrance with me to the grave.

Written at Charenton-Saint-Maurice in a state of reason and good health on the thirtieth day of January, in the year one thousand, eight hundred & six.

Signed, D. A. F. SADE

"Whoever wrote this page of such terrible bitterness," says M. Henri d'Alméras, "and whoever demanded to disappear entirely, body & soul into oblivion & nothingness, is certainly not, by any point of view, to be judged an ordinary man."

This was not an ordinary man. He had considerable faults, especially to his wife, but he did not like her, his marriage was to some extent forced, and love cannot be ordered. He was not crazy, unless it is thought as he said himself in a comedy:

All men are insane; it is necessary, if he is to see,
To lock him in his room and break his mirror,

He also said in a distich-epigraph which served as an epiphoneme to his works:

One is not a criminal if one paints
The odd inclinations which nature inspires.

While he flattered himself he would vanish from the memory of men, the Marquis hoped that before this he would be avenged "by posterity."

For a century, criticism treated him extremely cavalierly, caring much less for the ideas contained in his works than with inventing anecdotes which degraded his life and his character. Regarding his life, Doctor Eugen Duehren said with good reason: "Sade, as an individual, can be understood only if one examines him as an historical phenomenon."

Concerning his works, M. Anatole France wrote contemptuously: "It is not necessary to treat a text by the Marquis de Sade in the way one treats a text by Pascal." Some free spirits thought that the contempt and loathing inspired by works of the Marquis de Sade were perhaps unjustified. Already in 1882, in *Virilities* (A. Lemerre), Émile Chevé granted some power and grandeur to the books of the Marquis de Sade:

Marquis, your book is powerful, and in the future
No one will ever plunge as low in infamy,
After you, no one will ever be able to unite
All the poisons of the heart in a similar bouquet...

At least, you made yourself large in your obscenity!
Rape & parricide, incest & robbery
Stream from your pen, and our humanity
Howls at the flanks of your anthropophagous MUSE...

It was in Germany, where Nietzsche, it is said, did not disdain to systematically assimilate the philosophical, lyrical, energetic ideas of the Marquis. Dr. Eugen Duehren, with great courage, took on the task of elucidating the life of Sade & creating an awareness of his writings. "It was 2 June 1740," he said, "that saw the birth of the most remarkable man of the eighteenth century, perhaps even

of modern humanity in general. The works of the Marquis
de Sade constitute a subject of history and civilization as
much as medical science. This strange man has from the
outset inspired great interest. We wanted to understand
him in order to explain him, and we soon came to the
conclusion that the doctor, in the same way, can draw
from a similar case the most important information in
the history of civilization."

And later:

> There is yet another point of view that the works
> of the Marquis de Sade are for the historian who
> deals with civilization, for the doctor, the jurist, the
> economist and the moralist; a veritable well of learn-
> ing and new concepts. These books are especially
> instructive in the way they show us everything in
> life has a close connection with the sexual instinct
> which, as acknowledged by the Marquis de Sade with
> an undeniable perspicacity, has an impact on almost
> all human relations in any way. Any investigator who
> wishes to determine the sociological importance of
> love should read the major works of the Marquis
> de Sade. Not even at the level of hunger, but above,
> love powers the movement of the universe.

The love that moves sun & the other stars,

as Dante cried at the end of the *Divine Comedy*.

Doctor Jacobus X said that Doctor Duehren was a gallophobe, because he saw in the current events of the French policy a major agreement with the doctrines of the Marquis de Sade. Indeed, this agreement appears to be quite deep and progressive. Let no one be surprised to see that Sade was a supporter of the Republic. In about 1785, he would begin one of his tales thus:

> In the days when aristocrats lived on their estates like despots; in those glorious days when France had within its borders innumerable sovereign lords, instead of thirty thousand slaves grovelling in front of a single ruler, the Lord of the Château de Longeville, the owner of a rather large fief near Fismes in Champagne, lived with his wife on his large estate.[6]

A large number of writers, philosophers, economists, naturalists, and sociologists, from Lamarck to Spencer, met with the Marquis de Sade, and many of his ideas which terrified & disconcerted the minds of his time are still quite new. "One will perhaps find our ideas a little strong," he wrote. "What of this? Didn't we acquire the right to say everything?" It seems that the time has come for these ideas — which matured in the atmospheric hells of infamous libraries — and for this man — who appeared to count for nothing during all the 19th century — to dominate the 20th century.

The Marquis de Sade, the freest spirit that ever lived, had specific ideas on women and wanted them to be as free as men. These ideas, which will be published one day, gave birth to two novels: *Justine* and *Juliette*. It is not by chance that the Marquis chose heroines, not heroes. Justine is the former wife, enslaved, miserable and less than human; Juliette, on the contrary, represents the new women that Sade foresaw, a woman that no one else had any idea about, who emerges from humanity, who has wings and who will renew the universe.

The reader who approaches these novels often only notices that the style is disgusting and that deeper analysis unfortunately does not raise the spirits. It should be added, since it is impossible to give a portrait of the characters, that the Marquis de Sade believed that there was "an extreme connection between the moral and the physical."

Justine and Juliette are the daughters of a rich Parisian banker.[7] Up to the ages of fourteen and fifteen, they are raised in a famous convent in Paris. Unforeseen events: the bankruptcy of their father, his death, followed soon by that of their mother, completely alters the destiny of these girls. They find they must leave the convent and provide all of life's needs for themselves. Juliette, a lively, carefree, spontaneous, insolent beauty, is happy with this freedom. The younger Justine is a naïve, gentle, melancholic girl and feels the full extent of her misfortune. Juliette, aware of her own beauty, seeks at once to benefit from that beauty. Justine is virtuous & wants to remain so. They separate. Justine finds friends of her family who reject her. A priest tries to seduce her. She ends up going for help to a wholesale trader, M. Dubourg, who likes to make children cry. She does not hide her astonishment & disgust of him when he exposes his lecherous self to her. She resists him and he throws her out. During this time, a certain Mme Desroches, with whom she has fallen in with, steals everything she owns.

Justine is at the mercy of this woman who puts her in touch with Mme Delmonse, a kind of smart demi-mondaine, who tells Justine of the pleasures of prostitution. She tries to prostitute Justine, but after failing, takes her back to the old man, Dubourg. Justine still resists him, and after some deplorable adventures, Justine, in spite of her innocence, ends up going to prison after she becomes acquainted with Dubois, a rascal who has committed every crime imaginable. Both are sentenced to death. Dubois sets fire to the prison, after which they escape and join a band of the most infamous outlaws one could ever meet. Justine manages to run away with Saint-Florent, a merchant who delivered her from the hands of the outlaws and who tells her he is her uncle. He rapes & abandons Justine, who faints. When she regains consciousness, she sees a young man, M. Bressac who engages in unnatural "entertainments" with his lackeys. After they have made their advances, they end up leading her to the virtuous Mademoiselle de Bressac, who is moved to pity at the plight of Justine, and wants to take her back to Paris and occupy herself with her rehabilitation. Unfortunately, Delmonse has left for America, and the matter cannot be cleared up. Bressac, meanwhile, is engaged in appalling orgies, he poisons his mother and forces Justine to kill her. Justine runs away to the village of Saint-Marcel, near Paris, where she meets a surgeon named Rodin. Rodin & his sister, Célestine, run a co-educational school to which only children of exceptional beauty are admitted. There are one hundred boys and one hundred girls, with none younger than twelve years or older than seventeen. Rodin teaches the boys and Célestine teaches the girls. Justine becomes friends with Rodin's daughter, Rosalie. Rodin not only commits incest; he also engages — with criminal daring — in surgery with his colleague Rambeau. They submit the unfortunate Justine to this, who escapes death almost miraculously and then goes to Sens.

Sitting in the twilight at the edge of a pond, she hears somebody throw something into the water. On seeing that it is a very small girl, she saves her; but the murderer rejects the child and takes Justine to his château. He is a teetotaler & vegetarian with a mania for making women pregnant — and to see each of them only once. His name is M. de Bandole and he has rather curious ideas about conception. After congress, he leaves the women suspended head down for nine days, to be quite certain they have been fertilized.

Justine is taken out of the hands of M. de Bandole by the brother of Dubois, the brigand Coeur-de-Fer. Then Justine enters a Benedictine Abbey where Satanism is practiced. There is a harem of children of both sexes. The monk Jérôme tells her how his long, disgraceful life is filled with murder and incest. He describes the countries he has visited: Germany, Italy, Tunis, Marseille, & so on. Justine leaves the cloister. She meets Dorothy d'Esterval, the wife of a criminal innkeeper, who runs an isolated hostel and murders the travelers that stay there. Dorothy says she is afraid and begs Justine to go there with her. Justine follows her to the hotel where many crimes have been committed. Bressac arrives; he is a relative of d'Esterval. They then all go to the Comte de Gernande, who is also one of their relatives. He has taken to the hateful practice of torturing his wife, whose beauty is admirable. He draws "two bowls of blood" from her every four days.

Then Justine has a series of adventures which are difficult to summarize and which occur with the Verneuil family, among Jesuits, in the company of lesbians and inverts of all kinds.

Justine then meets Roland the counterfeiter and finishes by being locked up in Grenoble Prison. She is freed by a lawyer of the bar of this city, M. S… At the inn she meets Dubois who leads her to the country house of the archbishop of Grenoble, in which there is a cabinet of glass which can transform itself into a terrible room of torture where the archbishop decapitates the women after having ignobly abused them.

"When the women enter with the prelate, they find in this room a large abbot of forty-five years, whose physique is hideous and built like a giant; he is on a settee, reading *Philosophy in the Bedroom*."[8]

Justine escapes; she has a number of appalling adventures. She is incarcerated again and again, and is then sentenced to death. She escapes, wanders miserably and ends up meeting a lovely lady accompanied by four gentlemen. It is Juliette, who welcomes her sister with tenderness and then extols the criminal life to her. She says: "I followed the road of vice, my child; I only ever encountered roses."

This is the *Justine* that the Marquis de Sade always disavowed with such extraordinary tenacity. He had his reasons for this, knowing that the glory it earned would not be taken from him, while an admission on his part would have justified in the eyes of his contemporaries, in his case, to exercise against him any reprisals that they would want. He was capable of such disclaimers, and printed such a testimony. It was a response to Villeterque who had, in a serial, highly criticized *Les Crimes de l'amour (The Crimes of Love)* and had reproached the Marquis for having written *Justine*. Sade immediately wrote and printed a pamphlet entitled: *The Author of The Crimes of Love to Villeterque, Hack Writer*, and never has an author protested so vociferously against his own book.

But I have in front of my eyes the original manuscript — which has never before been mentioned — of the first version of Justine, the first spurt, the first draft of this work with all its erasures. The beginning is on page 69 of a notebook entitled *ninth notebook*, which contains other drafts by the Marquis. The work continues in three books entitled respectively *tenth notebook, eleventh notebook, twelfth notebook*, and ends in the *thirteenth notebook*. Consequently, *Justine* is included in five notebooks.

The Marquis de Sade entitled his first book: *The Misfortunes of Virtue*. Already, on the back of folio 451 of the manuscript collection kept in the *Bibliothèque Nationale*, he had inscribed in the margin this note, which indicates the initial idea that came to him for writing *Justine*:

Combine the treatise with the novel, in *The Misfortunes of Virtue*, a work in an entirely new style. From one end to another vice triumphs & virtue is dragged through every humiliation. The dénouement should restore to virtue any luster due to it and also make it as beautiful as it is desirable. There will be no one who, after reading it, does not abhor the false triumph of crime and not cherish the humiliation & misery experienced by virtue.[9]

As a result of its title, the Marquis de Sade noted: "19th century storytelling," indicating that he had abandoned his initial idea of writing a novel with this as the subject.

He was no longer interested in a story that would undoubtedly have been included in the *Tales and Fables of the 18ᵗʰ Century by a Provençal Troubadour* (manuscript in the Bibl. Nat. F. verso 450 and 451). Most of them were in the form of *The Crimes of Love*. But *The Misfortunes of Virtue* is a significant part of the contents written by the Marquis de Sade in these *Tales and Fables*, although he had not written it at the time it was listed, but had only imagined it. At that time, the Marquis de Sade had the idea to write this one novel. Having given it up, he marked — in advance — the end of his story on the cover of the *twelfth notebook* (actually the fourth): "End of *The Misfortunes of Virtue*."

On the cover of the *ninth notebook*, it states: "The notebooks used for *The Misfortunes of Virtue* are comprised of 192 pages in 8 notebooks; the draft has 175 pages, so the beautiful notebook has 17 pages more than the draft, and that is not too much for the projected increases." (The last four words are crossed out by the author.) This is the notebook from which the Marquis intended to recopy his story. The draft version has, in fact, 179 pages plus 6 pages of covers. At the end of his manuscript, the Marquis de Sade states in a footnote: "Finished after fifteen days. 8 July 1784." Therefore, he would have begun writing it on the 23ʳᵈ or the 24ᵗʰ of June.

Juliette, or Vice Rewarded is a continuation of *Justine*, and contrasts perfectly with that book.

After leaving the convent with her sister, Juliette enters a brothel, where she is introduced to a certain

Dorval, who is "the greatest thief in Paris," so named for having conned two Germans. She then meets the infamous Noirceuil who has caused the bankruptcy of his father and grown rich by depriving a great number of families of their wealth. He introduces her to the Minister of State, Saint-Fond who, although against certain kindnesses, provides the means for her to satisfy her taste for unbridled lust. He makes her the head of his department of poisons. Political poisonings start again, intermingled with the varied tortures to which one subjects the official victims.

An English friend of Juliette's, Lady Clairwill, goes to the Society of Friends & confesses to all of the crimes, including those committed by Saint-Fond. The minister has prepared a project on the depopulation of France; he forwards it to Juliette, who cannot suppress a reaction of shock and horror.

Saint-Fond notices. Juliette understands that her life is threatened. She runs away to Angers and works in another brothel. There she meets a wealthy gentleman who she marries and then poisons. She then leaves for Italy, visiting major cities everywhere while prostituting herself to the richest. She joins up with a criminal named Sbrigani. They travel to Florence, where they stay for some time. Juliet, as in all cities of royal residence she visits, is admitted to the Court. I shall not dwell on all the crime scenes that happen in the pages of this novel. There is even cannibalism in one particular place.

In Rome, Juliette is received by Pope Pius VII. She lists chronologically the crimes of the papacy. The Pope wants to interrupt: "Shut up, old monkey!" Juliette orders him, and Pius VII eventually exclaims: "O Juliette! I had been told that you had a considerable mind. I doubted it, but you outdo all reports; such a degree of elevation in ideas is extremely rare in a woman."

Juliette then travels to Naples. En route she gets involved in new adventures with a troupe of robbers, in which she finds Lady Clairwill. In Naples, King Ferdinand I receives Juliette with great respect. Then there are descriptions of Herculaneum, Pompeii, etc. Juliette ends up, with the complicity of Queen Marie-Caroline, by stealing a certain amount of millions from the King of Naples. The operation successful, Juliette denounces the Queen and makes her way back to France.

"These poor inventions," according to Alcide Bonneau, "show that the Marquis de Sade flattered himself as knowing the bedroom secrets of the Italian monarchs, whereas in truth, he knew nothing at all; however the intrigues of the Queen of Naples & her favorites were quite public. Even the most unrestrained imagination fell far short of history." Indeed, that very history was used to exonerate the philosophical stories of the Marquis, who in *Juliette* not only takes us for a wander in the Italian courts, but also in the Nordic courts, particularly those in Stockholm and in St. Petersburg.

In 1904, Dr. Duehren published a manuscript of the Marquis de Sade's which contained one of his most audacious works. It was the *120 Days of Sodom, or The School of Debauchery*, a manuscript that had been taken from the Marquis in the Bastille, the disappearance of which upset and angered him greatly. No doubt it is this libertine theory that Restif of Breton spoke about to M. Nicolas, but he undoubtedly had not seen it, confusing it with the public house project developed by Sade, and which, indeed, could seem to have similarities with Restif's *Le Pornographe*, according to the complaints of the latter:

> That's what that monstrous author proposes, in imitation of my *Le Pornographe*, the establishment of a place of debauchery. I worked to stop the degradation of nature, & the purpose of that infamous dissector of flesh in parodying a book of my youth was to outrage with excess this abhorrent, this infamous degradation…

The manuscript of *120 Days of Sodom* was described in 1877 by Pisanus Fraxi *(Index librorum prohibitorum, London, 1877)*. His description was not based on the evidence of his own eyes, but rather on a description that had been sent to him.

This manuscript was found in the Bastille cell that had been occupied by the Marquis de Sade by Arnoux

Saint-Maximin, who gave it to the grandfather of the Marquis de Villeneuve-Trans, in whose family the manuscript remained for three generations. Doctor Duehren sold it for a considerable sum to a German amateur collector through a Parisian bookseller. The manuscript is made up of 11 centimeter sheets bonded to each other and forming a strip that is 12.10 meters long. It is written on both sides, in almost microscopic writing. The last owner of the manuscript had locked it away in a phallic-shaped box. It was written in thirty-seven days at the Bastille, every night between 7 & 10 o'clock, and finished on 27 November 1785.

For Doctor Duehren, this work is of prime importance, not only in the works of the Marquis de Sade, but also in the history of humanity. He found a rigorously scientific classification of all the passions in their relationship to the sexual instinct. In his writing, the Marquis de Sade condensed all of his theories and created some new ones too, a hundred years before Doctor Krafft-Ebing's *Psychopathia Sexualis*.

By writing this book on *"those bizarre penchants inspired by nature"* the Marquis de Sade was aware of his novel's innovation and of its immense importance: "Who else," he asks, "could focus on and detail these variations in one of most beautiful works on manners — and perhaps one of the most interesting?"

And further, stressing the systematic and scientific side of this work, he adds:

Imagine that all the honest pleasures prescribed by the animal you call Nature and about which you speak unceasingly without knowing it, all these pleasures, I say, will be expressly excluded from this collection.

At the end of the reign of Louis XIV, shortly before the start of the Regency period, when the French people had been impoverished by the various wars of the Sun King, when a few had, vampire-like, sucked the blood of the nation & enriched themselves on the general misery, four characters of this species imagined the "strange game of debauchery," and whose conversations form the content of the book.

The Duke of Blangis & his brother, the Archbishop of … establish a plan which they share with the infamous Durcet and Judge de Curval. In order to be better related to one another, they each marry the first daughter of one another, & have an annual fund of two million set aside for their pleasures. They engage four procuresses to recruit girls and four pimps to find the boys, and four lovely dinners are given each month in four small houses in four different districts of Paris. The first dinner is devoted to Socratic pleasures. Sixteen young men from twenty to thirty years are used as "actives" and sixteen boys from twelve to eighteen years are used as "passives" in these orgies in which "men run everything even more lecherously than anything that Sodom &

Gomorrah invented." The second dinner is devoted to "girls of superior class."

There are twelve of them. The third dinner unites them with the most villainous and most disgusting girls in the city; there are one hundred of them. At the fourth dinner there are twenty virgin girls aged from seven to fifteen years. Moreover, each Friday there is a "secret" event attended by four young girls abducted from their parents and the four women of our original orgy. Each meal costs ten thousand francs, money we think is used to procure out-of-season rare foodstuffs, and wines from all countries. Then we enter the story itself which begins with the painting of the four libertines. These paintings are not embellished by lying colors; the features it offers are natural.

Above all, the author provides a portrait of the Duke of Blangis and makes us aware of his existence. He was the master, at eighteen years, of an enormous fortune, which he has increased with a large number of swindles and crimes. He has all the passions, all the vices; his heart is the toughest there is. He has committed all crimes, perpetrated all evils. He feels he must be completely evil and not "virtuous in crime" or "criminal in virtue." For him, vice is the source of "the most delicious pleasures." He believes that *the reason of the strongest is always the best.* He killed his mother and raped his sister. For twenty-three years he was associated with his "three companions in vice."

He engages in banditry, removes two pretty girls from the arms of their mother at the Comédie-Française. He kills his wife and marries the mistress of his brother, the mother of Aline, a heroine of the novel.

In fact in stature, he is a Hercules. This man, now fifty years old, is "a masterpiece of nature." We take this blasphemer to be the god of lewdness. He is so strong that he could crush a horse between his legs. His appetites are unimaginably excessive. He drinks ten bottles of burgundy with each of his meals…

The Archbishop, his brother, resembles him, and although he is not as strong, he is more spiritual. His health lacks his brother's vigor, he is more refined. He is forty-five years old, with beautiful eyes, an unpleasant mouth and an effeminate body.

The oldest of those debauchees is sixty years old. He is Judge de Curval. Tall, lean and dry, he looks like a skeleton. His long nose flares over a livid mouth. He is covered with hair like a satyr. He is impotent. He always liked crime: "He was looking for victims everywhere to sacrifice to the perversion of his taste." What he likes best is poisoning.

The fourth libertine, Durcet, is fifty-three years old; he is effeminate, short, fat & wide. His face is flabby. He has very white skin, the hips of a woman, and a soft & pleasant voice. This description indicates a passive homosexual, and in his youth he was the Duke's playmate.

After the portraits of the debauchees, here are those of their wives. Constance, the wife of the Duke and the daughter of Durcet, is a tall, thin woman, painted to look like a lily, and her features are smooth and full of nobility. She has big black eyes full of fire, and very small white teeth. She is now twenty-two years old. Her father had raised her as his mistress, rather than his daughter, but without being able to strip away her modesty or the goodness from her heart.

Adelaïde, wife of Durcet and daughter of Judge de Curval, has a different type of beauty to the brunette Constance. She is twenty years old; she is petite, blonde, and sentimentally romantic. She has blue eyes. Her features breathe decency. She has beautiful eyebrows, a noble face, a small aquiline nose, and a mouth that is a little wide. She is pleasant to look at and leans her head a little onto her right shoulder. However, she is the "outline rather than the model of beauty." She likes solitude and cries in secret. The Judge cannot destroy her religious feelings. She prays a lot. This earns her corrections from her father and her husband. She is a benefactor of the poor, for whom she is sacrificed.

Julie, wife of the Judge, is the eldest daughter of the Duke. She is large and slender, with a little puppy fat. She has beautiful brown eyes, a nice nose, playful features, hair, an ugly mouth, and rotten teeth. Because of his tendencies for uncleanliness, she attracts the love of the Judge, who has repugnant tastes. She has sworn eternal enmity to water. Greedy and drunk, she is totally insouciant.

Her younger sister, Aline, in reality the daughter of the Archbishop, is only eighteen years old. She has a fresh and piquant face, an upturned nose, lively brown eyes, and a delightful mouth. She also has a lovely figure, has smooth, soft, light brown skin. The Archbishop has kept her in the dark about everything; she can barely read and write, knows no religious beliefs, and has childish ideas & feelings. Her answers are unexpected & funny. She plays constantly with her sister, hates the Archbishop, and fears the Duke "like a fire." She is lazy.

Then comes the plan of the book and the delights devised by the four roués. It should be understood that in Sade's works, feelings that come from the language of the words are very powerful. The four roués decide to surround themselves with everything "which could satisfy the other senses by lechery" and to be told, "by order," all the depravities are roads of sexual perversion.

After a long search, the libertines find four old women who have seen and been used a lot. They know all of the sexual depravities and each has to include them in a systematic narrative.

The first must narrate one hundred and fifty of the simplest perversions; the most common, the least refined. The second must tell of the same number of "rarer & more complicated" perversions, in which several men act with several women. The third must tell of one hundred

& fifty criminal depravities related to law, nature &, religion. Excesses of this last category lead to murder, and these fatal pleasures are so varied that the fourth narrator must recount one hundred and fifty of these various tortures.

The four libertines want to practice the lessons of these stories on their wives and other "subjects."

These four "historians," whose science is extraordinary, are former prostitutes who have become procuresses.

Duclos is forty-eight. She is still in good health.

Champville is fifty years old. She is a promiscuous lesbian.

Martaine is fifty-two years old. Due to a vaginal obstruction, she has been a practitioner of sodomy from her youth.

Desgranges is fifty-six years old. She is "vice & lust personified," a skeleton with six teeth, three fingers & an eye missing. She limps & is corroded by a canker. Her soul is "the receptacle for all the vices." There is no crime which she has not committed. Moreover, her colleagues are not angels either.

Then the debauchees occupied themselves with the acquisition of "delicious specimens" of both sexes: eight girls, eight boys, eight men and four maidservants. They engaged the procuresses to recruit the material from the best in France; the choices were made with much refinement. They took from everywhere; from convents, from good families. They picked one hundred & thirty girls aged from twelve to fifteen years, for which they gave thirty thousand francs to the brothel-keepers. Of these one hundred & thirty girls they retained eight of them.

They do the same with the boys & men handed over by the "agents of sodomy."

The review of the girls in the country house of the Duke lasts thirteen days. They examine ten per day.

In the same way they examine the boys, the homosexual men, and the maidservants.

This assembly goes to the Duke's castle: for nine months it is the location of the stories and the orgies. The furniture is arranged carefully and food & wine are laid on. The castle is in the middle of a forest, which is surrounded by almost inaccessibly high mountains. The area is enclosed by a very high wall surrounded by a large ditch. Outside, the landscape is quiet and quasi-monastic, which is highly valued by the libertines. All the rooms open onto a large courtyard. On the first floor is a large gallery that leads to the dining room, which has the kitchens nearby. The dining room is furnished with Ottomans, armchairs, carpets. It is very comfortable. From there, one passes into the "living room of company," well furnished, close to the "cabinet of assembly" where the four old women hold forth. This room is the "battle field," the scene of the "lustful assemblies" and furnished accordingly. It is a semi-circle. There are four great niches decorated with glass. In one corner there is an Ottoman.

In the middle of the room a throne is prepared for the storyteller. On the steps of the throne are held the "subjects of debauchery" who, during the stories, must relieve the excited libertines. The throne and steps are covered in blue satin and black lace decorated with gold. The niches are lined with light blue satin. At the bottom of each niche is an open "mysterious wardrobe" in which the libertine withdraws with the object of his desires, and in which there is a sofa "& other items of furniture needed for all kinds of impurities." On both sides of the throne reaching up to the ceiling are tall hollow columns in which the libertines lock up people to be punished. The columns contain instruments of torture, the sight of which alone is appalling and causes the martyr great terror, which in turn "inspires the pleasure of delight in the soul of the persecutors." Close to this large room is a boudoir for the most voluptuous pleasures. In another wing of the castle are four beautiful guest rooms with boudoir, wardrobes, Turkish beds, Damas tricolor lights, and which are decorated with the most luxurious objects suitable to flatter "the lewdness of the most sensual."

On the two floors are some rooms for the narrators, the boys, the girls, the maidservants, etc. Outside the vault, at the end of the gallery, is a spiral staircase of three hundred steps leading to the basement, a dark arched room, with three closed iron doors, where the libertines have — with their refined & terribly cruel imaginations — prepared the finest & most barbaric instruments of the cruel art of torture.

They all enter the castle on 29 October at 8 PM. At the request of the Duke, all of the doors and exits are bricked up. The victims are allowed to rest until until 1 November (four days), and the four libertines establish the *rules*. It is a short day: up at 10 o'clock in the morning, and then visit the boys.

An hour for breakfast (chocolate, roast, wine) with the group of girls who serve them naked and kneeling.

Dinner from 3 to 5 PM, served by the wives & old women. Coffee in the lounge. Entry into the story room at 6 o'clock.

The women's costumes are changed every day. They vary between Asian, Spanish, Greek, nun, fairy, widow, and so on.

At the 6 PM bell, the historian begins her story, which lasts for four hours, interrupted by interludes for various kinds of pleasures chosen by the libertines. At 10pm, dinner. Then the orgies start in the cabinet of assembly, lit as bright as day. That lasts until 2 AM. There are a number of festivals, and every Sunday evening, there is the correction of boys & girls who have committed some peccadilloes. Only lascivious language is allowed. God is not to be mentioned, unless being blasphemed. No rest. The lowest & most disgusting are visited by the girls and the wives, who must act with grace.

After elaborating the rules, on 31 October the Duke harangues the women who have been brought together in the living room. His harangue is bleak; here is its conclusion:

the best that can happen to a woman is to die early. Sade then addresses the reader, requesting him to armor his heart. He will elucidate six hundred sexual passions which all exist: "We have carefully distinguished each one of these passions by a mark in the margin, below which is the name that we give this passion."

And so the *120 Days of Sodom* begins. On 1 November, Duclos opens the session by describing a hundred & fifty simple perversions, those of the first class. Each day, she describes five of them. The narrative is interrupted by discussions, observations, and various recreations.

Part One is the only part that Sade developed with all of the breadth that such a subject deserves. After that, he lacked paper.

The other parts, the second with Chanville's one hundred & fifty "double" perversions, the third with Martaine's one hundred & fifty perversions of the criminal kind, and fourth with Desgranges' one hundred & fifty perversions of death, are shortened, one could say outlined. Duclos speaks in November, Chanville in December, Martaine in January, Desgranges in February. The stories end on the last day, which culminates in the massacre of the last victims. Here is the *account of the total*:

Massacred before the 1st of March in orgies: 10

Massacred after the 1st of March: 20

Survived & came back: 16

TOTAL 46

This is the summary of a work which in the opinion of Doctor Duehren, puts the Marquis de Sade in the forefront of eighteenth-century writing, and in which he gives a scientific explanation of all the manifestations of sexual psychopathology.

Doctor Duehren also knows of the Marquis de Sade as the author of a rather long outline for a novel entitled: *Days of Florbelle or Nature Unveiled*, followed by *Mémoires of the Abbot of Modore*. This novel was to be formed of a number of volumes.

In the first volume, there were to be dialogues on religion, the soul, God.

In the second volume, the action happens in a grove of myrtles and roses; there are dialogues on the art of pleasure.

In the third volume there was a plan to establish thirty-two houses of pleasure in Paris.

In the fourth volume, there were the first twenty-four chapters of the history of Modore.

In the fifth volume, there were eleven chapters of the same story, including the story of the cruelties exercised on the unfortunate Eudokia.

In volume six there were twenty-six chapters on the history of Modore, etc., etc.

At the end, the Marquis indicates another title for his history of Modore: *The Triumph of Vice, or The True History of Modore.*[10]

The list of the manuscripts by the Marquis de Sade published as the *Michand Biography* indicates lost or seized works: *Tales*, 4 volumes; *The Portfolio of a Man of Letters*, 4 volumes. I think that it is these manuscripts that actually form the majority of the preserved collection in the National Library.

There are stories on the back of pages 451 & 453, the outline of *"Portfolio of a Man of Letters…"*

"Two sisters are in the countryside. One is a coquette; the other is kind, & more serious. Both have a regular exchange of letters with a man of letters in Paris."

Sade summarizes the contents of each volume. The most interesting, at least according to the outline, are the first & second volumes.

"The first volume contains essays on the death penalty, followed by a plan of employment to make criminals useful to the State, a letter on luxury, one on education in which is [the Marquis de Sade had written *are*, which he erased & wrote *is*] forty-four questions on morals…

"The second volume contains a letter on the art of writing comedy, the plan of an amusing comedy to be performed in verse, fifty dramatic precepts in which [a word here that I am unable to decipher] everything that can be useful for people who follow this career…"

The Marquis de Sade had developed the plan for this second part in folio 1 of the manuscript in which one reads:

Continuation of the portfolio.

Draft,

To be completed,

Pholoé and Zénocrate who [it is Pholoé] announces their plan to work on a comedy.

Zénocrate and Pholoé fight for the plan by sending nothing to the dramatic council.

Pholoé to Zénocrate. They [the two sisters] have done a comedy which will be shown to him on his return; *&* now they ask him for something funny.

Zénocrate to Pholoé. She sends (taken from the notebooks) anecdotes *&* etymologies; Miramas finishes the anecdotes — the words — *&* the stories.

Pholoé to Zénocrate. She left for Paris for the coronation.[11]

The Marquis de Sade was always very concerned with theatrical matters. We have a letter of his dated 1772, addressed to M. Girard, father of Philippe de Girard and who was, at the time of the coronation of the emperor, the judge of the cantonal assembly of Cadenet (Vaucluse).

The letter from the Marquis de Sade shows he presented a comedy on Monday, 20 January 1772. Here is the letter as published in the *Petite Gazette Aptésienne* of 11 December 1911:

The last time you played (sic) comedy with me, Monsieur, I had appointed several gentlemen of La Coste and Lourmarin to witness the pleasure that you gave me, although I have not yet been happy enough to have you with me as I fervently wished. I would be flattered to have the opportunity to perform a comedy that I have created and which will be presented on Monday, the 20th of this month and for which I would like your judgment. Perhaps I will finally get the pleasure that I have wished for so long by getting to know you. Spectators *&* judges have also informed me that you, Monsieur, are *prétieux* (sic), and I make no secret that I really would be sorry if you deny me what I am willing to put on that day. If not for the bad climate, I would have requested visiting you at your home. I hope that the season, soon less rigorous, will enable us to cultivate our friendship *&* repair any wrongs, for I have enjoyed your pleasant company.

I am, of course, Monsieur, your very humble *&* very obedient servant.

SADE

This 15 January 1772.

He dedicated a volume of the *Portfolio of a Man of Letters* to the theater; he wrote a great number of documents which, for the majority, are enumerated in the catalogue of the *Biography Michaud*, which, consequently, must still be in the hands of the Sade family. In folio 450 of the manuscript in the National Library, the Marquis de Sade listed three of his pieces. We are only familiar with the titles so far: *The Inconstant One*, a verse comedy in 3 acts; *The Double Test or the Corrupt Official*, a comedy in 3 acts; *The Credulous Husband or the Insane Competition*, a one-act comedy in free verse. On the back of pages 452 & 453, he gives an insight into his play *Les Ruses d'amour* that the *Michaud Biography* mentions under the title *L'Union des Arts*, ambiguous in genre like those that Aiguebelle gave in 1726, and those which are printed in the works of Morand. The plays of the Marquis de Sade include five pieces, the first of which serves as a prologue or connector to the others: *Les Ruses d'amour*, an episodic one-act comedy in prose; *Euphémie de Melun ou Le Siège d'Alger*, a one act verse tragedy; *L'homme dangereux ou Le Suborneur*, a one-act comedy in blank verse, performed at the Theater Favart in 1790 or 1791; *Azelis ou la Coquette punie*, a one-act fairy comedy in free verse, performed at the Théâtre de la Rue de Bondi in 1790. Everything ends as an amusement. There is also *La Fille malheureuse* which the *Biographie Michaud* does not mention.

Here, however, is the Marquis de Sade's note in his book *Les Ruses d'amour*:[12]

> A young Comte, in love with the daughter of a man who lives in a land near Paris, and knowing that he is on the eve of hosting Mondon, a very wealthy old rival, thinks he will disrupt this plan… He arrives at his château [the father's château] with a considerably skilled troupe of actors. He offers to provide entertainment, firmly resolved to take advantage of the freedom that the spectacle will provide, allowing him to either remove his mistress or get rid of his rival. The father accepts *&* [illegible word] to mingle with the Company troupe, in which the young Comte has disguised himself as an actor, in order to perform in the planned celebration concert… The young Comte, who wants to distinguish himself in every way, hoping that the more varied he is, the more he will find opportunities to succeed… offers to perform and then does perform a tragedy in one act entitled *Euphémie de Melun ou Le Siège d'Alger*, in alexandrines.

> A comedy of [illegible word] in decasyllabic verse: *Les Suborneur*.
> A tragedy in prose: *La Fille malheureuse*.
> A fairy comedy in free verse: *Azelis ou La Coquette punie*.

A comic-opera with music and comedy. Everything is sung. The whole thing is finished with a superb ballet-pantomime...[13] And the marriage of the young man and his mistress, which forms the dénouement of the whole piece, is concluded in the last important scene following this opera, and ballet-pantomime is to serve as entertainment.

This piece has 6000 lines of verse with as many different line lengths as prose. It requires five hours to present it. It is unique and is intended for Italians. [The last lines starting from *"This piece"* were erased by the author. He intended it for the *Italians* and took it to the *French*.]

The Marquis de Sade was associated with the Comédie-Française. It retains seven of his letters. Four have been published for the first time, in M. Octave Uzanne's introduction to the reprint of *Some Thoughts on the Novel (Idée sur les Romans)*. I now present the text of these letters in versions that are more exact than any published so far. Two of these letters have never been published in English; Dr. Duehren has just translated them into German, and which are as yet unpublished. The seventh, the longest, has never been published. I therefore present the seven letters of the Marquis de Sade, three of which are newly-published.

TO A GENTLEMAN,

M. de Laporte,
Secretary *&* Prompter of the Comédie-Française,
Rue des Francs-Bourgeois, Saint-Michel, № 127.

The Comédie-Française, Monsieur, has given me hope that it would like to compensate me for the [here I have erased an obscene word] little deserved and very bad reception which its assembly made the other day with the piece that I submitted for its consideration; I request that you, Monsieur, register me for a new reading, perhaps two or three similar to the last one [here are two or three erased words that I could not decipher], and you can be perfectly sure that I will not importune any more, Monsieur, either you or the Comédie-Française.

I sincerely have the honor to be, Monsieur, your very humble and very obedient servant.

Sade
17 February 1791[14]

Monsieurs,

Permit me the honor of constantly reminding you of the sentiments of esteem and attachment which, for years, have bound me to your theater. I have acted professionally at all times, I must say (and evidence exists), despite taking too much heat for your party during your recent troubles; your enemies have crushed me in the public papers, but never discouraged me. The reward for my loyalty has been your rejection of the latest work that I have read to you and which, I insist, was not created to be treated so harshly.

Despite this strict, severe, & general refusal of yours which has caused me some sorrow, I will be no less devoted to you in the future regarding what remains in my portfolio and what will be in it again. But, gentlemen, permit me to state that, having been treated by you so severely on the occasion I have just mentioned that I at least have your indulgence and your fairness on two other subjects.

For a long time you have had a piece of mine, unanimously received by you on the understanding that I accept the arrangements that you like to make for authors.[15] I ask with authority, Monsieurs, that you, as soon as possible, give me an answer, I implore you. It cannot be easy for you, if it is true, as has been said, that several authors, not wanting to adopt your arrangements, have withdrawn their works. I subscribe to everything, Monsieurs, and only ask that you do not make me languish.

My other request, gentlemen, because you have promised me compensation for the poor reception that you earned with my last comedy, is that you hear as soon as possible a reading of three or four of my other works, all of which are ready to be submitted and that I will not submit elsewhere.

As soon as you could kindly let me know the day you would like them from me, I will have the honor to present you with the four that I believe are the worthiest.

I have the honor to be, Monsieurs, with feelings of the highest regards, your humble and very obedient servant.

SADE

2 May 1791

I, the undersigned, declare it false and against my will and consent that my name is on the list of authors who took part in the deliberations that they should all be granted 700 liv. costs per day by the Comédie-Française. I have put my name on the list of those who signed that a minority should, by special consideration, be granted eight hundred pounds, and have certified that this is my way of thinking in a letter written to public gentlemen authors, signed by me, and I have also distributed copies to the gentlemen French actors, in order they be persuaded to my way of thinking.

SADE

In Paris, Monday, 17 September 1791

I have read the conditions in which the ordinary French actors of the King receive regular parts which they undertake to play, as well as the financial agreement they make regarding each work.

I agree with these regulatory conditions, and I promise to sign the financial agreement if my piece entitled *La Ruse d'amour ou l'Union des Arts*, a six act piece in verse, prose, & comedy is accepted.

SADE

In Paris, 27 January 1792

To citizen De La Porte,
Secretary of the Theater de la Nation.
The Theater.

CITIZEN,

I have the honor to send in, sealed, a one act comedy in free verse to be read at the Comédie-Française eighteen months ago. Your records show that it was by only one vote that this piece was not accepted, so the Assembly agreed to a second reading, when I would have made the changes that were prescribed. As they are now carried out, I beseech you accordingly to try and accept it as a tribute, and under the condition that I simply want it to be performed, I place in your hands this one act play, and renounce all the rights and fees of the author.

I am aware of the diplomacy of the Comédie-Française in this respect, but I beg it to notice and listen to mine, for it requires me to beg the assembly to accept this trifle. As the same favor was granted to M. De Ségur,

I would have the right to complain if they denied me. It is not from the gentlemen actors of the nation that I have to fear such an insult to the self-esteem.

I have the honor of fraternally being, citizens, your fellow countryman.

SADE

This 1st March 1793, year 2 of the Repub.: Rue Neuve des Mathurins, № 20, Chaussée du Mont Blanc.[16]

To Citizen De La Porte,
Secretary of the Comédie-Française.
The Theater.

If the Comédie-Française, Monsieur, does not approve the offer that I made of a one-act play, which I had the honor to send to you lately, I ask you to return it to me. I do not need to be subjected to the same time limits that we give to the things we buy & sell.

In a word, Monsieur, I ask you to instruct me as to the fate of this negotiation and believe that I am, with all the possible feelings,

Your citizen,
SADE

On 15 March 1793, the year of the Republic 2, Rue Neuve-des-Mathurins, Chaussée-d'Antin.[17]

It has taught me, citizen, that the Comédie-Française has some reasons to complain about me… it was surprised by my letter asking to be given a prompt reply to my offer of a short play, which, if it was appropriate, citizen, then it would be unfortunate to reject what one should politely want to accept.

I cannot let things remain in this state of confusion any longer; I do not deserve to lose the esteem of your company, I have loved, served, & advocated it for twenty-five years, which I now ask M. Molé to verify.

Justify me to them, citizen, I ask you, as is fair, and be assured for my part that I did and would never have done any real harm. In their opinion, this will be enough. I wished the reading of my short play; I still wish it, as I know that it is bound to succeed, I ask for the promptest presentation of it; it is a service that I beg of the Comedy. I have strong reasons to wish it, and as I do not want these authorities to believe that self-interest motivates me, for I do not want anything of this part, the diplomacy of the Comedy is opposed to this arrangement. Ah well, I will reconcile this for mine & its satisfaction; I offer to give up for war expenses whatever this trifle earns: but I beg that it is presented; citizen, I ask you for a response… to the Comédie-Française my regard, I am worthy from both & am with consideration,

Your friend,
SADE

12 April 1793, Year 2 of the Rep. Fran.

I have just this moment received the letter that you do me the honor of having written. I see with pleasure that you do not want to forget me. Well, I wait for the day you will want to show me it clearly. I request that you teach me this by agreeing to let me know if it is me or citizen Saint-Fal who must read it; in the first case, you will want to return the manuscript to me again, as it is useless sending it to the latter.[18]

The Comédie-Française had "unanimously accepted" *Le Misanthrope par amour ou Sophie et Desfrancs*, but although they had been in possession of this work of the author's for five years, they had never had it performed. Elsewhere the Marquis de Sade was happier. At the Theater Molière, he put on a performance of *Oxtiern ou Les Effets du libertinage*, a prose drama in three acts.

The Molière Theater was opened on rue Saint-Martin, on 11 June 1791. Its director was Jean-François Boursault, says Malherbe, who performed there himself. The Theater Molière represented everyone, but concerned itself with performances of patriotic pieces. "This theater, said *Le Moniteur* of 11 November 1791, has, since its opening, distinguished itself with patriotism and a love of the revolution." The company was unfortunate, and the theater was forced to close its doors a year later. It reopened soon after, but under various names: it suffered a large number of successive bankruptcies. The first theatrical success was: *La Ligue des fanatiques et des tyrans*, by Ronsin. Boursault was playing the role of the M P, Mademoiselle Masson appeared in it. Verse of this kind was heard:

> *But in the mists of time, your eyes regard*
> *The last of Louis, the first of Cæsar,*
> *Of the crimes of kings revealed by history;*
> *Of those whose virtues were devoted to glory*
> *Thousands are stained by the darkest attacks,*
> *As a thousand streams of blood flood their States.*

Also performed successfully was *La France régénérée*, a comic opera by Chaussard, with music by Scio.

Here is an extract, to give some idea:

THE PRELATE
Everything is reversed since you dared to write.

THE PRIEST
Reason has only reigned since you learned to read.

In the meantime, it put on *La Mort de Coligny ou La Saint-Barthélemy*, by Arnault-Baculard, *La Partie* de *chasse d'Hénri IV*, by Willemain d'Abancourt, and so on. On 22 October 1791, the Théâtre Molière gave the first performance of *Comte Oxtiern*, followed by *Henriot et Boulotte*, a parody of *Procureur arbitre*.

It was rather successful, and yet at the second presentation the name of the author caused enough of a storm that not one theater offered to put it on again, at least not in Paris. The second presentation took place on 4 November 1791. *Comte Oxtiern* was followed by *L'École des maris*. The presentation was so noisy that *Le Monitor*, which had never before mentioned the Théâtre Molière, included on on 6 November 1791 the following article:

> *Le Comte Oxtiern ou Les Effets du libertinage*, a prose drama in three acts, was successfully presented in this theater.
>
> Oxtiern, a great Swedish lord, and a determined libertine, rapes and abducts Ernestine, the daughter of the Comte of Falkenheim; he has her lover thrown into prison on a false charge; he brings his unhappy victim one mile to Stockholm, to an inn, whose maître, Fabrice, is an honest man. The father of Ernestine follows in the libertine's tracks and finds them. The young woman, in despair, imagines a way of being avenged against the monster that dishonored her: she makes an 11pm appointment with him in the garden, to fight with the sword. Her letter is written in order to make him believe that it is written by Ernestine's brother. Her father sends, in the brother's place, a substitute to fight Oxtiern, and this one, informed of the project by Ernestine, conceives the horrible scheme of putting the girl in the hands of her father. Indeed, both arrive at the appointment;

they attack each other and fight vigorously, until a young man runs in to separate them. He is the lover of Ernestine, whom the honest Fabrice has extracted from prison. The first use he makes of his freedom is to fight Oxtiern, whom he kills. He marries his mistress after having avenged her.

There is interest and energy in this piece, but the role of Oxtiern is an appalling atrocity. He is more infamous, and uglier than Lovelace and a lot less amiable.

A troubling incident disturbed the second performance of this play. At the beginning of the second act, a spectator, disgruntled or malicious, but certainly indiscreet, shouted: "Lower the curtain!" He was in the wrong, because demanding an interruption to the piece was prohibited. The theater's stage manager was wrong to obey this solitary order and lower the curtain over halfway. Finally, many spectators, after having it raised, shouted: "Out the door!" in unruly fashion. They were wrong in their turn, as they had no right to expel a man from a show for expressing his opinion. There was a kind of resulting split of attitude in the audience. A very small minority offered a few shy whistles, while the author was well compensated by much applause from the majority. He was asked after the performance: Are you M. Sade?

The Marquis used one of his tales in *Crimes de l'amour:* "Erneſtine. A Swedish Tale," as the subjeƈt of his drama. The draft of this tale is in manuscript and held in the National Library.

In the ſtory, the author meets Oxtiern working hard in the mines of Taperg, Sweden, and gets him to tell his story. In this tale, Ernestine dies, killed by her father, who, at the end of the ſtory, brings Oxtiern his freedom, which he has obtained from the King.

This drama reappeared eight years later, on 13 December 1799, in Versailles Theater, with the amended title: *Oxtiern ou Les Malheurs du libertinage.*

In Versailles, the Marquis de Sade created another part, a role which he filled. The faƈt is atteſted by the following letter, in the *Colleƈtion De La Porte.* It is dated 30 January 1798, but I have been unable to discover the name of the addressee.[19]

"God alive, here at leaſt is one letter that I like and I thank you; that's all I asked, I accept the arrangement proposed by M. Vaillant. It is the one he talked to me about and which was the subjeƈt of my letter of yesterday; here is my authority; send the money as soon as possible, I entreat you.

Now, regarding the subjeƈt of comedy; I herewith send you — free of carriage — two copies of a comedy which I have juſt had performed in Versailles and which, I now dare ſtate, was a great success there; I myself filled the role of Fabrice. One of the copies is for you; here's what I ask you to do with the other copy. I urge you to submit it to your best theater company leader and say that you are responsible on the part of the author to propose the performance of this play. You may tell him that if they want me to, I will perform the same role that I played in Versailles (that of Fabrice), but that, in any event, I pledge to go on rehearsing it in Chartres.

I have the honor to thank you and greet you with all my heart.

SADE.

10 pluviôse, Year 6, Versailles.'

Meanwhile, the Marquis de Sade sent to the Theater Favart *L'Homme dangereux ou Le Suborneur*, which had been part of his ambiguous *La Ruse d'amour*; the work was rejected in 1792. Another play, *L'École du jaloux ou Le Boudoir*, also received by the Theater Favart, was not performed. He had yet to have *Azelis ou La Coquette punie* — which was another ambiguous play — returned by the Theater de rue de Bondy, and *Le Capricieux ou L'Homme inégal* from the Theater Louvois. Neither play was performed, and the author himself withdrew the second. He tried in vain to impose his play *Jeanne Laisné ou Le Siège de Beauvais* on the Théâtre-Français (which had refused because it raised questions about Louis XI).

On 21 July 1798, he sent the *Journal de Paris* the following letter:

If there is a scientist in the world for which one can forgive a small error in the history of events on the earth, it is undoubtedly one that puts as much depth, sagacity, & precision into the history of the events in the sky. Occupied by such serious subjects, and such interesting calculations & such accuracy, isn't Lalande the citizen excusable for having been mistaken over the name of the heroine of Beauvais, when all modern historians trace this error to Presque? I therefore ask for his forgiveness if, much less to reveal this slight fault than to immortalize the real name of the heroine, I obviously prove that this girl never bore the name of *Hachette*.

Having tackled this subject in a comedy read at the Théâtre-Français on 24 November 1791, I took the most exact precautions to illuminate the historical facts relating to it. According to Hénault, Garnier, & a few others, it had become simple to think, like citizen Lalande, that the woman's name was Jeanne Hachette, but to make absolutely certain, I even consulted Beauvais for the *letters patent* granted by Louis XI to the famous warrior of this city, which are lodged in the city hall. I transcribed them, and one day they will be printed verbatim beside my play. Here's what we find in these letters, which I feel I must put here to give any authenticity, which should have the daring of the literary, to the criticism of scientists such as Garnier, Hénault, Lalande, & so on.

After the usual protocols, the *letters patent* expressed Louis XI's acknowledgement of the heroine in question: "Be aware of our respect for the good and virtuous resistance that was made last year (1472) by our dear and beloved Jeanne Laisné, daughter of Mathieu Laisné, residing in the town of Beauvais, against the Burgundians, etc."

That should be enough to publicize, in an unavoidable way, the name of the famous girl who, at the head of the city's women, vigorously repelled the troops of the Duke of Burgundy from the walls of Beauvais. The rest of this patent grants Jeanne Laisné and her lover Colin Pilon due awards & honors for this courageous action.

I ask that those who doubt and would dismiss this truth, to take the trouble to check, as I did, the Beauvais Letters patent that I have quoted, so that they will not oppose any more facts established by such strong evidence.

SADE.

It was because of this letter that the directors decided not to accept *Jeanne Laisné*, and on the 1 October 1799, Sade made a contractual appeal for intervention by Goupilleau de Montaigu, with whom he had established a relationship.[20]

"Citizen representative,

I must start by conveying to you thousands and thousands of thanks for the honor that you gave us recently when you agreed to come to Saint-Ouen, and to testify to you at the same time my regret at not being found there myself. I wished you well, for I was at home praying that you have the kindness to notify us when you want us to compensate.

I now have something else to share with you. Here it is:

You are all of the opinion, citizen representatives — & all good Republicans think the same — that one of the most important things is to revive the public spirit for good examples of good writing. It is said that my pen has some energy, which my philosophical novel[21] has proved: therefore I offer my medium to the Republic, and offer it with all my heart. Unhappy under the Ancien Régime, you know I fear the return of an order of things under which I would inevitably be one of the first victims. The means that I extend to the Republic are of no interest to me whatsoever; I have drawn up a plan, I will carry it out, and I believe that we will be satisfied.

But I tell you, citizen representative, a terrible injustice ceases to cool the feelings I have and which engulf me; why should I want to complain of a government for which I would give one thousand lives if I had them?

Why did it take over my property for two years, since which time, I am reduced to receiving charity, without having deserved this horrible treatment? Are you not convinced that instead of emigrating, I have not ceased to be employed at all, in the most terrible years of the Revolution? Do I not possess the most authentic certificates? If it is convinced of my innocence, why does it treat me as though I am guilty? Why does it want to place the hottest and most zealous of its supporters among the enemies of public affairs? There is, it seems to me, much injustice & much that is ill-advised about this process.

In any event, citizen representative, I offer the government my pen & my means, because that iniquity, misfortune, and misery no longer weigh on my head and make me scratch. I ask you, what difference does it make, being noble or not? Did I ever behave like a noble? Did you ever see me share their conduct & their feelings? My actions have erased the wrongs of my birth, and it is because of this manner of being that I have all the traits which have been crushed by the royalists, including Poultier, in his sheet of 12th of Fructidor. But I brave them as I hate them, and any wrong I feel for the government will remain with me until the last moment of my life, my choice, my pen & with all the feelings of my heart. Forgive my comparison, as that of the tender lover crying infidelity to a mistress at the foot of which he always sighs.

In a word, citizen representative, for my first offered attempt, I suggest a tragedy in five acts, a work most able to spark patriotism in all hearts, and which is, you will agree, far better in the theater than elsewhere, for there you can relight the almost extinct love that any Frenchman owes his country, and convince him of the dangers that exist for him if he falls into the hands of tyrants. He will speak of the excitement born in his heart at home and inspire his family and the effects will endure for longer. They are far different from those feelings that are momentarily lit within him by proclamations in newspaper articles, because in the theater the examples are lessons he has been given, and which he retains.

The subject of my tragedy is not caught up in the events of the day, which are still too close to us. Besides, an audience never has the same sort of interest in present events that the events of the past inspire; indeed it fears surprise, it fears the desire we may have to deceive, and the play is deserted by the second performance, as we have seen. My chosen text was from the history of France, which is a way to involve the French more deeply. It begins in the reign of Louis XI, when Charles, Duke of Burgundy, wanted to besiege the town of Beauvais, and which Jeanne Laisné, at the head of the women of the city, defended so bravely against the designs of the oppressor and inspired patriotism in those brave citizens, and during my five acts, I do not present only that emotion to them.

Are they susceptible to another tyrant such as Louis XI? I have taken care to say it, to prove it, and my work is of the school of the purest and most disinterested patriotism. The republican, the royalist, everyone who sees it will say: patriotism has always been the first virtue of the French, and it does not contradict the national character. We still loved the motherland under the rule of the tyrants. We always love it when we are afraid, or so the republican says; we love it even by wishing for them, or so the royalist says, but we learn to quell the danger by being prepared. Thus my play is essential… it is good… it is useful in all respects for all individuals, and, as I have just said, it has — far more so than the situation play — the great interest of the ancient & the certainty that it is not one of these paid-for vehicles which the republican laughs at and the royalist mocks.

That is, citizen representative, the work that I wish to submit to you. If you enjoy reading it, I ask your permission to have it put on, please. If you find that my intentions are good, I think it is important then to hasten the performance of it… it is absolutely of the moment. You may well want, in this case, to send an order to the appropriate authority at the Théâtre Français, to learn it and to perform it immediately. This order is essential to prevent the actors, if they do not like the work, or by being unwilling, causing the author to despair with their unbearable delays.

I apologize for such a long letter, citizen representative, but I think that the details it contains will not displease someone who, like you, loves both the Republic and the arts. Allow me to conclude by offering the tribute of my most respectful recognition.

Salutations & respect,

SADE

9th vendémiaire, year 8"

Goupilleau had to be approached diplomatically. Here is another letter from the Marquis dated 30 October:

8th brumaire year 8

Sade has the honor to accord citizen Goupilleau his respect; he begs him to have the kindness to take care of these two petitions, one to the commission in charge of debt cancellation, the other to the Minister of Justice. He awaits the day that citizen Goupilleau wishes him well in the reading of the *Siège de Beauvais*, for it is necessary that the part is read by the author himself. Sade will be quite at ease meeting citizen Goupilleau in his home on that day, although some people are in the position of judging the citizen representative. If he likes, it follows that the government should play the authority part as patriotic. Without that nothing will be achieved, and the moment when it is right to perform it will pass; our victories already age it a little.

Salutations and respect,
SADE

In September 1799, police intervened to prohibit a drama entitled *Justine ou Les Malheurs de la vertu*, which was undoubtedly by him and which was performed at the Théâtre Sans-Prétention.

We see that Sade appeared on stage, in public, in one of his plays at Versailles; perhaps he even played the same role in Chartres. Indeed, he was a good actor and shone particularly in the roles of lovers. There was some feeling in his playing and nobility in his bearing. He had taken lessons from Molé. Sometimes comedies were presented by the Marquis when he lived with his Justine, at rue du Pot de Fer-Saint-Sulpice. His taste for the theater, his talents as a writer and actor were very useful when he was locked up in Charenton, for his imprisonment had the effect of softening them.

The following documents, taken from the work of Dr. Cabanès (*Le Cabinet secret de l'histoire*, 4th série), showed that the Marquis de Sade could organize performances which were followed with great assiduity by the people in the best theater companies.

"The author of *Justine*, says Dr. Cabanès, obeyed his calling to the theater by giving these representations, which were also followed accurately, and which the ladies of the brave new world did not attend. Both letters reveal that the establishment's director gave the Marquis the opportunity to organize the show in the way he wanted.[22]

"Madam Cochelet, lady to the Queen of Holland.
Spectacle of 23 May 1810

Madam,

The interest that you seemed to take in the dramatic recreations of the residents of my house, make it a principle for me to offer you tickets to each one of their performances.

Spectators such as you, Madam, have such great power over their self-esteem which they find, only in the hope of your understanding and your pleasure, all that one needs to exalt their imagination *&* to nourish their talent.

They are performing, next Monday, the 28th of the current month, *l'Ésprit de contradiction*, *Marton et Frontin*, and the *Deux Savoyards*.

I await your instructions for sending the tickets that you want, and implore you to submit my respects to the ladies of the court of Her Majesty, the Queen of the Netherlands, the Princess whose rare *&* precious qualities join so deliciously & closely in the hearts of all French people, and which are a tribute to the sanctity of those she governs.

SADE"

"M. de Coulmier,
Director of the house of Charenton.

I have the honor to greet you, M. de Coulmier, and to send over the list as was agreed between us.

You are urged to approve it, as nobody wants to make any kind of changes, especially from memory, without the approval of the supervisor of projects.

Here, Monsieur, is the request in the form of M. and Mme. de Roméi, about who I had the honor to speak to you, and whose names are written on the list that I now present to you.

You will appreciably oblige me not to refuse them.

Accept this homage from your devoted servant,

SADE"

"It seems that this request was rejected, says Dr. Cabanès, because we do not find the Roméi name on the list that follows."

"List corrected by M. le Director:

M. Treillard............	3 places
Mlle Ronchoux, rue de Choiseui, № 12..........	2 —
Mlle Cochelet, lady to the Queen of N'Lands...	8 —
Mme D'Houdetot	3 —
The Irish doctor............	1 —
The house of Sauvan	4 —
The house of Finot............	2 —
The house of Guise............	3 —
Mlle Lambert............	3 —
Mlle Gonax............	4 —
The priest for M. Norvert............	4 —
The mayor of Charenton............	2 —
The Career............	1 —
M. Milet............	1 —
Mlle Quesnet............	7 —
M. de Sade............	7 —
M. Camp............	3 —
Mlle Adelaïde............	3 —
Mlle de Huteuil............	5 —
M. Roi............	2 —
Mlle Urbistandos............	6 —
M. Vivet............	2 —
M. Chapron............	3 —
M. Veillet............	4 —
Mlle Marchand............	2 —
M. le Couteux............	2 —
M. Florimond............	2 —
Three ladies of Nogent............	3 —
M. Flandrin............	1 —
	90 seats
Employees of the house............	36 —
Sick............	60 —
	186 seats *

The following letter, written by a certain Thierry, employee or resident of Charenton, provides interesting details on the character of the Marquis and on the theater he had organized. It seems to be addressed to the prison director. Dr. Cabanès provides the key elements.

"Monsieur,

Allow me to justify myself, as I promised you, concerning the scene that I had with M. Sade.

He told me in front of M. Veillet to do something necessary for decoration, and as I turned my back to him to go to seek what he asked me, he took me abruptly by the shoulders while saying to me: "Monsieur Rascal, have the kindness to listen to me." I answered him quietly that it was wrong to speak to me thus, since I had made myself available to him as the executor of his will. He answered me that that did not truly exist, that I had turned my back impertinently on him, and that if I laughed, he would give me 50 blows of his stick. Then, Monsieur, patience escaped from me, and I could not prevent myself from answering him in the same tone in which he spoke to me. I must inform you that for a few days I avoided M. Sade, because I was tired of his brutality; he had kindness for me, I agree, but, Monsieur, I paid with my zeal to do everything that I could to be useful and please him.

Company is an exchange of benefits, and I dare say that I have done more for M. Sade than he has done for me, because, after all, he has never invited me to dinner. I am tired of pretending to be his valet *&* to be treated as such, as it was only out of friendship that I served him.

As a result, M. Sade has given me more roles in his comedies, and so on."

Here, finally, is the letter of Dr. Royer-Collard, chief physician of the hospital of Charenton. In the letter, he violently attacks the Marquis de Sade.

"From the Senior Doctor of the Hospice of Charenton to His Excellency, Monsignor, Senator, and General Minister of the Police of the Empire.

Monsignor,

I have the honor of reporting to the authority of Your Excellence a subject of interest, primarily my duties, as well as the good order of the house whose medical department is entrusted to me.

In Charenton, there is a man whose bold immorality has unfortunately made him too famous, and whose presence in this hospice causes the most serious disturbances: I am referring to the author of the infamous novel *Justine*. This man is not unhinged. His only delirium is vice, and this species of delirium cannot be suppressed in a house devoted to the medical treatment of psychiatric disorders. It is necessary that this affected individual is either subjected to the most severe sequestration, or, to make the other patients safe from his fury, to isolate him from all the objects which could exacerbate or maintain his hideous passion. However, the house of Charenton, in this particular case, fills neither one nor the other of these two conditions.

M. Sade enjoys too much complete freedom. He communicates with a fairly large number of people of both sexes, receives them in his quarters, or goes to visit them in their respective rooms. He has the faculty to walk in the park, and there he often encounters patients who have been granted the same privilege. He preaches his terrible doctrine to some, he lends books to others. Finally, the general gossip in the house is that he lives with a woman who passes for his daughter. That is not all. He had the imprudence to form a theater in this house, on the pretext of creating a comedy drama for the insane, without necessarily considering the disastrous effects that such a tumultuous display would reproduce in their imagination.

M. Sade is the director of this theater. It is he who allocates the parts, distributes the roles and chairs the rehearsals. He is the *maître de déclamation* of the actors and actresses, and performs with them with great artistry. On the days of public performances, he always has a number of admission tickets at his disposal, which are usually distributed to his assistants, partly because it guarantees the room is favorable to him. He is always the chosen author for special occasions; on the birthday of M. le Director, for example, he is always careful to compose a complimentary allegorical piece in his honor, or at least a few verses praising him.

It is not necessary, I think, to make Your Excellency aware of the scandal of such a life, and to present the dangers inherent to anyone who may become attached to him. If these details were known to the public, what ideas would be formed about an institution where such strange abuses are tolerated? How could it be, moreover, that the moral part of treatment for derangement would be compatible with them? The patients, who are in daily communication with this abominable man, are constantly unaware of his deep corruption, and the sole notion of his presence in the house is not enough to shake the imagination of those who do not see him?

I hope that Your Excellency will find these reasons powerful enough to order that M. Sade be assigned to a place of confinement other than the Hospice de Cha-renton. It would renew his defense to leave in any way by communicating with the people in the house, for the defense might be better executed than in the past, and the same abuses still occur. I ask that the subject be referred to Bicêtre, where he was previously placed, but I cannot help but suggest to Your Excellency that a

secure house or a fortress would be much better than
an institution for the treatment of patients requiring
the most assiduous monitoring and the most delicate
moral precautions.

I have the honor to be, with the deepest respect,
Monsignor, Your Excellency, your very humble & obedient
servant.

ROYER-COLLARD, D. M."

"It is astonishing [adds Doctor Cabanès] that the police
force could thus enter an establishment intended for
the treatment of mental illness, and, in this context, it
is inappropriate to seek out, when the Marquis under-
goes his detention there, the real location of the house
of Charenton.

We could not do better than to send the address to
the man who is an authority in these matters, Esquirol, the mental specialist. In a work that has become a
classic, Esquirol gave a very comprehensive history
of the establishment in which the Marquis de Sade
had been confined, for reasons of law and order. We
are going to examine the principal elements of this
luminous work.[23]

Two years after the abolition of the establishment,
on 15 June 1797, the Executive Director ordered that the
charity hospice of Charenton was created in a principal
location; that it would be housed in an ancient property

founded by the Frères de la Charité; that it would use all necessary means to establish comprehensive treatment for the healing of madness; that the insane of both sexes would be allowed there; and finally that the institution would be under the immediate supervision of the Ministry of Interior, who was authorized to make whatever payments he deemed suitable for the organization's new facility in Charenton.

The management of the property is entrusted, under the title of general manager, to M. Coulmier, of the religious Order of Prémontré, a member of the Constituent Assembly & a legislative. M. Gastaldy, a former doctor in the d'Avignon madhouse, called Providence, is appointed Charenton physician. M. Dumoutier takes the place of economics-supervisor, & the late M. Deguise shall function as a surgeon. These appointments are made on 21 September 1798 (…).

Article 4 of the Ministerial Order of 5 June 1797, said that the manager of Charenton immediately returned monies for the economic administration of this establishment to the Minister of the Interior. This amount was never returned and would never have been. Article 5 of the same Order urged the Paris School of Medicine to write a payment suitable to stabilize the various services of Charenton; this payment was not made, and M. de Coulmier remained independent, the maître absolute and the supreme supervisor of the administration and the medical department.

Also, when M. Gastaldy died, at the beginning of 1805, M. de Coulmier did not want the Minister to provide a successor to this doctor; it was necessary that the Medical School intervened and nominated Doctor M. Royer-Collard as the chief doctor of Charenton Insane Asylum.

In the absence of any rules, the chief doctor had no real authority because of the control that the director had assumed. Considering the application of moral means to be one of his most important functions, the director believed to have found, in drama & in dance, a sovereign remedy for madness. He established, in the house, dancing & theater. Storage space above the old hall of the hospital accommodation, once a room for mentally ill women, became a theater, with room for an orchestra and an audience in front of the stage, as well as a dressing room reserved for the director and his friends. In front of the theater and on each side of the dressing room, which jutted from the stalls, were steps intended to seat, on the right, fifteen or twenty women, and on the left, as many men, all more or less deprived of reason, almost all insane & usually quiet. The rest of the room — the stalls — was filled with unknowns & a few convalescents. The too-famous Sade was the authority figure at these entertainments, these performances, these dances, and does not hesitate to call in "dancers" and "actresses" from the smaller Paris theaters.

As the director's protégé, the Marquis de Sade some-times put on dramas that were devoted to the tastes of the director. But the terrible Royer-Collard, after watching one of them, complained again, and the performances were stopped by a Ministerial Decree of 6 May 1813."

In *Juliette,* there are some new examples of sadistic dramaturgy.

One could multiply the notes since I began compiling these *Extraits.* One could now cite a large number of authors, scholars, philosophers, as well as many of our contemporaries who express ideas very similar to those of the Marquis de Sade. He was victimized out of fear that he would weaken or erode some very fixed ideas and suggest new ones, which are now enshrined in the *Opus Sadicum.*

And to conclude this essay on one of the most amaz-ing men who has ever lived, it is advisable to transcribe this phrase in which the Marquis de Sade, aware of what he was, and with quiet pride announced to a shocked world that was filled with terrified men:

"I address only the people who are able to hear me, for they will read me without danger."

The Marquis de Sade and the Gothic Novel
Maurice Heine

"... and we too know how to create."
D. A. F. DE SADE
Some Thoughts on the Novel

1

On the cover of the manuscript of his *Tales*,[24] which immediately precedes the *Catalogue of the Planned Works of the Author in October of the Year 1788*, Sade has handwritten this singular-toned note: "There is neither tale nor novel in all the literature of Europe where the "noir" genre is taken to a more terrifying and more pathetic degree."

If one is allowed to take the time to examine the works that Sade created while he was a prisoner in the Bastille, how can we fail to recognize in those revealing lines the defining elements of the *gothic novel*? To be too terrified to move is the very central idea that Mrs. Ann Radcliffe would put into her works three years later, starting with *The Romance of the Forest*. Therefore, let us ascertain as to whether the Marquis de Sade is mistaken in claiming that he already excels in a genre of which an English novelist and her follower and compatriot, Matthew Gregory Lewis, are commonly held to be the major writers *&* innovators.

To this end, we resort to a thesis: Miss Alice M. Killen has devoted time and effort to producing *The Novel of "Terror," or the "Gothic" Novel and its Influence on French Literature since 1840*.[25] This erudite scholar seems to be unaware of the works *&* the name of Sade. The copious alphabetical index at the Sorbonne appears to have been too rigorous for her. We will imitate this indulgence, only noting and implicitly confirming that her work highlights the view already expressed — in 1800 by the author of *Some Thoughts on the Novel* [26]— regarding the masters, Richardson *&* Fielding *&* their works, and the innovations of Radcliffe *&* Lewis:

> *Finally, the English novels — the vigorous works of Richardson and Fielding — have arrived to teach the French that it is not by portraying the tedious languor of love that one can obtain any success in this genre.*[27]

But Sade's testimony contains a combination of high regard for and a number of reservations regarding his own contemporaries:

> *Perhaps here we should analyze these new novels; the ones in which magic and fantasy constitute their entire merit; foremost amongst them I would place* The Monk...[28]

This critique shows that Sade was particularly well informed on the subject of English literature, despite it all being in translation. The epigraphs that decorate the four volumes of *The Crimes of Love* are borrowed from *The Night of the Young*. We have no formal proof that he read *The Castle of Otranto* by Horace Walpole, translated into French in 1767, or *The Old English Baron*, by Clara Reeve, whose translation appeared in 1787, but nothing accounts for the Gothic influence in his work better than the assertion of it in his work as a storyteller.[29] It is likely that Sade read these works, as did the English masters, particularly Radcliffe & Lewis. Nor is it surprising that, being older than them both by a quarter of a century, Sade had — long before them — colored his "noir" work by drawing from the same sources they drew from.

2

From about 1785, from his cell in the Bastille, Sade created, with meticulous artistry & care, the first text in his body of major works. On small sheets, stuck end to end, and assembled in a light, easily dissimulated roll, he recopied the draft written in his regular notebooks. A useless precaution in itself, if not for posterity: the storming and subsequent plundering of the Bastille will cause the author to lose first one and then the other manuscript. Incredibly, the frail roll will avoid destruction and will be passed from hand to hand, until it reaches us. Thus we can study in a pure state, the most powerful, the most original, and the most terrifying creation of the Marquis of Sade.

For a long time, the public was uncertain of the importance of works such as *The 120 Days of Sodom*, and refused to accept that its author's bizarre genius had slowly progressed; that he had been learning to develop, little by little, the latent cynicism of his first compositions; that perhaps he found encouragement in the extreme license of public morality at the beginning of old age. And everyone seemed to be in agreement with the silence that greeted the *Catalogue of Planned Works* of 1788.

But that reassuring assumption is now demolished, & in the works that some like to call "too simple" lies the Marquis de Sade's obscenity, identified at the outset as the essence of his genius. It is enough to undertake a reading of *120 Days* to be convinced, as he claims in his "Introduction," that this infernal microcosm excludes any element unsuitable for the synthesis of fear.

Set during the last years of the reign of Louis XIV, we are asked to imagine a feudal castle, deep in the heart of the Black Forest in winter. Durcet the financier, lord of the place, recalls the young Elvire, who was tortured and murdered there for pleasure. It is his dream to find new and more exquisite victims. Linked by marriage and friendship to his companions of vice — a duke, a magistrate, a bishop — at first it was the perfect surrounding isolation which provided protection & shelter for their imminent crimes.

It was necessary to first arrive in Basel, then to cross a retractable bridge... the castle itself was defended

*by a thirty foot high wall that surrounded the castle;
beyond the wall was a very deep moat full of water,
and finally, a defensive circle of servant's quarters,
forming an inner courtyard.*[30]

All the trappings of the English *Gothic* appear to have
been recreated here. But instead of opaque ghosts materializing in deserted, damp, & cold corridors during
the night, instead of empty and gloomy rooms in which
ancient armor turns to rust, instead of unexplained noises, strange apparitions, disturbing wonders — in a word,
so much childishness — what is revealed to us in this
intimate retreat?

*From the gallery you enter a very attractive dining
room, furnished with cupboards shaped like towers.
The gallery communicates with the kitchens and
provides the facility to serve hot food promptly and
with no need of any waiters... On either side of the
throne, an isolated column rises to touch the ceiling:
these two columns are designed to support the subject
whose misconduct might be in need of correction.
All the instruments required for this correction are
hanging from hooks attached to the columns, and
this imposing view is used to maintain the subordination that is essential to the parties of this nature;
subordination from which arises all the charm of
delight in the persecutor's soul.*[31]

The strange and quite appropriate scene setting, with the deceitful and inexorable cruelty which it implies, gives us our first impression of such people, even if the author had not painted their full portraits. Wouldn't it be better, though they are reproduced here, to eschew analyzing this masterful gallery of four? The sole reason we have for noting that this romance is terrifying is because Sade is its organizing engineer. Apart from the four protagonists, all of the characters — although their physical and moral characters are analyzed and defined with control — play at other roles, including those of assistants or animals in a laboratory. And what a laboratory it is!

It seems that the writer has evoked it in order to provide, a half-century later, a template for Edgar Allen Poe.

> *But depravity, cruelty, disgust, shame, all these passions, anticipated or experienced, had erected another room of which it is now urgent to give a sketch, for the laws essential to narrative demand that we depict it in the fullest and most careful detail. A fatal stone, skillfully made, rose from beneath the back of the altar... Woe, a hundred times woe to the unlucky creature who, in the midst of abandonment, finds himself at the mercy of a lawless and irreligious villain who is amused by crime and whose only interest lay in his passions, and who obeys nothing but the imperious laws of his own perfidious lusts!* [32]

What we are promised is a terrible work in which experimental vice is practiced. But before that, following the subtitle of the novel, *The School of Libertinage,* Sade will introduce his readers to all the phases of terror which progress rationally with the eroticism of his protagonists, each supported & developed by a theoretical graduate course. It is good that the "noir" genre was taken to "a more alarming & more pathetic degree," to use his own phrase, for Sade became — with the first of his great works — the very man who remains without equal in any literature with "a book the likes of which has never been seen or accepted by the ancients or by us moderns."[33]

3

Publicly debuting in letters at the age of fifty is certainly not a common destiny, especially when the value of his literary start proved equal to the political power of the revolution he supported. However, such was the adventure of Sade in 1791, when he published *Justine, or The Misfortunes of Virtue,* that this exceptional situation did not escape him when he presented himself, his book, and his heroine.

> *… I show Vice triumphing everywhere, & Virtue as the victim of its own sacrifices, I show an unfortunate woman wandering from misfortune to misfortune, a plaything of wickedness & vice; a woman exposed*

to the cruelest and most barbarous tastes; who is stunned by the boldest and most specious sophisms; and who is prey to the most skillful seductions, the most irresistible subordinations; a woman who has only the tenderness of her soul, a sensitive heart, a natural spirit and great courage with which to oppose the great number of reverses and so many plagues, and to push back corruption. In a word, I have painted the boldest dangers, the most extraordinary situations, and the most alarming maxims, with the most energetic strokes of the pen, for the sole purpose of obtaining from it one of the most sublime moral lessons that man has ever received. It is all so that one can arrive at the goal by a road not much travelled until now. [34]

Besides, who does not recognize in this tableau "the young, innocent, & virtuous girl, both unfortunate & persecuted, who will become the habitual protagonist of the novel of terror," the one that Alice M. Killen shows us has an affiliation to the unfinished *Marianne* by Marivaux and to *Pamela* by Richardson, omitting, of course, to make any reference to France and the character of Justine? [35]

This is not the only point where Sade shows he is already in possession of the English Gothic school methods. The draft of *Tales*, the second manuscript saved from among those he had written in the Bastille, is quite instructive in this respect. It is accompanied by several summary lists, where the different stories are distinguished by genre and subject. The letter S marks the *somber tales*, and a mysterious letter L indicates those where the author introduced what he calls the *dénouement of light*, an artistic device he uses that is a parallel to what Ann Radcliffe called the "supernatural explained." It is the skill of this particular novelist to suspend until the end of her stories the explanation of the dark circumstances which occur within them.

However, the first version of *Justine* — the one that bears the subtitle *The Misfortunes of Virtue* — was fully completed in 1787, according to the evidence of the manuscript.[36] It is listed among the first contents page of the *somber tales*, then disappears from it in subsequent ones, for its projected developments by the author obliged him to quickly qualify his work as a novel. The reader who compares the 1787 and 1791 versions of *Justine* will undoubtedly admit that Sade has, in the interval, transformed his *somber tale* into a "noir" novel.

But this metamorphosis was accomplished by 1788, the final date of the revisions made to the manuscript in the Bibliothèque Nationale, which, with its corrections, additions and marginal references in an unfortunately lost *book of supplements*, survives only because of a clean text given to Girouard, the printer. It is necessary to stress that in 1788, the English "Gothic novel" has yet to be born, since the first book by Ann Radcliffe — which falls far short of her future style — will not be published until the following year in London. It was with her third work, *The Romance of the Forest,* that her style is established; and, in the first memorable coincidence in the chronology, the year 1791 also sees Sade appearing & affirming Radcliffe's work.

In fact, it can be assumed that these two writers, different in sex, age, and origin, had in common their deployment of the same tropes, and most often their differences are obvious in a comparison of their works. In the English novel, the terrifying factors are reduced to a Gothic abbey, sufficiently ruined to provide a framework for the moral concerns and the nocturnal nightmares of a pure & beautiful heroine. However, a happy outcome does not fail to clarify the disturbing mysteries. It is very different, have no doubt, to Sade's novel, whose preliminary statements in the form of an *Editor's Note* are enough to outline his intentions:

> *…Who would attempt to censor the novelist? Are not all imaginable species of defects, all possible crimes available to him? Does he not have the right to depict them all to make men hate them?* [37]

However, the author is not in the least reluctant "to use the elements of nature to increase the terror caused by other circumstances." [38]

This pure & brilliant vault... This imposing silence of the night... This fear that freezes my senses... This image of nature at peace, so close to the upheaval of my lost soul, spreads a dark horror within me, from which is born a need to pray.[39]

While it is true that "the use of nature, and especially nature at its most frightening, is one of the most significant characteristics of Ann Radcliffe," there is no denying that Sade uses it just as well.[40]

The shadows of night began to spread throughout the forest a kind of religious horror which gives birth simultaneously to fear in timid souls, and the planning of crimes in wild hearts.[41]

Neither does he omit the depiction of disturbing and virtually inaccessible feudal buildings.

At about four in the afternoon, we arrived at the foot of the mountains... this alarming den, resembled more an asylum of robbers, rather than the dwelling of virtuous people.[42]

But these are average accessories for the novelist who has an unlimited arsenal of tortures & murders. And when Justine discovers skeletons, one understands so much better her fear that they lack the elegant patina of the centuries:

I hastened to flee… perhaps this skull is that of my dear Omphale, perhaps it is that of the unhappy Octavie, so beautiful, so gentle, so good, and who — while she lived — was like the rose; her charms were in its image! [43]

However it is not in the accumulation of adventures & dramatic episodes external to the characters that it is necessary to seek the genuine springs of the "gothic novel" in Sade. It is rather among the human defects & social iniquities that the elements of fate are found, made bitter with unhappy virtue. Also, when the author consents to set a scene of the dark kind, he transposes it, according to the practice of Radcliffe, into the thoughts of his heroine, although he presents it with more realism and audacity, so it resembles the result of the arrangements of materials devised by libertines for the satisfaction of their own lust.

Imagine, Madam, a circular vault, twenty five feet in diameter, whose walls were covered with black hangings, which were decorated with the most gloomy objects, skeletons of all sizes, crossed bones, severed heads… the floor of the vault was occupied by a large black divan, an eloquent testimony to the atrocities of this dismal place. [44]

Finally, with supreme and decisive dissimilarity, the dénouement, far from turning pink as in Radcliffe, remains obstinately "noir" here. If the men weary themselves by tormenting their victim, and their inconsistency seems to offer her safety, isn't this the same sky that will not change in Sade's story of languid persecution?

> *Monsieur de Corville still lived in the countryside; it was at the end of the summer, they planned an outing when a terrible storm approached, forcing them to postpone their walk... Thérèse hastened to calm her sister, then ran to the windows which were already being broken; she would fight the wind, she fought for a minute, and drove it back, and in that moment a bolt of lightning struck her where she stood in the middle of the living room.*[45]

As it is, such a work prompted the following lines: "The appearance of this novel is a true literary event. It meets the need for strong emotions that follow great social disturbances; it flatters sensualism with its voluptuous depictions, & the irreligious due to the boldness with which it treats holy things."[46] But it is *The Monk* of Lewis and not the *Justine* of Sade that this note should be about.

4

After the publication of *Justine* in Paris, five years were to pass before the original edition of *The Monk* appeared in London. Lewis immediately became alarmed by threats of litigation, and prepared a new expurgated edition of his novel. At the same time, Sade was working on a third draft of *Justine*, carefully making its contents more gruesome. It was published in 1797, under the title of *The New Justine*, on the same date as the first French translation of the amended text of *The Monk*.

1797, a really crucial date in the history of the "gothic novel," was not limited to the publication of those two literary efforts. It was also the year that Victorine de Chastenay chose to reveal to French readers *The Mysteries of Udolpho*, which Ann Radcliffe had published in London three years earlier. Meanwhile, A. Morellet & Mary Gay Allard hurried, each on their own account, to translate *The Italian, or the Confessional of the Black Penitents*, which Ann Radcliffe had published earlier that year.

At the same time, Sade showed his own extraordinary productivity: he carefully added to the four volumes of his *New Justine*, and created a six volume continuation of it: i.e., *The History of Juliette*.

What appears at first glance to be *rapprochement* is actually the remarkable simultaneous appearance of characteristic works in both English & French, from 1791, subject to the incontestable primacy gained by Sade for his creation of *The 120 Days of Sodom* (1785) and *Justine* (1788). Therefore, let us examine more closely the possibilities of mutual influence between 1791 and 1800; in England, from Radcliffe's *The Romance of the Forest* to the appearance of Lewis's *The Castle Specter*, and in France, from *Justine* to the publication of *The Crimes of Love*.

One striking fact is particularly worth paying attention to: Lewis's literary debut was as early as Sade's was late. The fuss over *The Monk* made Lewis famous at the age of twenty, and that extreme precocity by no means excludes the huge number of readings (in a variety of languages) he undertook.

But if it's really "in French literature that he sought what he had been unable to find in fantastic or noir fiction," then one can readily agree that it is not in the fiction of Diderot, as Alice M. Killen suggests, with which he could have satisfied his curiosity.[47] If we are allowed, in our turn, to offer an assumption, we rather see this young man at sixteen years of age, taking advantage of the trip he made to Paris in 1792 to acquire a copy of *Justine*, the third edition of which had just been published in the famous collection of Cazin.

Moreover, Lewis very quickly exhausted his apparently exceptional gifts. His second work, *The Castle Specter*, a drama, played in London in 1797 and was published the following year, scarcely justifying the success it achieved, to the extent that his literary activities did not survive beyond the 18th century.

By a strange coincidence, Ann Radcliffe — whose *The Mysteries of Udolpho* had, in 1794, so effectively stimulated the ambition of her young rival — only responded to him in 1796 with her last novel, *The Italian*. Then, from 1797 until 1823, the date of her death, she was condemned to silence.

Finally, by a no less remarkable accident; the start of the political persecutions — of which he would become the victim — resulted in Sade, from 1801, having almost every means of expression withdrawn or restricted. With only one or two exceptions, he was unable to publish his works, for the manuscripts on several occasions were seized and destroyed: we are ignorant of the works of a writer who was forced to remain fertile until the approach of his death, which occurred in 1814.

Thus, in France as in England, as happened during the 19th century, imitators took care, with varying fortunes, but generally without talent, to prolong a genre which its originators no longer considered valid.

It goes without saying that the works published by Sade after 1791 were not kept with the documents of the reciprocal reactions of the two schools. We have explained our reasons for the probable influence of *Justine* on *The Monk*; but we accept that Ann Radcliffe would have benefited the least from Sade's creations, even had she been aware of them.[48]

The reverse is less certain; because if no translation of Ann Radcliffe's works appeared in France before 1797, it is likely that Sade was aware of her first work, either from the original texts or by analysis, at the time he composed *Juliette*. At all events, this last work seems to be the best among his known writings, the richest in episodes that are specific to the novel of adventure as Radcliffe conceived it. From it, one only wants, for example, the account of the visit of the witch and the poisoner Durand; or the various phantasmagorias which are held in his small, detached house in the suburb of Saint-Jacob; or better still the fabulous evocation of "The Hermit of Apennin," the kind giant ogre, so curiously related to those who the author scoffed at on the front-piece of the first editions of *Justine*.[49] To us, it was worth at least a page that, in our language, can pass for the most beautiful of its kind.[50]

Is this point enough to invalidate the opinions of Alice M. Killen, according to whom, in France, "the premier period of the school of terror is remarkable for an almost complete absence of literary value"?[51]

Miss Killen, admittedly, does not make the error of including the Marquis de Sade "among the very many writers entirely forgotten today, who at that time filled their literature with cries of terror and death."[52]

5

Still, literary value is not at issue here, and Sade differs from so many of his obscure contemporaries by the sheer power of his thought. It may be that, in the English school, talent alone distinguishes the works of Radcliffe or Lewis from those of their many imitators; but, in France, the great figure of Sade dominates — along with Laclos — the last twenty years of his century. And to find reasons for their brilliant superiority, one needs to look initially into their pessimistic philosophical system, one that these two writers based on a serious knowledge of the world and of man. Sade shows weakness by not naming his rival in his *Some Thoughts on the Novel*, but, as was pointed out by M. Andre Monglond, the critic of the time, that although Sade was malevolent, he was not mistaken.[53] Later, in the year that *The Crimes of Love* appeared, Joseph Rosny wrote in *The Court of Apollo:* "It has been demonstrated that it [the novel *Dangerous Liaisons*] has done more harm to morality in recent years than all other works of this kind have done in a century. The infamous novel *Justine* is the only one that challenges it for criminal superiority by the number of its victims."

In fact, it was his philosophical culture that allowed Sade his invention; the development of characters and unbridled atrocities from which his compositions drew their dramatic intensity. If he wanted to terrify, then he needed artificial, incredible, or puerile circumstances.

It will suffice to invite his readers to contemplate in his latest work the naked & ugly truth. When he opposes nature and prefers the fable, when he criticizes the use of spells and phantasmagoria; when he makes available to the novelist "every imaginable vice and all possible crimes" despite knowing that from his appeal human monsters will arise, he is as frightening as the ghosts of Radcliffe or the wonders of Lewis. Sade thus discovered, in an area of psychology & introspection, the elements of respectful terror for natural laws, in the literature of terror, he pleaded & won the cause for the novel of manners & character against that of the adventure novel.

Thus it was not only the chronology, but also the analysis of the means deployed that showed the independence, at least in their creators, of the two parallel temporary trends — French & English — that lead the novel to its objective of terror. To support the lack of originality of the French trend, it was necessary, as Alice M. Killen maintains — and she did not leave it at that — to exhume the evidence of a forgotten literary mercenary. Still, even in this field, we should close our eyes so as not to see the frequently made loans against the work of Sade by imitators generally lacking scruples as well as merit. But the real fruitful exchange from one literature to another never takes place. In terms of superior talents, we have for example ignored the great thesis of G. Lafourcade, which was on the importance of Sade on the spiritual formation of Swinburne.[54]

In a final flowing backwards from past to present, the intellectual waves that flow from Marivaux to Richardson, from Richardson to Abbé Prévost and the Marquis de Sade, and finally from Sade to Swinburne, reveal the existence of a great affinity between the two types of literature.

Sade has admitted his essential debt to the masters of the English realistic school; he has agreed on the merits of their translators and named Abbé Prévost; he has praised, but with reserved good grace, the early success of young novelists of the "black" romance genre. But having paid tribute to these writers, *&* before moving to a personal plea, he finishes his *Some Thoughts on the Novel* with this claim: "…Is it not better to say to these proud rivals, *and we too know how to create.*"[55]

However, in Year VIII, by ironic fate, Sade was forced to receive no profit from the major part of his works. There is decisive evidence that his manuscripts were lost, or that he denied authorship of some of his works. This was because of the very real threat that weighed heavily on his freedom; any claiming of authorship would have prevented him from taking issue with various presumptions. At that time in the realm of thinking, aversion to — or a propensity for — moral conformism was no longer a criterion. It is a small dispute in our time, for the work of Sade has fully resumed its place among the works of the spirit. Indeed, an interpretation of the sadistic nature of man, whether one agrees or not, has already had many consequences that are no longer possible to ignore. In particular, if the novel of terror cannot be banned from literary art, it is inevitable that Sade should regain the rank of its creator, a title to which he is entitled.

A Revolutionary Intelligence: The Marquis de Sade (1740–1814)
Paul Éluard

No man was more feared, reviled, & hated than the one who is now known as the Divine Marquis. He was, and he remains, the most feared of philosophers. Because he never acknowledged any barrier to his desire for freedom; because his genius shamelessly revealed every human instinct; because he denounced man's hypocritical relationship with others; and because he developed a system that would have given humans of both sexes their natural freedom and allowed them a real life together, Sade was persecuted throughout his life, and for over a century, his truthful and courageous works have been outlawed and prohibited.

Sade wanted to restore to civilized man the power of his primitive instincts; he wanted to deliver the amorous imagination from its own objects. He believed that out of this, and this alone, true equality would come. Since virtue is its own reward, he labored, in the name of everything that suffers, to drag it down and humiliate it, to subject it to the supreme law of unhappiness, with no illusions and no lies, so that those it normally condemns might build here on earth a world on the immense scale of mankind.

It is extremely difficult to disentangle the true facts of Sade's life from the web of false accusations that he was subject to. The whole of society seems to have constantly united against him. No evidence has ever been provided to prove the seriousness of the offenses that saw him successively imprisoned in Vincennes, Saumur, Lyon, Miolans, Aix, & in the Bastille.[56] He was sentenced to death in 1772 for what is known as "The Marseilles Case," in which his innocence was proven. The verdict was quashed in 1778, but his mother-in-law made no attempt to utilize her power to obtain his release.[57]

In 1789, the Marquis de Sade was imprisoned in the Bastille for five years. In 1788 he had written: "A great revolution is brewing in our country: France is weary of her rulers' crimes, their cruelty, their debauchery and their stupidity. She is tired of despotism and she will break her bonds." In prison, he developed his revolutionary principles. He used his writings to attack — with the utmost savagery — the monarchy and the clergy; he attempted to destroy the idea of God and show that Christian morals have always forced man to resignedly accept a repressive state, and to be the slave of the stupidest masters.

On July 2, 1789, Sade managed to fashion a makeshift megaphone, which he immediately used to shout to passers-by that the prisoners were being murdered; that the guards were hanging them from the towers of the Bastille. From the window, he threw out pamphlets inciting people to rescue the inmates, *&* he managed to cause so much agitation in the street outside the building that the governor of the Bastille arranged for him to be transferred to Charenton on 4 July.

The Constituent Assembly finally awarded Sade his freedom on 23 March 1790. He immediately took an active part in the Revolution and became Secretary of the Section des Piques. An ardent admirer of Robespierre and Marat, but a decided opponent of the death penalty, he was considered suspect and detained on 6 December 1793. By a singular stoke of fate, he was released on 9 Thermidor II (27 July 1794), the date of the fall of his heroes.

An ardent materialist, Sade believed that "the power to destroy is not granted to man: he has at most the ability to vary forms, but he does not have the right to destroy them." The death penalty, according to him, could not be justified because the law, contrary to man, acted without passion: "Man, who receives his impressions from nature, may be forgiven for this action [of murder]; the law, however, which is always in opposition to nature and receives nothing from her, cannot be allowed to have the same choices: not having the same reasons, it cannot have the same rights."

Aged almost sixty, Sade appears to have had a peaceful end to his terribly turbulent life. But even he could not withstand the power of Bonaparte, the emerging tyrant. Sade wrote *Zoloé and His Two Acolytes*, a satirical pamphlet of unprecedented savagery directed at the First Consul, Josephine, Tallien Barras, & Visconti. With no publisher willing to accept the work, he was obliged to print it himself.

Arrested and imprisoned in 1801 in Sainte-Pélagie, he was transferred shortly after to Bicêtre, then to Charenton. It was in this asylum that he died, on 1 December 1814, in full possession of his reason. The precursor of Proudhon, Fourier, Darwin, Malthus, Spencer and also of all modern psychiatry, this apostle of absolute freedom simply desired that all men follow the course of their own instincts and thoughts, and thereby have the courage to see themselves as they truly are and to yield only to their real needs.

Notes on the Sadistic Imagination
André Masson

One would vainly search in any of Sade's books for an example of one irrational step. Dedicated solely to researching the laws of the erotic, Sade's females — descendants of Laura — are never able to stop what they cannot understand. They are moved by their author with the utmost precision and meticulousness — toward a perfectly logical narrative conclusion.

Sade's prose, occasionally feverishly overwritten, sometimes dominates a page of *The 120 Days of Sodom*. Of course, heated descriptions of barbarities often continue until they culminate in the death of the object of desire. But above all, reason and science triumph, for by their acts, these characters solve problems — perfectly described problems of desire.

In *Justine*, a group of monks share her: she is circulated amongst these antagonists. The novel's "style" shines a light on the monstrousness that one frequently finds in an individual: be it your next-of-kin, your brother, or even yourself. But the extremes in Sade's fictions are presented in a very sophisticated way; they are shown in a "theatrical" light, where ceremony, rite, & mystery occur — right at the very borders where prose meets poetry.

However, there was, far from these deviations, the development of the "murals of Paris" — an extreme example, since the fortuitous surrealism of a great writer of the 16th century makes the undulating — & vaguely sexual — constructions of Gaudí diminish.

Sade's work is far from Sorel's dream of *Francion*, which features a certain charming meadow in which the hero of our comic novel prostrates himself. This is because the ways in which the sadistic scenes are depicted is partly dependent on English novels — particularly the fantastic ones — or *Gothic* stories, as they are known. However, sacred ground, underground caves, court-yards and mazes do not seem to belong to any important symbolic system.

This said, it is necessary to go to *Juliette* to find the highpoint of the divine Marquis's imagination: a large Italian decoration on blood-soaked armor, which depicts — as it should — an erupting volcano. The episode of the naked women being used as furniture (so neatly & precisely selected by André Breton for inclusion in his *Anthology of Black Humor*) represents the extremes of reverie for the neglected philosopher. Here, although all these positions are possible, the hyperbole of demanding healthy sensuality dominates to such a degree that it could discourage imitation by the vainest participants in their homes — including critics — if they could. On the other hand, these visions will fill an honest reader with ease; a reader who can then cultivate, without remorse, fear or denial

the holy flower of pleasure.

Notice
Anatole France

I

We did not request the task of writing about this rare subject, this beautiful and rich subject of literary pathology. But, since he has presented himself to us, we must make it our duty to analyze him. However, before writing a few notes on the surprising case he offers us, let us warn the discerning readers to whom this essay is addressed that the *Stories, Tales, and Fables* which are published here for the first time will not serve as a document that supports our thesis.

Although these are stories by the Marquis de Sade, they are not sadistic; on the contrary, they are very innocent and bear no trace of the mental illness which afflicted its author. This is what we wish to state at the outset. Now, let's consider the afflicted *&* the affliction.

Donatien Alphonse François de Sade was born in the Hôtel de Condé, Paris, on 2 June 1740.[58] His parents were Jean Baptiste François Joseph, Count de Sade and Marie Eléonore de Maillé de Carman, distant cousin and lady-in-waiting to the Princess de Condé, and the niece of Cardinal Richelieu. The de Sade family came from an old *&* noble line which dated back to Comte Hugues de Sade *&* his wife, Laura de Noves (1310–1348), the lady whose beauty *&* grace were extolled by Petrarch in his sonnet sequence *The Canzoniere.*

Sade spent his childhood partly in Provence, where his family had land, *&* partly in Exeuil, Auvergne, with his uncle, the Abbé de Sade, the Grand Vicar of Toulouse *&* Narbonne, who combined the gallantry of a court Abbé with the knowledge of a politician, *&* with witty erudition that was far in advance of Fauriel, particularly regarding Provençal poetry. The young marquis studied at the Lycée Louis-le-Grand in Paris, a Jesuit college, where he was tutored by Abbé Jacques-François Amblet, a priest. After studying there for four years, he left the Lycée at the age of fourteen, to enter the cavalry.

At the age of fourteen, Sade began attending an elite military academy. After twenty months of training, on 14 December 1755, Sade was commissioned as a second lieutenant in the King's regiment, then he was made a lieutenant in the Carbine Regiment. During the war in Germany he earned the rank of cavalry Captain on the battlefield. He eventually became Colonel of a Dragoon regiment and fought in the Seven Years' War. He returned to Paris in 1763, and those who knew him then say that that was when he formed the idea of becoming an amiable libertine. His youthful follies went far beyond what was permitted and acceptable at that time for a young man *&* Sade began to attract scandal, which his father resolved to curtail by arranging for his son to be married.

Aware of his father's intentions, Sade began courting a rich magistrate's daughter, Anne-Prospère de Launay de Montreuil. She was the daughter of Monsieur de Montreuil, judge of the Court of Aix, a friend of Sade's father. The judge rejected Sade's suitorship and instead Sade's father made an arrangement for his friend to give his eldest daughter, Renée-Pélagie de Montreuil, in marriage to the Marquis. She was an attractive, honest, pious and reserved young lady. Her younger sister, Anne-Prospère de Launay, was more vivacious, far less reserved and consequently, more delightful company than her sister. The Marquis de Sade was immediately smitten with Anne-Prospère and declared that it was her that he wanted to marry. Sade's father and Monsieur de Montreuil refused. They demanded that he marry Renée-Pélagi, the elder daughter. After constant pressure from his own father and from Renée-Pélagi's father, the Marquis reluctantly agreed to the marriage.

A year after this arranged marriage, the death of his father meant that the Marquis inherited a large fortune along with the hereditary title of Comte, a title always bestowed on the eldest male of a noble family. For reasons he never bothered to explain, Sade rejected the title of Comte, despite it being legally conferred on him as the male successor, preferring instead to retain the title of Marquis; the erroneous title that history has preserved for him. He then proceeded to throw himself into a life of furious debauchery with roués, men of letters, lackeys

& sycophants. This was ignoble behavior, but not all that unusual for young noblemen.

The first scandalous act that became known to the public is one that reveals an aberration that is characteristic of the moral sense in this man. It dates from 3 April 1768. On that day, his valet had taken two young prostitutes to Sade's *petit maison* in Arcueil, Paris, where they waited for the Marquis, who was in the city center. Sade met a prostitute named Rose Keller, to whom he offered payment & supper and who readily agreed to his proposal.

When he entered the house with her, the two women were at the table, crowned with roses in the Greek fashion. But, instead of letting Keller sit down at the table for supper, Sade dragged her into an attic room with the help of his valet, stripped her naked, bound her, and whipped her with a blood-stained whip. He then sat down to supper with the two other women. It was daytime when Rose Keller, mad with terror, managed to break her ties & threw herself through the window and fell naked into the garden, where shrubs broke her fall. Once she had climbed over the garden wall and was in the street, people gathered around her. Cries & threats broke out, and the Marquis de Sade, who had chased after her, fled, pursued by indignant peasants. Rose Keller lodged a complaint, and the Marquis, whose adventure became the main source of conversation in the salons, was detained in the Château de Saumur, then in the prison of Pierre-Encize, in Lyon.

Within six weeks, the Marquis's family had obtained a royal *letter d'abolition*, in which it was claimed that the delirium suffered by Sade on 3 April was a new type not covered by any law. The letter was expedient; the incident was regarded by the king and his advisers as embarrassing enough to bring shame on France's nobility, and obscene enough for it to be necessary to expunge it from everyone's memory as quickly as possible. Whatever the case with the letter, the contents of which cannot now be verified, the accusation was nullified after its withdrawal by the complainant who, for a sum of one hundred louis, paid to her by Sade's mother-in-law, was happy to report she had received nothing more than a light spanking. With those hundred louis as a dowry, Rose Keller found a husband the following year. Besides, although she was a prostitute, the act committed on her by Sade was nonetheless an outrage.

If we are to believe the various reports we have heard of the Marquis, he was often overwhelmed by violent urges, combined with a sort of amorous despair, which often precipitated the Marquis into the seventh circle of the hell of debauchery. As much as he disliked his wife, Renée-Pélagi, he adored his sister-in-law, Anne-Prospère. He had some reason to believe that she was correspondent to his feelings, and no matter how discreet they were, no matter their public acts of indifference toward each other, Monsieur de Montreuil felt it was his paternal duty to take the precaution of sending his daughter to a convent, specifically one that Sade knew nothing of.

In addition, he obtained an order from the police for his son-in-law to be exiled to Provence, to the Château la Coste. Sade went to La Coste, taking with him a young woman from the theater whom he passed off as his wife and introduced as such to the nobility of the area.

The Marquise de Sade went to stay at the château owned by Sade's paternal uncle, the Abbé Jacques François de Sade, in Saumane, not far from the Fontaine de Vaucluse. Her sister, on leaving the convent, joined her there. The Marquis hurried to join them. He begged his wife's forgiveness for having offended her. But he had only gone there to see Anne-Prospère, to whom he was still very strongly attracted.

To his wife, he swore that he had never loved Anne-Prospère and then threatened to impale himself on his own sword, to drown himself in the Sorgue, or to throw himself from the top of the towers of the château de Saumane if she refused to forgive him & reciprocate with the love he thought he deserved having entered into their arranged marriage.

He told Anne-Prospère of his desire for her and claimed that his only faults were his behavior which was simply the result of his being driven to despair at being without her. He recognized, from the effect of his words, that the young woman still loved him, and he resolved to take her away.[59]

In June, the Marquis went to Marseilles with Latour, the servant who assisted him in his debauchery. Provided with chocolate pastilles into which he had injected a large dose of cantharides, which is an aphrodisiac, he went to a brothel where he lavished wines, liquors, & pastilles on the women there. The aphrodisiac was too concentrated a dose, rendering it toxic. Those women, at first excited and then becoming nauseous, became so frenzied and uttered such loud cries that a crowd gathered around the house. One unfortunate woman, driven completely mad, threw herself out of the window. Sade and his valet fled, but the court of Aix was notified of this scandalous affair. Two girls died from injuries they sustained during the bout caused by the cantharides.[60]

The Marquis, although he had gone into hiding, had a letter written by a counsellor announcing the inevitable outcome of the trial: the wheel. Armed with this letter, he made a secret journey to Saumane and threw himself at his sister-in-law's feet & kissed them, sobbing. He called himself a monster unworthy of pity; accused himself of the vilest crimes & declared that he intended to punish himself with suicide. Anne-Prospère trembled, she cried, and said she sympathized & felt pity for him.

He handed her the letter and then told her the cause of his despair. "I know you don't love me; I know you despise me! It was this thought that drove me to crime… I prepared the poisoned pastilles with my own hands… Several people died… pure luck saved me… I am going to do the right thing — justice. Farewell!"

The young woman understood little of what he said. But she cared for him and did not want him to die a horrible death on the wheel. So she held on to him and begged him not to leave.

"Very well!" he cried, "In that case, I choose to live, but I must leave here. But do not abandon me, not if you love me! Otherwise, farewell! let me die."[61]

An hour later, Mademoiselle de Montreuil got into the carriage that Sade had prepared and it carried them off together to Italy.

The Marquis de Sade was sentenced *(in absentia)* to death in effigy, by decree on 11 September 1772.

On that date, in a secluded palazzo, the Marquis enjoyed the incest he had carefully prepared by means more abominable than the goal itself. Mademoiselle de Montreuil died in his arms of a violent illness, at the age of twenty-one, and her lover, whose mind was becoming increasingly disturbed, returned to France, where he was arrested under the power of a *lettre de cachet*, taken to Vincennes, and from there transferred to the Bastille. His mental illness grew more bizarre, more warped under the prison regime, which was initially very harsh: no laundry permitted in the summer, nor wood for the stove in the winter. Always attentive to her spousal duties, the Marquise de Sade took him, as soon as she could, clothes, books, and paper.

It was then that he wrote those tales of the darkest eroticism, each book full of flagellation, orgies of blood

& wine, corpses, stabbings and rapes and mutilated children. They are abominable novels with their own particular moral code, their own philosophy and their own doctrine. They are complicated manuals of debauchery and cruelty, compared to which, all of the other books of the XVIIIth century are innocent. *Justine*, since it is necessary to name the monster's novel, does not resemble Diderot's *Bijoux Indiscrets* any more than Sophie Arnould[l] resembles the Marquise de Brinvilliers.[62]

While the Marquis de Sade was in the Bastille writing his mentally disturbed monstrous dreams, there was pre-revolutionary agitation in the Faubourg Saint-Antoine suburb that housed the prison. The governor, Louis de Launey, fearing that the sight of his prisoners would incite the mob gathered beneath the prison walls, curbed Sade's daily walk around the tower. The Marquis de Sade, angered by this measure, seized a long conical tin pipe which had been made for him to empty his waste-waters into the ditch outside, and used it as a megaphone to call to the people outside, begging them to storm the prison as prisoners were being murdered by the guards.

Monsieur de Launey wrote about the incident to his superiors in Versailles. He was told that he could dispose of his prisoner as he saw fit, so he contented himself with sending him to Charenton. On 17 March 1790, the decree of the Constituent Assembly, which granted freedom to all prisoners imprisoned by *lettres de cachet* freed the Marquis de Sade. His mother-in-law, on hearing that he was free, contented herself with saying: "I hope that he is happy!"

He had been treated too badly under the old regime not to be a supporter of the new one. Besides, the revolutionaries welcomed him with enthusiasm as a victim of tyranny. His long captivity earned him municipal honors. Secretary of the Société des Piques, he used his influence with a thoughtfulness one would not expect from someone whose mind was distorted by such furious eroticism. During the Terror, he showed himself to be humane & labored and petitioned to save his father-in-law and his mother-in-law from execution, knowing they hated and despised him, and aware that they would not have not spared him. His kindness & his name made him a suspect. Accused of "moderantism," he was imprisoned at Madelonnettes. When he was finally released by the Thermidorians, he was more mentally disturbed than ever, due to the combination of the guillotine being erected directly outside his rooms on the Place de la Révolution, & because of his constant view, from the same rooms, of the provocative nudes adorning the entrance to the Palais-Égalité.

Le Directoire, which is the name given to the final four years of the French Revolution, was remarkably favorable to Sade. During that time, he wrote several not very good plays in an attempt to earn a living. He found a publisher to print his books for him in fine print, on fine paper, with illustrations; he found booksellers to sell them. Five copies were printed on vellum paper for presentation to the Directorie, as a present from the author. No doubt the Marquis thought he was being courteous by presenting gilded copies of his work to General Bonaparte. Josephine's husband was not flattered by this present, seeing the cynical and self-serving motive behind the gift. Since he had become emperor, he had become more concerned than ever with the moral order, since it was *his* moral order. He had a clandestine edition of *Juliette*, illustrated with one hundred erotic drawings, seized from the Marquis' publisher and had the author locked up in Charenton. The Marquis de Sade spent the remaining fourteen years there.

He was a handsome old man, with white hair, whose manners were impeccable. He spoke softly, but his talk was mostly abominable nonsense. He traced obscene figures on the sand of the courtyard with the end of his cane, and wrote bloody infamies in his cell. He composed comedies which he had performed by madmen in a theater that had been built in the asylum. And beautiful ladies, it is said, attended these performances. Sade remained healthy and robust right to the very end of his life, and died quietly, peacefully, on 2 December 1814.

His skull was studied by Dr. Ramon, a disciple of Gall, who found there was a great resemblance to the skull of Héloïse.[63] This ridiculous conclusion has no importance, since the study of the bumps of the head teaches about the morale of the man exactly as much as it does about the flight of birds and the position of the stars. It is the brain that a modern physiologist should have examined, and it is in the central grey matter of the optic layer that he would have looked for the lesion, because it is there that the genital excitations of notorious perversions are disseminated from. But he probably would not have found anything. The brains of people with satyriasis have been studied without noticing anything abnormal. If it is certain that the Marquis de Sade was a patient with a severe mental illness, although the fundamental clinical feature of his illness is still today impossible to grasp, and the pathology ends, in this case, in the somewhat vague fields of psychological analysis.

First of all, let us note that the madness of the Marquis de Sade was rigorously localized. In matters not involving sex, he was harmless, and sometimes even, as we have seen, humane and generous. He has been compared to Gilles de Rais; this is very unfair. Rais actually committed lustful mutilations. Sade, who only told stories, admittedly stories which are extremely violent, never mutilated children or women. The flagellation of Rose Keller & the aphrodisiac-laced chocolate pastilles offered to the Marseille prostitutes were scandalous acts, but they do not amount to the atrocity of the mutilations of which Nero was suspected and for which Rais was convicted. I know very well that the facts regarding the Arcueil and Marseilles scandals only became public knowledge due to the exceptional nature of their perpetrator, and although it reasonably suggests that there are other incidents, just as detestable, what is certain is that Sade, in his madness, never went so far as murder. When this madness took hold of him, in the prison dungeon, the outcome was a theoretical one; he indulged in writing down his villainous ideas. Even someone with the most severe morality would not consider crimes of the imagination to be equal to crimes actually committed.

Our madman would have been far less dangerous if we had burned his books instead of printing them. He was intelligent; in his *Some Thoughts on the Novel (Idée sur les romans)* there are judicious observations & evidence of a fairly straightforward literary sensibility at work. His remark, "it is only as you work that ideas will come" will doubtless strike all those who have some experience of intellectual production as correct.

The way in which Sade writes of the *Princess of Clèves, Manon Lescaut,* and *Clarissa Harlowe,* suggests that these charming works were reflected in his soul without distortion or ugliness.[64] Sade's novella, *Dorci, or The Unpredictability of Fate,* which we are publishing for the first time, resembles those short Romanesque tales that Abbé Prévost included in *Le Pour et le Contre,* and it is not inferior to most of those dark tales.

Mental disorder, which is manifest in the Marquis de Sade's deeds & in his writings, results from the association, and consequently from the confusion, of two ideas which remain perfectly distinct & even opposed in all healthy minds: pleasure and suffering. Images of pleasure and torture were simultaneously forming in the mind of this unfortunate man. This combination was there in his first crime & it is the hallmark of his literature. On one of his last manuscripts, written in Charenton, Jules Janin read this sentence: "I forgot the two torture rooms. A few years ago, in an autograph room, I saw a plan of a brothel drawn by that incurable old man; the function of each room was marked; those at the back had these captions: 'Here we cripple.' 'Here we kill.'"

This madness is rare, but it is not unique; the Roman world felt its effects under some of their emperors. The era Sade was brought up was not infested with it. We printed a lot of nonsense in the XVIIIth century, and we will print more.

But they are all quite pleasant books, & that is what makes them forgivable. I will mention Doctor Tardieu's book in which he recounts the fairly recent history of the sergeant who unearthed & molested the dead, and whom the authorities decided to put in a madhouse; there is a certain moral kinship between this man & the Marquis de Sade. However, I do not wish to deviate from my literary teratology. A book, published about twenty years ago, in Belgium, and which I will be careful not to name, contains a large number of scenes in which debauchery & cruelty are closely united & confused in order to create scenes of disgusting obscenity.

The author, whoever he is, of this infamous work, produced it in a fit of villainous eroticism such as the Marquis de Sade never expressed in his violent works.

The author of *Justine* has had the lamentable glory of having a malady named after him: sadism, which is still not recognized as a mental illness. Sade is regarded favorably by several writers who do not want his name to die. It would be odious to compare a dishonored writer's name with the name of another writer who is, unlike Sade, worthy of honor. It is the name of a poet who has found a new and rare form of beauty. But how can we fail to note on these pages of literary nosology the irresistible penchant of the author of *Les fleurs du Mal* to associate crime and pleasure, so that we no longer know if he chants in his stanzas of dark brilliance, the crime of pleasure or the pleasure of crime?[65] The diseased influence of Sade did not kill this magnificent and singular poet, but it did affect him, just as it has affected several other writers of this era. They have not all succumbed, but have all been infected.

II

This novella, *Dorci, or The Unpredictability of Fate*, which we are publishing here for the first time, from the signed autograph manuscript, was to be included in the collection entitled *Crimes de l'Amour* (Paris, Massé, year VIII (1800), 4 vol. in-12), as indicated by a note written in pencil by the author in the margin of the first sheet:

The crime of love, in this tale, is the only episode, because the main subject is really the action of the virtuous being who wants to save a victim from the law.

The Marquis de Sade is right, and his story falls into this virtuous genre, a genre much appreciated at the approach of the Revolution. *Dorci, or The Unpredictability of Fate* was certainly written under the old regime, during the Marquis' incarceration. The author refused to include it in *the Crimes of Love*, where it did not fit, as he prudently recognized. Instead, he considered including it in another collection. This is from the note that we read in the margin of the last page:

> To the editor.
> This tale is a moral one. It is effective. It must be put in a collection of other good stories.

But we were then in the midst of a revolution, and the original draft, which dated from the old regime, was subjected to a curious system of corrections: *"Dorci, or The Unpredictability of Fate"* became *"Les Dangers de la bienfaisance."* "The Comte *&* the Marquis de Dorci" became "Paul and François Dorci." These alterations were necessary. Paul Dorci had "sensitivity *&* virtue" instead of being "gentle, sensitive, honest." Obviously, he cannot be an aristocrat, so the "château," which would have awakened anger in the souls of patriots, became the "house"; the "land" became the "garden." A free man cannot plough the land of an aristocrat, but any citizen can work in a "garden," which is quite different, isn't it? In the original draft, the young peasant girl named Annette was about to take "her first communion." This was removed from the story. An innocent child can no longer be left the victim of fanaticism & deception.

These corrections were made because of the spirit of the time. Censorship demanded them from the authors whose comedies and melodramas were examined. I find, in a very interesting book by M. Henri Welschinger on the theater of the Revolution, reports from censors who conclude that all noble titles & all feudal terms had to be deleted from the documents submitted to them.[66] In 1794, an author had given his protagonist the name of Louis. The administration crossed out this name for one very simple reason: one cannot give the name of Louis to a man, especially to a virtuous man. Also, all men of letters did as Citizen Sade did: they erased from their writings even the smallest vestiges of the old regime. The more zealous did not stick to their own works. There was one patriot who put civility in Corneille's *El Cid*.

This war on words was pitiful; but, in reality, it was more odious than inept. In matters of government, the word matters more than the thing. The politicians know that we are often killed for a word. In Sophocles' *Philoc-tetes*, Ulysses quite rightly says: "But now I've entered adult life and faced some of its trials, I see with mortal men it is words & not actions that rule over everything." Ulysses was wise.

We reproduce here the Marquis de Sade's manuscript exactly as he wrote it, complete with its incorrect but generally regular spelling. We have punctuated the text to make it readable. We could have re-instated all of the crossed-out passages; they are numerous, and although the original word or phrase is visible beneath the word or phrase which effaces it, we have only altered the more curious changes. It is not necessary to treat a text by the Marquis de Sade like a text by Pascal.

AF

Notes

Foreword — D.A.F. DE SADE

1. This foreword is essentially a shorter first draft of Sade's essay, *Some Thoughts on the Novel*.

Foreword — MAURICE HEINE

This is Maurice Heine's foreword from *Stories, Tales, and Fables* (*Historiettes, contes et fabliaux*) published by the Société du roman philosophique in 1927. The details of this book, a copy of which is in the Bibliothèque nationale de France, are as follows:

Title: *Historiettes, contes et fabliaux* / Marquis de Sade; publiés sur le texte authentique de la Société du roman philosophique avec un avant-propos par Maurice Heine

Author: Sade, Donatien Alphonse François de (1740–1814). Auteur du texte

Publisher: S. Kra (Paris)

Publication date: 1927

Contributor Heine, Maurice (1884–1940). Préfacier

Language: French

2. Apart from the changes of name, the two stories, *Done As You Require* and *The Obliging Husband*, are almost the same story, or extended joke. It is Maurice Heine's contention that *Done As You Require* is simply the short story, *The Obliging Husband*, rewritten as a fable.

Stories

The Effective Subterfuge

1. This story in this translation first appeared in May 2021 as an audio recording, read by Gerald Cox for `listentopoetry.com`

The Murdered Brothel-Keeper

2. The *Régence* (*Regency*) was the period in French history between 1715 and 1723, when King Louis XV was a minor and the country was governed by Philippe d'Orléans, a nephew of Louis XIV of France, as prince regent.

3. [*we will now present the various*] is a conjectural phrase to fill a gap in the original text where Sade's intended phrase is missing.

4. "He was a legless cripple." (Sade's original footnote to this story.)

5. There is no rue des Déjeuneurs in Paris, but there is a rue des Jeûneurs, which is in the 2nd arrondissement of Paris, in the area of Mail.

The Obliging Husband

6. This story in this translation first appeared as *The Compliant Husband*, published in July 2021 by Spontaneous Poetics.

The Horse-Chestnut Flower

7. This story in this translation first appeared in May 2021 as an audio recording, read by Gerald Cox for listentopoetry.com

Tales & Fables

Augustine de Villeblanche, or A Strategy for Love

1. Augustine de Villeblanche, or A Strategy for Love is an Eighteenth Century short story with a lesbian theme. There are very few stories from the eighteenth century that tackle that specific theme or subject. The opening monologue is notable for its defense of lesbianism, combined with its request for tolerance, acceptance, & understanding.

2. Jacques Cujas (1522–4 October 1590) was a French legal expert.

3. The temple of Aphrodite (Venus) in Old Paphos was the center of Aphrodite worship for the whole Aegean world.

— There were several temples devoted to Venus (Aphrodite) through-out the world, but the temple of Venus in Old Paphos on the island of Cyprus was considered to be the most significant as devotees believed that Aphrodite had risen from the sea and made her first home on the island in Paphos.

Done As You Require

4. Apart from the changes of name, this is almost the same story, or extended joke, as *The Obliging Husband*. It is Maurice Heine's contention that *Done As You Require* is simply the short story, *The Obliging Husband* rewritten as a fable.

The Duped Judge

5. This story in this translation under the title *A Judge Deceived* first appeared as a stand-alone chapbook in November 2022 as number 24 in the Pocket Erotica Series, published by New Urge Editions/Black Scat Books.

6. Flora is a Roman Goddess of flowers and of the season of spring. She is a fertility Goddess and the Goddess of youth

— In Greek mythology, the Graces are three or more goddesses of charm, beauty, nature, human creativity, goodwill, and fertility. In art, the Graces are usually depicted as three naked women.

7. Themis is an ancient Greek Goddess of justice, described as "the lady of good counsel." She is the personification of divine order, fairness, law, natural law, and custom. Her symbol is the Scales of Justice, which show that justice is balanced and pragmatic.

8. "The reader is reminded that he must try to imagine the judge's distinctive Provençal accent as the written word cannot convey it." (Sade's original footnote to the story.)

9. Prospero Farinacci (30 October 1554–30 October 1618) was an Italian lawyer and judge, known for his particularly harsh sentencing.

— Jacques Cujas (1522–4 October 1590) was a French legal expert. He was prominent among the legal humanists who sought to ascertain the correct text and social context of the original works of Roman law.

10. The Ostrogoths were a Roman-era Germanic people. In the 5th century, they followed the Visigoths in creating one of the two great Gothic kingdoms within the Roman Empire, based upon the large Gothic populations that had settled in the Balkans in the 4th century, having crossed the Lower Danube. Sade is using the term Ostrogothic as shorthand.

    — Flavius Petrus Sabbatius Iustinianus (482–14 November 565), also known as Justinian I and Justinian the Great, was the Byzantine emperor from 527 to 565. His reign is marked by the ambitious but only partly realized "restoration of the Empire." His general, Belisarius, along with some of his other generals conquered the Ostrogothic kingdom, restoring Dalmatia, Rome (still under Papal dominion), Italy, and Sicily to the empire after more than half a century of rule by the Ostrogoths.

11. Sade noted that he finished writing *The Duped Judge* on 16 July 1787. The Saint-Germain Fair (Foire Saint-Germain) was an annual event and it generally ran for three to five weeks around Easter. During the 18th century, the Foire Saint-Germain consistently opened on 3 February & ended on Palm Sunday which, in 1787, fell on Monday, 11 April. Sade began writing *The Duped Judge* shortly after the fair had ended, and obviously decided to include a reference to it in his story.

12. Jean-Baptiste Nicolet (16 April 1728–27 December 1796) was an 18th century French actor & manager. He was the eldest son of puppeteer, dance master, and violinist Guillaume Nicolet. He set up the Grands-Danseurs du Roi, the predecessor of the Théâtre de la Gaîté.

13. Nicolas-Médard Audinot (also *Odinot, Oudinot*) (7 June 1732–21 May 1801) was a French actor, singer, impresario, and puppeteer. He first played at the Comédie Italienne. In 1762, he set up a puppet theater at Foire Saint-Germain where each character was an imitation of an actor of the Comédie-Italienne. His wooden comedians attracted the crowd, and soon Audinot founded the Théâtre de l'Ambigu-Comique where he substituted children for puppets.

14. Quintus Horatius Flaccus (8 December 65–27 November 8 BC), known in the English-speaking world as Horace, was the leading Roman lyric poet

during the time of Augustus. Most famous for his *Odes*, he also crafted elegant hexameter verses (*Satires* and *Epistles*) & caustic iambic poetry (*Epodes*).

15. "A Provençal swearword." (Sade's original footnote to this story.)

16. Clovis (c. 466–27 November 511) was the first king of the Franks to unite all of the Frankish tribes under one ruler, changing the form of leadership from a group of royal chieftains to rule by a single king and ensuring that the kingship was passed down to his heirs. He is considered to have been the founder of the Merovingian dynasty, which ruled the Frankish kingdom for the next two centuries. Clovis is important in the historiography of France as the first king of what would become France.

17. The fleur-de-lis (plural fleurs-de-lis or fleurs-de-lys) is a lily (in French, fleur and lis mean "flower" and "lily" respectively) that is used as a decorative design or symbol. The fleur-de-lis is particularly associated with France, notably during its monarchical period. The fleur-de-lis became a much-recognized religious, political, judicial, dynastic, monarchic, artistic and emblematic symbol, especially in French heraldry.

18. Asclepius is a hero and god of medicine in ancient Greek religion and mythology. He is the son of Apollo & Coronis or Arsinoe, or of Apollo alone. Asclepius represents the healing aspect of the medical arts; his daughters are Hygieia (Hygiene, the goddess of cleanliness), Iaso (the goddess of recuperation), Aceso (the goddess of the healing process), Ægle (the goddess of good health) & Panacea (the goddess of universal remedy).

19. Hippocrates of Kos (c. 460–c. 370 BC) was a Greek physician during the Age of Pericles, and he is considered one of the most outstanding figures in the history of medicine. He is traditionally referred to as the Father of Medicine in recognition of his lasting contributions to the field, such as the use of prognosis and clinical observation, the systematic categorization of diseases, or the formulation of humoral theory.

— Ælius Galenus or Claudius Galenus (September 129–216 CE), often Anglicized as Galen or Galen of Pergamon was a Greek physician, surgeon, and philosopher in the Roman Empire. Considered to be one of the most accomplished of all medical researchers of antiquity, Galen influenced the development of various scientific disciplines, including anatomy, physiology, pathology, pharmacology, and neurology, as well as contributing to philosophy and logic.

20. A temple sacred to Asclepius (see note 16) in Epidaurus, a small city in ancient Greece, on the Argolid Peninsula at the Saronic Gulf. The Temple was the main holy site of Asclepius and was built in the early 4th century BC. The temple would have been closed during the persecution of pagans in the late Roman Empire, when the Christian Emperors issued edicts prohibiting non-Christian worship.

21. This is Sade's reference to himself, specifically to what is now known as the Marseilles Affair, an incident involving Sade & a group of prostitutes.

22. Lycurgus was the son of Pronax, son of King Talaus of Argos, and therefore, the brother to Amphithea, wife of Adrastus. He was one of those raised from the dead by Asclepius.

23. In Greek mythology, Comus is the god of festivity, revels, & nocturnal dalliances. He is a son and a cupbearer of the god Dionysus. He was represented as a winged youth or a child-like satyr and represents anarchy and chaos. His mythology occurs in the later times of antiquity. During his festivals in Ancient Greece, men and women exchanged clothes. He was depicted as a young man on the point of unconsciousness from drink. He had a wreath of flowers on his head and carried a torch that was in the process of being dropped. Comus was a god of excess.

24. Hymen, Hymenaios, or Hymenaeus, in Hellenistic religion, is a god of marriage ceremonies, inspiring feasts, and songs. Related to the god's name, a *hymenaios* is a genre of Greek lyric poetry sung during the procession of the bride to the groom's house in which the god is addressed. He is one of the winged love gods, the Erotes. Hymen is the son of Apollo and one of the Muses, either Clio, Calliope, Urania, or Terpsichore.

25. Tenares is a town in the Hermanas Mirabal Province of the Dominican Republic.

26. This is yet another reference by Sade to himself and his constant clashes with the judiciary because of his indiscrete libertine lifestyle.

27. The Province of Salerno (*Provincia di Salerno*) is a province in the Campania region of Italy. The Port of Salerno *(Porti di Salerno)* is a port serving Salerno, southwestern Italy. The port of Salerno is located in the gulf of the Tyrrhenian Sea.

— Mérindol is a commune in the Vaucluse department in the Provence-Alpes-Côte d'Azur region in southeastern France. The village is located south of the Luberon massif, *&* has some prominence in the plain of the Durance River which demarcates the Vaucluse and Bouches-du-Rhône departments. Its history, like that of several other villages in the Luberon, was marked by the French Wars of Religion.

— Cabrières-d'Avignon is a commune in the Vaucluse department in the Provence-Alpes-Côte d'Azur region in southeastern France. The Château and the village were the scene of the massacre in 1545 of about 700 Vaudois, or Waldensians — a reformist group declared heretical by the Catholic Church. Men, women, and children were tortured and killed. The events are known as the Massacre of Mérindol, after the campaign that began in nearby Mérindol and resulted in the destruction of between 28 villages.

28. Ibn Rushd (14 April 1126–11 December 1198), often Latinized as Averroës or Averroes, was a Muslim Andalusian polymath and jurist who wrote on many subjects, including philosophy, theology, medicine, astronomy, physics, psychology, mathematics, linguistics, Islamic law, and Islamic jurisprudence. He was the author of more than one hundred books and treatises. His philosophical works include numerous commentaries on Aristotle, for which he became known in the west. Ibn Rushd also served as a chief judge and a court physician for the Almohad Caliphate.

29. A *toise* is a unit of measure equal to six feet or 72 inches. Fifteen *toises* would have been the equivalent of 90 feet, or just over 27 meters.

30. *lex talionis* (Latin for "law of retaliation") is a principle developed in early Babylonian law and early Roman law that criminals should receive as punishment precisely those injuries and damages they had inflicted upon their victims. Lex Talionis is also the principle of retributive justice expressed in the phrase "an eye for an eye," from Exodus 21:23–27. The basis of this form of law is the principle of proportionate punishment, often expressed under the motto "Let the punishment fit the crime," which particularly applies to mirror punishments (which may or may not be proportional). At the root of the non-biblical form of this principle is the belief that one of the purposes of the law is to provide equitable retaliation for an offended party.

31. Themis' halter is a reference to the parameters that apply to a person who is a servant of Themis, in other words, the law. See note 7, p. 560.

32. "Another Provençal swearword." (Sade's original footnote to this story.) *Pechaire*: An obsolete, regional interjection used in the South of France to express pain, pity, or astonishment. From Occitan *pecaire*, from Latin *peccator* ("sinner"), corresponding to Old French *pechiere*, subject case of *pecheor* ("sinner"), also used as an interjection in the past.

33. Bluebeard (*Barbe-bleue*) is a fairy tale by Charles Perrault. It first appeared in *Contes de ma mère l'oye* (English: *Tales of Mother Goose*), published in 1695. It included four other tales by Perrault. Bluebeard is the story of a cruel man who murders his wives so that he will inherit their wealth. He puts their corpses in a secret room that can only be opened with a magic key.

34. Jean Calas (1698–10 March 1762) was a merchant living in Toulouse, France, who was tried, tortured, & executed for the murder of his son, despite his protestations of innocence. Calas was a Protestant in an officially Catholic society. Opponents of the Catholic Church raised doubts about his guilt and he was exonerated in 1764. In France, he became a symbolic victim of religious intolerance. Despite Calas claiming that the death was a suicide, the court in Toulouse held that he had murdered his son. Calas was also sentenced to be tortured after being judged & found guilty. His arms and legs were stretched until they were pulled out of their sockets. Thirty pints (more than 17 liters) of water were poured

down his throat. He was tied to a cross in the cathedral square where he had each of his limbs broken twice by an iron bar. On 9 March 1762 the regional court of Toulouse sentenced Calas to death on the wheel. On 10 March, at the age of 64, he died while being tortured on the wheel, still firmly claiming his innocence.

35. This is another reference by Sade to himself, this time regarding the trial at which he was sentenced to death in absentia and at which an effigy of him was burned.

36. Areopagus referred, in classical times, to the Athenian governing council, later restricted to the Athenian judicial council or court that tried cases of deliberate homicide, wounding, and religious matters, as well as cases involving arson of olive trees.

37. Demosthenes (384 BCE–Oct 12, 322 BCE) was an Athenian statesman, recognized as the greatest of ancient Greek orators, who roused Athens to oppose Philip of Macedon and, later, his son Alexander the Great. His speeches provide valuable information on the political, social, and economic life of 4th-century Athens.

38. Yet another self-referential passage. This concerns the Rose Keller incident, when Sade whipped a prostitute and she ran into a nearby town & reported that he had committed all sorts of atrocities, after which his lifelong clashes with the authorities began.

39. Pégu or Pegoo is one of the islands of Sumatra, northern Borneo, on the Malay Peninsula.

40. An *aune* is an old French unit of measurement for fabrics, equivalent to about 47 inches or 119 centimeters. Twenty *aunes* of gauze would therefore have been a piece of material about 80 feet (24.38 meters) long.

41. Paphos is a coastal city in southwest Cyprus, the site of the temple of Aphrodite at modern day Kouklia, erected in 1200 BC, once the most important shrine to the Goddess of Love in the Mediterranean. In classical antiquity, men who worshipped Aphrodite showed their devotion to her by having sex with her temple maids.

— The *ferme générale* was, in *ancien régime* France, essentially an out-sourced customs, excise, & indirect tax operation. It collected duties on behalf of the King (plus hefty bonus fees for themselves), under renewable six-year contracts. The major tax collectors in that highly unpopular tax farming system were known as the *fermiers généraux* (singular: *fermier général*).

42. René Descartes (31 March 1596–11 February 1650) was a French philosopher, mathematician, and scientist who invented analytic geometry, linking the previously separate fields of geometry and algebra. One of the most notable intellectual figures of the Dutch Golden Age, Descartes is also widely regarded as one of the founders of modern philosophy and algebraic geometry. His best-known philosophical statement is "cogito, ergo sum" *(I think, therefore I am).*

— Nicolaus Copernicus (19 February 1473–24 May 1543) was a Renaissance polymath, active as a mathematician, astronomer, and Catholic canon, who formulated a model of the universe that placed the Sun rather than Earth at its center. In all likelihood, Copernicus developed his model independently of Aristarchus of Samos, an ancient Greek astronomer who had formulated such a model some eighteen centuries earlier. The publication of Copernicus' model in his book *De revolutionibus orbium coelestium* (*On the Revolutions of the Celestial Spheres*), just before his death in 1543, was a major event in the history of science, triggering the Copernican Revolution and making a pioneering contribution to the Scientific Revolution.

43. "Although gas-filled balloons had not at that time become a matter of public knowledge, one had been constructed in 1779." The French brothers Joseph-Michel and Jacques-Étienne Montgolfier developed a hot-air balloon in Annonay, Ardeche, France, and demonstrated it publicly on 19 September 1783, making an unmanned flight that lasted for ten minutes. After experimenting with unmanned balloons and flights with animals, the first balloon flight with humans aboard, a tethered flight, was launched on or around 15 October 1783, by Jean-Francois Pilâtre de Rozier, who made at least one tethered flight from the yard of the Réveillon workshop in the Faubourg Saint-Antoine. Later that same

day, Pilâtre de Rozier became the second human to ascend into the air, reaching an altitude of 26 meters (85 feet), the length of the tether. The first free flight with human passengers was made a few weeks later, on 21 November 1783. King Louis XVI had originally decreed that condemned criminals would be the first pilots, but de Rozier, along with Marquis François d'Arlandes, petitioned successfully for the honor. Sade is therefore manipulating dates and events to suit his story. His claim is both fictional and written nearly four years after the fact, as *The Duped Judge* was completed in July 1787.

44. "It's surprising that the people haven't risen up and done exactly that, although it seems that the day is not that far off and it won't be much longer before they do..." Sade shows his prescience and his awareness of the general mood of the French people by predicting the French Revolution two years before it began. This is not the only story in this collection in which he does this. *The Marquise de Télême* also contains a paragraph on the imminent revolution. In that story, it is suggested that Fondor changes his mind about helping the Marquise because he realizes that the aristocracy is going to lose everything and it would therefore be foolish of him to provide the Marquise with funds for her legal battle.

45. See the passage on Mérindol in note 27 of this section, p. 564.

46. Charles III (17 February 1490–6 May 1527) was a French military leader, the Comte de Montpensier, Clermont, and Auvergne, and dauphin of Auvergne from 1501 to 1523, then duke of Bourbon and Auvergne, count of Clermont-en-Beauvaisis, Forez, and La Marche, and lord of Beaujeu from 1505 to 1521. He was also the constable of France from 1515 to 1521. Also known as the constable of Bourbon, he was the last of the great feudal lords to oppose the king of France.

47. Charles III made a secret agreement to betray his king and offer his services to Emperor Charles V. The emperor, the constable, and King Henry VIII of England devised a grand plan to partition France. This however came to nothing because the plot was discovered; Charles was stripped of his offices and proclaimed a traitor. He fled into Italy in 1523 and entered the imperial service.

48. The Catholic League of France (*Ligue catholique*), sometimes referred to by Catholics as the Holy League (*La Sainte Ligue*), was a major participant in the French Wars of Religion. The League, founded and led by Henry I, Duke of Guise, intended the eradication of Protestantism from Catholic France, as well as the replacement of King Henry III.

49. *Lettres de cachet* (Letters of the signature or Letters of the signet) were letters signed by the king of France, countersigned by one of his ministers, and closed with the royal seal. They contained orders directly from the king, often to enforce arbitrary actions and judgments that could not be appealed. The best-known *lettres de cachet*, however, were penal, by which a subject was imprisoned without trial and without an opportunity of defense (after inquiry and due diligence by the *lieutenant de police*) in a state prison or an ordinary jail, confinement in a convent or the General Hospital of Paris, transportation to the colonies, or expulsion to another part of the realm, or from the realm altogether. The *lettres* were mainly used against drunkards, troublemakers, squanderers of family fortune, prostitutes, or insane persons. The wealthy sometimes petitioned such *lettres* to dispose of inconvenient individuals, especially to prevent a scandal (the *lettre* could prevent court cases that might otherwise dishonor a family) or to prevent unequal marriages (nobles with commoners).

50. "This tale was finished on 16 July 1787, at 10 o'clock in the evening." (Sade's original footnote to this story.)

The Marquise de Télème, or The Effects of Libertinism

51. *The Marquise de Télème, or The Effects of Libertinism* has two incomplete final pages in manuscript. Sade took the initial idea for the story from an anecdote he read in a letter, as he mentions in his preface to this collection. Sade states:

With regards to the genesis of "The Marquise de Télème," if the reader turns to volume 2, page 202, of the Letters of Madame du Noyer, then they will find an anecdote about a woman from Champagne who travelled to Paris to take part in a court case. It was not long before it became obvious she would lose her case. A rich moneylender who was infatuated with her offered to pay for the best lawyer and to cover all of her legal fees, in order to ensure that she won her case. In return, she had to make herself sexually available to him. She agreed to his terms and went on to win her case. She returned home to her husband, but soon guilt began to make her very ill.

Her husband questioned her, insisting on knowing the cause of her unhappiness. Finally, she confessed everything. She was forgiven by her husband, who informed her that what happened was not her fault and that she did what she had to do to win her case. The woman recovered and subsequently lived with her forgiving husband as happily as could be expected.

That was the basic situation, the crude, slightly ludicrous outline that we used to create one of our most tragic and hopefully absorbing tales. If anyone takes the time to compare that rather vague outline with our finished tale of virtue and nobility under duress, then we are certain it will be seen that we can quite rightly claim the honor of being the actual and the original author of "The Marquise de Télème."

Sade intended to rewrite the story so that it took place during the Terror, but the story remained in its incomplete form. The last few paragraphs of the story appear in note form, with several narrative lacunae. The translating process has thereby necessitated a small amount of reconstruction of the missing parts, simply for narrative cohesion.

Retaliation

52. This story in this translation first appeared in August 2021 as an audio recording read by Gerald Cox for listentopoetry.com

This story in this translation first appeared as a stand-alone chapbook in November 2021 as number 17 in the Pocket Erotica Series, published by New Urge Editions/Black Scat Books.

Room for Two

53. This story in this translation first appeared in May 2021 as an audio recording, read by Gerald Cox for listentopoetry.com

The Husband Who Said Mass

54. A viguier is a magistrate.

Dialogue Between a Priest & a Dying Man

55. "Socinian, so I had a range of points ready to refute you, ..." A Socinian rejects the views of orthodox Christian theology regarding the doctrine of the Trinity and the divinity of Christ.

Non-Fiction

Some Thoughts on the Novel

1. This essay in this translation first appeared as a stand-alone bilingual edition paperback book in November 2021, published by Oneiros Books.

2. Hercules is a generic name, composed of two Celtic words, Her-Coule, which means, Sir Captain. *Hercoule* was the term used to designate an army captain, which resulted in there being many Hercoules. Fables that describe the wonderful adventures *&* daring actions of *Hercules* are referring to many men, not just one particular *Hercules.* — See *History of the Celts*, by Pelloutier. (Sade's original footnote to this essay.)

3. Pierre Daniel Huet (8 February 1630–26 January 1721) was a French churchman and scholar, editor of the Delphin Classics, founder of the Académie de Physique in Caen (1662–1672) and author of *Traité de l'origine des romans* (1670).

4. *The Æthiopica (Ethiopian Stories)* or *Theagenes and Chariclea* is an ancient Greek novel that has been dated to about 350 AD. It was written by Heliodorus of Emesa (also Heliodorus Emesenus or Heliodorus of Emesa) and is his only known work. He identifies himself at the end of this work as: "a Phoenician from Emesa of the line of Helios, Theodosius' son Heliodorus."

5. Milesian Tales are a genre of fictional story prominent in ancient Greek and Roman literature. A Milesian tale is a short story, fable, or folktale that features love and adventure, usually of an erotic or titillating nature. *The Oxford Companion to Classical Literature* suggests that the Milesian tale is the literary model for Giovanni Boccaccio's *The Decameron* and Marguerite de Navarre's *The Heptameron.*

— *Metamorphoses* by Apuleius, commonly referred to as *The Golden Ass,* is the only ancient Roman novel in Latin to survive in its entirety.

— Aristides of Miletus was a 2nd century BCE writer of shameless and amusing tales that were notable for their salacious content & unexpected plot twists. He is the author of the *Milesiaka.*

6. Antonius Diogenes was the author of an ancient Greek romance entitled *The Incredible Wonders Beyond Thule.*

— "The Loves of Dinias and Dercyllis" is Sade's reference to the subtitle of *The Incredible Wonders Beyond Thule.*

— J.L. Le Sueur is the writer of *Dinias et Dercillide Fragment traduit du grec d'Antonius Diogenes, par, suivi de Poésies diverses (Diana and Dercillade, A Fragment Translated from the Greek by Antonius Diogenes, followed by Various Poems),* published in 1745.

7. *The Adventures of Sinonis* refers to Iamblichus's novel, which was about two lovers, Rhodanes and Sinonis. Garmus, a legendary king of Babylon, forces Sinonis to marry him and throws Rhodanes into prison. The lovers manage to escape, and after many singular adventures, in which magic plays a considerable part, Garmus is overthrown by Rhodanes, who becomes King of Babylon.

— Rhodanes is a central character from Iamblichus's *Babylonian Stories.*

— Iamblichus (c. 165–180 AD) was an ancient Syrian Greek novelist. He was the author of the *Babyloniaca (Babylonian Stories),* which has the distinction of being, if not the earliest romance novel in Greek, it is at least one of the first of its kind in Greek literature.

— The Loves of *Theagenes and Chariclea* is Sade's reference to Heliodorus's *The Æthiopica.*

8. Gaius Petronius Arbiter (c. 27–66 AD) was a Roman courtier during the reign of Nero. He is generally believed to be the author of the *Satyricon,* a picaresque satirical novel believed to have been written during the Neronian era (54–68 AD).

— Marcus Terentius Varro (116–27 BC) was one of ancient Rome's greatest scholars and a prolific author. He is best known for his *Saturarum Menippearum libri CL (Menippean Satires in 150 books).*

— Xenophon of Athens (c. 430–354 BC) was an Athenian-born military leader, philosopher, and historian. He was the author of *Cyropedia*.

— *Cyropedia*, sometimes spelled *Cyropaedia*, is a partly fictional biography of Cyrus the Great, the founder of the Achaemenid Empire, the first Persian Empire. It was written around 370 BC by Xenophon.

— Longus, sometimes Longos, was the author of the ancient Greek pastoral romance novel, *Daphnis and Chloe*. Nothing is known of his life; it is assumed that he lived on Lesbos (the setting for *Daphnis and Chloe*) during the 2nd century AD.

— *Daphnis and Chloe* is an ancient Greek pastoral romance novel written in the Roman Empire, the only known work of the second-century AD Greek novelist & romance writer Longus.

— *Ismene and Theoclymenus*. The 7th-century BC poet Mimnermus tells the story of Ismene being murdered by Tydeus, one of the *Seven Against Thebes*. In Mimnermus's account, Ismene and her lover Theoclymenus meet outside of the city during the siege.

9. Marcus Annaeus Lucanus (3 November 39 AD–30 April 65 AD), better known as Lucan, was a Roman poet. He is known for his epic *Pharsalia*.

10. Charlemagne, or Charles the Great (2 April 748–28 January 814), also Charles I, was King of the Franks from 768, King of the Lombards from 774, and Emperor of the Romans from 800.

— Archbishop Tilpin (died 794 or 800), also called Tulpin, a name later corrupted to Turpin, was the Bishop of Rheims from about 748 until his death. He was for many years regarded as the author of the *Historia Caroli Magni*, which is also known as the *Pseudo-Turpin Chronicle*.

— The Round Table is the legendary gathering place of King Arthur's knights in the Arthurian legend.

— Tristan (also known as Tristram or Tristain) is the hero of the legend of Tristan and Iseult, a story of misdirected love.

— Lancelot du Lac, or Lancelot of the Lake (also written as Launcelot), is a character in some versions of Arthurian legend, where he is typically depicted as King Arthur's close companion and one of the greatest Knights of the Round Table.

— The Lady of the Lake is the name or title used by several enchantresses in the medieval literature and mythology associated with the legend of King Arthur.

— *Perceforest* or *Le Roman de Perceforest* is an anonymous prose chivalric romance, with lyrical interludes of poetry that describes a fictional origin of Great Britain and provides an original genesis of the Arthurian world.

11. A *fabliau* (plural *fabliaux*) is a comic, often anonymous tale written by jongleurs in northeast France between c. 1150 and 1400. They generally have a sexual or scatologically obscene subject or theme. Several of them were reworked by Giovanni Boccaccio for *The Decameron* and by Geoffrey Chaucer for *The Canterbury Tales*. About one hundred and fifty French *fabliaux* are extant and are considered to be the first expression of literary realism in Europe.

— Hugh Capet (c. 939–14 October 996) was the King of the Franks from 987 to 996. He is the founder and first king from the House of Capet. Hugh was descended from Charlemagne's sons Louis the Pious and Pepin of Italy through his mother and paternal grandmother, respectively, and was also a nephew of Otto the Great.

12. Jean-François de La Harpe (20 November 1739–11 February 1803) was a French playwright, writer, and literary critic. La Harpe's main work is his *Lycée ou Cours de littérature* (1799).

— Dante Alighieri, often referred to simply as Dante (c. 1265–14 September 1321), was an Italian poet, writer, and philosopher. His *Divine Comedy* is widely considered to be one of the most important poems of the Middle Ages and the greatest literary work in the Italian language.

— Giovanni Boccaccio (16 June 1313–21 December 1375) was an Italian writer, poet, correspondent of Petrarch, and an important Renaissance humanist. His most notable work is *The Decameron*, a collection of one hundred short stories.

— Alessandro Tassoni (28 September 1565–25 April 1635) was an Italian poet and writer. Tassoni is best known as the author of the mock-heroic poem *La secchia rapita (The Rape of the Pail)*; it is by virtue of this work that he is remembered as Modena's poet laureate.

— Francesco Petrarca (20 July 1304 – 18/19 July 1374), commonly Anglicized as Petrarch, was a scholar and poet of early Renaissance Italy, and one of the early humanists. His most famous work is *Il Canzoniere*, also known as *Rime Sparse*, but originally titled *Rerum vulgarium fragmenta*, a collection of poems in praise of Laura Du Noves, wife of Comte Hugues de Sade (an ancestor of the Marquis de Sade).

13. Honoré d'Urfé, Marquis de Valromey, Comte de Châteauneuf (11 February 1568–1 June 1625) was a French novelist and miscellaneous writer. His most renowned work was *L'Astrée*, a pastoral novel published between 1607 and 1627. It has been described as the single most influential work of 17th century French literature.

14. Gomberville Marin le Roy, sieur du Parc et de Gomberville (1600–14 June 1674), was a French poet and novelist. He wrote a *Discours sur l'histoire* and a pastoral, *La Charité*. His most ambitious work is *Polexandre* (5 vols 1632–1637).

— Gauthier de Costes, seigneur de la Calprenède (1609/1610–1663), was a French novelist and dramatist. La Calprenède wrote several long heroic romances, most of which are mentioned in Charlotte Lennox's *The Female Quixote* (1752). They are: *Cassandre* (1642–1650); *Cléopâtre* (1648); *Faramond* (1661); and *Les Nouvelles ou les Divertissements de la princesse Alcidiane* (1661).

— Jean Desmarets, Sieur de Saint-Sorlin (1595–28 October 1676), was a French writer and dramatist. He is known for his romance, *L'Ariane* (1632), a comedy, *Les Visionnaires* (1637), a prose-tragedy, *Erigone* (1638), a tragedy in verse, *Scipion* (1639), and a long epic, *Clovis* (1657).

— Georges de Scudéry (22 August 1601–14 May 1667), the elder brother of Madeleine de Scudéry, was a French novelist, dramatist, & poet. He is known for his *CURIA POLITIÆ, OR, THE APOLOGIES OF SEVERALL PRINCES: Justifying to the WORLD Their Most Eminent Actions.*

15. Madeleine de Scudéry (15 November 1607–2 June 1701), often known simply as Mademoiselle de Scudéry, was a French writer. She is best known for her lengthy novels, *Artamène, ou le Grand Cyrus* (1648–53), *Clélie* (1654–61), *Ibrahim, ou l'illustre Bassa* (1641), and *Almahide, ou l'esclave reine* (1661–63).

— *Artamène ou le Grand Cyrus (Artamène, or Cyrus the Great)* is a novel sequence, originally published in ten volumes in the 17th century. The title pages credit the work to French writer Georges de Scudéry but it is usually attributed to his sister & fellow writer Madeleine. At 1,954,300 words, it is considered one of the longest novels ever published.

— *Clélie* (1654–61) is a ten-volume novel by Madeleine de Scudéry. It is a *Roman History* that contains Scudéry's most celebrated passage, the *Carte de Tendre*, a map of love, which describes the various obstacles (depicted as rivers, deserts, & mountains) that affection must overcome as it attempts to reach the summit of spiritual love.

Cyrus — The central character of Madeleine de Scudéry's ten-volume novel, *Artamène, ou le Grand Cyrus* (1648–53).

16. *El ingenioso hidalgo don Quijote de la Mancha (The Ingenious Gentleman Don Quixote of La Mancha)*, or simply *Don Quixote*, is a Spanish novel by Miguel de Cervantes. Originally published in two parts, in 1605 and 1615, it is founding work of Western literature, considered to be the first modern novel and one of the greatest works ever written. It also holds the distinction of being one of the most-translated books in the world.

— Miguel de Cervantes Saavedra (29 September 1547–22 April 1616) was a Spanish writer widely regarded as the greatest writer in the Spanish language & one of the world's pre-eminent novelists. He is best known for his novel *Don Quixote*

17. Charles de Marguetel de Saint-Denis, seigneur de Saint-Évremond (1 April 1613–29 September 1703), was a French soldier, hedonist, essayist, and literary critic. After 1661, he lived mainly in England. He is buried in Poets' Corner, Westminster.

— *Novelas ejemplares (Exemplary Novels*, or more commonly, *Exemplary Tales)* is a series of twelve novellas written by Miguel de Cervantes between 1590 and 1612 and published in Madrid in 1613.

— Alain-René Lesage (also spelled Le Sage) (6 May 1668–17 November 1747) was a French novelist and playwright. Lesage is best known for his 1707 comic novel *Le Diable boiteux (The Devil on Two Sticks)*, his comedy *Turcaret* (1709), and his picaresque novel *Gil Blas* (1715–1735).

18. *L'Ariane* (1632) is a romance novel written by Jean Desmarets, Sieur de Saint-Sorlin (1595–28 October 1676). See note 41, p. 379.

— *Cléopâtre* (1648) is a long heroic romance novel written by Gauthier de Costes, seigneur de la Calprenède.

— *Faramond* (1661) is another long heroic romance novel also written by de Costes.

— Polixandres is a popular heroic novel, written by Marin le Roy, sieur du Parc et de Gomberville (see note 39), in which the hero wanders through the world in search of the island home of Princess Alcidiane.

— Marie-Madeleine Pioche de La Vergne, Comtesse de La Fayette (18 March 1634–25 May 1693), better known as Madame de La Fayette, was a French writer; she authored *La Princesse de Clèves*, France's first historical novel, and one of the earliest novels in literature.

19. François VI, Duc de La Rochefoucauld, Prince de Marcillac (15 September 1613–17 March 1680), was a noted French moralist & the author of *Maximes*, a series of (105) philosophical aphorisms. *Maximes*, or *Réflexions ou sentences et maximes morales*, was published in 1665. The collection of maxims focus on the merciless nature of human conduct, with a cynical attitude towards virtuosity and avowals of affection, friendship, love, and loyalty.

— Jean Regnault de Segrais (22 August 1624–25 March 1701) was a French poet and novelist born in Caen.

— *Zaïde, histoire espagnole*, also Zayde (1670), is a French novel that was written by Marie-Madeleine Pioche de La Vergne, Comtesse de La Fayette, published in 1670. It is a Hispano-Moorish romance that was signed by Segrais (see note 61) but was almost certainly written by La Fayette.

— *La Princesse de Clèves (The Princess of Cleves)* is a French novel that was written by Marie-Madeleine Pioche de La Vergne, Comtesse de La Fayette, but published anonymously in March 1678. One of the earliest psychological novels, and also the first *roman d'analyse* (analysis novel), *La Princesse de Clèves* marked a major turning point in the history of the novel, which to that point had largely been used to tell romances, implausible stories of heroes overcoming odds to find a happy marriage, with myriad subplots, often in several volumes. *La Princesse de Clèves* turned that on its head with a highly realistic plot, introspective language that explored the characters' inner thoughts and emotions.

20. François de Salignac de la Mothe-Fénelon (6 August 1651–7 January 1715) was a French Catholic archbishop, theologian, poet, and writer. He is the author of *The Adventures of Telemachus*, first published in 1699.

— Jeanne-Marie Bouvier de la Motte-Guyon, known as Madame Guyon (13 April 1648–9 June 1717), was a French mystic accused of heresy and imprisoned from 1695 to 1703, after publishing the book *A Short and Very Easy Method of Prayer*.

21. Paul Scarron (c. 1 July 1610–6 October 1660) was a French poet, dramatist, and novelist, born in Paris. Scarron was very prolific. His *Virgile travesti* (1648–1653) is a parody of the *Æneid*. *Roman comique* (1651–1657) is now considered to be Scarron's best work.

22. Madeleine-Angélique de Gomez, also M.P.V.D.G. (22 November 1684–28 December 1770), was a French author and playwright, the daughter of actor, Paul Poisson. While most of her work was published under the name Madame de Gomez, some of her works have been published under the pseudonym M.P.V.D.G.

— Paul Poisson (1658–28 December 1735) was a French actor.

— *Les journées amusantes* is a novel written by Madeleine-Angélique de Gomez.

— *Cent nouvelles nouvelles* is a collection of short stories by Madeleine-Angélique de Gomez.

23. Marie Louise d'Esparbès de Lussan, by marriage Vicomtesse, then Comtesse de Polastron (19 October 1764–London, 27 March 1804), was a French lady-in-waiting, known as the mistress of the Comte d'Artois, who later reigned as Charles X of France.

— Claudine Alexandrine Guérin de Tencin, Baroness of Saint-Martin-de-Ré (27 April 1682–4 December 1749), was a French salonist and author. She joined her sister Madame de Ferriol in Paris, and as the Mesdames de Tencin, they soon established a salon, frequented by intellectuals, wits, and roués. De Tencin was the mother of Jean le Rond d'Alembert, who later became a prominent mathematician, philosopher, and contributor to the *Encyclopédie*.

— Françoise de Graffigny (11 February 1695–12 December 1758), better known as Madame de Graffigny, was a French novelist, playwright, and salon hostess.

— Jean-Baptiste Armand Louis Léonce Élie de Beaumont (25 September 1798–21 September 1874) was a French geologist.

— Marie-Jeanne Riccoboni (25 October 1713–7 December 1792), whose maiden name was Laboras de Mézières, was a French actress & novelist. She wrote & published *Les Lettres de Juliette Catesby* in 1759.

— *Lettres d'une Péruvienne* is an epistolary novel, written by Françoise de Graffigny and published in December 1747.

— *Les Lettres de Juliette Catesby* (1759) is an epistolary novel written by Marie-Jeanne Riccoboni.

24. Anne "Ninon" de l'Enclos, also spelled Ninon de Lenclos and Ninon de Lanclos (10 November 1620–17 October 1705), was a French author, courtesan, and patron of the arts. She is mentioned by name in Edgar Allan Poe's short story, *The Spectacles*.

    — Marion Delorme (3 October 1613–2 July 1650) was a French courtesan known for her relationships with the important men of her time. She is said to have numbered among her lovers and benefactors Charles de Saint-Évremond (1610–1703) the wit and litterateur, George Villiers, 2nd Duke of Buckingham, Louis II de Bourbon, Prince de Condé (called The Great Condé), and even Cardinal Richelieu.

    — Charles de Sévigné (1648–1713) was a French aristocrat and soldier. He was the son of French literary icon Madame de Sévigné. He was one of Ninon de l'Enclos's many lovers.

    — Philippe-Charles de La Fare, or Marquis de La Fare, 4th Marquis of Monclar, Conte of Laugères (15 February 1687–14 September 1752), was a Marshal of France.

    — Guillaume Amfrye de Chaulieu (1639–27 June 1720), French poet and wit, was born at Fontenay, Normandy. He became the trusted and devoted friend of Mlle Delaunay, with whom he carried on an interesting correspondence. Among his poems the best known are *Fontenay* and *La Retraite*. His works were edited with those of his friend the Marquis de La Fare (See note 33) in 1714, 1750, and 1774.

    — Cythera is a small Greek island, southeast of the Peloponnesus, and the birthplace of the goddess Aphrodite (Venus). The island is therefore consecrated to love. The god of Cythère would be the god of love, Eros.

    — Georges-Louis Leclerc, Comte de Buffon (7 September 1707–16 April 1788), was a French naturalist, mathematician, cosmologist, and encyclopédiste.

25. Louis XV (15 February 1710–10 May 1774), known as Louis the Beloved, was King of France from 1 September 1715 until his death in 1774. He succeeded his great-grandfather Louis XIV at the age of five. His reign of almost 59 years (from 1715 to 1774) was the second longest in the history

of France, exceeded only by his predecessor, Louis XIV, who had ruled for 72 years (from 1643 to 1715.) Historians generally criticize his reign, his corruption, which embarrassed the monarchy, and his wars, which drained the treasury while producing little gain. His grandson and successor Louis XVI would inherit a kingdom in need of financial and political reform that would ultimately lead to the French Revolution of 1789.

26. Claude Prosper Jolyot de Crébillon (13 February 1707–12 April 1777) was a French novelist.

— *Le Sopha, conte moral (The Sofa: A Moral Tale)* is a 1742 libertine novel written by Claude Prosper Jolyot de Crébillon. On publication, *Le Sopha, conte moral*, an erotic political satire, quickly became Crébillon's most popular work, although it forced him into exile from Paris for several months.

— *Tanzaï et Néadarné, histoire japonaise* (1734) is a novel written by Claude Prosper Jolyot de Crébillon. On publication, it proved popular, but as it contained thinly veiled attacks on the Papal Bull, Unigenitus, the cardinal de Rohan, and others, it meant that Crébillon was suspected of writing a religious satire that landed him briefly in the prison at Vincennes, the same prison de Sade would be sent to in 1776.

— *Les Égarements du cœur et de l'esprit ou Mémoires de M. de Meilcour (Strayings of the Heart and Mind, or Memoirs of M. de Meilcour)* is a novel written by Claude Prosper Jolyot de Crébillon, which appeared in three parts from 1736 to 1738.

27. Pierre Carlet de Chamblain de Marivaux (4 February 1688–12 February 1763), commonly referred to as Marivaux, was a French playwright and novelist. He parodied François Fénelon's *Telemachus*, which he updated as *Le Telemaque travesti* (written in 1714 but not published until 1736). He started writing articles for the *Mercure*, the chief newspaper of France, in 1717. His work was noted for its keen observation and literary skill.

28. François-Marie Arouet (21 November 1694–30 May 1778), known by his *nom de plume* Voltaire, was a French Enlightenment writer, historian, and philosopher famous for his wit, his criticism of Christianity, especially the Roman Catholic Church, as well as his advocacy of freedom of speech, freedom of religion, and separation of church & state.

— *Candide, ou l'Optimisme (Candide: or, The Optimist,* also *Candide or, Optimism)* is a French satire first published in 1759 by Voltaire. The novella concerns a young man, Candide, who is being indoctrinated with Leibnizian optimism by his mentor, Professor Pangloss.

— *Zadig ou la Destinée (Zadig; or, The Book of Fate)* is a 1747 novella of philosophical fiction by the Enlightenment writer Voltaire. It tells the story of Zadig, a Zoroastrian philosopher in ancient Babylonia. The author does not attempt any historical accuracy, and some of the problems Zadig faces are thinly disguised references to social and political problems of Voltaire's own day.

29. Jean-Jacques Rousseau (28 June 1712–2 July 1778) was a Genevan philosopher, writer, and composer. His political philosophy influenced the progress of the Enlightenment throughout Europe, as well as aspects of the French Revolution and the development of modern political, economic, and educational thought.

30. *Julie, ou la Nouvelle Héloïse (Julie; or, The New Héloïse),* originally entitled *Lettres de Deux Amans, Habitans d'une petite Ville au pied des Alpes* (Letters from Two Lovers, Living in a Small Town at the Foot of the Alps), is an epistolary novel by Jean-Jacques Rousseau and published in 1761.

"What tears are shed on reading this exquisite book! Nature is painted in its true colors, interest is sustained, and is increased by degrees. Many difficulties are overcome. A deep understanding of philosophy was needed to have brought about all this interest in a courtesan. Would it be too bold of us to suggest that this book can make a claim as being our finest novel? It was in its pages that Rousseau saw how a heroine, despite all her recklessness and foolishness, could still be able to move us deeply. Perhaps we would never have had *Julie,* without *Manon Lescaut.*" (Sade's original footnote to this essay.)

— In Greek mythology, Momus was the personification of satire and mockery. Two stories about him are in Æsop's *Fables.* During the Renaissance, several literary works used him as a mouthpiece for their criticism of tyranny, while others later made him a critic of contemporary society.

31. Jean-François Marmontel (11 July 1723–31 December 1799) was a French historian, writer, and a member of the Encyclopédistes movement.

— *Contes moraux* is a collection of short stories by Jean-François Marmontel, published in 1755–1759.

32. *Bélisaire* is a banned 1767 French novel written by Jean-François Marmontel. It focuses on the life of the Byzantine general Belisarius and popularized the apocryphal tale of his being reduced to beggary by Justinian I despite his great services to the empire. The novel presents Belisarius' story as an example of the ingratitude of those in power towards their faithful servants and it indicts the French king Louis XV by proxy as another such ungrateful monarch.

33. Samuel Richardson (19 August 1689–4 July 1761) was an English writer and printer, best known for three epistolary novels: *Pamela or, Virtue Rewarded* (1740); *Clarissa: Or the History of a Young Lady* (1748), and *The History of Sir Charles Grandison* (1753).

— Henry Fielding (22 April 1707–8 October 1754) was an English novelist and dramatist known for his earthy humor and satire. His comic novel *Tom Jones* is still widely appreciated. His *Shamela* parodied Richardson's *Pamela*, and was his first literary success. Fielding and Samuel Richardson are seen as founders of the traditional English novel. He also holds a place in the history of law enforcement, having used his authority as a magistrate to found the Bow Street Runners, London's first intermittently funded, full-time police force.

34. Aristotle (384–322 BC) was a Greek philosopher and polymath during the Classical period in Ancient Greece. Taught by Plato, his writings cover many subjects, including physics, biology, zoology, metaphysics, logic, ethics, aesthetics, poetics, theater, music, rhetoric, psychology, geology, linguistics, economics, politics, meteorology, and government.

35. Denis Diderot (5 October 1713–31 July 1784) was a French philosopher, art critic, and writer, best known for serving as co-founder, chief editor, and contributor to the *Encyclopédie* along with Jean le Rond d'Alembert. He was a prominent figure during the Age of Enlightenment.

36. *Clarissa; or. The History of a Young Lady: Comprehending the Most Important Concerns of Private Life. And Particularly Shewing, the Distresses that May Attend the Misconduct Both of Parents and Children, In Relation to Marriage* is an epistolary novel written by Samuel Richardson, and published in 1748. It tells the tragic story of a young woman, Clarissa Harlowe, whose quest for virtue is continually thwarted by her family. The Harlowes are a recently wealthy family whose preoccupation with increasing their standing in society leads to obsessive control of their daughter, Clarissa. It is considered one of the longest novels in the English language (based on estimated word count). It is generally regarded as Richardson's masterpiece.

37. Antoine François Prévost d'Exiles (1 April 1697–25 November 1763), usually known simply as the Abbé Prévost, was a French author and novelist. His novel, *Manon Lescaut*, separately published in Paris in 1731 as *Histoire du Chevalier des Grieux et de Manon Lescaut*, made him famous. The book was eagerly read, chiefly in pirated copies, being forbidden in France.

38. See note 12, p. 574.

39. *Mémoires et aventures d'un homme de qualité qui s'est retiré du monde*, his most famous novel, the first four volumes of which were published in Paris in 1728.

— *Le Philosophe anglais, ou Histoire de Monsieur Cleveland, fils naturel de Cromwell, écrite par lui-mesme, et traduite de l'anglois* is a romance novel written by Antoine François Prévost d'Exiles, the material of which had been written in London. It was published in Paris in 1731–1739.

— *Histoire d'une Grecque moderne* (*The Story of a Modern Greek Woman*) is a novel written by Antoine François Prévost d'Exiles, and published in 1740.

— *Le Monde moral, ou Mémoires pour servir a l'histoire du cœur humain* (*The Moral World, or Memoirs to Serve the History of the Human Heart*) is a novel written by Antoine François Prévost d'Exiles and published in 1760.

— *Histoire du Chevalier des Grieux, et de Manon Lescaut (The Story of the Chevalier des Grieux and Manon Lescaut)* is a novel written by Antoine François Prévost. Published in 1731, it is the seventh and final volume of *Mémoires et aventures d'un homme de qualité (Memoirs and Adventures of a Man of Quality)*.

40. Dorat Claude Joseph Dorat (31 December 1734–29 April 1780) was a French writer, also known as Le Chevalier Dorat. He became fashionable for his work, *Réponse d'Abélard à Héloïse* (Abelard's Answer to Heloise), and a number of heroic epistles, *Les Victimes de l'amour, ou lettres de quelques amants célèbres* (1776) (Victims of Love, or Letters from some famous lovers). Besides light verse, he wrote comedies, fables, and, among other novels, *Les Sacrifices de l'amour, ou lettres de la vicomtesse de Senanges et du chevalier de Versenay* (1771).

41. Stanislas Jean, chevalier de Boufflers (31 May 1738–18 January 1815) was a French statesman *&* writer, known primarily for his story, *Aline, reine de Golconde (Aline, Queen of Golconda)*, which became extremely popular on its publication in 1761.

— Pūblius Ovidius Nāsō (20 March 43 BC–17/18 AD), known in English as Ovid, was a Roman poet who lived during the reign of Augustus. He is often ranked as one of the three canonical poets of Latin literature. Although Ovid enjoyed enormous popularity during his lifetime, the emperor Augustus banished him to a remote province on the Black Sea, where he remained until his death. Ovid is today best known for the *Metamorphoses*, a 15-book continuous mythological narrative written in epic meter, *&* for works in elegiac couplets such as *Ars Amatoria (The Art of Love)* and *Fasti*. *Metamorphoses* remains one of the most important sources of classical mythology.

— Napoléon Bonaparte, born Napoleone di Buonaparte (15 August 1769–5 May 1821), usually referred to as simply Napoleon in English, was a Corsican military and political leader who rose to prominence during the French Revolution. He was the *de facto* leader of the French Republic as First Consul from 1799 to 1804. As Napoleon I, he was Emperor of the French from 1804 until 1814 and again in 1815.

42. François-Thomas-Marie de Baculard d'Arnaud (8 September 1718–8 November 1805) was a French writer, playwright, poet, and novelist. His five-volume series of novellas *Les Épreuves du sentiment* (1775–1778) inspired Bellini's opera *Adelson e Salvini*.

43. Nicolas Restif de la Bretonne, born Nicolas-Edme Rétif, or Nicolas-Edme Restif (23 October 1734–3 February 1806), also known as Rétif, was a French novelist. He is reputed to have coined the term "pornographer" in his book, *The Pornographer*. He and the Marquis de Sade maintained a mutual hatred after Bretonne wrote *Anti-Justine*, a pornographic novel he published in 1798. It was written to parody and to oppose the political philosophy of the Marquis de Sade as expressed in the earlier edition of Sade's 1791 novel, *Justine, ou Les Malheurs de la Vertu (Justine, or The Misfortunes of Virtue)*.

44. *The Monk: A Romance* is a Gothic novel by Matthew Gregory Lewis, published in 1796. This quickly written book was published before Lewis turned twenty. It is a prime example of the Gothic horror novel. Its convoluted *&* scandalous plot has made it one of the most important Gothic novels of its time.

— Ann Radcliffe (9 July 1764–7 February 1823) was an English author and a pioneer of Gothic fiction. Her technique of explaining apparently supernatural elements in her novels (*The Mysteries of Udolpho* (1794), *The Italian* (1797), and *The Romance of the Forest* (1791)) is credited with gaining Gothic fiction a degree of respectability in the 1790s. Radcliffe was the most popular writer of her day and almost universally revered, particularly in France, where her admirers included Victor Hugo, Charles Baudelaire, the Marquis de Sade, and Alexandre Dumas.

45. *Encyclopédie, ou dictionnaire raisonné des sciences, des arts et des métiers (Encyclopedia, or a Systematic Dictionary of the Sciences, Arts, and Crafts)*, better known as *Encyclopédie*, was a general encyclopedia published in France between 1751 and 1772, with later supplements, revised editions, and translations. It had many writers, known as the Encyclopédistes. It was edited by Denis Diderot and, until 1759, co-edited by Jean le Rond d'Alembert.

46. Titus Aelius Hadrianus Antoninus Pius, known as Antoninus (19 September 86–7 March 161) was Roman emperor from 138 to 161. He was one of the Five Good Emperors from the Nerva-Antonine dynasty.

— Titus Caesar Vespasianus (30 December 39–13 September 81 AD) was Roman emperor from 79 to 81. A member of the Flavian dynasty, Titus succeeded his father Vespasian upon his death.

— Andronikos I Komnenos (c. 1118–12 September 1185), usually Latinized as Andronicus I Comnenus, was the Byzantine emperor from 1183 to 1185. The reign of Andronikos was characterized by his harsh measures. He resolved to suppress many abuses but above all else to check feudalism and limit the power of the nobles, who were rivals for his throne.

— Nero Claudius Cæsar Augustus Germanicus (15 December 37–9 June 68 AD), originally named Lucius Domitius Ahenobarbus, was the fifth emperor of Rome, and the last in the Julio-Claudian dynasty line of emperors. He was adopted by the Roman emperor Claudius at the age of thirteen, and succeeded him to the throne at the age of seventeen. Nero was popular with the lower-class Roman citizens during his time and his reign is commonly associated with unrestricted tyranny, extravagance, religious persecution and debauchery.

47. In Greek mythology, the Titans were the pre-Olympian gods. According to the *Theogony* of Hesiod, they were the twelve children of the primordial parents Uranus (Sky) and Gaia (Earth) with six male Titans: Oceanus, Coeus, Crius, Hyperion, Iapetus, and Chronus, and six female Titans, called the Titanides, (also Titanesses): Theia, Rhea, Themis, Mnemosyne, Phoebe, and Tethys.

— Mount Vesuvius is a somma stratovolcano located on the Gulf of Naples in Capania, Italy. It is nine kilometers east of Naples and a short distance from the shore. Vesuvius consists of a large cone partially encircled by the steep rim of a summit caldera. The eruption of Mount Vesuvius in AD 79 destroyed the Roman cities of Pompeii, Herculaneum, Oplontis, and Stabiae, as well as several other settlements. The only surviving eyewitness account of the event consists of two letters by Pliny the Younger to the historian Tacitus.

48. "The Enchanted Tower" is the subtitle of Sade's own short story, *Rodrigo*, which first appeared in his short story collection, *Les crimes de l'amour (The Crimes of Love)*, published in 1800.

— "The Amboise Conspiracy" is Sade's reference to his own 18,000 word short story *Juliette et Raunai, ou la conspiration d'Amboise, nouvelle historique (Juliette and Raunai, or The Amboise Conspiracy, A Historical Tale)*. Because it was based on a significant French historical event, Sade used it as the opening tale of his short story collection, *Les crimes de l'amour*.

49. Sade wrote his short story, *Rodrigo or, The Enchanted Tower* based on a story he half-remembered by Miguel de Luna, who sometimes used the pseudonym Abulcasim Tarif Abentarique. "It would appear more likely that the name of this historian, unfamiliar to all the specialists we have consulted, should be written: Abul-selim-terif-ben-tariq." (Sade's original footnote to this essay.)

50. Jean-Jacques Garnier's *Histoire de France, Vol. 24: Depuis l'Établissement de la Monarchie, Jusqu'au Regne de Louis XIV (History of France, Vol. 24: From the Establishment of the Monarchy, Until the Reign of Louis XIV)* includes details of the Amboise Conspiracy. Also called The Tumult of Amboise, the Conspiracy was a failed attempt by a Huguenot faction in France to gain control over the young King Francis II and to reverse the policies of the current administration of Francis, Duke of Guise and Charles, Cardinal of Lorraine, through their arrest & execution.

51. *Aline et Valcour; ou, Le Roman philosophique (Aline and Valcour; or, The Philosophical Novel)* is an epistolary novel by the Marquis de Sade. It contrasts a brutal African kingdom, Butua, with a South Pacific island paradise known as Tamoé and it is ruled by the philosopher-king Zamé. Sade wrote the book while incarcerated in the Bastille in the 1780s. Published in 1795, it was the first of Sade's books published under his true name. Sade found out that certain sections of it had been pirated and published under different titles, all without his consent. Understandably, he railed against this and let his readers know of this: "This anecdote is the same one that Brigandos begins, in the episode of the novel my *Aline and Valcour*, with the title: *Sainville and Léonore*, and that interrupts the

circumstance of the corpse found in the tower; the counterfeiters of this episode, by copying it word for word, did not fail to copy also the first four lines of this anecdote, which are in the mouth of the leader of the Bohemians. It is therefore as essential for us, at this moment, as for those who buy novels, to warn that the work that is sold at Pigoreau and Leroux under the title of *Valmor and Lidia*, and at Cérioux and Moutardier, under that of *Alzonde and Koradin*, are absolutely the same thing, and both literally looted sentence for sentence of the episode of *Sainville and Léonore*, forming about three volumes of my novel *Aline and Valcour*." (Sade's original footnote to this essay.)

52. The manchineel tree (*Hippomane mancinella*) is a species of flowering plant in the spurge family (Euphorbiaceae). Its native range stretches from tropical southern North America to northern South America. The name "manchineel" is from Spanish manzanilla ("little apple"), from the superficial resemblance of its fruit and leaves to those of an apple tree. It is also known as the beach apple. The manchineel is one of the most toxic trees in the world: the tree has milky-white sap that contains numerous toxins. The sap is present in every part of the tree: the bark, the leaves, and the fruit.

53. *Justine, ou Les Malheurs de la Vertu* (*Justine, or The Misfortunes of Virtue*) is a 1791 novel by de Sade. *Justine* is set just before the French Revolution in France and tells the story of a young girl who goes under the name of Thérèse, who explains the series of misfortunes that have befallen her. De Sade's denial of his authorship was an act of attempted self-preservation. Napoleon Bonaparte ordered the arrest of the anonymous author of *Justine* and *Juliette*, and as a result de Sade was incarcerated for the last thirteen years of his life. The Cour Royale de Paris ordered the book's destruction on 19 May 1815.

To Madame de Sade (My Grand Letter)

54. Written while Sade was imprisoned in a dungeon of Vincennes on 20 February 1781. The Château de Vincennes is a former fortress and royal residence in the town of Vincennes, on the eastern edge of Paris next to the Bois de Vincennes. It was built between 1361 and 1369. In 1787 the Château took on a new role as a military base and prison. De Sade was held there from 1777 to 1784.

55. Out of fear of possible blasphemy charges from the censor, Sade refused
to reveal the names of the divinities he had chosen. In 1781, blasphemy
laws were repressive and punishment for actual or perceived blasphemy
was severe.

56. *Les Arsacides:* A historical tragedy in six acts, written by Bernard de La
Fortelle in 1775. The Arsacids were the dynasty of Parthian kings who
ruled Iran to form the Parthian Empire.

57. Madame Marie de Montreuil was Sade's mother-in-law through his
arranged marriage in the spring of 1763 to Renée-Pélagie Cordier de
Launay de Montreuil. Madame de Montreuil personally wrote to King
Louis XVI, asking that Sade remain imprisoned.

58. Sade's "serious occupations" were writing, editing, & publishing his works.

59. Sade's phrase, "the first and the most important of all its rules," is a reference to the Christian philosophy of forgiveness, a central tenet of Christianity as articulated in *The Lord's Prayer*, part of which states: "and forgive
us our trespasses, as we forgive those who trespass against us."

60. Sade's reference to *a party involving some girls* is a reference to what became known as the Arcueil affair or scandal.

61. The "first incident" was the Arcueil affair, which Sade maintained never
amounted to anything and never would have except that Sade's mother-
in-law took legal action due to being concerned that by association Sade
would defile the de Montreuil family's good name.

62. The Marseilles incident In 1772, the Marquis de Sade was visiting Marseilles when he and his manservant, Latour, drugged, whipped, and sod-
omized several local prostitutes. Sade was thirty-two years old at that
point and his father had already died, so he was heir to his family's fortune and legacy. He took Anne, his sister-in-law/nun, whom he'd deflow-
ered in her youth, and fled to Italy to escape execution. There, he lived
incognito as the Comte de Mazan. He was found guilty of sodomy in
absentia and sentenced to death. Either his portrait, or a straw figured
dressed like him, was burned in effigy on 12 September 1772.

63. procuress

64. whore

65. Rose Keller was the "lying, scheming woman." In 1768, a prostitute named Rose Keller accused Sade of flagellating her. He was imprisoned in the Château de Pierre-Encise, but was released once Rose withdrew her complaint after being paid off by Sade's mother-in-law.

66. Sade's uncle was the Abbé de Sade, vicar general of Toulouse, later vicar general of Narbonne. The Abbé's main residence was the Château de Saumane in the Vaucluse region of southern France.

— *"what happened to her"* was that the Abbé sent her to a hospital at l'Isle-la-Sorgue, also L'Isle-sur-la-Sorgue, a Provençal town and commune on the Sorgue River in southeast France. The commune is in the arrondissement of Avignon within the department of Vaucluse, in the region of Provence-Alpes-Côte d'Azur.

— "Another one" refers to a cook named Marie.

67. The third of Madame de Montreuil's disgraceful acts took place in 1775, when Sade left for Italy, following the third time his mother-in-law attempted to have him arrested.

— The postmaster of Courthézon was Louis Charvin and he travelled with Sade to Italy in 1775.

68. A procuress named "Nanon" that Sade used in Lyons had a twenty-four year old niece named Anne Sablonnière who was also known as "Nanon."

69. "I intend, at the very least, to publicly cover them with ignominy, shame, and confusion" is similar to Sade's epigram to *The Duped Judge*, in which he states: "Oh, believe me when I say I want to praise them so much… that for twenty years they will not dare show themselves."

70. This was a young man named Andre, who Sade and his wife had employed as a secretary for the Marquis. Andre was aged fifteen or sixteen and he was one of the seven staff the Sades hired that month to accompany them to La Coste.

71. She knew about the one hundred *louis* paid at Arcueil by Madame de Montreuil to Rose Keller.

72. Monsieur de Castillon was the Chief Prosecuting Attorney for the Court of Aix.

    — Monsieur de Mende was the King's Prosecuting Attorney at Marseilles, and the cousin of Monsieur de Castillon.

73. *Juniperus sabina*, an evergreen shrub that produces an oil believed to induce abortions.

74. "the little doctor from Rome" was Giuseppe Iberti, whom Sade first met during his trip to Italy in 1775–76.

75. The Château Saint-Ange, formerly the Château Challuau, was built in 1540, renamed in the 17th century, & destroyed in the early 19th century.

76. *Histoire des Celtes, et particulièrement des Gaulois et des Germains* (1740), by Simon Pelloutier.

77. "an herb called *linveum*" is mentioned in *Omnium Rerum Propia Nomina Variis Linguis Explicata Indicans by Hadrianus Junius.*

    — Pliny the Elder, *Naturalis Historia, Vols IV–VI.*

    — Aulus Gellius (c. 125–180 AD) was a Roman author and grammarian, best known for his book *Attic Nights*, a commonplace book, or compilation of notes on grammar, philosophy, history, antiquarianism, and other subjects, preserving fragments of the works of many authors who might otherwise be unknown today.

    — *Hellebore* is the Eurasian genus *Helleborus* that consists of over twenty species of herbaceous or evergreen plants, many of which are poisonous.

78. *"very similar to those you were accused of."* Madame de Sade had been accused of tampering with the religious faith of her young servants at La Coste.

79. The mass of the magpies was a daily morning mass held in memory of an unjust condemnation of a French servant girl accused of theft who was tried, convicted, & executed. Later the true culprit was revealed to be a magpie that had in fact committed the crime. *La Pie voleuse*, a play written by Jean-Marie-Théodore Baudouin (or d'Aubigny) in collaboration with Louis-Charles Caigniez, was based on this event. The play served as the basis for Rossini's 1817 tragicomic opera entitled *La Gazza Ladra* (*The Thieving Magpie*). After finding out that the French servant girl was innocent of the crime and that a magpie had committed the theft, the town organized an annual "Mass of the Magpies" to pray for the girl's soul.

80. Jean Calas (19 March 1698–10 March 1762), a Huguenot cloth merchant, was arrested and charged with having murdered his son to prevent or punish his conversion to Catholicism. On 13 October 1761, Calas's eldest son, Marc Antoine, was found hanged in his father's textile shop in Toulouse. Anti-Huguenot hysteria broke out among the local Roman Catholic populace, and Calas was arrested and charged. At first he attributed the crime to an unknown intruder, but he later insisted that his son had committed suicide. Found guilty, he was condemned to death on 9 March 1762. The following day he was publicly broken on the wheel, strangled, and then burned to death. His son was buried as a martyr to the Catholic faith. The philosopher Voltaire took an interest in the case & due to his influence, a panel reversed Calas's conviction on 9 March 1765, and the government paid the family an indemnity.

81. Évry was where the de Montreuil family had their family home. Évry is a former commune in the southern suburbs of Paris, France, prefecture of the department of Essonne.

82. The Marquis de Poyanne was a friend of Sade's father. He was the commander-in-chief of the Carabiniers, a distinguished regiment of the French Royal Army. It was Poyanne who nominated the Marquis de Sade for a commission in the Dragoons, a regiment in which he served for seven years, quickly rising to the rank of Colonel.

The Last Will and Testament of D. A. F. de Sade, Man of Letters

83. This document in this translation first appeared in *Philosophy Now*, Issue 143 (April/May 2021). It also appeared in May 2021 as an audio recording, read by Gerald Cox for `listentopoetry.com`

Essays on Sade

The Divine Marquis — **Guillaume Apollinaire**

1. Paul Ginisty, *The Marquis de Sade* (Paris: Carpenter, 1901).

— Dr. Eugen Duehren, *Der Marquis de Sade und seine Zeit* (Berlin: Verlag von H. Barsdorf, 1901), tr. by Uzanne Octave as *The Marquis de Sade and His Time* (Paris: Michalon, 1901); *Neue Forschungen über den Marquis de Sade und Seine Zeit* (Berlin: max Harrwitz, 1904).

— Dr. Cabanes, *The Alleged Madness of the Marquis de Sade* in *The Secret History of the Cabinet*, 4th series.

— Doctor Jacobus X, *The Marquis de Sade and his Work Before Medical Science and Modern Literature* (Paris: Charles Carrington, 1901).

— Henri d'Alméras, *The Marquis de Sade, the Man and the Writer* (Paris: Albin Michel, (s.d.)).

2. *Répertoire où Journalier du château de la Bastille à commencer le mercredi 15 mai 1782*, published in part by Alfred Bégis, *Nouvelle Revue* (Nov. & Dec. 1882); *The Revealed Bastille*, by Manuel; *The Marquis de Sade*, by Henri d'Alméras.

3. It also appeared as the front-piece to an edition of *The Correspondence of Madame Gourdan*.

4. L.-A. Pitou *Analysis of my Misery & Persecution During my Twenty-Six Years*, by the author of *Journey to Cayenne* and *The Stuart and Bourbon Reign* (Paris: 1816), p. 98.

5. *A General History of Prisons during the Reign of Bonaparte, with Strange and Interesting Anecdotes about the Conciergerie, Vincennes, Bicêtre, Sainte-Pélagie, the Force, the Château de Joux, and so on., and the Notable Characters who were Detained There*, by P.-F.-T.-J. Giraud (Paris: 1814), in-8.

6. This story is entitled *La Châtelaine de Longeville, ou la Femme vengée (The Lady of the Château de Longeville, or A Woman's Revenge)*. It is one of the tales that appears in *Stories, Tales, and Fables*. The manuscript is in the Bibliothèque Nationale.

7. This is an analysis of the third draft of *Justine*.

8. M. Henri d'Alméras thinks *Philosophy in the Boudoir* is not by the Marquis de Sade. This is a mistake that this quotation could dispel. Besides, no one else is so deceived, neither Restif, who was very familiar with the works of Sade, or anyone else. Everything in *Philosophy in the Boudoir* reveals the genius of the Marquis, and his easily recognized style. Perhaps this is the major work, the *Opus Sadicum* par excellence.

9. An unpublished note.

10. I will not give an analysis here of the Sade books which are published openly. Regarding *Philosophy in the Bedroom*, it is too easy to imagine the fable being necessarily able to cause discomfort and stress.

11. The quotations concerning the *Portfolio of a Man of Letters* are unpublished.

12. An unpublished note.

13. We read in the margin: "It is worth noting that each of these acts, despite particular intrigues, contributes to the general plan and purpose of the Comte."

14. An unpublished letter.

15. *Le Misanthrope par amour ou Sophie et Desfrancs*, "a three-act comedy in free verse."

16. An unpublished letter.

17. This letter is preceded by the unpublished response that is sent by De La Porte to the Marquis de Sade: "To answer, the Comédie-Française does

not customarily accept any piece without providing remuneration for its author, and that I have subsequently read your play and am considering it for a regular run, but as our concerns do not allow us to fix its performance on the date that M. De Sade asks for, we hereby return your play."

18. An unpublished letter. The annotation also stated: "Received 13 April '93, at one o'clock in the morning." Allow me to thank for his kindness, M. Couët, the distinguished librarian of the Comédie-Française.

19. This letter and the following were published in 1859 by the *Correspondance littéraire*; they were provided by Baron Girardot, Secretary General of the Prefecture de la Loire.

20. Published by the *Revue anecdotique*, new series, t. I, first semester (1860), pp. 103–106. (Note of Dr. Cabanès.)

21. *Aline et Valcour; ou, Le Roman philosophique (Aline and Valcour, or The Philosophical Novel)* (1795).

22. Published by the *Revue anecdotique, op. cit.* pp. 103–106. (Note of Dr. Cabanès.)

23. Cf. Esquirol, *Some Mental Maladies*, Vol. II, pp. 561, *passim.*

The Marquis de Sade and the Gothic Novel — Maurice Heine

24. Bibliothèque nationale; *New French Acquisitions, ms. 4010, fol. 449.*

— First published as *The Crimes of Love; Heroic and Tragic Stories*, by D.-A.-F. Sade, author of *Aline and Valcour*, Paris, in the year 1800, 4 vols in-12, and reprinted separately by Octave Uzanne (Paris: E. Rouveyre, 1878) in-12.

25. Alice M. Killen, *The Novel of "Terror," or the "Gothic" Novel and its Influence on French Literature since 1840* (Paris: G & Crês, & Cle, 1915).

26. *Some Thoughts on the Novel* is included in this volume.

27. *Some Thoughts on the Novel.*

28. See, for example, *The Lady of the Château of Longeville* and the episode of the ghosts in *The Duped Judge*. These two stories were written in 1787 and published for the first time in *Historiettes, Contes and Fabliaux (Stories, Tales, and Fables)*, Paris, by the Société du roman philosophique, 1926, in-4. However it would be a fundamental error to confuse the Gothic novel with the true "noir" novel that succeeded it by a quarter of a century. According to Walpole, in his second preface (*The Castle of Otranto*, translated in the second edition by M [arc-Antoine] E [idous], Amsterdam *&* Paris, 1767, in-12), its purpose for Sade was less to terrify the reader and more an attempt to "blend the two kinds of romance, the ancient and the modern." However "nothing is as difficult," because "in the former all was imagination and improbability: in the latter, nature is always imitated… and imagination has not been wanting, but the great resources of fancy have been dammed up, because one sticks too scrupulously to the ordinary circumstances of life." Such a conception, which *Justine* was going to vividly contradict, appears to us from the start so artificial that it becomes superfluous to analyze the puerile mechanisms of the gothic stories of Walpole, those frozen fictions of an amateur enthusiast of the romances of the Middle Ages. Furthermore, no viable outcome is in line with *The Castle of Otranto*, whose only decoration would be taken and used in a better arrangement. Both Ann Radcliffe and Lewis failed there, but these novelists were born with other gifts, independent of a medieval convention whose vogue was going to dominate the next romantic era. The snobbery of their precursor Walpole has served his memory well, although none of the puppets that haunted the daydreams of the lord of the manor of Strawberry Hill, had the fabric of the characters that we have the right to expect from an authentic literary creation.

29. *The 120 Days of Sodom* (1931) in-4, pp. 54–56.

30. *Ibid.*, pp. 56–58.

31. *Ibid.*, pp. 59–60.

32. *Ibid.*, p. 74.

33. *Justine or the Misfortunes of Virtue*, in Holland (Paris: J. V. Girouard, 1791), in-8, t. I, pp. 4–5.

34. *Ibid.*, p. 3.

35. Alice M. Killen, *op. cit.*, p. 3.

36. *The Misfortunes of Virtue*, text established from the original manuscript autographed and published for the first time (Paris: Éditions Fourcade, 1920), in-16.

37. *Justine*, 1791, in-8, preliminary page not listed (missing from the majority of the examples).

38. Alice M. Killen, *op. cit.*, p. 60.

39. *Justine*, 1791, in-8, T. I, p. 83.

40. Alice M. Killen, *op. cit.*, p. 60.

41. *Justine*, 1791, in-8, T. I, p. 81.

42. *Ibid.*, p. 67.

43. *Ibid.*, pp. 279–280.

44. *Ibid.*, pp. 77–78.

45. *Ibid.*, pp. 188–189.

46. *Hoefer Biography*, Lewis article.

47. Alice M. Killen, *op. cit.*, p. 77.

— In particular, *La Religieuse* did not appear in the original edition of 1796, the year in which Lewis found time to create the first two editions of *The Monk*, circumstances which would be enough — in addition to the times of drafting and of composition — to cause doubt about the value of such a comparison.

48. Alice M. Killen, *op. cit.*, p. 62: "Ann Radcliffe knew her limits. Her task was not that of the psychologist. She was satisfied to show the passions and their results, and, instead of giving individuality to her characters, to make them play their roles well in the melodrama."

49. *The History of Juliette* (1797), in-18, T. III, pp. 220–259.

50. *Ibid.*, pp. 316–319.

51. Alice M. Killen places this period between 1797 and 1802.

52. Alice M. Killen, *op. cit.*, p. 126.

53. *French Pre-Romanticism* (Grenoble: 1930), in-8, T. I, p. 6.

54. *The Youth of Swinburne* (1837–1867) (Strasbourg and Paris: The Belles Lettres, 1928) 2 vols in-8.

55. In italics in the printed text.

A Revolutionary Intelligence: D.A.F. de Sade — Paul Éluard

56. Sade spent twenty-seven years in prison.

57. We must do justice here to the legend that Sade was arrested and imprisoned in 1793 after having attempted to intercede on his parents-in-law's behalf. There is no actual evidence that they were ever directly or seriously threatened. At the time, Sade's credit was not great. And finally, everything suggests that this aristocratic family did what they could to protect the memory of the Marquis from the more serious charges — in the eyes of all others — of harboring a sincere and relentless revolutionary will. The rest passes for the debauchery that was generally prevalent in the eighteenth century and does not taint anyone's honor. What is impossible, really, deeply immoral, is to allow those who do not understand his principles of sedition to continue to disavow his name. Besides, we do not know enough the spirit of Sade to suppose him capable of returning good for evil, able to advocate for those who, by *lettre de cachet*, caused him to remain in prison for twelve years.

Notice — Anatole France

58. Cf. *Le Marquis de Sade*, by Jules Janin, in the *Revue de Paris* of 1834, t. XI, p. 321; — *The Truth about the Two Criminal Trials of the Marquis de Sade*, by Paul L. Jacob, bibliophile, in the *Revue de Paris* of 1837, t. XXXVIII, p. 135. — See also the Michaud biography.

59. These words are quoted by M. Paul Lacroix *(Loc. Cit.)* on the verity of the testimonies he invokes in these terms: 'I have often questioned respectable people, some of whom still live, being more than octogenarians (1837); I asked them with indiscreet curiosity some strange revelations about the Marquis de Sade...'

60. The *Mémoires de Bachaumont, Nouvelles à la main*, 1772, relate this affair quite differently. It is to his sister-in-law, according to the short story writer, that the Marquis would, at a dinner in Marseille, have offered the chocolate pastilles containing the cantharides. There is no evidence to support this version of events.

61. For the authenticity of this dialogue, I have only the references indicated in the note on page 8. Yet the aesthetic that the Marquis de Sade expressed in his essay *Some Thoughts on the Novel (Idée sur les romans)* is quite sustainable and is by no means the underpinning philosophy of his works. In this essay, after having praised the naturalness of *Clarissa*, he adds: "Writers working in this genre must be able to capture nature, they must be able to capture the heart of man, that most singular of nature's creations, and not virtue, because virtue, however beautiful, however necessary it may be, is nevertheless only one of the manifestations of this astounding heart, the profound study of which is essential for every novelist, because the novel if it is to be a faithful mirror of the human heart, must inevitably reflect every part of it" (p. xxv).

62. *Les Bijoux indiscrets (The Indiscreet Jewels, or The Talking Jewels)* is the first novel by Denis Diderot, published anonymously in 1748. It is an allegory that portrays Louis XV of France as Mangogul, Sultan of Congo, who owns a magic ring that makes women's vaginas ("jewels") talk.

— Sophie Arnould (13 February 1740–18 October 1802, in Paris) was a French operatic soprano.

— Marie-Madeleine d'Aubray, Marquise de Brinvilliers (22 July 1630–16 July 1676), was a French aristocrat who was accused and convicted of murdering her father & two of her brothers in order to inherit their estates.

63. Héloïse (c. 1116–May 1163), variously Héloïse d'Argenteuil or Héloïse du Paraclet, was a French nun, philosopher, writer, scholar, and abbess.

64. Further on in *Some Thoughts on the Novel,* Sade states that the author who wants to gain knowledge of the human heart must fulfill two conditions, conditions which summed up his life, at least as he imagined it. He said: "important knowledge is acquired only through *suffering* and *travel.*" He added: "One must have encountered men of all nations to know them, and one must have suffered at their hands to know how to appreciate them" (p. xxxiii).

65. Read especially in this regard Charles Baudelaire's *A Martyr* from *Les fleurs du Mal.* However, the poem is still conventional in structure, but it is beautiful, and does not depart from aesthetic rules which, in short, come under public morality.

66. M.H. Welschinger & M.M. Charavay, his editors, kindly communicated to me the contents of this book that is being printed at the moment.

COLOPHON

STORIES, TALES, & FABLES
was handset in InDesign CC.

The text font is *Warnock*.

The display font is *Henrietta*.

Book design & typesetting: Alessandro Segalini

Cover design: CMP

Front cover image: Francisco Goya, *Vuelo de Brujas* (1798).
Oil on canvas, 43.5 × 30.5, Museo del Prado, Madrid, Spain.

Opening image: Félicien Rops, *The Human Parody* (1879–1881)
watercolor, pastel, chalk (22.5 × 15 cm).

STORIES, TALES, & FABLES
is published by Contra Mundum Press.

Contra Mundum Press   New York · London · Melbourne

CONTRA MUNDUM PRESS

Dedicated to the value & the indispensable importance of the individual voice, to works that test the boundaries of thought & experience.

The primary aim of Contra Mundum is to publish translations of writers who in their use of form and style are *à rebours*, or who deviate significantly from more programmatic & spurious forms of experimentation. Such writing attests to the volatile nature of modernism. Our preference is for works that have not yet been translated into English, are out of print, or are poorly translated, for writers whose thinking & æsthetics are in opposition to timely or mainstream currents of thought, value systems, or moralities. We also reprint obscure and out-of-print works we consider significant but which have been forgotten, neglected, or overshadowed.

There are many works of fundamental significance to *Weltliteratur* (& *Weltkultur*) that still remain in relative oblivion, works that alter and disrupt standard circuits of thought — these warrant being encountered by the world at large. It is our aim to render them more visible.

For the complete list of forthcoming publications, please visit our website. To be added to our mailing list, send your name and email address to: info@contramundum.net

Contra Mundum Press
P.O. Box 1326
New York, NY 10276
USA

OTHER CONTRA MUNDUM PRESS TITLES

2012   *Gilgamesh*
Ghérasim Luca, *Self-Shadowing Prey*
Rainer J. Hanshe, *The Abdication*
Walter Jackson Bate, *Negative Capability*
Miklós Szentkuthy, *Marginalia on Casanova*
Fernando Pessoa, *Philosophical Essays*

2013   Elio Petri, *Writings on Cinema & Life*
Friedrich Nietzsche, *The Greek Music Drama*
Richard Foreman, *Plays with Films*
Louis-Auguste Blanqui, *Eternity by the Stars*
Miklós Szentkuthy, *Towards the One & Only Metaphor*
Josef Winkler, *When the Time Comes*

2014   William Wordsworth, *Fragments*
Josef Winkler, *Natura Morta*
Fernando Pessoa, *The Transformation Book*
Emilio Villa, *The Selected Poetry of Emilio Villa*
Robert Kelly, *A Voice Full of Cities*
Pier Paolo Pasolini, *The Divine Mimesis*
Miklós Szentkuthy, *Prae, Vol. 1*

2015   Federico Fellini, *Making a Film*
Robert Musil, *Thought Flights*
Sándor Tar, *Our Street*
Lorand Gaspar, *Earth Absolute*
Josef Winkler, *The Graveyard of Bitter Oranges*
Ferit Edgü, *Noone*
Jean-Jacques Rousseau, *Narcissus*
Ahmad Shamlu, *Born Upon the Dark Spear*

2016   Jean-Luc Godard, *Phrases*
Otto Dix, *Letters, Vol. 1*
Maura Del Serra, *Ladder of Oaths*
Pierre Senges, *The Major Refutation*
Charles Baudelaire, *My Heart Laid Bare & Other Texts*

2017   Joseph Kessel, *Army of Shadows*
Rainer J. Hanshe & Federico Gori, *Shattering the Muses*
Gérard Depardieu, *Innocent*
Claude Mouchard, *Entangled — Papers! — Notes*

2018   Miklós Szentkuthy, *Black Renaissance*
        Adonis & Pierre Joris, *Conversations in the Pyrenees*
2019   Charles Baudelaire, *Belgium Stripped Bare*
        Robert Musil, *Unions*
        Iceberg Slim, *Night Train to Sugar Hill*
        Marquis de Sade, *Aline & Valcour*
2020   *A City Full of Voices: Essays on the Work of Robert Kelly*
        Rédoine Faïd, *Outlaw*
        Carmelo Bene, *I Appeared to the Madonna*
        Paul Celan, *Microliths They Are, Little Stones*
        Zsuzsa Selyem, *It's Raining in Moscow*
        Bérengère Viennot, *Trumpspeak*
        Robert Musil, *Theater Symptoms*
        Miklós Szentkuthy, *Chapter on Love*
2021   Charles Baudelaire, *Paris Spleen*
        Marguerite Duras, *The Darkroom*
        Andrew Dickos, *Honor Among Thieves*
        Pierre Senges, *Ahab (Sequels)*
        Carmelo Bene, *Our Lady of the Turks*
2022   Fernando Pessoa, *Writings on Art & Poetical Theory*
        Miklós Szentkuthy, *Prae, Vol. 2*
        Blixa Bargeld, *Europe Crosswise: A Litany*
        Pierre Joris, *Always the Many, Never the One*
        Robert Musil, *Literature & Politics*
2023   Pierre Joris, *Interglacial Narrows*
        Gabriele Tinti, *Bleedings — Incipit Tragœdia*
        Évelyne Grossman, *The Creativity of the Crisis*
        Rainer J. Hanshe, *Closing Melodies*
        Kari Hukkila, *One Thousand & One*
2024   Antonin Artaud, *Journey to Mexico*
        Rainer J. Hanshe, *Dionysos Speed*
        Amina Saïd, *Walking the Earth*
        Léon-Paul Fargue, *High Solitude*
        Gabor Schein, *Beyond the Cordons*

SOME FORTHCOMING TITLES

Nuriá Perpinyà, *And, Suddenly, Paradise*
Sara Whym, *dreamscapes*

AGRODOLCE SERIES Æ

2020   Dejan Lukić, *The Oyster*
2022   Ugo Tognazzi, *The Injester*

HYPERION
On the Future of Æsthetics   2006–PRESENT

To read samples and order current & back issues of *Hyperion*,
visit contramundumpress.com/hyperion
Edited by Rainer J. Hanshe & Erika Mihálycsa (2014 ~)

 CONTRA MUNDUM PRESS

is published by Rainer J. Hanshe
Typography & Design: Alessandro Segalini
Publicity & Marketing: Alexandra Gold
Ebook Design: Carlie R. Houser

THE FUTURE OF KULCHUR

THE PROJECT

From major museums like the MoMA to art house cinemas such as Film Forum, cultural organizations do not sustain themselves from sales alone, but from subscriptions, donations, benefactors, and grants.

Since benefactors of Peggy Guggenheim's stature are rare to come by, and receiving large grants from major funding bodies is an infrequent and unreliable source of capital, we seek to further our venture through a form of modest support that is within everyone's reach.

Although esteemed, Contra Mundum is an independent boutique press with modest profit margins. In not having university, state, or institutional backing, other forms of sustenance are required to move us into the future.

Additionally, in the past decade, the reduction of the purchasing budgets across the nation of both public and private libraries has had a severe impact upon publishers, leading to significant decreases in sales, thereby necessitating the creation of alternative means of subsistence.

Because many of our books are translations, our desire for proper remuneration is a persistent point of concern. Even when translators receive grants for book projects, the amount is often insufficient to compensate for their efforts, and royalties, which trickle in slowly over years, are not a reliable source of compensation.

WHAT WILL BE DONE

With your participation we seek to offer writers and translators greater compensation for their work, and in a more expeditious manner.

Additionally, funds will be used to pay for translation rights basic operating expenses of the press, and to represent our writers and translators at book fairs.

If the means exist, we will also create a translation residency, providing opportunities to both junior and more established translators, thereby furthering our cultural efforts.

Through a greater collective and the cultural commons of the world, we can band together to create this constellation and together function as a patron for the writers and artists published by CMP. We hope you will join us in this partnership.

Your patronage is an expression of your confidence and belief in visionary literary work that would otherwise be exiled from the Anglophone world. With bookstores and presses around the world struggling to survive, and many even closing, joining the Future of Kulchur allows you to be a part of an active force that forms a continuous & stable foundation which safeguards the longevity of Contra Mundum Press.

Endowed by your support, we can expand our poetics of hospitality by continuing to publish works from many different languages and reflect, welcome, and embrace the riches of other cultures throughout the world. To become a member of any of our Future of Kulchur tiers is to express your support of such cultural work, and to aid us in continuing it. A unified assemblage of individuals can make a modern Mæcenas and deepen access to radical works.

The Oyster ($2/month)

- Three issues (PDFs) of your choice of our art journal, *Hyperion*.
- 15% discount on all purchases (for orders made directly through our site) during the subscription term (one year).
- Impact: $2 a month contributes to the cost to convert a title to an ebook and make it accessible to wider audiences.

Paris Spleen ($5/month)

- Receive $35 worth of books or your choice from our back catalog.
- Three issues (PDFs) of your choice of our art journal, *Hyperion*.
- 18% discount on all purchases (for orders made directly through our site) during the subscription term (one year).
- Impact: $5 a month contributes to the cost purchasing new fonts for expanding the range of our typesetting palette.

Gilgamesh ($10/month)

- Receive $70 worth books of your choice from our back catalog.
- 4 PDF issues of our magazine *Hyperion*.
- A quarterly newsletter with exclusive content such as interviews with authors or translators, excerpts from upcoming titles, publication news, and more.
- 20% discount on all merchandise (for orders made directly through our site) during the subscription term (one year).
- Select images of our books as they are being typeset.
- Impact: $10 a month contributes to the production and publication of *Hyperion*, encouraging critical engagement with art theory & æsthetics and ensuring we can pay our contributors.

The Greek Music Drama ($25/month)

- Receive $215 worth of books.
- 5 PDF issues of *Hyperion* ($25 value).
- A quarterly newsletter with exclusive content such as interviews with authors or translators, excerpts from upcoming titles, publication news, and more.
- 25% discount (for orders made directly through our site) on all merchandise during the subscription term (one year).
- Impact: $25 a month contributes to the cost of designing and formatting a book.

Citizen Above Suspicion ($50/month)

- Receive $525 worth of books.
- 6 PDF issues of *Hyperion* ($30 value).
- 1 tote.
- A quarterly newsletter with exclusive content such as interviews with authors or translators, excerpts from upcoming titles, publication news, and more.
- 30% discount on all merchandise (for orders made directly through our site) during the subscription term (one year).
- Select one forthcoming book from our catalog and receive it in advance of release to the general public.
- Impact: $50 a month contributes to editorial & proofreading fees.

Casanova ($100/month)

- Receive $1040 worth of books.
- 7 PDF issues of *Hyperion* ($30 value).
- 1 tote.
- A quarterly newsletter with exclusive content such as interviews with authors or translators, excerpts from upcoming titles, publication news, and more.
- 35% discount on all merchandise (for orders made directly through our site) during the subscription term (one year).
- A signed typeset spread from two forthcoming books.
- Select two forthcoming books from our catalog and receive them in advance of release to the general public.
- Impact: $100 a month contributes to the cost of translating a book, therefore supporting a translator in their craft & bringing a new work & perspective to Anglophone audiences.

Cybernetogamic Vampire ($200/month)

- Receive $2020 worth of books.
- 10 PDF issues of *Hyperion* ($50 value).
- 1 tote.
- A quarterly newsletter with exclusive content such as interviews with authors or translators, excerpts from upcoming titles, publication news, and more.
- 40% discount on all merchandise (for orders made directly through our site) during the subscription term (one year).
- A signed typeset spread from four of our forthcoming books.
- The listing of your name in the colophon to a forthcoming book of your choice.
- Select four forthcoming books from our catalog and receive them in advance of release to the general public.
- Impact: $200 a month contributes to general operating expenses of the press, paying for translation rights, and attending book fairs to represent our writers and translators and reach more readers around the world.

To join the Future of Kulchur, visit here:

contramundumpress.com/support-us